THE STRATFORD MURDER

By Mike Hollow

THE STRATFORD MURDER

Mike Hollow

Allison & Busby Limited
11 Wardour Mews
London W1F 8AN
allisonandbusby.com

First published by Lion Hudson as *Firing Line* in 2018.
This edition published by Allison & Busby in 2020.

A CIP catalogue record for this book is available from
the British Library.

10 9 8 7 6 5 4 3 2 1

ISBN 978-0-7490-2603-5

Typeset in 11/16 pt Sabon LT Pro by
Allison & Busby Ltd.

The paper used for this Allison & Busby publication
has been produced from trees that have been legally sourced
from well-managed and credibly certified forests.

Printed and bound by
CPI Group (UK) Ltd, Croydon, CR0 4YY

For Jackie: my sister, my friend

CHAPTER ONE

She wondered what it would feel like in the instant your body was blown to pieces. Would there be time for you to register the sensation before you ceased to exist? Or would some part of you live on beyond death, able to remember the pain? She brushed the thought from her mind. There were more pressing things to focus on, like not falling down a broken manhole in the blackout.

She was used to brushing thoughts from her mind. At work they called her a no-nonsense sort of woman. The sort who got on with the job. The sort who coped. Now she was coping with holding down a job in the daytime and being an air-raid warden at night. At first, when the really big raids started at the beginning of September, she'd been twitchy, yes, but even then not panicky like some – men included. As always, she'd just got on with it. Now, six weeks later, if a bomb landed round the corner and took out a house or two she barely flinched. Some people said it wasn't natural for a woman to cope like that, but she knew that's what women always did.

Not all women, of course. There was one she saw every night in one of the public shelters she patrolled, a worn-looking creature about her own age, muttering prayers for her husband, her children, her home, quivering with the fear of losing them. But that was the difference: Sylvia Parks had nothing to lose.

Next birthday she'd be forty-nine, if she managed to dodge the bombing that long. Past her prime, people would say, if they knew. At forty-eight she'd already been a war widow half her life, a leftover, one of the tens, the hundreds of thousands seen but unnoticed every day on every street, slowly ageing women married to ghosts.

She paused to pull her scarf tighter against the chill as a train rumbled across the bridge over Carpenters Road and on into the night. Pushing her steel helmet back from her forehead, she mouthed a silent curse at the planes that droned with their irregular engine-beat in the darkness above. For twenty-four years she'd felt numb, adrift, and only now had the nightly risk of death made her feel alive.

She glanced down at the pavement and stepped over a cat's cradle of fire hoses. A house to her right – or what was left of it – was still smouldering, but one of the other wardens had told her they'd got the old lady out just in time. Sylvia knew the type. 'It'll take more than Hitler to get me out of my bed,' she'd have said, silly old fool. Well, she was wrong, wasn't she?

It had been cold like this on their wedding day, November 1915, with Sylvia shivering in borrowed white lace and Robbie spotless in his Royal Field Artillery uniform, a pair of corporal's stripes on each sleeve. She was twenty-three, and he a year older. Four days' leave from shelling the Germans for him, two days as a married woman for her before he had to go back. And by May he was dead.

She heard the crash of three bombs landing somewhere towards the London and North Eastern Railway works the other side of Stratford station. A target the German aircraft would be pleased to hit, she thought, like so many other places in West Ham. Big bombs too, by the sound of it, but no threat to her here. She'd wait till they came a bit closer before she thought of taking cover.

This wasn't her own sector, but she could imagine Carpenters Road, crammed with factories and works, would be another important target. The post warden, her superior in the Air Raid Precautions service, had sent her over from her regular patch to gather information on the situation here. Not long ago he'd described her to a visiting dignitary as fearless, and her conduct as an ARP warden under bombing conditions as exemplary, but the truth was she simply didn't care. What was the worst that could happen? Yes, a hundred pounds of high-explosive bomb might blast her to anonymous shreds of flesh on the back streets of Stratford, but there'd be no husband, no children, no parents, no siblings to mourn her. No hearts stabbed through by grief at her death, no unfillable void left by her passing. In her oblivion she might even be reunited with Robbie – who could say?

Up ahead, just before the bridge, she could see flames raging skywards from the site of the old William Ritchie and Sons jute factory. She checked her watch as she approached it: just coming up to three o'clock in the morning, but no chance of a break yet. Her job was to find out the extent of damage from the firemen, as well as details of any casualties and possibly unexploded bombs, and then take her report back to the ARP post.

She crossed the road, then stopped as something caught her eye. Not another one – would these people never learn? At the back of one of the houses adjoining the jute works site a ground-floor window was shining like a beacon. Of course, even an idiot should be able to see there was no serious risk of light in a kitchen window guiding the German air force to its target when there was a huge blaze like that right next door, but nevertheless she wasn't allowed to ignore it. She'd have to tell whoever lived there to turn the light off or obscure it with their blackout curtain. That was if there was anyone at home, of course. If there wasn't, she'd have to find a policeman or a fireman to break in – as an ARP warden, for reasons best known to the people who made the regulations, she wasn't permitted to do so.

She strode up to the house and was about to reach for the door knocker when she saw a pair of bell-pushes to her left. So the house must be two flats. She jammed her forefinger onto the lower one and held it there for two or three seconds. Nobody came. She pressed again, for longer this time, then bent down and shouted through the letterbox. Still no answer. She tried the upper bell, but this too went unanswered. She stepped back and looked up to the first floor of the house. All the curtains were open and the rooms behind them in darkness: the whole house had a bleak and lonely air. With a sigh of exasperation she set off briskly up the road towards the blaze. No policemen in sight: she'd have to ask a fireman.

Fire hoses snaked in all directions across the factory site, each one terminating in a cluster of firemen wrestling to direct what must have been tons of water into the burning buildings, too focused on their task even to notice Sylvia approaching. She looked around for help and spotted one man sitting alone on a doorstep away from the inferno. He was wearing a fireman's tunic, and as she approached she could see the Auxiliary Fire Service badge on its breast, and the letters AFS on the front of his steel helmet. He looked exhausted, and when she drew close enough to see his eyes by the light of the fire they were vacant, as if in his mind he was somewhere else, far away.

'Excuse me,' she said. 'I'm looking for some help. Are you injured?'

Her question made him snap to attention, like a man caught dozing on duty.

'Me?' he replied, with a sudden brightness and a hint of Welsh in his voice. 'No, not injured, love, but bless you for asking. I had a bit of a slip off the ladder over there, and it knocked the wind out of me. I'm just sitting here for a moment to recover. How can I help you?'

'I'm Sylvia Parks. I'm an ARP warden.'

'I can see that,' he replied, glancing at her helmet. 'Hosea Evans – Auxiliary Fire Service, as you can also no doubt see. So what's up?'

'I've got a house over the road with a light on, and there's no answer when I ring the bell, so I need you to break in so we can turn it off.'

'Break in? Why me?'

'Because firemen are allowed to, and wardens aren't. I don't make the regulations, but I don't want some bobby nicking me for breaking and entering.'

'They wouldn't do that, love.'

'Wouldn't they? We've put their noses out of joint enough already when it comes to who does what. They kicked up a right stink when someone said the ARP should be in charge of everything in an air raid, not them.'

'Except fire-fighting.'

'Yes, all right, except fire-fighting. Anyway, the fact remains that I need you to break into that house for me. There may be someone in there who's hurt or can't get to the door for some reason. If so, they're in danger.'

'All right,' said Evans, hauling himself to his feet. 'Lead, kindly Light, amid th' encircling gloom, lead Thou me on.'

Sylvia recognised the hymn, but wasn't sure whether his intention was poetic or patronising.

'This way,' she said. 'Welsh, are you?'

'Oh, yes. I expect you could tell.'

'It wasn't difficult. Now come along – as quickly as you can.'

She set off towards the house, with Evans limping along beside her.

'You really could, you know,' he said.

'Could what?'

'Break in for yourself. They've changed the regulations. You're fully entitled to smash your way into some poor soul's house now, especially if you think they need rescuing. No need to bring a boy like me along.'

'Well, they haven't told me. Not that anyone tells us much – we spend so much time enforcing the blackout, they must think we like being kept in the dark.'

'Oh, yes, very good,' said Evans with a laugh, although Sylvia wasn't sure whether it was genuine.

'Here we are,' she said as they arrived. She rang the bell again, but there was no answer. She turned to Evans and jerked her thumb towards an alleyway that ran along the side of the property. 'Down there,' she said. 'Back gate. Off you go.'

Evans hobbled down the alleyway, followed by the warden. They turned left at the end, into another narrow lane bounded on one side by a brick wall that enclosed the small yards behind the houses. He reached the first gate and rattled it.

'It's locked,' he said. 'Do you want me to break it down?'

'No,' she replied. 'We don't want to create more

damage than we have to. That wall looks manageable –
over you go.'

Evans seemed suddenly to regain his agility, and
Sylvia was surprised to see him clambering over the
wall without difficulty. She followed him, thankful for
the protection of her sturdy tweed overcoat and leather
gloves, and for the fact that like many of her fellow
female wardens she'd taken to wearing slacks since the
air raids started.

At the end of the back yard was an Anderson shelter,
sunk into the ground to the requisite depth and covered
with soil. She shone her flashlight in at the entrance: it
was empty. Crossing to the back door of the house she
tried the handle. It was locked.

'Open it, please,' she said to Evans.

'Righto,' he replied, and took his fire axe from its
pouch on his belt. He pushed the spike end of its head
into the gap between the door and the frame, and with
a couple of twists the door was open. He swung it
wider and held it open with a flourish, inviting Sylvia
to enter first.

She stepped past him without a word and went into
the scullery. It was dark, but beneath the door leading
to the kitchen she could see the light glowing. She went
on, with Evans following her. The kitchen was empty
too. She drew the blackout curtains across the window,
leaving the light on, and went into the hall. There was
an open door on the left, leading into what must have
been the front room. This was in darkness too, but

as she went in she swept her flashlight quickly round it. The first thing she saw was a dazzling reflection of her own light from a tall mirror – a wardrobe. As the realisation dawned that this was the bedroom, her light picked out a bed.

She stopped, and let out an involuntary gasp. On the floor beside the bed there was the unmistakeable shape of a body dressed in a jersey and slacks, curled on its side, face to the bare polished floorboards. It was lying unnaturally, one arm twisted behind it. The head was shrouded in a tangle of blonde hair.

'Look,' she whispered to Evans. 'It's a woman.'

She knelt down beside the body and gave it a gentle shake, but the woman did not stir.

'She must be unconscious,' said Evans. 'Passed out, by the look of it.'

Sylvia gripped the woman by the shoulder and rolled her onto her back, and gasped again.

'Worse than that,' she said. 'Look at that thing round her neck. I think she's been strangled.'

CHAPTER TWO

It was a quarter to four in the morning when Detective Inspector John Jago arrived at the scene. He was not in the brightest of moods. When the bomb blasts ceased and a measure of silence fell, he'd tried to settle down in the damp tomb of his Anderson shelter for some belated sleep, only to be roused by the noise of what proved to be a uniformed constable rapping his truncheon vigorously on the shelter's corrugated iron wall.

'Sorry, sir,' his unexpected visitor had said. 'You're wanted in Carpenters Road. A body's been found in a house next to the old jute works by the railway bridge.'

'What?' said Jago, struggling out of his uncomfortable bed and sticking his head out of the shelter.

'Foul play suspected,' the officer added in a theatrically gloomy tone. 'PC Gracewell's down there waiting for you, sir, guarding the scene.'

Jago thanked him as courteously as he could. Not the best start to a Monday morning, but the poor man was only doing his duty. He threw some clothes on and dragged a comb through his hair, then set off in his car to the scene of the crime.

He found PC Gracewell waiting for him in Carpenters Road, but there was no sign of Cradock.

'Morning, sir,' said Gracewell. 'I'm sorry we had to disturb you, but it looks like a suspicious death.'

'Where's Detective Constable Cradock?' said Jago. 'Did you get him out of bed too?'

'I contacted the station, sir – the phone box down the road's still working. He's living in the section house, isn't he? I expect they'll have told him. They said they'd try to get hold of the pathologist at the hospital and get him down here as soon as possible, but he hasn't arrived yet. They said they'd get the police surgeon too, but apparently he's not been very good at answering his phone in the night of late.'

'Don't tell me – I assume he hasn't turned up either.'

'That's correct, sir.'

'Well, let's get on with it,' said Jago. 'What do you know?'

'It's a young woman, sir. Looks like she's been murdered. She was found in that house there by an air-raid warden name of Mrs Sylvia Parks, but she's had to go off and make a report. I told her you'd want to speak to her, but she hasn't come back.'

'So what did she have to say before she disappeared?'

'She said there was a light on in the downstairs flat and no answer when she rang at the door, so she got a fireman to break in and they found the woman dead. The fireman's still here – Evans, he's called. I told him to stay until you got here. He's waiting just across the road there.'

'Good work. I'd better get in the house and have a look at the body.'

'I'm very sorry, sir, but it's not there.'

'Not in the house, or not anywhere?'

'Not in the house, sir. I'm afraid it's been moved from where it was found.'

'Wonderful. That's just what we need.'

'I'd have made sure nobody touched it or moved it before you came, but unfortunately by the time I got here they'd already done it. It's just over there on the pavement, by the wall. They covered it with a blanket.'

Jago was about to give vent to his feelings about members of the public who thought they were being helpful by moving bodies when he spotted Cradock hurrying down the street towards him.

'Good morning, Peter,' he said when Cradock arrived. 'Good of you to join us.'

'Very sorry, guv'nor. I had to—'

'Never mind. You're here now, and we've got work to do. Tom Gracewell's just told me the body's already been moved, and there's a fireman that we need to talk to.'

'Yes, sir.'

'I think we can manage without you now,' said Jago to the uniformed constable. 'I'm sure you've got better things to do than hang around here waiting for the CID to arrive. Thanks for your help – you've done everything right.'

'Thank you, sir. I think the fireman's keen to get away – he's been on duty all night.'

'Very well, we'll have a quick word with him straight away. That'll be all.'

PC Gracewell nodded, thanked Jago again and set off down the road in the direction of Stratford High Street.

'Now, then, Peter,' said Jago to Cradock, 'to work. The victim's a young woman, strangled it seems. She was found by an air-raid warden and a fireman, but the warden's had to go and deliver some report to her post and isn't back yet. The fireman's over there, so we'll see what he's got to tell us first.'

They crossed the road to where the fireman was sitting with his back against a garden wall. He got to his feet as they approached.

'Mr Evans?' said Jago.

'That's me,' said the fireman.

Jago thought he sounded surprisingly cheery for a man who'd been up all night fighting fires during an air raid.

'I'm Detective Inspector Jago of West Ham CID,' he said, 'and this is Detective Constable Cradock.'

'Good morning, gentlemen. Hosea Evans at your service. I'm afraid you'll have to excuse the mess.' He gestured over his shoulder towards the jute works site and its ruined buildings, glowing red in the darkness. 'I don't think this is quite what my illustrious countryman had in mind – you know, "keep them burning".'

'What?'

19

'The home fires. You know – Ivor Novello. "Keep the Home Fires Burning".'

He sang the first line of Novello's song from the last war in a mellow baritone voice.

'I see,' said Jago. 'The song, yes – very stirring. More popular at home than at the front, though, I'd imagine. So would I be right in thinking you must be Welsh?'

Evans laughed. 'That's right. I suppose if the voice doesn't give me away the name will.'

'I understand it was you who found the body.'

'Well, strictly speaking it was that ARP warden who found the body, but I was with her, see?'

'And what time was that?'

'About three o'clock, as I recall.'

'Where did you find the body?'

'It was in the downstairs flat at number 28 over there. In the bedroom – that's the front room.'

'And can you tell me why you moved the body?'

'Well, we thought we had to, really. The fire next door looked like it might spread, you see, so we had to make a quick decision – leave her there and risk any evidence of who did it being destroyed by fire, or pull her out. So that's what we did. We got her out and covered her with a blanket, out of respect, like – respect for the dead. The ARP warden said she'd find a policeman, and I went back to my work. But look, couldn't I tell you all this later? I'd like to get away if it's all the same to you.'

'No, I'll need you to show me where you found her. I'll—'

Jago was interrupted by a familiar voice calling his name. He turned round and saw Dr Anderson, the pathologist, emerging from the darkness.

'Sorry I'm late,' said Anderson. 'I was actually asleep when your chaps called me. I came as soon as I could. What have you got for me?'

'Mr Evans,' said Jago to the fireman, 'I'll have to ask you to excuse me for a moment. Perhaps you'd like to get yourself a cup of tea – I saw a mobile canteen parked in the High Street on my way here.'

'Very well,' said Evans with a sigh. 'Can I get one for you and your boy too?'

Jago took 'boy' to be a reference to Cradock, but in view of his colleague's evident youth he didn't think it inappropriate.

'That would be kind of you. One spoonful of sugar for me, two for my colleague here. And Dr Anderson?'

'Not for me, thanks,' said Anderson. 'I confess I grabbed one in the hospital canteen before I left.'

'Just the two, then,' said Jago. 'Thank you, Mr Evans.'

Evans sauntered off towards the High Street, in no apparent hurry.

'Right, let's see what we've got,' said Anderson, rubbing his hands together. Jago was unsure whether this was because of the night chill or simply a reflection of the unseemly enthusiasm the pathologist seemed to have for poking about in dead bodies. He pulled back the blanket and played his flashlight over the dead woman's body.

Her clothes were loose-fitting and ordinary-looking: the kind of things he imagined a woman might wear for comfort rather than show, when she wasn't expecting visitors or when she'd got home from work and changed. She was slim, of average build and height, with nothing visibly exceptional about her. But his hand twitched as he shifted the flashlight to her face and saw her eyes. They were bulging, staring forcefully at nothing, a picture of terror.

He tried to imagine what she would have looked like before she was consumed by those last terrible moments of fear and agony. If he ignored her eyes he could see an attractive young woman with shoulder-length blonde hair and a confident chin. What his mother would probably have called presentable. And she had what looked like a stocking tied tightly round her neck.

'Do you know who she is?' said Anderson.

'Not yet. I'm going to take a look at her flat as soon as you've finished here, so I might find out more in there.'

'Presumably not married, though – no rings on her finger.'

'So I see.'

'If you've seen enough, I think I'd rather like to get her back to the mortuary. I can put her under some proper light there. I just need to take her temperature before I go, to help establish an estimated time of death.'

Jago took a deep breath.

'Tell me when you've finished,' he said, turning away and motioning Cradock to come with him. He understood that pathologists had to do these things, but he had always found it such an undignified procedure that he felt guilty if he watched. Even the dead deserved their dignity.

'All right, gentlemen, you can come back now,' said Anderson moments later. 'All done.'

'Can you give us an indication of when she died?'

'I'll let you know when I've had a look at her in the mortuary. Right now her temperature's still a little above the normal 98.4 degrees, but that's nothing unusual.'

'But she's dead,' said Cradock. 'Shouldn't it be lower?'

'Not in this case,' said Anderson. 'As I'm sure you can tell from that thing round her neck, she's been strangled, and in cases of asphyxia the body temperature actually rises.'

'Right,' said Cradock, sounding surprised.

'But Doctor,' said Jago, 'surely the fact that she's got a stocking tied round her neck doesn't necessarily mean that's what killed her.'

Anderson laughed. 'Good point, Inspector. We should get you to train our forensic pathologists. You're absolutely right – I'll need to make a closer examination before I can be as categorical as I sounded.'

'There's something odd about it too,' said Jago. 'It looks much thinner and finer than any stocking I've ever seen – not that I've made a study of such things, of course.'

'I think it must be one of those new ones, sir,' said Cradock. 'I've read about them.'

'There you have the advantage of me, Peter. I don't make a habit of reading the women's page in the newspaper.'

'Neither do I, sir. I just happened to hear about this new thing they've invented in America – they call it nylon.'

'And they make stockings out of it? I've heard of nylon toothbrushes, but not stockings.'

'That's probably because they're only made in America – you can't get them here, as far as I know. I've never seen one either, so I'm just guessing.'

'Well,' said Jago to Anderson, 'I'll need to take that stocking. I've never come across one like it, so I'd like to get an expert to identify it.'

'Can you wait until I've finished the post-mortem examination?'

'Of course. Is there anything else you can tell us at this stage?'

'No. I'll just clear up now and get her taken to the mortuary. I'll do the post-mortem immediately, so if you'd like to stroll up to the hospital at about six this morning I should be finished.'

'Very well, I'll see you then. Come along, Peter, let's find out where that fireman's got to with our cups of tea.'

They left the pathologist to complete his work and headed away towards the High Street. As soon as they were out of earshot Jago thought he heard Cradock make a strange noise like a suppressed chuckle, which then turned into a rather unconvincing cough.

'You all right, Peter?'

'Yes, sir, I'm fine. I was just wondering, though – who's that expert you want to show the stocking to?'

'The only person I can think of who probably knows enough about ladies' hosiery to identify an American nylon stocking,' said Jago.

'Ah, yes, sir, I see,' said Cradock in a knowing way. He said no more, turning his head slightly aside lest Jago should see his amused grin.

CHAPTER THREE

When they got to the bottom of Carpenters Road Cradock spotted Evans: he was holding a mug of tea in his right hand and two more in his left, and appeared to be deep in conversation with a small group of men in AFS uniforms. On seeing them approaching, the fireman bade a quick farewell to his friends and hurried over to them.

'Sorry, Inspector,' he said. 'You must've wondered what'd happened to me. I was discussing the night's fires with my colleagues, you see.'

Jago thought it was just as likely he'd been discussing the rugby results, but he let it pass. He took one of the mugs of tea that Evans was offering and sipped: it was little more than lukewarm, but he drank it. Cradock did the same.

'Now then, Mr Evans,' said Jago. 'I want you to take us into the flat and show us exactly where you found that unfortunate young lady's body.'

Evans led them round to the back of the house.

'That gate's still locked,' he said, 'so you'll have to climb over, like we did.'

Jago and Cradock followed him over the wall and to the back door.

'Wait a moment,' said Jago. 'I want to have a look at this.'

He shone his flashlight on the door and could see it was as flimsy as most of them on these cheap old houses. He gave it a push, and it swung open. Stepping inside, he saw on the back of the door a small deadlock: the key was still in it, and the bolt was protruding. The wooden door frame was splintered where Evans said he had forced it.

They moved through the scullery and into the kitchen, which was in darkness.

'Where was the light showing?' Jago asked Evans.

'Here, in the kitchen. The blackout curtains were open, so the warden drew them.'

'I see.' Jago switched on the light. 'And you found the body in the bedroom, right?'

'That's it, yes. Follow me.'

He led them towards the front of the house, where Jago quickly verified that the lock on the front door was a Yale. The door was closed and locked to bar intruders, but the latch was positioned to allow anyone to open it from the inside and close it behind them.

The door to the bedroom was open, and Evans showed them in.

'She was here,' he said. 'On the floor, like, lying on her side, but awkward. Terrible shock, it was.'

'I'm sure,' said Jago. 'Now, tell me, did you touch anything or move anything?'

'No, nothing, apart from getting the poor woman out.'

'Right. Well, thank you, Mr Evans, you've been very helpful. I'm sorry we've kept you from your duties. Please give your name and address to Detective Constable Cradock here before you go – we may need to ask you a few more questions. When might we find you at home?'

Evans gave a hearty laugh. 'That's a good question. I've been on duty now for about eleven hours, but with a bit of luck I should be finished in another four or five. Try me this afternoon. If all goes well I might have grabbed a bit of sleep by then.'

'And I hope you won't mind letting us take your fingerprints.'

The laughter went out of the fireman's voice. 'Fingerprints? What? You don't think I—'

'It's just so we can eliminate you from our enquiries. We can expect to find your fingerprints on the back door, and those of the lady you found here, so if we know they're yours we can concentrate on any we don't know.'

'Well, if I must. I can't say I like the idea, but I suppose I don't have much choice, do I?'

'Thank you, Mr Evans. My colleague here will see to that.'

Jago opened the front door with a handkerchief over his fingers and let the fireman out. Evans looked back over his shoulder with a hesitant expression, as if he were about to say something, but seemed to think better of it and went on his way.

Jago and Cradock went back to the kitchen. It was almost empty, with just a table and a couple of upright chairs for furniture. The table was bare, save for a single plate bearing the remains of a portion of beans on toast, with a knife and fork propped on its edge, and beside it a glass half full of water.

'It's like the *Marie Celeste*,' said Cradock.

'Except we've found one more body than they did. Check those cupboards – see if we can find out anything more about her.'

Cradock searched while Jago looked in the drawers.

'Not a thing, sir,' said Cradock when he'd finished. 'There's nothing here.'

'Nor in the drawers,' said Jago. 'Curious.'

They moved to the bedroom. Jago checked that the blackout curtains were in place, then switched on the light. The room was furnished sparsely: just a bed, a single wardrobe and an easy chair, all looking as if they'd seen better days, and a threadbare red-and-black carpet of indeterminate pattern that covered three-quarters of the floor. In one corner stood the gas and electricity meters, both thick with dust. The walls were bare, except for a crucifix.

The bed was a double, covered in a green counterpane, with two pillows in pillowcases that had once been white but now looked past their useful life. Cradock moved to the far side of it and noticed a light wheel-back chair lying on its side on the floor, with a woman's stocking crumpled beneath it.

'Sign of a struggle, do you think, sir?' he said.

'Possibly,' said Jago. 'That stocking looks the same as the one round that poor woman's neck – the other half of the pair, I'd say. Take it with us.'

While Cradock picked up the stocking, Jago moved to the wardrobe and opened the door.

'Only women's things in here,' he said across the room. 'That would suggest she lived on her own. And I'm no expert on women's clothes, but these look quite smart – fancy dresses and the like. Not the kind of things she was wearing when we saw her.'

'Maybe she was a party girl – or maybe just had to dress smart for work and was off duty when she was killed,' Cradock replied. 'Hang on, there's a handbag on the floor over here.' He picked it up and tipped the contents onto the bed.

'There's a purse,' he reported. 'Money still in it, but not much. And here – that's handy. An identity card. It says her name's Joan Lewis.'

'Good,' said Jago. 'At least we know who she was now, although it would've been helpful to know whether she was a miss or a missus. I don't know why the government didn't include marital status on those blessed cards. All the money they must've spent on them and then they leave that out.'

'This is a bit funny, though.'

'What is?'

'Well, we're at 28 Carpenters Road, but that's not what she's got on her card. It says 166 Carnarvon Road. Looks like she didn't live here. But what was she doing here if she didn't, and with clothes in the wardrobe?'

'Interesting. We'll need to check the other address.'

Cradock put the items back into the handbag and shut it. He stepped back from the bed and looked down at the floor: something had caught his eye. He crouched down and pulled it out from under the bed.

'That's odd too, sir. Funny thing to find in a young lady's bedroom, I mean.'

He held it up so that Jago could see. It was a round navy blue cap encircled by a black ribbon bearing the letters 'HMS'.

'So, the navy's here, eh, sir?' he said with a grin. 'That's what they said when they rescued those prisoners in Norway, wasn't it?'

'Yes, very amusing,' said Jago. 'All very well when it was Jolly Jack Tar seizing the *Altmark*, but what's this tar been doing in Carpenters Road, Stratford?'

'Hang on, there's a name stamped inside – it says E. G. Sullivan. Must be a careless fellow to leave his cap behind. Friend of Joan's, do you think, sir?'

'Maybe – or a relative, or even someone she didn't know. All we know is he's in the navy, and it's a rating's cap, so he's not an officer.'

'Could it be significant?'

'Your guess is as good as mine, but if he left it here Sunday night it could be very significant.'

31

'Should we try to find him, though?'

'Yes. You'll have to ask the navy. Make some enquiries later – find out where he's stationed. If he's at sea we won't be talking to him for some time, but it could be he's shore-based. And bring that cap and the handbag back to the station with you.'

'Aye aye, sir.'

'That'll do, Peter.'

'Sorry, sir. Will do.'

'If it turns out he's not at sea and he left it here recently, we'll have to find out what he was doing here, and why this Joan Lewis was entertaining a sailor.'

'Well, they do say all the nice girls love a sailor.'

'Yes, but the question is, was our Joan a nice girl?'

CHAPTER FOUR

Jago and Cradock let themselves out through the front door and emerged into Carpenters Road. It was almost six o'clock, and soon the sun would be rising. The fire was close to extinction, and only one AFS crew could still be seen, playing water onto a heap of smouldering timber wreckage.

'Where's that ARP warden got to?' said Jago.

'Caught up in some other emergency on her way to the post, perhaps?' said Cradock.

'Possibly, but we can't wait for her. I want to see what Dr Anderson's found out. We'll take the car back to the station, then stroll up to the hospital.'

They set off up the road to where Jago had left his Riley.

'We'll catch up with Mrs Parks later,' Jago continued. 'I want you to get fingerprints from Evans, and Mrs Parks and the dead woman too. See what prints you can find on the door handles and windows. And when we get back to the station, arrange for someone to come and secure that back door.'

'Yes, sir. What did you make of it, sir? The door, I mean.'

'In what sense?'

'Well, there's a woman murdered in the house, but the door was locked on the inside. So does that mean she must've known her killer – let him in?'

'Of course not. The fact that the door was locked when the body was found doesn't mean it was locked when she was killed. Someone could've found the door unlocked and got in, then locked it behind them, killed her and let themselves out the front way, as we did.'

'Yes, of course. And they wouldn't necessarily have had to come in through the back door anyway, would they? They might've just knocked on the front door.'

'Indeed. On the face of it that would be simpler. But there's the question of when she was killed too. If it was after dark, she might not have wanted to risk opening the door to a stranger, in which case it might suggest she knew them, might even have been expecting them. But on the other hand, these days if someone like an ARP warden had knocked and asked to be admitted she might well have let them in.'

'And that business of the blackout curtains, sir. It's a bit unusual for people to put a light on without closing them, isn't it? Especially when it means they might get fined. So maybe she came home with the murderer and switched the light on, but before she had time to realise she hadn't drawn the curtains she was dragged into the bedroom and killed. If the murderer left in a hurry via the front door, he might've just forgotten to go back to the kitchen and turn the light off.'

'An interesting theory.'

'Or perhaps it was that thing that sometimes happens with the meters. You know – the electricity runs out and all the lights go off, so you put another shilling in the slot and they come on again, but you forget to go and turn off the ones you don't need. Maybe she did that and never went to check the light in the kitchen was off.'

'Yes, but don't forget it's possible that she came home and never got as far as the kitchen before she was killed. The murderer might've gone looking for something in the kitchen after he'd killed her, and put the light on without thinking, then left. Who knows? We've got too many possibilities to be sure of anything.'

Their route from Carpenters Road to the police station in West Ham Lane was free of obstruction, and they arrived within minutes. A little later they took the short walk back up the road to Queen Mary's Hospital. As far as they could see, no bombs had fallen close during the night, but ambulances were still edging through the brick-and-stone entrance archway. The hospital had lost a whole wing to a direct hit in the opening days of the Blitz the previous month, but it was still functioning as a casualty centre for victims of the air raids. Dr Anderson welcomed them at the mortuary.

'Good morning again, gentlemen,' he said breezily. 'I trust you've had some breakfast.'

'Yes, thanks,' said Cradock.

Ah, so that's why you were late, thought Jago, but he declined to voice his suspicion. The very mention of food in close proximity to the human remains that lay in the mortuary was enough to make him take kindly to the idea of fasting. If the bombs hadn't mutilated those bodies, the forensic pathologist soon would – and with an unfathomable air of enthusiasm, if Jago's experience was anything to go by.

'Not yet, thank you,' he replied. 'I'll get something later. I want to know what this woman died of.'

'Very well, that's simple,' said Anderson. 'Come in here and I'll show you.'

They followed him into the post-mortem room. It was cold and forbidding, the very opposite of what a hospital should be, thought Jago – but this was a place for the dead, not the living. The chilling array of saws, chisels and scalpels laid out beside the table gave notice that this was the final destination for those who were now beyond the reach of hope.

'There you are,' said Anderson, gesturing towards the body. 'She died from asphyxiation caused by strangling, as I said at the scene. But you were right to challenge my initial judgement – the presence of a ligature such as that stocking doesn't necessarily confirm strangulation. I've had a look inside now, though, and I've found damage to the larynx consistent with strangulation.'

Jago looked down at the dead woman.

'Poor kid,' he said. 'It's not fair, is it? Here we are fighting a war so people can be safe in their own homes, but nowhere's safe when there's someone creeping around ready to kill a young woman like this. And we're supposed to be the country that's pulling together.' He turned back to Anderson. 'No question of doubt, then?' he added.

'No. There are also some tell-tale signs in the lungs. Would you like to see?'

'I'd rather not, thank you.'

'Very well. As you may know, they're marks under the pleural surface that are caused by the rupture of the air cells – very characteristic of violent asphyxia. And then finally we have the tiny spots you may be able to see on her face.'

'Petechiae?'

'You've done this before, haven't you?'

'Too many times. I don't take as much joy in it as you seem to.'

'Ah, well. One man's meat, as they say . . .'

'Exactly, although perhaps not the most delicate way of putting it. Where did they train you?'

'At Guy's. In fact it was the clinical tutor who recommended I go into pathology – he said I had just the right bedside manner for it.'

'Very amusing. Now, what about the time of death?'

'Well, allowing for the initial rise in temperature, as I said, and then the usual decline, I estimate that death occurred sometime between five and seven hours before I took her temperature. In other words between about nine o'clock and eleven o'clock last night. I've also taken into account the fact that the body was moved outside and left in the open air on a cold pavement before we got to it. But in any case, a dead body doesn't cool at a consistent rate. It can vary considerably according to the conditions. Establishing a time of death is inevitably an approximate affair – it could easily vary by half or three-quarters of an hour in either direction.'

'Good – thank you. Now, have we finished here?'

'Yes, I think that just about covers it.'

'And there's no possibility that she did it herself?'

'Suicide, you mean? I don't think so. It's possible, of course – you can't strangle yourself with your hands, because you start to lose consciousness and release your grip, but you can if you use a ligature. In this case, though, I think someone killed her.' He pointed at the woman's neck with a scalpel. 'Look at those scratches – they could've been made by her as she struggled to pull the stocking away. And there's also some bruising that I didn't notice when we looked at her on the street – some on her arms, which would be consistent with her having been grabbed or held, and one on the left side of her face, which is less easy to be specific about.'

'Could she have got that from falling? The body was found lying on the floor.'

'Yes, she could have, but it would also be consistent with, say, being slapped. You have to bear in mind that women bruise much more easily than men, so it wouldn't necessarily take much force to have that effect.'

'Is it right that dead bodies don't bruise? It's just that

she was carried out of the house after she'd been found dead. I understand a fireman was involved and it was an emergency, so it may not have been the most delicate of operations.'

'It's not strictly correct. It is possible to bruise a dead body, but bruises formed before death are quite different. All I can say is that in my opinion the bruising that I found took place at about the time of death. I can't be more precise than that.'

'I see. Thank you.'

'And the stocking, by the way – whether it's nylon, as DC Cradock said, or something else, I've noticed that it seems to stretch more than normal stockings. Silk or rayon ones, I mean. It would've been hard work to kill her – asphyxiation isn't immediate, and it's difficult to strangle someone to death if they're fighting back. So it's possible the murderer may have needed an accomplice, to help hold the victim down while she was strangled.'

'Thanks, that's helpful. Can I take the stocking, if you've finished with it?'

'Of course,' said Anderson. 'I didn't find anything on it to help you.' He handed the stocking to Jago, who slipped it into a buff envelope and gave it to Cradock.

'There are one or two other things I'd like to ask you,' said Jago, 'but we don't need to be in here. Could we step outside?'

'Yes, certainly.'

Anderson led them out of the post-mortem room and into his office.

'What else can I help you with?' he asked.

'Well, it's just that there's something about this case that's bothering me,' said Jago. 'It's the thought of that poor girl fighting for her life – and losing. Ever since we saw her I've been thinking about some other cases a few years ago. Do you remember the Soho Strangler?'

'Vaguely. There was something in the papers a few years ago, wasn't there? It was probably when I was a junior doctor, working all hours and not having much time to read the news.'

'Yes, there was. It was a pretty grim tale. Four women were murdered between 1935 and 1937, and as far as I know we're no closer to working out who did it now than we were then. Most of them were what we used to call ladies of desire, and they were all found dead in their flats. The first one was known as French Fifi, but that was only her working name, of course, and she was strangled with a stocking. The others were all strangled too.'

'And all in Soho?' said Cradock.

'Three of them had flats there, I believe, and the other was somewhere else in the West End, so that's why the papers called the killer the Soho Strangler, but one of the women was originally from East Ham.'

Cradock's face registered surprise. 'Really? A local connection, then. So he might've struck a West Ham girl now? You think this Joan Lewis could've been on the game?'

'What do you think?'

'Well, a good-looking young woman, living on her own in a little flat, found strangled. It's possible.'

'And then there's the furniture in her bedroom.'

'Furniture, sir?'

'Yes. There wasn't much of it, was there? Nothing fancy. I've noticed in the past that some of these girls don't like to make their place too comfy. They keep things a bit spartan. They say that when they're bringing men back, if it looks too much like home it's not good for business. Also, there's the bed. It's a double. Not necessarily what you'd expect a single woman to have.'

'But if it's a furnished flat, sir, it might just be an old bed the landlord decided to stick in it.'

'Absolutely, there could be a very good reason for it. But two pillows? I could imagine it being annoying enough for her to have to wash and iron double sheets when she's sleeping on her own – so why would she want to iron an extra pillowcase for nothing?'

'An interesting observation,' said Anderson. 'A detective's observation rather than a medical man's, but a good point, I would think. I did notice she didn't have any rings on her fingers. Could that be significant?'

'Possibly,' said Jago. 'As a matter of interest, did you find any tattoos when you were examining her?'

'No, I didn't, but then I wouldn't normally expect to find tattoos on a woman. Why would that be of interest?'

'The absence of them wouldn't be significant, but if she had some, it could be – it's a bit of a tradition among

41

prostitutes to have them, especially on their arms and chest.'

'Well, this body doesn't have any. So does that mean she was a respectable lady?'

'Not necessarily, but in any case I don't think it's as simple as that. I've known a lot of these girls over the years, and it's not their fault that that's how they make their living. Some of my superiors would disagree, but I say it's not our job to divide women into respectable and unrespectable. If someone's arrested and charged and goes to court, it's their alleged offence that they're on trial for, not their character, but all too often that type of woman seems to be convicted just because the court decides she's "unrespectable".'

'Very interesting,' said Anderson. 'But you haven't asked the obvious question.'

'No, but I was about to. I assume you've examined the body for evidence of sexual activity?'

'Of course, and I think you'll find it interesting. There was evidence of sexual experience.'

'There you are, then,' said Cradock.

'But,' Anderson continued, ignoring him, 'no evidence of recent sexual activity, so if she is a murdered prostitute, she wasn't working last night.'

'That doesn't mean she wasn't on the game, though, does it?' said Cradock.

'No, of course not, but it's worth noting. And there's something even more interesting I've discovered.'

'What's that?' said Jago, his eyes fixed on Anderson's face.

'I checked for any sign that she'd experienced childbirth. There was none, but that was going to change. She was expecting – about twelve weeks pregnant, in my estimation. She would probably have known for some weeks, but she'd reached the stage when it was just beginning to show.'

CHAPTER FIVE

'Where to next, guv'nor?' said Cradock as they left the hospital. 'Any chance of a bite to eat on the way?'

'You said you'd already had some breakfast,' said Jago.

'Yes, but that was just a quick snack on my way out of the section house, and it was hours ago. These early starts always make me hungry.'

Jago checked his watch in the morning twilight. It was ten to seven. The sun wasn't up yet, and the blackout still had about a quarter of an hour to run. Besides, the all-clear siren had only sounded about half an hour before, so it was perhaps a little too early in the morning to go knocking on doors.

'All right,' he said. 'We'll nip back to the station and get something in the canteen. But no dawdling.'

Jago himself felt sufficiently recovered from the ordeal of the mortuary to tuck into a breakfast of egg and bacon when they got there, but he was surprised at how much food Cradock managed to pack away.

'Not expecting to eat again today, are you?' he enquired.

'Yes, sir – I mean no, sir. I mean, it's just that you never know in this job, do you, sir? Got to keep your strength up.'

'You have to be able to move, too. Supposing you have to chase someone down the street as soon as we get out of here?'

'Don't you worry about that, sir. I fancy my chances.'

'Right, well let's just hope we don't have to put your confidence to the test. Now finish that – it's time to go.'

'Yes, sir,' said Cradock, cramming in a last mouthful. 'Where to?'

'I think we need to check that address on Joan Lewis's identity card – Carnarvon Road's only about five minutes' walk from here, so it shouldn't deplete your energy stores too much.'

Five minutes proved to be an optimistic estimate. They stopped when they saw a house on the way that looked badly damaged by fire, and an elderly couple standing on the pavement outside it amidst a jumble of salvaged possessions.

'Incendiary,' said the man. One word was enough to tell the whole story, now that incendiary bombs had become familiar nightly arrivals: little silver cylinders crashing through roof tiles in a dazzling white flash of magnesium that turned to yellow as the flames took hold.

'If I'd been twenty years younger . . .' he added disconsolately.

Yes, thought Jago, twenty years younger and he could have scrambled into the loft with a bucket of earth or a stirrup pump and saved the day. Another twenty years and he might have been up in the sky shooting the bomber down before it could do its deadly work. These were not good days to be old. The woman said the local council was sending a van to collect their remaining things and put them in storage, and she asked if they could help stack them neatly so they wouldn't block the pavement. The sort of people you'd want for neighbours, thought Jago, as he and Cradock shifted the couple's pathetic belongings into some sort of orderly pile.

It was all done in minutes, and by just after eight they were knocking on the door of 166 Carnarvon Road.

The house was large, solid and Victorian, with a patch of garden in front of it and stone steps up to the front door. Four or five bedrooms, if not more, Jago guessed, and worth a bob or two. He rapped the substantial brass knocker on its plate and heard the sound echo down what was presumably a spacious hallway. He hoped he wasn't waking anyone. The door opened, and he realised his concern was groundless. The woman standing before him had clearly not just got out of bed, nor did she look about to busy herself with housework.

The steps were contrived to position callers at a lower level than whoever opened the door, so Jago and Cradock both found themselves looking up at her. She was dressed in a navy blue fitted suit that didn't look cheap, with dark grey woollen stockings and black laced shoes. If asked to estimate her age, Jago would have guessed mid-fifties.

'Good morning,' he said. 'I'm Detective Inspector Jago of West Ham CID, and this is Detective Constable Cradock. I'm sorry to disturb you at this time of the morning.'

He paused, expecting the conventional polite acceptance of his apology, but the woman simply stared at him, her face impassive.

'May I ask your name?' he continued.

'Yes,' she replied. 'It's Lewis, Mrs Audrey Lewis.'

'I'm calling in connection with Miss Joan Lewis, and I believe she lives here. Is that correct?'

The woman's voice was as expressionless as her face. 'No.'

Jago produced the identity card from his pocket. 'This document says she does.'

She took the card from him and gave it a cursory glance. 'Well, this document's wrong then, isn't it? She moved out of here three weeks ago. And before you tell me, yes, I'm aware that she's supposed to notify the authorities, although whether she did I have no idea. Knowing her, she's probably been too busy out dancing or partying to go and get it changed. I wouldn't be surprised if she doesn't even know where the National Registration Office is. Not the most responsible of women.'

She folded the card shut and handed it back to him.

'And another thing,' she added. 'She's not Miss Joan

Lewis. She's Mrs Lewis, and she's only related to me by marriage. She's my son's wife.' She paused, then added with what seemed like a hint of distaste, 'I'm her mother-in-law.'

'I see, thank you,' he replied. 'I'm sorry, but the cards don't give marital status. May we come in?'

She nodded briefly and admitted them to the house, then showed them into the living room. It was comfortably furnished, but she didn't invite them to sit.

'I'm afraid we have some difficult news,' Jago began. 'You might like to take a seat.'

For the first time, a hint of emotion crossed her face. 'It's not about Richard, is it?'

'Richard?'

'My son, Richard.'

'No, it isn't. It's about your daughter-in-law.'

The flash of concern that had illuminated Mrs Lewis's face faded, and she sat down. Jago and Cradock followed suit.

'What is it?' she said.

'I'm very sorry to have to tell you this, but your daughter-in-law was found dead this morning in a flat in Carpenters Road.'

She nodded slowly, as if taking the news in.

'Dead?' she repeated flatly. 'What happened?'

'I'm afraid she'd been strangled.'

'Strangled? You mean someone killed her?'

'Yes.'

She shook her head in disbelief. 'But why would anyone want to do that?'

'We don't know yet. Can you think of anyone who might've wished her harm?'

'Of course not. She's a foolish young woman, but that's no reason for someone to strangle her. It doesn't make sense.'

'What do you mean when you say she was foolish?'

'You know, typical of the young girls of today, I suppose – flighty, irresponsible, more interested in dressing up and putting on make-up and having a good time than in buckling down to some hard work and taking life seriously.'

'You mentioned your son, Richard. Would he be her husband?'

'Yes, he's my only son.'

For the first time her expression softened. She stood up and crossed the room to the mantelpiece, on which a framed photograph of a man in military uniform stood beside the clock. She brought it back and handed it to Jago.

'That's Richard. He's twenty-six now, and in the Territorial Army – he volunteered last year, before the war started.'

'Can you tell me where I can contact him? We'll obviously need to speak to him as soon as possible.'

She replaced the picture on the mantelpiece, tracing her hand across the frame in an almost imperceptible caress.

'That won't be possible, I'm afraid.'

'Oh, I'm sorry.'

'No, it's not what you think. I'm sure he's alive – it's

just that he's been reported missing, so we don't know where he is. He's serving in the Queen Victoria's Rifles, a Territorial Army motorcycle battalion. They were particularly keen to recruit well-educated young men who were already experienced motorcycle riders. He's always loved motorbikes, you see, and he had one of his own until he went away. It was a BSA, I think, and he paid nearly forty pounds for it. He was always down at the stadium in Custom House, watching the speedway racing. He said he'd be back there as soon as he got some leave, but I believe they've closed it down now because of the war . . .' Her voice faded away, and she seemed to be lost in thought about him.

'Went away?' said Jago.

'His unit was sent out to Calais to defend it against the Germans when the army was retreating in France.'

'When was that?'

'He left on the twenty-first of May. We had a telegram later, saying he was missing. I saw in the paper that an officer from his battalion who'd been missing had now been reported a prisoner of war, but Richard isn't an officer, he's just a private, so it isn't him. I expect that's what's happened to him, though – either he's a prisoner of war and we'll find out soon, or he's escaped. There was something else in the paper about one of the men being captured by the Germans but escaping and rowing back to England in a dinghy. That's the kind of thing Richard would do – he's fit, and very resourceful, and he can speak some French too. He's a young man of great ability, with a successful future ahead of him. His father would have been very proud of him.'

'His father?'

'Yes. That's him there.'

She gestured to a second photograph on the opposite side of the clock to her son's, then walked over to it and handed it to Jago.

'That's my late husband, Charles.'

'Oh,' said Jago, 'I'm sorry.'

'Thank you, Inspector. He passed away the year before last – just before Christmas 1938. It was a heart attack, out of the blue. The doctor said he wouldn't have known a thing – it would've been like switching off a light. A mercy, really.'

'Yes, I'm sure.'

'He was a good husband, and our son takes after him in that respect. Charles was a self-made man who started with nothing but ended up a very successful businessman and an investor, very good with money. He always provided for us as a family, and thanks to him I'm glad to say I have no financial worries – not something a lot of widows can say these days, unfortunately.'

She took the photograph frame from Jago, replaced it carefully on the mantelpiece and fell silent again. Reaching for a silver cigarette case that was sitting beside the photograph, she took out a cigarette and then waved the case in Jago's direction.

'I'm sorry, Inspector,' she said, 'I didn't offer you a cigarette. Would you like one?'

'No, thank you,' he said.

She glanced at Cradock, extending the case vaguely towards him, but he declined with a shake of his head. She lit her own cigarette and slowly exhaled a stream of blue smoke.

'Your daughter-in-law, Joan, Mrs Lewis,' Jago continued. 'You said she moved out of here three weeks ago. So was that flat in Carpenters Road her new home?'

'I expect so, yes. What I mean is I don't know the address, but it was in Carpenters Road. I haven't been to visit her yet.'

'So when did you last see her?'

'I don't know. Probably when she moved out.'

'Can you tell me why she moved out?'

'She just wanted a place of her own, I think.'

'Does she have any next of kin apart from your son? Parents? Brothers or sisters?'

'She doesn't have parents. She has one sister, a girl called Beryl. Beryl Hayes, I expect, if she isn't married yet. I don't know her address, but she works at the cinema, like Joan.'

'So Joan worked at the cinema?'

'That's what I said, Inspector.'

'Which one?'

'When she was living here she worked at the Broadway Super, but since she left I've heard that she's been at the Regal, in Stratford High Street.'

'What was her job?'

Audrey Lewis paused as she drew on her cigarette,

and Jago caught a fleeting impression of disdain in her voice when she replied.

'She was what I believe is called an "usherette". What a ridiculous word.'

'Just one last question, Mrs Lewis. Would you be willing to come to the mortuary and identify the body?'

'I'd prefer not to, if you don't mind. I've been under some considerable nervous strain since Richard went missing, and I don't think visiting a mortuary would be good for me. Could you possibly ask her sister? I'll do it, of course, if she can't, but that would be my preference.'

'Very well, I'll bear that in mind. Just one last question before we go, if you don't mind. Can you tell me what kind of wedding ring your daughter-in-law wore?'

'Yes, it was just a simple thin golden one, and I think her engagement ring's gold too, with a small square emerald. Why do you ask?'

'We're just collecting information at this stage, Mrs Lewis. We'll be on our way now. Thank you for your time, and I hope you get some good news about your son soon.'

'Thank you, Inspector. You're most considerate.'

She showed them to the door, cigarette in hand, and Jago heard it click behind them as soon as they left.

'Where to now, sir?' said Cradock as he closed the garden gate behind them.

'To the Regal,' said Jago. 'We need to find this sister, Beryl.'

'Right. Odd about the rings, isn't it? Why did you ask her about them?'

'Simply because it turns out she was married, and you don't expect a married woman not to be wearing rings. I don't want anyone in the family to know just yet that she wasn't wearing them when we found her, but I'd like to find out why.'

'There's one obvious possibility, isn't there?'

'Yes? And what's that?'

'Well, like we were saying at the flat – maybe she was on the game. Her husband's away somewhere, maybe hiding in France, maybe a prisoner in Germany, maybe even dead, and she's moved into a little flat. She wouldn't want to keep her rings on, would she? Maybe she takes them off when she's working, as you might say.'

'Possibly, but we're only guessing. There could be a perfectly legitimate explanation – perhaps she was meeting someone for some entirely innocent reason and didn't want them to know she was married. Maybe she'd lost them. Maybe she was hard up and had pawned them for a few days. It may be of no significance at all.'

'Can I ask another question?'

'Of course. What is it?'

'You didn't ask Mrs Lewis whether she knew Joan was expecting.'

'That's right.'

'Well, I just wondered why.'

'Work it out for yourself. She's been pregnant for twelve weeks and her husband's been out of the country for five months, so it's clearly not his child, and from what we've seen of Audrey, I don't think Joan would've confided in her. In fact, it wouldn't be surprising to find she hadn't told anyone. If it's a secret and we reveal it, it'll be common knowledge before you can say Jack Robinson. I think I'd rather wait for a bit and see if anyone tells us – I'd like to know who knew the secret before we did.'

CHAPTER SIX

The Regal cinema on Stratford High Street, near the Black Bull pub, was an eye-catching building in the bold art deco style favoured by some of the big cinema companies. The front entrance boasted a row of fully glazed steel doors, their glass still intact, and as Jago pushed one open he was struck by how heavy it was. The whole place had an air of elegance, and inside it was lavishly decorated. No wonder they were called picture palaces, he thought: the owners seemed to have gone all out to impress.

A uniformed page boy who looked about fourteen greeted them politely. Informed by Jago that he and Cradock were from the West Ham CID and wished to see the manager, the boy led them across the entrance hall and past the pay box to a plain, unmarked door. He knocked on it and waited until bidden to open it by an authoritative voice sounding faintly from inside, whereupon he announced them, showed them in and scuttled away.

The room was spacious and well furnished in the modern style, but with no windows. To Jago it looked more like a wealthy person's living room than an office, with a sofa and matching armchairs upholstered in leather, a coffee table and framed paintings offsetting the more conventional filing cabinets and desk.

The desk, like the room, was imposing and of contemporary design, uncluttered by anything except a blotting pad, inkstand and telephone, and it was from behind this desk that a man rose to greet them. To Jago's eye he was too young to be the manager of a showpiece cinema, but the only other person in the room was a woman of similar age seated behind a typewriter on a smaller and cheaper desk in the corner, which he took as a signal that she was a subordinate.

'Good morning,' said the man, approaching them with an outstretched right hand with which he gripped Jago's firmly. 'My name's Sidney Conway, and I'm the manager here. And this,' he added, waving his other hand in the direction of the woman, 'is my secretary, Miss Carlton, although I'm sure she won't mind if you call her Cynthia, will you, Cynthia?'

Miss Carlton rose and nodded briefly to the visitors, giving a half-smile which suggested an unspoken appeal for patience with her boss's patronising style.

Conway looked about twenty-five at the most and was dressed in a well-cut double-breasted suit in navy serge with a chalk stripe. His hair was oiled and his black shoes spotless. Flash Harry, thought Jago. It had not escaped his attention that among the paintings on the wall there was also a mirror, and he wondered which of the two colleagues using this office made more use of it. Cynthia Carlton seemed to take care of her appearance too: heavily made up, she wore a tightly tailored suit of jacket and skirt in a lighter shade of blue than the manager's, and matching two-tone high-heeled shoes. Her hair was immaculately styled, but nevertheless she kept touching it at the back and sides as if to check that it was still in place.

'Welcome to the Regal,' said Conway, the roughness of his voice in striking contrast with the quality of his tailoring. 'Regal by name, regal by nature, that's what we say here. Isn't it, Cynthia?' The secretary gave another weak smile. 'We may not be the biggest cinema in West Ham, but I think I can confidently say we're the finest, and we're going places. Did you know there are thirty-five cinemas in this borough, Inspector?' He raised his eyebrows to accompany the question but continued without waiting for a reply. 'Or at least there were, until the air raids started. There'll be fewer than that now, but that means less competition, so it's not all bad news – especially since the Broadway Super down the road copped it. I don't mind telling you I've got big plans for this place. Fortune favours the brave, eh? That's what they say. There's a whole world out there, and if you want it, it's all there for the taking. We're living in difficult days, but when our patrons step through our doors we offer them a dream, something better than their real life – glamour for people whose life is a misery.'

All that and a choc-ice too, thought Jago, but his face remained attentive.

'If I had my way, of course, I'd be making the movies, not showing them. I'm a very good photographer, so film's the logical next step. Hollywood, that's the place to be. It's just a pity it's a bit tricky getting over there these days, what with the U-boats and all.'

He paused for a moment, as if checking back over what he'd just said.

'But don't get me wrong,' he added swiftly. 'I'd much sooner be out there somewhere doing my bit in the forces. Truth is, I failed the medical. Spot of heart trouble, you know.'

'I'm sorry.'

'Yes, grade four, they said, totally unfit for military service. But luckily it's not enough to stop me running the best cinema in town and bringing a real benefit to our community. We're here to serve, just like you and your colleagues in the police. Which reminds me . . . thank you for coming so promptly. I really didn't expect to see you that quickly.'

'You were expecting us?'

'Well yes, of course.'

'So you've heard about Mrs Lewis already?'

Conway looked puzzled. For the first time in their conversation, it seemed to Jago, the man was listening to a voice other than his own.

'Mrs Lewis? You mean Joan? No, I haven't heard anything. What do you mean?'

'I understand Mrs Lewis is an employee here. Is that correct?'

'Yes, she's one of our usherettes. She used to work at the Broadway Super, and I gave her a job here when it was bombed. I couldn't take on many of them, but Joan was outstanding.'

'I'm very sorry, Mr Conway, but I have some bad news for you. I'm afraid Joan Lewis has been killed.'

Conway stared at him, as though straining to understand what Jago had said. His mouth began to form a word, but no sound came out. He walked slowly back to his chair behind the desk and slumped into it. It seemed to Jago that the man's air of aggressive confidence had slipped off him like an unfastened cape.

'I can't believe it,' he said, his voice little more than a whisper. 'That's shocking. She was here on duty only last night. And I thought you were here because . . . but no, this is much more important. What happened?'

'I'm sorry to say she's been murdered.'

His face registered shock and then puzzlement, in rapid succession.

'Murdered? But that's dreadful. Who'd want to murder Joan? She's such a sweet soul.'

Jago heard a sniff coming from the corner of the room, and on looking round he noticed a distressed expression on Cynthia's face.

'It's a shock for Cynthia too,' said Conway. 'I believe she's known Joan for a long time, since before Joan came to work here. Isn't that right, Cynthia?'

Cynthia nodded, but did not speak.

'I'm very sorry, Miss Carlton,' said Jago.

'Do you have any idea who did it, Inspector?' Conway asked.

'No, not yet. But there's something you can help us with. We want to speak to Joan's sister, Beryl Hayes. I believe she works here too.'

'That's right – she's an usherette, like Joan. She's not due in until later, but I'll send for her. Cynthia, get one of the pages to go round to Beryl's flat and ask her to come in immediately. And tell Bert Wilson to come in here too.'

'Yes, Mr Conway,' said Cynthia.

There was an unmistakeable quavering in her voice, and Jago noticed that she didn't look up as she left the room.

CHAPTER SEVEN

It took some time for Conway to compose himself. As soon as Cynthia had gone he took a bottle from an anonymous-looking piece of office furniture behind his desk that proved to be his drinks cabinet and poured himself a Scotch. He raised the bottle before his two visitors by way of an invitation to them to partake too, but Jago declined for both of them.

'You said you were expecting us, Mr Conway, but it wasn't to do with this unfortunate incident,' Jago began. 'May I ask why you were expecting a visit from the police?'

'Yes, of course,' Conway replied, 'although it hardly seems important now. The thing is, you see, we've been robbed. And actually it is important, because we've lost a lot of money. I don't know who did it, but I've got a pretty good idea when. It seems we had a break-in overnight.'

'Perhaps you could give me the details while we wait for Miss Hayes to arrive.'

'Certainly. You'd better hear what Bert Wilson has to say too – that's why I've sent for him. He's one of our doormen and he was here overnight. Normally there'd be no one in the building after we close up, but of course nowadays we have a fire-watchers' rota – members of staff take it in turns. He'll know more than me about what happened. But what I do know is that the takings have gone. Come and see.'

He took Jago and Cradock to the door through which they had entered his office.

'You may not have noticed when you came in,' Conway continued, 'but you can see here where a bit of the door frame's splintered away on the inside next to the lock. There are some marks on the outside too, but the damage is mostly on this side. It looks as though someone's jemmied their way in, doesn't it? The lock's not very strong, because we keep anything of value in the safe.'

'Have you found any signs of forced entry into the cinema itself?' asked Jago.

'No. I've had a good look round and haven't seen anything to suggest that.'

'Who had keys to the building?'

'Apart from myself, of course, only Cynthia, who keeps a spare set. Then we have one set that we issue to the duty fire-watcher, which on this occasion was Wilson.'

Conway took off his jacket and draped it carefully over the back of a chair, then took the two men back across to the other side of the office, where he opened a door that gave access to a corridor.

'Take a look in there,' he said.

Jago could see that this door bore signs of forced entry too. Beyond it, the corridor was dark, with no windows, and when he flicked the electric light switch nothing happened.

'Lights are busted,' Conway explained.

In the gloom Jago could see a mess of unidentifiable debris on the floor. Taking out his flashlight, he spotted two further doorways, one on either side of the corridor. The door on his left was no longer attached to its frame but instead had fallen at an angle against the opposite wall. He looked back at Conway.

'The one on the right's a storeroom,' said the manager. 'On the left is where we keep the safe. If you go in you can see we've had visitors.'

Jago entered the room on the left, followed by Cradock and Conway, and surveyed the scene. The safe was at the far end, and the space in front of it was littered with tatters of paper and cardboard, all covered in dust and lumps of plaster that had fallen from the ceiling.

'It used to be where we kept our confidential files too,' said Conway with a sigh. 'Looks like a bomb's hit it, doesn't it? But not a German one this time, I reckon.'

Jago stepped through the mess to what appeared to be its source. The door on the safe was about as useless as the one that had hitherto secured the room. It hung drunkenly open on one hinge. The safe was empty except for a few manila envelopes. He glanced around the floor and bent down to pick something up.

'I think this probably explains it,' he said, showing it to Cradock and Conway. It was a waxed paper wrapper with the words 'Polar Ammon Gelignite' printed on it. 'Do you know how much money's been stolen?'

'Yes, it was our weekend takings, so it would've been more than three hundred pounds. Mostly coins, of course, and a few used notes, so quite heavy for the thieves to carry away, but I imagine they'd have had the time to do that in the night. During the week I bank the takings every day – I just put the cash into a stout bag and take it down to the National Provincial with one of the doormen with me for protection, but of course the banks aren't open on Sundays, so on Monday mornings I'm banking the whole weekend's takings, for Saturday and Sunday. That must be why they chose to break into the safe last night.'

'Was there anything else of value in the safe?'

'There were a few bits and pieces, like contracts and other legal documents, as well as some private correspondence, but that's what's in those envelopes, so the thieves can't have been interested in them. They only took the cash, and it was lucky I didn't have the staff's wages in there. There was one other little thing in there that was mine, though, and they seem to have taken it. It's just a brown envelope with some personal papers inside. I'd be grateful to have it back, if you manage to recover it.'

'We'll keep it in mind, sir.'

They heard the office door open and Cynthia's voice. 'Bert's here, Mr Conway.'

'OK, bring him in, then go and wait outside until Beryl gets here.'

Conway went back into the main office, followed by Jago and Cradock. Bert Wilson looked about the same age as Conway but was taller. He was a burly, fair-haired man with a healthy, good-looking face, and the sports jacket and flannels that he was wearing didn't obscure his athletic build.

'This is Bert Wilson, Inspector,' said Conway. 'As I said, he's one of our doormen. You'll be familiar with them – mostly their job's to keep the queues under control and be a bit of handy muscle if there's any trouble in the cinema, or one of the patrons tries it on with the usherettes, that sort of thing. And chucking out anyone who tries to sneak in without paying, of course.' He looked askance at Wilson's jacket. 'He'll be changing into his uniform later, and then he'll look the part rather more than he does at the moment. Bert's someone else I took pity on when the Broadway Super got bombed, like poor Joan. I expect he'd have been out of work if I hadn't. Isn't that right, Bert?'

'Yes, sir,' he said meekly. 'But Mr Conway, what's happened to Joan? Cynthia said she's—'

'Not now, Bert. She's been killed – I'll tell you about it later.'

'But—'

'Not now, I said. The inspector's a busy man, and he wants to know about our break-in last night. I've told him you might know something, so I want you to answer

66

his questions. I hope this won't take long, Inspector – we've got a lot of clearing up to do today.'

'I shall be as quick as I can, Mr Conway. Now, Mr Wilson, tell me what you know.'

'Well,' said the doorman, 'I was up on the roof when the second air raid started. That was at half past eleven – I know, because I have to keep a log. By about a quarter to midnight the bombing was getting heavier, and there was lots of noise, and explosions, and fires starting. But I was sure I heard one blast from under my feet, in the cinema. I thought we'd been hit, but I was on the roof, so if a bomb had gone down through it I would've known – or else I wouldn't be here talking to you. I went clattering down the ladder and two blokes grabbed me from behind, tied me up and gagged me. Mr Conway found me when he came in this morning.'

'So you think the noise you heard was the safe being blown?'

'Yes. Obvious, isn't it? If you're going to blow a safe, what better time to do it than in the middle of an air raid? No one's going to notice another explosion with all that racket going on, unless they happen to be in the building – or on the roof.'

'These men who attacked you, did they say anything?'

'No, they didn't speak to me, just grunted a bit as they tied me up.'

'Not a word?'

'Well, one of them did – he just said something like shut up and keep still and you won't get hurt. But that was all.'

'Could you identify either of them?'

'No. They got me from behind, so I didn't see them.'

'So it wasn't necessarily two men. It could've been a man and a woman, for example?'

'Yes, but safe-breakers are always men, aren't they? Anyway, I didn't stand a chance of seeing them. I had my torch, but they jumped me in the dark and knocked it away. I reckon I know when they blew the safe, though. I heard that odd explosion at exactly fourteen minutes to midnight, you see. I made a note in my log before I came down from the roof – it should still be up there. So that's obviously when the safe was blown, isn't it?'

'I think the inspector would prefer to draw his own conclusions about when the safe was blown, Wilson,' said Conway. 'Do you have any other questions for my doorman, Inspector?'

'No, that will do for the time being. Thank you, Mr Wilson.'

'In that case cut along now, Wilson, there's a good fellow. I'm sure you've got things to do. Oh, and one more thing – those boots of yours need polishing before the patrons arrive.'

Wilson gave the slightest of nods to Conway and left the room.

'It's the little details that count, you know, Inspector. One pair of scuffed boots can make a whole business look slipshod,' said Conway. 'I run a tight ship, but I like to think it's a happy ship.'

The door opened and Cynthia Carlton came into the office.

'I've got Beryl here, Mr Conway. Shall I bring her in?'

Conway looked at Jago. 'Would you like to speak to Miss Hayes now, Inspector?'

'In a moment,' said Jago. 'First I have to ask you where you were last night – it's simply a technicality, since you're a keyholder.'

'That's simple. I got home by about ten or ten-thirty, and after that I was trying to get some sleep in my Anderson shelter in between the air raids.'

'Can anyone vouch for that?'

'No, I was alone.'

'And you, Miss Carlton. Where were you?'

'Me? Why are you asking me?'

'Mr Conway's told me that you keep a set of keys to the cinema, so I'm afraid I have to ask you.'

'Well, if you must know, I was at home too – and I was alone.'

'Thank you. Perhaps you could bring Miss Hayes in now.'

Cynthia slipped out of the door and returned with a young woman dressed in a maroon uniform of skirt and jacket trimmed with gold braid. Jago noticed that her eyes looked red, as if she'd been crying.

'Now, Beryl,' said Conway, 'Inspector Jago just wants a brief word with you.'

'I know,' said Beryl. 'Cynthia's just told me. She said Joan's been murdered.'

Beryl pulled a handkerchief from her pocket and pushed her face into it as she burst into tears. Conway moved to comfort her, but Cynthia placed herself between him and Beryl, putting her arms round the distressed woman and holding her. Beryl seemed to struggle to control her crying, but eventually she pulled herself away a little from Cynthia to face Conway.

'I'm sorry, Mr Conway, I didn't mean to do that. It's just a terrible shock. It's all right, though, I won't miss my shift – I've put my uniform on, because I didn't know whether there'd be time to go home and change before I start, and I knew you wouldn't want to be left one usherette short. I won't let you down.'

Jago thought Conway wasn't quite sure how to respond to this, so he stepped in.

'I'm sorry, Miss Hayes. I just need to ask you a few questions. Please accept my condolences on your sad loss. This must be very difficult for you.'

'Thank you,' she replied. 'But how could it happen? It doesn't make sense. Who'd want to kill Joan?'

'We don't know yet, but we'll endeavour to find out. I'm sorry to have to ask you this, Miss Hayes, but would you be able to come with us and identify the body?'

'Yes, of course.'

She began to cry again and thrust her face back into Cynthia's shoulder.

'Mr Conway,' Jago continued, 'when we've done

that, I'd like to come back and have a word with Miss Carlton, if that's all right.'

'Yes, of course,' said Conway.

'And I think it would be a good idea if Miss Hayes had the rest of the day off. Don't you?'

'Oh, er, yes, of course. Just what I was going to suggest.'

'Very well. I'll take her home when we've finished at the mortuary.'

Conway nodded quickly. 'Yes, yes, of course.'

'And just one last question before we go,' said Jago. 'You said Joan was on duty here last night. Is that the last time you saw her?'

'Yes, that's correct.'

'What time did she go off duty?'

'Well, the evening programme finishes at nine o'clock nowadays, because of the bombing, and normally once all the patrons have gone Joan and the other usherettes go round pushing the seats up if they've been left down and emptying the ashtrays, that sort of thing. But last night Joan said she wasn't feeling very well, so I said she could slip away as soon as the national anthem finished. I mean, I wasn't going to keep her back, was I? Some people say I'm a hard taskmaster, Inspector – that all I care about is filling this place every day and making money – but they've got me wrong. Yes, I run a tight ship, and if people don't like it they can get out, but I care about my girls, you know. I see my job as being like a . . . like a . . . well, not a father, I'm obviously too young to be that, thank the Lord, but a big brother – someone who'll keep an eye out for their welfare. I like to think I look after my girls – I always try to be sensitive to their needs.'

Jago thought he heard Cynthia snort, but when he looked at her, she was staring blankly over Beryl's head, her face betraying no identifiable emotion. It was only when he announced that it was time to go that she released Beryl from her grasp.

CHAPTER EIGHT

It was a little after half past ten when Jago and Cradock returned Beryl to her lodgings in Cross Street, just off the northern end of West Ham Lane. On seeing Joan's lifeless body in the mortuary she had stood as if frozen, with only a silent inclination of her head to confirm that this was her sister. On the short journey back she had barely spoken, but when they reached her home she gave a faint smile and thanked them.

'Would it be all right if we asked you a few questions?' said Jago.

'Yes, of course,' she replied. 'I'm sure it's your duty.'

She took a key from her handbag and opened the front door. Inside, the narrow hall was gloomy, and blocked by a hard-faced middle-aged woman with her arms folded intimidatingly across her chest.

'Hello, Mrs Jenks,' said Beryl in a tired voice. 'These gentlemen just want to have a word with me.'

'You know the rule, Miss Hayes. No gentlemen visitors in your room.'

'My landlady,' said Beryl, turning to Jago and raising her eyebrows slightly. She turned back to the woman barring their way.

'These are police officers, Mrs Jenks.'

Jago extended his warrant card for the landlady's inspection, and she stepped aside.

'All right, then,' she said. 'But don't get any ideas, young lady. I'm not having any funny business going on under my roof. It's bad enough you coming in at all hours of the day and night – I don't know what the neighbours must think.'

'But it's my job, Mrs Jenks. If you work at a cinema you have to come home late in the evening.'

'That's as may be, but this is a respectable house, and that's the way it's going to stay. They can have ten minutes, and then they're out, or you're out with them.'

Beryl led Jago and Cradock past Mrs Jenks and up the stairs, where she opened a brown-painted door.

'This is my room,' she said. 'Do go in. As you can see, there's hardly the space for any funny business to go on, whatever she means by that.'

It didn't take long for Jago to survey the contents of her bed-sitting room. A single divan with a pink candlewick bedspread was ranged along one wall, with a wardrobe at its foot. On the opposite side of the room stood a chest of drawers, a small table with two chairs, and an easy chair with threadbare arms.

The fireplace housed an antique-looking gas fire, and on the floor beside it a dented aluminium kettle was perched on a gas ring.

'Welcome to my home,' said Beryl with a sweep of her arm. 'One room, comfortably furnished, shared bathroom, use of kitchen by arrangement, eight shillings a week. And, as you've just heard, no gentlemen visitors.'

Her voice sounded frail, and Jago spoke quickly, worried that the sight of this miserable room might send her into tears again.

'I'm grateful to you for coming to the mortuary with us, and I'm very sorry to have to put you through something like that. It can't have been easy for you.'

'You're right, it wasn't. But at least it meant I could say goodbye to poor Joan – not everyone gets that chance these days, do they?'

Jago nodded.

'It all seems a bit unreal,' she continued. 'I mean, you think about your sister maybe dying some day, but we always think it'll be when we're old and grey, not when we're still in the prime of life. I can't quite get it into my head that she's really passed away. And to go in such a terrible way – why would anyone want to strangle Joan? And in her own home, too. We weren't the closest of sisters, but we were sisters all the same. It's just awful, shocking.'

'It is a shock, yes. Perhaps you should sit down and have a good hot cup of tea with plenty of sugar. Peter, would you mind?'

'Thank you,' said Beryl slowly, as if her thoughts were wandering elsewhere. 'There's water in the kettle, and a teapot in the cupboard behind you.'

Cradock found a box of matches and lit the gas under the kettle.

'Tell me about Joan,' said Jago.

'What's there to say?' Beryl replied. 'None of it seems very important, now she's gone. She was my big sister, two years older than me. I suppose that makes her the only person I've known for my whole life.'

'And what kind of person was she?'

'Just an ordinary girl. You know, normal. She didn't have any peculiar hobbies or habits. She liked a bit of fun from time to time, but nothing outrageous. She wasn't unkind to people.'

'Was she religious?'

'Why do you ask that?'

'It's just that we found a crucifix on the wall in her flat.'

'Oh, that. She was raised a Catholic, same as me, but neither of us are what people call devout. I think that crucifix was something our dad gave her years ago – she probably kept it to remind her of him.'

'Is he still alive?'

'No, he died a few years back. He was Irish. He grew up in the slums in Dublin, then joined the army in the Great War – it was still the British Army in those days, of course – and spent three years in the Royal Dublin Fusiliers. But when it was all over and he came home everything in Ireland had changed, and men who'd fought for the king weren't welcome. He decided to move to England – to get work, but also to get away from all that. He met our mum over here, and they got married. Joan came along pretty quickly, and then me a couple of years later. She was named after Joan of Arc. That was Dad's choice – not because she fought against the English, but because she stood up for what she believed in. It was a good Catholic name.'

'But I don't think Beryl's a Catholic name, is it?'

'No, I don't think it is. Mum and Dad had an agreement that he'd choose the name of their first child and she could choose the second. She named me Beryl after her mother.' Beryl's voice caught, and she wiped her eyes with her finger.

'I'm sorry,' said Jago. 'I didn't mean to upset you.'

'No, it's all right,' said Beryl. 'It just reminded me of when I was little and we were all together, a family.'

'Is your mother still alive?'

'No, she died before Dad. He was working, of course, so Joan had to take over running the house – he expected her to do all the chores. Then he died when Joan was seventeen. I think by then she felt he'd stolen her childhood, forcing her to be an adult when she wasn't.'

'And do you have any other family?'

'No, it was just us. Now with her gone it means I've got no family at all in the world. It's like being orphaned twice – I don't feel connected to anything or anyone.'

'You said you weren't the closest of sisters. What did you mean?'

'Well, I suppose I meant we were close, but not very. She was my only family, so we were close in that sense, but once we'd grown up I think we didn't need each other so much. And then she got married, of course, and her life was very different to mine. She still looked out for me, though – she got me my first job. That's how we both ended up in the same line of work.'

'Yes, her mother-in-law Mrs Lewis mentioned that you both worked at the cinema. That's how we found you.'

'Ah, yes, Audrey.'

'You know her, presumably?'

'No, I've never met the woman. Joan used to say she was a funny old stick. Those weren't the precise words she used, but I could tell she thought Audrey was a bit odd. When a girl marries a bloke, his parents are supposed to say they welcome her into the family like an extra daughter, aren't they? From what Joan said, Audrey never did that. It was like she already had one daughter, and a son, and that was all she wanted or needed.'

'She didn't mention she had a daughter when we spoke to her.'

'Well, she has, although I've never met her either. She's called Elsie, a couple of years younger than her brother. Lives at her mum's place with her husband and works in a pub – mainly evenings, I believe. The Green Man, on the corner of Stratford High Street and Carpenters Road. Don't know what days, though.'

'Tell me, please – when did you last see Joan?'

'Last night. We were both at the Regal.'

'When we were at the cinema with you and Mr Conway he said Joan hadn't been feeling well last night and he'd told her she could go home as soon as the national anthem had finished, which would've been just after nine o'clock. Did you see her leave?'

'No, I didn't. When I said I was at the Regal I didn't mean I was working. I was off last night, but I went with my boyfriend to watch the film.'

'Isn't that an odd thing to do when you work there? Hadn't you seen the film already?'

Beryl giggled, but then seemed to remember she was talking to a police officer and composed herself.

'I hadn't seen it all the way through – I mean you don't when you're working, do you? Besides, he lives at home with his dad, and you can see I could never bring him back here, but I can get boys into the Regal for free, if I'm careful. It doesn't really matter much to me whether I've seen bits of the films before. The cinema's a good place if you want to have a nice time together, in the dark, if you know what I mean.'

Jago had a good enough idea of what she meant not to enquire further.

'But anyway,' she continued, 'even when we're both working at the same time I don't necessarily always see her go. This place is the opposite direction to Joan's flat from the Regal, so it's not as though we were in the habit of walking home together or anything.'

'So did she normally walk home on her own?'

'As far as I know, yes.'

'Did she have any friends? Close friends, I mean.'

'I'm not sure – I didn't know everything about her life, so she may've done. To be honest, though, I think she was lonely. You know her husband's a soldier, missing in France?'

'Yes, Mrs Lewis told us that, too.'

'Well, I think since Richard went away she's felt even less part of the family. I don't think they've rallied round her, like some would. Mind you, to tell the truth, I don't think her marriage was exactly Fred Astaire and Ginger Rogers, even when he was here. Not entirely happy, if you know what I mean. I got the impression there was something wrong, but I couldn't tell you what it was.'

'Do you know whether Joan had any men friends?'

'What do you mean? She was married.'

'Of course, yes, but we need to find out who was in her circle of acquaintances – just to eliminate them from our enquiries.'

'Well, if you must ask, I don't know of any close male friends. But then she wouldn't tell me, would she? I was her little sister.'

'What about close female friends?'

Beryl thought for a few moments. 'There's one person I can think of who seemed to be quite good friends with Joan. I've met her a couple of times. She's called Carol something – Hurst, I think. Yes, that's it, Carol

Hurst. I don't know where she lives, but she works at the National Provincial Bank on the High Street.'

'Thank you, that's very helpful. Now, before we go, do you recall Joan being worried about anything recently?'

'No, I don't think so.'

'Or anything about her behaviour that struck you as out of the ordinary?'

'No, it just seemed to be life as usual, except for her moving from the Broadway to the Regal.' She thought for a moment. 'There was just one thing, though. Hang on a minute.'

She crossed the room to the bed, knelt down and felt beneath it, then hauled something out and handed it to Jago.

'This was a bit odd,' she said.

Jago looked it over. It was a cardboard suitcase, scratched and dented on one side, with the result that the lid barely fitted it.

'Have a look inside,' she said. 'Joan asked me to look after this when she moved out of her mother-in-law's place. Said she didn't want the old girl coming round to her new flat and finding some excuse to nose around.'

Jago put the case on the table and opened it. Carefully emptying its contents onto the table, he found some items of strange-looking clothing: a green tunic, a green hood, a green pair of shorts and a leather belt.

'Odd, isn't it?' said Beryl. 'I've no idea what it is, and Joan never said why she didn't want Audrey to find it.'

'Odd indeed,' said Jago. 'If you don't mind, I'd like to take this away with me.'

'Be my guest,' Beryl replied with a shrug. 'This place is pokey enough as it is, without cluttering it up with someone's old fancy dress costumes.'

CHAPTER NINE

Cross Street was quiet, almost deserted. The only sound was the dreary cry of the rag and bone man and the clip-clop of the horse pulling his cart slowly round the corner from Mark Street. Jago stood for a moment, thinking, then thrust the suitcase into Cradock's hand.

'Here, take this,' he said. 'You can look after it till we get to the station. We need to pop back to the cinema and see if we can get a word with that secretary, Cynthia Carlton, in private. I've got a feeling she might be able to add something to the pot if her boss isn't hanging around listening to her every word.'

They returned to the Regal and found Conway at his desk in the manager's office and his secretary at hers, typing.

'Excuse me, Mr Conway,' said Jago, 'but I need to have a word with Miss Carlton. Do you mind if I take her out for a few minutes? We won't be long.'

'Out? But I'm sure there's nothing she would say that she can't say in here.'

'I need to speak to her in private.'

'But she's busy. She's typing some urgent correspondence for me.'

'Mr Conway, I'm investigating the murder of one of your employees. I'm asking you for the sake of politeness, but if you prefer, I'll just tell you. I'm taking Miss Carlton out for a talk and I'll return her to you as soon as possible.'

'Oh, I see. Very well, then. But be as quick as you can.'

'Come along, Miss Carlton. I expect you could do with a cup of tea.'

Cynthia got her coat and hat, and left with the two detectives. A few doors down the road from the cinema there was an ABC tea shop that didn't look too busy.

'Actually, Inspector,' said Cynthia once they were inside, 'if you don't mind, I think I'd rather have a hot chocolate.'

'Certainly. And something to eat?'

'Well, I shouldn't, but . . . perhaps a little toasted tea cake.'

'And perhaps—' Cradock began.

'Yes, I know,' said Jago. 'Perhaps a little something for you too.'

'Thanks very much, sir.'

Cradock settled for a plate of ham sandwiches and a pork pie with his cup of tea, but Jago preferred just a slice of Dundee cake.

'Now, Miss Carlton,' Jago began, 'tell me, please – how long have you worked at the Regal?'

'Ooh, I don't know, it must be three years, I think. It was before Mr Conway came, when the old manager was still there – a right one he was. Mr Conway was like a breath of fresh air. At first, anyway. This tea cake's lovely, you know.'

'Good. And what did you do before that?'

'I worked for the Gas Light & Coke Company. I was just a typist then, at Beckton gasworks, but now I'm a secretary – much more responsibility. It's people like me that keep places like the Regal going. Not that I'll be there for ever, of course. I've got plans, you see.'

'I'm sure. Now, the set of keys that you hold for the cinema – do you have any reason to believe they could've got into anyone else's hands recently?'

'No, they've been with me all the time. I keep them in my handbag.'

'And I assume you still have them.'

'Yes.' She opened her handbag, pulled out some keys on a ring, and dangled them in front of him. 'See? I don't think Mr Conway would ever say I was anything less than a very trustworthy employee.'

'Thank you. How do you get on with Mr Conway? Personally, I mean.'

'He's all right.'

'He seems a very enterprising man.'

'Oh yes, very enterprising. He'll try anything.' She snapped her handbag shut and hung it on the back of her chair.

'What's he like to work for?'

'He's very particular, wants the Regal to be the best cinema in the area. I think he sees himself sailing on to greater things in the future, so he wants everything he touches to be a success.'

'He told us he runs a tight ship.'

'Yes, he talks like that – likes to be in command, if you know what I mean. He gets all the doormen and usherettes lined up every day for a uniform inspection, like an admiral on a battleship. Always keen to check everything's where it should be – he expects them all to be up to scratch.'

'And Joan Lewis – was she up to scratch?'

'As far as he was concerned, I'd say very definitely yes, she was.'

'What do you mean?'

'I mean he had his eye on her, and I don't mean he thought she tore her tickets in half neatly. He has an eye for the ladies, does our Mr Conway, and he had his eyes on her.'

'Are you suggesting there was some sort of relationship between them?'

'I'm not suggesting anything, Inspector. But we learn things in life, don't we? And something I've learnt is that he's one of those men who'll chase anything in a skirt – and these days in trousers too, as long as it's a pretty girl who's wearing them.'

'But she was a married woman.'

'Yes, but you know what they say. While the cat's away . . .'

'Do you have any evidence for that?'

'No, but I know Mr Conway. Let's just say he and I have a little history, and I've probably got to know him better than the rest of the staff have. If you ask me, it's a pity they haven't taken him for the army. That might've given him something different to think about.'

'He told us he'd been exempted from military service.'

'Oh, yes, I expect he told you about his spot of heart trouble.'

'That's right. He said he'd failed the medical examination.'

'Yes, well, I reckon he failed it because when they looked for his heart they couldn't find one. Will that be all, Inspector?'

'For the time being, yes, thank you.'

'So, Peter, what do you make of it all so far?' said Jago when Cynthia had departed for the cinema. 'We've got a young woman murdered. Her husband's in the army, missing in France, possibly captured, possibly worse. Her mother-in-law doesn't think much of her character or her sense of responsibility, but her boss at the cinema seems to have thought highly of her.'

'Maybe it wasn't just her character he was thinking of, sir,' said Cradock.

'Quite. Then we've got her sister, Beryl.'

'She seems a sweet girl.'

'Yes, I suppose she would, to you. Like a younger sister, eh?'

'No, just a younger member of the public, sir.'

'Good. Now, it seems Beryl wasn't especially close to Joan, and her mother-in-law Audrey certainly wasn't, from the sound of it. That leaves this Carol Hurst as the only close friend anyone's mentioned, so we'll need to find her. That kitchen's troubling me too.'

'Whose kitchen?'

'Joan's. We had a good look round, but there were no photos, no letters, no books, nothing to tell us anything about her. Same in the bedroom. As if she'd made sure there was nothing there to help anyone find out.'

'Or someone else wanted to make sure and removed it.'

'Possibly, but if you'd just murdered her you wouldn't want to hang around collecting up all her stuff before you got away, would you?'

'No. So maybe she just didn't want anyone to know who she was. A bit weird. And what about that Soho Strangler business, sir? Do you think she was on the game?'

'It might explain why she moved out to a place of her own, and also why she let a stranger into her flat at night, if that's what she did. We need to find out more about how she spent her time when she wasn't being an usherette. I want you to have a word with Tom Gracewell – ask him if he's seen or heard anything on his beat that would suggest she was a lady of the night. And check whether Scotland Yard's got any fingerprints for her on record. If she's ever been charged with a prostitution offence anywhere in the Metropolitan Police district she'll have been fingerprinted. Meanwhile I'll talk to whoever was responsible for investigating those Soho stranglings.'

'There's also the question of someone else, isn't there? Someone she presumably knew rather well. What I mean is, who's the father of her child?'

'Indeed. The only person we know it can't possibly be is her husband. He may be resourceful, but not that resourceful.'

'We need to find that sailor, too, don't we? The one whose cap we found in Joan's flat.'

'That's right. And there's also the small matter of the break-in at the Regal. If Conway's right about the takings, it's a serious amount of money, so we'll have to get onto it.'

'Do you think it could've been an inside job, sir? None of them look like explosives experts to me, but then if one of the keyholders was involved, all they'd have to do is let the professionals in.'

'That's if the people who blew the safe were professionals. It's certainly dangerous work for amateurs, but if someone told them what to do they might manage it. They'd have had to get hold of the explosives, too, of course.'

'Yes, but that can't be difficult in a war. There must be hundreds of factories making munitions now.'

'On the contrary, that's just it. The idea of fifth

column types or saboteurs getting hold of explosives must frighten the life out of the government, so those places are all guarded. And in any case, munitions use TNT, but this was Polar Ammon Gelignite. That's an industrial explosive, so it's more likely to have come from a mine or quarry, and there's nowhere like that in this area.'

'No obvious explanation, then.'

'No. And what did you make of Conway, the cinema manager?'

'He's a pompous little – sorry sir, I mean he certainly fancies himself. Too cocky by half, if you ask me.'

'In what way?'

'Well, he obviously likes being the boss, and he reckons he's quite a success story because he's got the job so young. Likes chucking his weight about a bit though, doesn't he?'

'Perhaps he thinks that's what seniority's all about.'

'He seemed to take it all in his stride – the break-in and the theft of all that money. I got the impression he was just as concerned about his precious little envelope as he was about the company losing a weekend's takings.'

'Yes. Just some personal papers, he said. I wonder what those were, and what made them so important he had to put them in the safe?'

'They could be something suspicious, you mean?'

'I don't know – it's just curious. But he's not the kind of character I'd buy a second-hand car from, if you know what I mean. It's that smooth manner of his, I think. He definitely strikes me as a man with an eye to the main chance.'

'Too smart for his own good, if you ask me.'

'Quite possibly,' said Jago. 'He should go far.'

CHAPTER TEN

If the bomb had fallen a mere two or three yards farther down the street the National Provincial Bank would have been flattened, but in the randomness of aerial bombing it had been spared, while the adjacent furnishings store had been blasted to ruins. On the outside the bank's stone-clad walls still exuded their customary air of security and permanence, but when Jago and Cradock went inside they found a scene of quiet but urgent industry, with staff endeavouring to maintain normal business while others swept up dust and other debris blown in through the shattered windows. A clerk took them to the manager, secluded in his office at the back of the bank.

'I realise this is not a good day to deprive you of a member of staff, even for ten minutes, but I need to speak to Miss Carol Hurst in connection with our enquiries,' said Jago once they had been introduced.

'Of course. Miss Hurst – one of our shorthand

typists,' said the manager, Harold Pemberton. He was a studious-looking man in his fifties, crisply turned out in the habitual black jacket and striped trousers to which his occupation still clung. To Jago this was quaint, since the professional world in general seemed to have defected to lounge suits. But he assumed it reflected the conservative nature of banking: an air of sober respectability was everything. He thought the man would be mortified to know there was what looked like a smudge of ash on his wing collar.

'As you can see,' Pemberton continued, 'we've had a slight disruption to our business today, but we must be thankful we're still here. We're doing our very best to maintain our normal service, and so far I think we're succeeding. So you want to speak to Miss Hurst. I do hope she isn't in any trouble.' He said this with an amused grin, as if the idea of one of his staff being in trouble was so improbable as to be laughable.

'No, she's not in trouble, but we think she may be able to help us.'

'I'll send for her, then. The office next to this one is empty today, so you can use that if you wish.'

'That will be perfect, thank you.'

When Carol Hurst arrived she presented quite a contrast to her staid manager. She was young, in her early twenties to Jago's eye, and despite her demure dress – he assumed the bank had rules about that sort of thing – she seemed bursting with life. She joined Jago and Cradock in the empty office, took a seat, and straightened her skirt in a somewhat exaggerated manner. Jago broke the news of Joan's death to her, and she seemed genuinely upset.

'I'm sorry to be the bearer of bad news,' he said, 'but we understand you and Joan were friends. Is that the case?'

'Yes, it is,' said Carol. 'I got to know her about four years ago. We were both in the Women's League of Health and Beauty. We used to like that kind of thing in those days – fresh air, exercise, keeping fit. We were supposed to be the flower of English womanhood, but actually, looking back now I think we were just a bunch of conceited young women prancing round in baggy satin knickers and waving our arms about thinking we were changing the world. I think that's how she met her husband – he was a fresh air type at the time, liked camping and all that. But I think the charm wore off for him too. Mind you, I suppose being a part-time soldier and going on training camps in the summer means a bit of outdoor life, so maybe he hadn't given it up completely. Not like her. I reckon the closest she's got to that sort of thing in the last couple of years is watching cowboy films at work.'

'So you know her husband?'

'Richard? Yes. I was her bridesmaid – me and her sister Beryl. The wedding was in January of last year, so they only had a year and a bit together before he was sent off to France. You know he's in the Territorial Army, don't you?'

'Yes, I do. What else can you tell me about him?'

'Well, no one knows where he is at the moment – it's a bit of a mystery. Joan told me someone from the same battalion as Richard came to see her when he got back to England. He said they'd been sent over there to defend Calais, but they'd run into a spot of trouble. Rather serious trouble, in fact – he said most of the battalion were killed or captured, and Richard had gone missing. It must've been terrible news for Joan, and she was never a very strong person. I think she went to pieces a bit, but she tried to cover that up. I did my best to comfort her – Richard's only missing, after all, not killed, and we're all hoping there'll be some good news soon.'

She paused, as though taking in the significance of what she'd just said, then looked at Jago with a pained expression.

'That'll be too late for her, though, won't it?'

Jago nodded sympathetically. 'I understand Richard volunteered for the Territorials before the war started,' he said.

'Yes, in April of last year, I think. He said he joined up because of Hitler occupying Czechoslovakia – he said that was the last straw. But I think there was more to it than that. He had a boring job, and maybe joining the Territorials sounded like a bit of adventure. I expect his mother's told you all about him volunteering, though.'

'We have spoken to Mrs Lewis, yes. Do you know her?'

'What – Audrey? Yes, I've met her a few times, but I don't know her well. She's done nothing but worry about Richard since he went to France – but then she's always been the same, from what I've heard. What you might call a possessive mother, a bit overbearing at times.'

'She seemed confident that he's still alive.'

95

'Oh, yes. But I think that's mainly because her friend Madame Zara says so.'

'Madame Zara?'

'Yes. She's a spiritualist – a medium. I believe Audrey's consulted her about her late husband, Richard's dad, but I don't know why. Audrey's a bit of a crackpot, if you ask me.'

Jago wondered whether she spoke this freely about all her acquaintances and how she might later describe himself to her friends.

'Tell me,' he said, 'did Joan have any men friends?'

She smiled and gave him a sly look. 'That's a bit of a naughty question, isn't it? I mean, she was a married woman.'

'It's a question I have to ask in a case like this.'

'Well, I can't give you any names, if that's what you're thinking.'

'Do you mean you have some names but can't tell me, or that you don't know of anyone?'

'I don't know of anyone, of course. What kind of girl do you think she was? Mind you, she wasn't what I'd call shy. She could be a flirt – you know, looking all coy talking to the boys, but then giving the eyelashes a bit of a flutter if she felt like it.'

'Do you know if it ever went further than flirting?'

'Well, that I couldn't say, Inspector. I think she was just a bit tired of life. I mean, you know – husband's gone overseas to fight and hasn't come back, and for all she knows maybe he never will, and she's cooped up with a mother-in-law who'd barely give her the time of day, in what's probably a dead-end job. Not much chance of a social life, either, with the shifts she worked at the cinema. I think she was looking for a bit of excitement, a thrill – but not for something serious.'

'How was she financially?'

'She told me she earned twenty-seven and six a week at the cinema. Not a king's ransom, is it? I get two pounds at the bank. But I think she got another eighteen bob or something family allowance for her husband being a private in the army. So what's that altogether? Two pounds five and six a week. Still not a lot when you're paying rent.'

'I see. Now, forgive me for asking, but at times like this some women have to do things they wouldn't normally consider doing to earn enough money to live.'

Carol gave a short, tinkling laugh. 'Oh, aren't you sweet? Don't worry, I know what you mean.'

'Do you know whether this might've applied to Joan?'

'If it did, it would've been her own business, and I don't think she'd have broadcast the news to all and sundry. I wouldn't have judged her if she'd been tempted, but the fact is I don't know – she never said, and I never saw.'

'Thank you.'

'Look, Inspector, some men think there are perfect women out there – always faithful to their husband in thought and deed, devote their life to his happiness and welfare, never flirt, never even smoke or drink, but make allowances for everything he does. That's what they think, but I doubt whether they've ever met one in real life. I've already told you she was a flirt, so that's one bad mark against her, and she might've failed on some of those other points. I don't know everything about her life, but she was a good friend to me when I needed one, and that's all that matters to me.'

CHAPTER ELEVEN

Jago walked into West Ham police station, followed by Cradock, who was still carrying the suitcase, and raised a hand in mock salute to Station Sergeant Frank Tompkins on the front desk.

'Afternoon, Frank,' he said. 'Everything under control as usual, I assume?'

'Afternoon, sir,' said Tompkins. 'All shipshape and Bristol fashion, if I say so myself. Although what Mr Soper's going to say about you two turning up for duty on a Monday morning at half past three in the afternoon I don't know.'

'Well, you know what it's like, Frank – it can be difficult getting out of bed when you're old. Heaven knows what I'll be like when I'm as old as you.'

'Don't remind me. But I've got one advantage over you – I've got a missus to kick me out of bed. Don't need an alarm clock – it works like a charm. You should think about getting one yourself, sir. A missus, I mean, not an alarm clock. Oh, and that reminds me, how are you getting on with that nice young—'

'I don't know what you're talking about, Frank,' Jago interrupted. 'But I didn't need either this morning – I got a personal early morning call from one of your men, as I'm sure you know.'

'Well, yes, a little dicky bird did tell me there'd been an unfortunate incident over in Carpenters Road, and I thought that might've detained you.'

'While you were still tucked up in bed with your missus, no doubt. Did that little bird tell you what time DC Cradock and I started work today?' He glanced up at the clock on the wall. 'Twelve hours ago almost to the minute – for me, at least. A little later for him.'

Cradock was about to spring to his own defence, but thought better of it.

'Sorry,' said Tompkins. 'My mistake.'

'You don't make mistakes, Frank, you're too long in the tooth to get anything wrong. You must be the longest-serving officer on the division.'

'No need to rub it in. I used to hate being retired, but now I'm back serving His Majesty again I miss it more every day.'

Tompkins peered down his nose at Cradock.

'Anyway, you two going off on holiday?' he said. 'I've heard Eastbourne's very nice at this time of year if you don't mind the barbed wire on the beach. Only one suitcase, though?'

'Ah, that,' Jago replied. 'Give it here, Peter.'

Cradock handed him the suitcase, and Jago set it down on the desk in front of Tompkins. He opened it so the sergeant could see the contents.

'What do you make of these, Frank?'

'Well, let's have a look.' Tompkins took out the garments and turned them over in his hands. 'Hmm, green shirt, green hood, a natty pair of green shorts. No accounting for taste, is there? My guess is you're on your way to the theatre and you're going to be appearing in a pantomime. Robin Hood, is it? Can I be one of your merry men? You'll need a Maid Marian too, won't you – got anyone in mind?'

'If I didn't know you better, Sergeant, I'd say there was a hint of impertinence in that remark, but I'm sure I'm mistaken.'

'Oh, absolutely, sir,' said Tompkins with a broad grin. 'And do give her my best wishes when you next see her, sir.'

'Thank you, I'll keep that in mind. Now, about these clothes. I'm trying to work out what they are. There's a badge on the tunic that looks vaguely familiar, but I can't quite place it. You've seen everything in your time, Frank, and your memory's better than mine, so I thought you'd be able to put your finger on it.'

Tompkins took a closer look at the badge.

'Yes, now I look at it again it rings a bit of a bell with me too. A green tree, a red shape like smoke from a campfire and a blue thing like a letter K. I

101

remember seeing this back in the twenties, I think. I've an idea it was something to do with those blokes who wear shirts.'

'That narrows it down to the entire male population.'

'No, I mean the ones who wear coloured shirts and like to strut about in the street. You know – you've got Hitler with his Brownshirts, and Mussolini with his Blackshirts, and then we had Mosley and his mob in black shirts too, and the Irish with their Blueshirts. They wear them like a uniform. And then on top of all that we had Greenshirts. I can't say I know exactly what the Greenshirts were all about – from what I recall it was a bit complicated. But this lot, with this badge, I think they were something to do with them.'

Tompkins held the tunic up and checked its length. 'I'm not sure whether it's meant to be for a man or a woman. It's about the right size for a dress for a woman, or it could be a sort of tunic for a small man.'

'And the shorts go with it?'

'Looks like it, sir. In that case I'd say it was all made for a small man or a boy. Wouldn't you?'

'Yes, I would. Well, thanks, Frank, you've been very helpful. It's connected in some way with the murder victim, you see. But you're right, it definitely does have a bit of a theatrical look about it. More a costume than a uniform.'

'Yes, sir. Suitable for pantomime, like a lot of what goes on inside this nick. All it needs now is a little bow and arrow to go with it. And speaking of Robin Hood and his merry men, that reminds me. The Sheriff of Nottingham would like a word with you.'

He nodded his head towards the corridor leading to Divisional Detective Inspector Soper's office, a conspiratorial look on his face. 'Wants to know how you're getting on with the unfortunate strangled lady, I believe.'

DDI Eric Soper presided over all CID operations on K Division of the Metropolitan Police, and therefore presided over Jago. The latter didn't know how old the DDI was, but reckoned he must surely be at retirement age by now. The powers that be had presumably kept him on because of the current shortage of men, and so Jago accepted the situation as just one more troublesome variety of collateral damage to be put up with for the duration. He braced himself and knocked on the door.

'Come,' said a voice from within.

He opened the door and went in. Soper was sitting at a heavy old mahogany kneehole desk. He looked up and stubbed out the last finger's width of his cigarette into an ashtray, then blew a cloud of smoke into the air.

'Take a seat, John,' he said, motioning to the chair on the opposite side of the desk. Close up, Jago noticed how battered the edge of the desk was – it looked as if it must have been brought down from the old police station on the corner of Langthorne Street when the present one was built at the end of the last century. He wondered which was older, the desk or its current occupant.

'Making progress with that Carpenters Road case?' said Soper, glancing at his watch.

'Yes, sir,' said Jago. 'Early days yet, but we've identified the victim and established one or two possible lines of enquiry.'

'Strangled with a stocking, I hear. Gruesome business, by the sound of it. The work of a maniac?'

'At this stage I couldn't say, sir. But you remember the Soho Strangler?'

'What? You don't mean to say it's another one of those? That's the last thing we want on our doorstep. This woman was a prostitute, then?'

'No, sir, we don't know, and I'm not jumping to any conclusions. It's just a bit reminiscent of those very unpleasant murders.'

'Have you ever seen a pleasant one?'

'No, sir.' Jago felt his patience was being tried already.

'I remember what it was like in the Great War,' said Soper. 'I don't know what four years of fighting did for the national economy, but as far as prostitution was concerned it was boom-time. Morals went to pot. Time was when a copper knew who all the ladies of easy virtue were and could keep an eye on things, but it seems in wartime even respectable women get involved in the trade. And as for unfaithfulness – where do I start? Some men are barely arrived at the front before their wives' eyes start wandering, and we know what that leads to. I say we should never have given them the vote. Look at the clothes they started wearing once they'd got it, and the things they started doing. And it'll be worse in this war, you mark my words.'

'Yes, sir.'

'So what are you doing next?'

'We've been tracking down family, friends and work colleagues and talking to them, and we've found a hat at the dead woman's flat that looks like it shouldn't have been there – a sailor's cap. I'm going to try to find the owner when we've finished here.'

'Good. And that safe-blowing business at the cinema?'

'You've heard about it, then, sir? It comes at a bad time, what with the murder to investigate.'

'That's too bad. We've no one to spare, so you'll have to take care of that too. If word gets around that picture houses are easy prey there'll be more of the same, and we need to keep the cinemas going – they're vital for morale, apparently, although I can't see why, given the frightful tosh they put on most of the time. If you ask me, we need more good old-fashioned patriotic films – the cinemas still have far too many feeble-minded comedies, and they're always showing that ridiculous romantic nonsense that comes from Hollywood.'

'Really, sir? I very rarely go.'

Soper stared at him. He sometimes wondered whether Jago treated these meetings as seriously as he should.

CHAPTER TWELVE

'Right,' said Amy Evans. 'There's some sausage toad keeping warm in the oven for your supper, and I'll make you a cup of tea before I go.'

'I wish you didn't have to,' said her husband, sneezing into a large handkerchief that had been more grey than white for some years. Hosea Evans was hunched in an easy chair only inches from the oven, trying to keep himself warm as what felt like a developing cold tormented his nose.

'You won't make it any better by sitting right next to that wet coat,' she replied, busying herself with the teapot.

'But I can't go back on duty in that. I'll catch my death.'

The Home Office in its wisdom had decreed that AFS men would be issued with only one set of uniform, so every time he got home from duty he had to hang up his tunic and trousers in front of the range, in the hope that the heat from its fire would dry them before his next shift. It didn't always work.

'Surely you don't have to go every night,' he said. 'You can't just abandon me to fend for myself when I'm working all hours like this.'

'I'm sorry, Hosea, but I'm not spending the night here until all this bombing's finished, and that's final.'

Amy Evans was a short, stout woman of forty-three, who, unlike her Welsh husband, was a native of Plaistow. Born in Brighton Road, she had lived there until she married Hosea, and then had moved into the next street, Stephen's Road, and lived there ever since.

'Look at the clock,' she said. 'I can't wait around any longer.'

She already had one arm in the sleeve of an old black overcoat and was struggling to get the other in while propping up a grubby canvas bag with her foot to stop it toppling over. Once she had the coat on, she poured a cup of tea as quickly as the pot allowed and handed it to him.

'I'll be back in the morning, same as always,' she continued, 'but my nerves just won't stand it. I don't think this old place would stand up to a decent clap of thunder, never mind high explosives. You know what I was like when the air raids started. It wouldn't be so bad if you were here with me, but six nights a week you're out fighting fires and suchlike. Now don't get me wrong, I think you're very brave for doing that, but there's no use pretending. I'm not made of the same stuff as you, and I'm not ashamed to admit it. It's men that start wars and men that fight wars. That Hitler must be a coward to bomb women and children, but he's doing it, and that's a fact. It's not going to change anything by me staying here and getting killed too. I'm just thankful Cissie's said I can spend the nights out there. At least I might get some sleep, and that means I can come back here in the morning and look after you properly. I only wish we could move out there ourselves.'

'Oh, yes, let's move out to the country. And what would we live on? I don't like this war any more than you do, and I can think of plenty of things I'd like to do all night more than trying to put out fires when half the German air force is up there dropping bombs on our heads. But at least it means I've got a job. When have I ever earned three pounds a week in the last ten years?'

'Yes, and when have I ever seen three quid coming into the house? I know a good wife isn't supposed to begrudge her husband a drink, but a pint here and a pint there and it soon dribbles away, doesn't it? I'm sure you're a valued customer down at the King George, aren't you? Not to mention the dog track. But I'd appreciate seeing a bit more of it in my purse, paying our bills.'

'We'd have a bit more to spare if you weren't spending it on train fares to Epping every night too, wouldn't we?'

'That's not fair. It's an emergency. I don't think we can say the same about your pint down at the King George, can we?'

'All right, love, you win. Look, we don't want to start arguing, do we? I mean, when I'm out at night fighting fires I feel like I'm just one step away from an early grave.

You've only got to be in the wrong place at the wrong time and you've had it, like those couple of lads when that wall fell on them last week. You go and see your sister, and have a good sleep, and God bless you, Amy. You're more than I deserve, and I know it.'

Her expression softened, and she crossed the room to give him a hug.

'And I love you too, Hosea. Just you look after yourself tonight.'

Before he could reply there was a knock at the front door. Amy opened it, to find Jago and Cradock standing on the pavement outside.

'Is Mr Evans at home?' said Jago, showing her his identity card. 'I think he'll be expecting us.'

She looked them both up and down, then beckoned them in.

'I'm on my way out, as you can probably see. I've got a train to catch, but if it's my husband you want to talk to you won't need me. Now, if you'll excuse me, I'll be off.'

She swung her bag over one shoulder, turned back to give Evans a brief kiss on the head, and went.

'Good afternoon, gentlemen,' said Evans. 'Do come in and take a seat. She's not walking out on me, by the way, if that's what you think.' He smiled. 'We've been happily married for nigh on twenty-five years. Got our silver wedding anniversary coming up next spring, although as you can see we're not the sort of people to have a lot of silver about the house. No. Thing is, she's a trekker.'

Jago was familiar with the term: he'd heard people using it since the first heavy air raid in September. But this was the first time he'd met one.

'She doesn't go and sleep out in the forest, like some of them,' Evans continued. 'I don't know what they're going to do when the winter comes, if this bombing hasn't let up by then. It's pathetic, really, isn't it? I mean, people having to cart their bedding and everything out to Epping Forest every night just to get away from the bombs? Fortunately for Amy, she's got a sister in Epping – Cissie, her name is. Got a nice little bungalow, and she doesn't mind Amy going out there. It's been weeks now, though. Every night. And there's no sign of the air raids easing off, is there? If they did, I might get a chance of a bit of sleep myself, but as it is I seem to be on duty morning, noon and night. I don't mind, though. I'm happy to take my chance with everyone else, and I can do my bit with the AFS. Plenty of work for us now, isn't there?'

'How long have you been a fireman, Mr Evans?' asked Jago.

'Since March of last year, when the council started recruiting people to join the AFS. I think we must've been one of the last places to start – the council here wasn't very keen to get ready for a war, it seems. Only part-time at first, of course, but then a couple of days before war was declared we were mobilised, and from then on I've been full-time.'

'And what did you do before that?'

'Not a lot. It's funny, really – the last proper job I had was stoking a furnace at Beckton gasworks, slaving away eight hours a day to keep the fires going, and now I'm seeing more fires than I ever wanted to see again and doing my hardest to put them out. Apart from that it was just bits and pieces, here and there. The last time I had good regular work was during the Great War. I got a job in a munitions factory. That was in 1915, when the government got caught short because the artillery at the front were running out of ammunition, and they built new factories everywhere. You remember that?'

'I remember hearing about it.'

'That packed up when the war ended, of course. There was no work, and I didn't have any real skills, so I had to leave Wales. Most of us did, you know. I had no desire to live in England – the English have never done anything for Wales except send us underground so they can make money. It's the same with Ireland, isn't it? Just exploited people, although at least the Irish have got rid of the English, or most of them anyway. I can't see the Welsh ever fighting the English, though, except on the rugby field. If you ask me, there's only one thing about living in England that's better than Wales, and that's that the pubs don't shut on Sundays here. Mind you, we've found plenty of ways round that in Wales, but I probably shouldn't be saying that to a policeman, should I?'

'We're not here to enquire into your drinking habits, Mr Evans. I'd like to know if you can tell us anything more about what happened last night.'

'Last night? Well, it was a big fire, I can tell you that for nothing. It had got a good hold on those old buildings before we got there. Incendiaries mainly, I expect. It's not so bad if there are fire-watchers on duty, but some of those places in Carpenters Road still don't have any. And even when they do, some of them skive, you know. It's too easy for them to slope off for a rest or a sleep, or anything else that might take their fancy, for that matter – you'd be shocked at what some of them get up to.'

'Perhaps we would, Mr Evans. Now, there's just a few questions I'd like to ask you about last night. First of all, just to confirm – you said it was you and Mrs Parks, the ARP warden, who found the body, yes?'

'That's right.'

'And I understand she'd asked you to help her get into the building.'

'Yes, although I wouldn't say asked – told, more like it. She was a bossy sort of woman – ordered me about like a flunkey. I think I heard her say "please" once, if that. I've seen her type before, mind – English, you know.'

'You went in through the back door?'

'Yes, she told me to break it open. It was a pretty flimsy affair, though. She probably could have kicked it open herself.'

'So why did she need you to do it?'

'Something to do with regulations. It used to be that firemen were allowed to break into a place but wardens weren't, but the government changed the regulations last

112

week, so she could've done. She said she didn't know, but I can't see how she wouldn't. I reckon she just wanted to get someone else to do the dirty work for her.'

'Dirty work?'

'Well, you know, if someone complained about having their door broken down, or if something else happened, she could say she wasn't the one who did it, like.'

'I see. As you were leaving us this morning, I had the impression that perhaps there was something else you were going to say. Was there?'

Evans looked as though he were trying to recall the moment, and his face took on an expression of puzzlement.

'Something else? No, I don't think so.'

'I wondered whether perhaps you'd seen something. Did you notice anything suspicious or unusual last night?'

Evans shook his head.

'Did you know the dead woman?' Jago continued.

'No. Never seen her before. She was a good-looking girl, though. Not your usual run-of-the-mill spinster wasting away in a lonely little flat.'

'What makes you say she was a spinster?'

'I don't know. I just assume she was, I suppose. She wasn't wearing any rings.'

'You noticed that, then.'

'Yes, but that wasn't suspicious or unusual, was it? There are women living alone in every street.'

'So you didn't see anything else that might shed some light on what happened in that flat?'

'No, I was too busy fighting those fires to notice anything else.'

'You know that area, though?'

'No better than any other.'

'Where are you stationed?'

'I'm at West Ham No. 4 station, in Abbey Road – just down the road from here.'

'Not far from Carpenters Road, then.'

'Yes, but we go wherever we're needed – some of these fires we've had recently have needed thirty pumps, and more, so they have to come from all over. Did you know? Before the war there were three fire stations in West Ham. Now there's twenty-three, and we're still fully stretched nearly every night. So I'm not in Carpenters Road often enough to know whether anything's out of the ordinary. Besides, when you're trying to control a fire hose with a hundred and fifty gallons of water a minute pumping through it you don't have much time to study your surroundings. No, I'd say apart from finding a dead body in a bedroom, the only thing I saw last night that was a bit odd was that ARP warden, Mrs Parks.'

CHAPTER THIRTEEN

By half past five on Monday evening Jago had been at work for nearly fourteen hours by his own reckoning, so he felt no guilt about keeping his appointment. He had arranged to meet Dorothy outside St Thomas's Hospital and he was anxious not to keep her waiting. When they'd first met, she was just an American journalist he'd been instructed to chaperone round some of the bombed areas of West Ham, but of late – well, he'd noticed himself becoming increasingly concerned not to displease her in anything. It had come as something of a surprise to him to discover what an effect a woman could have on a man in a few short weeks, especially when that man was a police officer with twenty years' service.

One of his pleasures in life was to see the Thames from Westminster Bridge, so instead of driving to the hospital he parked his car in Great Smith Street, behind Westminster Abbey, and walked back to the bridge. The late-afternoon light had begun to fade, but when he reached the river he could still clearly see on the other side of the water the hospital's turreted Victorian blocks ranged elegantly along the foreshore. He could also see the effects of the recent weeks' air raids. The block closest to the bridge was wrecked, as were two others farther south along the row.

Dorothy had said she'd be visiting the hospital this afternoon to interview staff about how they were coping with the bombs. She planned to write a feature for her newspaper in Boston, the angle of which, she'd explained to him on the phone, was to bring to life for the American reader the indiscriminate destruction of twentieth-century total war. Since the start of the Blitz in early September, more bombs had fallen on St Thomas's than on the Houses of Parliament facing it across the river, and there was no way of knowing whether this was by design or just bad luck.

The wind off the river was cold, and by the time he was nearing the far side of the bridge it was beginning to bite through his overcoat. His watch reassured him that he was on time, and he was pleased to spot her making her way towards him. Even from a distance there was something about her that stirred an unforced sense of admiration in him.

It wasn't long since he'd summoned up the courage to admit to Dorothy that he wanted to see more of her, but circumstances, his work and the war seemed to have conspired to keep them apart. Even worse – and he shuddered now with embarrassment at his own audacity – he'd confessed that his feelings for her were more than friendship. It wasn't in his nature to throw caution to the winds like that, and as soon as the words left his mouth he'd felt a stab of anxiety that he'd gone too far, that he'd probably frightened her off. It was comforting, then, to see her looking so relaxed, greeting him with a warm smile.

'Hello,' he said, then stopped, uncertain what to say next.

'Hello, John,' she replied. 'It's good to see you.'

'It's, er, good to see you too.' He hesitated again. 'Look, I've got the car parked across the river and I thought we could walk back over the bridge, but it's getting chilly, so shall we hop on a tram instead?'

'Sure.'

They crossed the road to where the trams ran back and forth on the northern side of the bridge and waited at the stop until a red number 72 slowed to a halt. They climbed the stairs to the upper deck as it moved off, and sat down. The seat was small, and as they squashed in together Jago held on to the seat in front, careful to ensure the swaying of the tram didn't bring them closer than Dorothy might think appropriate.

'How was your visit to the hospital?' he asked.

'Very interesting,' said Dorothy. 'Inspiring, too. They've had a bad time there. You could probably see for yourself it's taken quite a beating. The first block, the one in ruins next to the bridge, that was where the nurses lived. A doctor told me it was hit in one of the first raids, at half past two in the morning, and three floors collapsed – one poor nurse was trapped in the wreckage for hours before she died. He said he was amazed that only five of the women in there were killed.'

'I could see damage to some of the other blocks too as I came over the bridge.'

'Yes, they said they've had other bombs since then that've killed more nurses and doctors, and they took me for a look around. The hospital's been turned into a casualty clearing station, so they have to keep open day and night to look after people in the neighbourhood who've been injured in the raids. Everything's in the basement now – the staff live and sleep down there. They've got wards there, even an operating theatre, and they have to do all their sterilising on primus stoves, so it's pretty tough for them. One thing made me smile, though.'

'Yes? What was that?'

'You remember the time you showed me that statue outside the House of Lords that survived a bomb? One of your kings?'

'Yes. Richard the Lionheart. He was still on his horse, but his sword was bent.'

'That's the one. Well, I was looking around the yard outside that smashed-up nurses' home and I noticed a statue. It was another one of your kings, King Edward the something, from way back, and it was the only thing still standing. It made me think your kings must be built to last – with the possible exception of your most recent King Edward, of course. The eighth, I mean.'

'Let's not talk about him.'

'I know. Another Englishman with a great career ahead of him until it was all ruined by an American woman?'

Jago smiled at her. 'No comment,' he said. 'So anyway, you think you've got enough information to put your readers in the picture?'

'I think so. I just wanted to make one simple point – that when you drop bombs on a city from the sky, you're as likely to hit a hospital as you are an aircraft factory. In a modern war, no one's out of range. I notice, of course, that your own newspapers here always say the RAF bombers only hit what they call "selected military targets", but I don't think anyone seriously believes that, do they?'

'I think people who read newspapers believe what they want to believe.'

Jago stood up. 'We get off at the next stop. Let's go.'

The tram halted on the western side of the river. They descended the narrow, winding staircase, Dorothy first, and as they stepped down onto the road she continued the conversation.

'And what do you think people here want to believe?'

'That's simple, isn't it? They want to believe this war's worth fighting, that we're in the right, and that we'll win. The trouble is, I expect a lot of Germans probably believe the same about themselves, and some of them might be looking at a bombed hospital of their own and thinking it right now.'

'No one can accuse you of being jingoistic, can they?'

'By jingo, no,' said Jago with a laugh. 'Come along, let's have a drink. I know a nice little place just up the road.'

They headed away from the river, up Bridge Street, with the Palace of Westminster on their left.

'Would you mind if we took a small detour for a moment first?' he said. 'We've got about twenty minutes before blackout time, and there's a place here that's important to me.'

'Of course, yes. What is it?'

'The Cenotaph. I expect you've already seen it, and it may sound silly, but I was thinking recently that I'd just like to bring you to it sometime. I can't really explain why. Perhaps it's a bit like taking you to meet my family, except I haven't got one – more like meeting part of my past, I suppose.'

'Let's go, then.'

The cold wind he'd felt on Westminster Bridge blew into their faces as they walked up the wide avenue of Parliament Street to the white Portland stone war memorial. Its smooth surface was now pitted by the blast of a bomb that had hit the Colonial Office on the corner of Downing Street since his last visit.

'Maybe it's just me being sentimental,' said Jago, 'but sometimes if I'm in the area I like to come here and look at this.'

'To remember the Great War? I don't think that's sentimental – I think it's honourable. You're showing respect for your comrades. I can understand why that's important for you.'

'Can you? I appreciate that. There's no names on it, of course, but when I'm here I remember the men I knew – the ones who didn't come back. That's all, really. They're gone, and there's nothing to remember them by except monuments like this. I know some of them had families who might still mourn them, but I'm thinking of all the ones who died before they could marry or have children. Who'll remember them when the rest of us have gone? There were so many of them.'

'Yes, it's unbearably sad – all those young lives cut short. I haven't seen a lot of England yet, but it seems like every town and village has some kind of memorial with the names of their men who died engraved on it. I guess at least that means their names live on.'

'Yes. And have you heard of the thankful villages?'

Dorothy shook her head.

'That's what they call the English villages where every man returned alive from the war. I once heard that someone had worked out there were just thirty-two of them in the whole country. So almost every village lost someone.'

'But you can't live in the past, John. You know that, don't you? Life has to go on.'

'It does, yes. And it did, for me – I've had another twenty-odd years that those men didn't have. It's just that I feel I can never leave them behind or forget them. It would be like a betrayal.'

'It sounds as though you feel guilty for surviving.'

Jago fell silent as he reflected on her words.

'Yes,' he replied slowly, 'I think that's it. I do feel a kind of guilt because I'm still here and they're not. I see young people being happy and I think I can't be like that, I don't deserve it, I'd be denying what happened to my friends.'

'Don't you think they'd want you to be happy?'

'Maybe, but that's not how it seems to work inside me. Look, I hope you don't mind me talking like this – it's a bit gloomy, I know, but it's important to me because it's what makes me who I am. And there's a whole generation of us walking the streets who must feel the same way.'

Dorothy flashed him a warm smile. 'So what would you do if you met one of those lost and forgotten men now?'

'I don't know. You tell me.'

'I think you'd take him for a drink.'

'I get it,' said Jago, smiling back at her. 'You're right. OK, let's go to that little place I mentioned.'

Five minutes later they were standing outside a pub on the corner of Bridge Street and Cannon Row. Through an open window they could hear the clamour of animated conversation.

'Here it is,' said Jago. 'I told you it wasn't far.'

He opened the door for Dorothy and they went in. The bar was small, but he found them somewhere to sit and went off to buy drinks.

'I think you'll like it,' he said on his return, handing a glass to Dorothy. 'It's got character.'

'It has,' she replied, gazing round the bar. 'I hope this won't disappoint you, but actually I already know this

122

place. I've been here before – some of my newspaper colleagues brought me. They say it's very popular with journalists – in fact I'd say the place is probably full of hacks. But that doesn't matter. It's a cosy old joint, and I do like it. Now, tell me how your case is going. You said on the phone that it's a murder, right?'

'Yes, it's a poor young woman who was found strangled in her flat. You'll understand that I can't tell you much about it, and I certainly don't want you writing about it in that *Boston Post* of yours.'

'Don't worry. I'd have to get past your censors first, and I don't think they'd allow me to file any copy to the States that mentions things your own press isn't allowed to say about a case. Just tell me what you feel you can.'

'Well, in some ways it's what you might call a fairly conventional murder, but there's one thing that's worrying me. There seem to be similarities with some other crimes that were committed in the mid thirties, and pretty unpleasant they were too. Four women were murdered in their flats, most of them prostitutes, and all strangled – the first one with a silk stocking. The papers called the murderer the Soho Strangler, and it was big news.'

'Yes, I remember hearing about it. I'm sure it was reported in the US press sometime back then. So was this woman a prostitute too?'

'We're not sure. There are indications that she might've been, but no proof, so we're keeping an open mind. The thing is, there's one point I'd like to confirm, and you're the person most likely to be able to help me.'

'Well, I'm surprised to hear that, but I'll help if I can.'

Jago reached into the inside pocket of his jacket and pulled out a buff envelope.

'This is the stocking that was used,' he said, opening the envelope and pulling out a few inches of the item it held. 'I won't take it out, otherwise someone here might think I'm a black-market trader.'

'And call the police?'

'Exactly. I just wondered – can you tell me what it's made of?'

Dorothy took the material between her forefinger and thumb, and rubbed it gently.

'Yes, I can – it's nylon. They're the latest thing.'

'That's what we thought – or rather, what Cradock thought. Apparently you can't buy them in Britain, so neither of us has ever seen one. I've heard of nylon bristles on a toothbrush, but I've never seen it in this form. How's it made?'

'They call it the new miracle material – at least, I guess that's what the people who are trying to sell it call it. It was invented in the States last year, and they say it's made from coal. Mind you, that sounds like someone's simplified the chemistry involved – I don't suppose the DuPont Corporation wants the recipe to get out. Stockings like this only went on sale back home at the beginning of the year.'

'It'll be a long time before we see them in the shops here, then. It said in the paper today that people won't even be able to buy silk stockings from the end of next month. Apparently the government's going to stop the shops selling them, because we need all the silk we can get for barrage balloons and parachutes.'

'That's why women are starting to wear slacks,' said Dorothy. 'A lot of men seem to think that's going against the natural order of things, but British girls I've talked to say if they can't buy stockings they're going to wear slacks instead, and the men will have to like it or lump it.'

'So the question is, how did our murderer get his hands on a nylon stocking?'

'Only on the black market, I guess.'

'Well, the war seems to be doing wonders for the black market – it's thriving on all the shortages. But look, let's talk about something else. I'm determined not to go on about work all the time, but I was sure you'd know a nylon stocking if you saw one.'

'I don't mind you talking about your work. It's interesting.'

'Yes, but I told you I'd like to spend time with you, and I meant just for its own sake, not because work demands it. And what've I done? I've taken up your time asking you to identify evidence.'

'And I have to be going pretty soon. I have work of my own to do this evening.'

'Writing about everyday life in a London hospital?'

'Correct. But I'll tell you what I'd like to do. Let's eat together.'

'Certainly. Lunch tomorrow?'

'No, I'm going to be very busy tomorrow with meetings and writing. How about we meet up the day after tomorrow, Wednesday, for breakfast?'

'Breakfast? Where would you like to go?'

'Well, I have to say it's been very nice of you to introduce me to so many of your, er, exotic English eating places, but I like seeing you on your home ground. Let's go to Rita's place. What time does she open?'

'Seven o'clock, usually. Could you manage half past seven?'

'That would suit me fine.'

'OK, it's a deal. I'll tell Cradock I'll be in a little late.'

'No, bring him along.'

'Really?'

'Sure. He's sweet – and besides, I want to ask him how his love life's going.'

CHAPTER FOURTEEN

'Good morning, Peter,' said Jago with a glance at the clock as Cradock entered the CID office on Tuesday morning. 'I trust you slept well.'

'Morning, guv'nor. Better than yesterday, thank you. I could've done without that murder – nearly put me off my breakfast.'

'Not quite, though, eh? In fact I was under the impression that you'd had two breakfasts yesterday.'

'Can't work on an empty stomach, can we, sir?'

'No – and speaking of work, which I believe is what you're here for, have you spoken to Tom Gracewell yet? I want to know whether he can tell us anything about what kind of life Joan Lewis lived.'

'Not yet, sir. I thought I'd catch him on my way in this morning, but it turns out he's been given a day's compassionate leave – his mother's been bombed out of her house in Harwich and she's in hospital. And you'll never guess who did the bombing. I couldn't believe it – they said it was the Italian air force.'

'Well, I suppose they had to join in eventually – do their bit, as it were.'

'Yes, but it's a long way from Rome to Essex, isn't it?'

'It is, Peter, but just because they're the Italian air force it doesn't necessarily mean they have to take off in Italy. Hitler's conveniently defeated France for them, so now they're probably based just over the Channel somewhere, if only to save petrol.'

'Oh, yes,' said Cradock, regretting having provided what had seemed to him an interesting detail.

'Anyway, give my best wishes to Gracewell and his mother when you see him. When's he due back?'

'Tomorrow morning, sir. He's on early turn, so I'll try to catch him when he comes off duty at two.'

'No. I'd like you to see him before he starts – see if you can catch him at half past five, before they parade for duty.' He saw Cradock's face sink. 'What's the matter?' he asked. 'You must've done plenty of early starts in your time, when you were in uniform, surely.'

'Yes, sir, but then we knocked off at two in the afternoon. I can't see us doing that tomorrow. Can you?'

'Definitely not, but you're a young man and fighting fit. And if you need consolation, turn up at Rita's by half past seven and I'll treat you to breakfast.'

Cradock's face brightened visibly. 'Thanks, guv'nor.'

'You're welcome. Now, no word yet on Joan's fingerprints, I suppose?'

'No. The Yard said they had a lot of record cards to

check but they'd let us know as soon as possible.'

Cradock pulled a chair out behind the desk across the office and sat down.

'Very well,' said Jago. 'But don't get yourself too comfortable – I want to have a word with Sylvia Parks before she goes off duty.'

The ARP post was in the basement of a derelict house that appeared to be otherwise uninhabited. Jago went down the outside steps at the front, followed by Cradock, and knocked on the half-open door. There was no answer, so he pushed it and peered in. The sole occupant, as far as he could see, was an exhausted-looking middle-aged woman in a dirty coat sitting at a battered table, writing something on a sheet of paper. She glanced up to see who it was, then returned to her writing.

'Mrs Parks?' he enquired. 'I'm sorry to disturb you.'

'Don't tell me,' she sighed. 'You're from the town hall and you need to inspect our milk bills – or is it to check we're using the right forms for our incident reports? Well, you can do what you like, but don't expect any help from me – I've been up all night and now I'm going home.'

'We're the police, actually – West Ham CID. I'm Detective Inspector Jago and this is Detective Constable Cradock. We're making enquiries in connection with the body you found at 28 Carpenters Road yesterday morning.'

She put her pen down on the table and stood up.

'I'm sorry, Inspector, I just assumed you were more of those fusspots from the council. They don't seem to actually do anything except go around inspecting what other people are doing. You'd better come in. How can I help you?'

The two men stepped into the room.

'We were told by one of our officers at the scene yesterday morning that you'd gone,' said Jago, 'and we were hoping you'd return so we could speak to you, but you didn't. I wonder if you could tell me why that was.'

'Certainly. The constable said you'd want to speak to me but he didn't tell me to come back, and I couldn't hang around waiting for you because I had a report to send in from the post. Then when I eventually got here through all the usual chaos I discovered the phone was dead, so I had to take it all the way to the next post. By the time I'd done that I had to go to work.'

'I see. You're not a full-time warden, then?'

'No, I do two or three nights a week as a volunteer. It's hard, but we take it in turns to grab a bit of sleep whenever we can between air raids. You get to the point where sleep's the thing you need most in the world – even more than food. Only trouble is, sometimes you're so tired you can't sleep – either that or the things you've seen in the raids make it impossible to sleep.'

Her face was streaked with grime from the night's work, but Jago could still see the signs of strain.

'Where do you work?' he asked.

'At the Co-op – the London Co-operative Society, I suppose I should say. At the head office in Maryland Street. I'm a comptometer operator – it's skilled work, and I get paid more than I would as a full-time warden, so I can't afford to give it up. Besides, I need to be sure I've got a job when all this ends. I'm a widow.'

'I'm sorry.'

'Yes, well, it's a long time ago now.'

'Not a result of the war?'

'No, at least not this one – it was the last one, which you look old enough to remember.'

Jago nodded, still studying her face.

'There's nothing exceptional about my story,' she said. 'Robbie and I had been walking out together for six weeks or so. We had a lovely quiet stroll one Tuesday evening, then we said goodnight with a little kiss and I returned to my lodgings and went to bed. When I woke up the next morning I discovered we'd declared war on Germany while I was asleep. Two days later he told me he'd volunteered for Kitchener's Army with a few of his pals. I was shocked and told him not to, but he said it was too late, he'd taken the king's shilling, and that was that. Next thing I knew, he was off. I wrote to him all the time, of course, and he wrote back when he could. Everyone said the war would be over by Christmas and Robbie'd come home a hero, and I believed them. But Christmas came and went, and he was still in France. They gave him a few days' leave the next year and we got married, but he had to go straight back. Six months later he was killed.'

'I'm very sorry to hear that.'

'Thank you. It was in May 1916 – he was in the Royal Field Artillery and was killed in a German attack near Vimy Ridge. They told me later it was the heaviest shelling of the war up to then. His battery was eight miles behind the front-line trenches, but even so a German shell hit his gun pit and they were all killed.'

Jago nodded again, not wanting to intrude too quickly with his questions.

'That sort of thing leaves you numb,' she continued. 'You feel like you might as well be dead yourself. But don't get me wrong – it was still a shock to find that woman strangled. It's bad enough having the enemy coming over and bombing us, without some swine of our own going round murdering innocent women – assuming she was an innocent woman, of course. I didn't know her.'

'But you're an ARP warden,' said Jago. 'Aren't you supposed to know everyone who lives in your area?'

'Yes, but that wasn't my sector. I'd just been sent over to prepare a damage report for the post warden. I didn't even clap eyes on the warden responsible for Carpenters Road.'

'I see. Now can you just clarify something for me? Was it you who told the fireman to break in?'

'Yes.'

'Why didn't you just kick the door open yourself? It looked pretty flimsy to me.'

'As far as I knew, that would've been against regulations. And anyway, I didn't know what it looked like until we got there. I'd tried the front door but there was no answer, so I assumed we'd probably have to break in. By the time I saw the back door, the fireman was there with his axe, so I asked him to do it.'

'Did you disturb anything in the flat, touch anything?'

'I don't think so. The only thing I did was close the blackout curtains. The light was on, you see.'

'Did you turn the light off?'

'No – I mean not at first, but I did turn it off when we left.'

'Who went in first?'

'That was me. Mr Evans opened the door and let me go in, then he followed.'

'And which of you found the body?'

'I did. It was in the bedroom.'

'Did you notice whether the dead woman was wearing any rings?'

'Rings? I've no idea. I didn't have time to examine the body. We had to get it out.'

'Whose idea was it to remove the body from the flat?'

'I'm not sure. I think we just decided.'

'Did you discuss it?'

'Yes. I said we ought to get the body out, because it looked as though the poor woman had been murdered – I don't suppose it's very easy to commit suicide in that way.'

'And Mr Evans agreed?'

'No, he didn't, actually, now you mention it – not at first. He said, "Let the dead bury their dead" – you know, like in the Bible. He's Welsh, of course, or at least he said he was, and they're always quoting the Bible, aren't they? Anyway, he said that, and when I asked him what he meant, he said she was dead, and nothing was going to bring her back, and he ought to be outside putting fires out and saving the living, not wasting time getting a body out of a building. I said, "But I can't get her out by myself, and besides, what would people think of us if we left her in here and the place caught on fire? And what about the police, too?" This poor woman would've been murdered and we would've destroyed all the evidence. I said to him, "If we leave her in here and it burns down, the police might even think we had something to do with it.'"

'And then what?'

'Well, that seemed to make sense to him, because he suddenly changed his mind and started picking her up. Got her in one of those fireman's lifts, you know – I could never have done it. I just helped holding doors open and so on. So we got her out and put her on the pavement, where you found her. I took a blanket from the bedroom as we left so I could cover her up – I didn't know how long it would be before the police came, and I didn't want her to be lying out there for all the world to see.'

'So it was your idea to get the body out and preserve the evidence?'

'Yes, that's right. Why?'

'Oh, nothing. I'm just making sure I get the facts straight. I got the impression from Mr Evans that it was more of a joint decision.'

'Well, I suppose it was – in the end.'

'Thank you.'

'Will that be all? It's just that I'm very tired.'

'Of course. I'm grateful for your assistance. I hope your next shift isn't quite so dramatic.'

'There's no need to worry about me, Inspector. I'm used to it now. In fact, to tell you the truth, there's nowhere I'd rather be at night than out among the bombs and the fires. The risk of dying is the only thing that makes me feel alive and worthwhile.'

CHAPTER FIFTEEN

On their return to the police station Jago pulled out from under his desk the suitcase that Beryl had entrusted to him the previous day. Cradock gave him a quizzical look.

'You still think that stuff's got something to do with this murder, sir?'

'I've no idea, Peter, but it's the only thing we've got that might tell us something about Joan. I'd especially like to find out why she didn't want Audrey to get her hands on it.'

'Sounds like we should drop in on Audrey, then, sir.'

'Indeed we should. Get your coat.'

Jago reckoned it would be quicker to walk than to try taking the car. At this time of the morning the streets would still be blocked by wreckage from the night's air raids, and it would probably be easier to scramble past any obstructions on foot. His decision was vindicated soon after they set off, when they found their route blocked by a yellow sign saying 'Danger: unexploded bomb'. They took a side road instead, and from here to their destination the streets were clear. Ten minutes later they were in the living room of 166 Carnarvon Road.

'I'm sorry to disturb you again, Mrs Lewis,' said Jago, 'but I thought you'd want to know the body we found has now been formally identified as your daughter-in-law. Her sister, Beryl, identified her for us. There was no reason for us to doubt it was Joan, but we still have to go through these formalities, just to be certain.'

'I understand, Inspector. You have your job to do, thankless drudgery though it must be at times.'

This wasn't the term Jago would have chosen to describe his work, but he hadn't come here to discuss his professional life with her.

'There's something I'd like to ask you, too,' he continued.

'Be my guest. But if you're thinking I can provide you with revealing insights into the deeper workings of young Joan's mind, I'm afraid you're in for a disappointment. I can't say I ever detected much depth to the woman. As I understand it, her job was to walk up and down the aisle and shine a torch onto vacant seats. That says it all, doesn't it?'

'You think she was capable of more?'

Audrey shrugged. 'I think she lacked ambition. Or perhaps she simply lacked ability – I don't know.'

'But she was your daughter-in-law.'

'You don't need to tell me that. Clearly my son thought a lot more of her than I did, but that was his prerogative as her husband. Unfortunately in this day and age one does not select one's children's marriage partners, more's the pity. They make their bed and regrettably they must lie in it.'

'It seems she was well regarded by her employer and colleagues.'

'Was she really? Well, that's as may be, but I'm afraid it's a subject I can't comment on. Now, what else did you want to know?'

Jago picked up the suitcase and showed it to her.

'Do you recognise this?' he asked.

'If you mean do I know what it is, then yes, of course I do. It's a suitcase, and a rather cheap one too. If you mean do I know whose suitcase it is, then I do not. It's certainly not mine.'

Jago put the case down again and opened it. He took out the green tunic and handed it to Audrey.

'Do you recognise this garment?'

Audrey looked at it warily. 'Where did you get it?' she said.

'We were given it by someone Joan had asked to look after it, and we wondered whether you might be able to shed any light on it. I'd like to know whether it might've belonged to her husband.'

'My son, you mean?'

'Yes – Richard.'

Audrey fell silent. She draped the tunic across her lap and stroked it slowly, then raised it to her face and nuzzled her cheek against it. She seemed to become aware that Jago was watching her and abruptly stopped.

'Yes,' she said, putting it down beside her, 'it was my son's. She must have stolen it when she moved out of my house.'

'Stolen it?'

'Yes, she took it without my permission. It belonged to my son long before he met her. It's part of who he was when he was younger, not who he is now, and she should have left it with me when she went.'

Jago reached out to take it back, but she snatched it away and held it close to her.

'I have to take it, Mrs Lewis.'

'No, you're not having it. It's mine. I'm not having anyone—'

'Anyone what?'

'I'm not having anyone else get their hands on this. It belongs to me. It's private.'

'I'm sorry, Mrs Lewis, but it may be required as evidence in our enquiry.'

'Evidence? How can this possibly be evidence?'

'Just let me have it, Mrs Lewis.'

The tone of his voice indicated that this was not a matter for discussion. She slowly handed the tunic to him.

'Look after it, please, Inspector. I'd like it back when you've finished with it.'

'Thank you, Mrs Lewis. Now, can you tell me about it?'

'No. I don't want to talk about it. Just go away and leave me alone.'

'Very well,' said Jago, carefully folding the tunic. 'If you change your mind, let me know – I'd like to have a little more information about this. But I can see it's important to you and I don't want to distress you. Goodbye, Mrs Lewis. We'll see ourselves out.'

'Well,' said Jago as he and Cradock walked away from the house. 'That was interesting.'

'Certainly was. One minute butter wouldn't melt in her mouth, next thing I thought she was going to fight you for that stuff. It obviously meant something to her, but I couldn't tell whether that was a good something or a bad something.'

'If she's right and the tunic was Richard's, maybe it just reminded her of his younger days when the world was a different place and he would've been safe, which it sounds like he isn't now. But maybe it's not as simple as that. It may have nothing to do with Joan's death, but it's an odd thing all the same – curious.'

Jago turned right into Romford Road, and Cradock followed him. He was about to ask where they were going next when Jago stopped and looked at his watch.

'Ten to eleven,' he said. 'Nearly opening time.'

'Are we going for a drink, guv'nor?' he asked, his voice at once hopeful and surprised.

'Not necessarily, but I do think we should drop in at the Green Man and see who's behind the bar.'

CHAPTER SIXTEEN

The clock on the saloon bar wall at the Green Man showed six minutes past eleven, soon enough after opening time for only the more committed drinkers to have arrived. The landlord was pulling a pint for a short, elderly customer in a shabby black suit, who handed over his coins and shuffled away, sipping appreciatively from the glass. When he had gone, the landlord cast a knowing eye over the two men who had just entered, and particularly over the cheap-looking suitcase the younger one was carrying.

'Morning, gents,' he said. 'You selling something?'

'No,' said Jago, 'we're the police. Are you the landlord?'

'Er, yes, I am, as it happens. And before you start, I was just about to say I don't want any black-market stuff going on in here. This is a respectable public house, you know.'

'I'm sure it is,' said Jago, quite certain that the conversation would have taken a different direction if the man hadn't been entertaining two members of the Metropolitan Police. 'I understand you have a barmaid called Elsie. Is she here?'

'Elsie Marwell? Yes, she is. Only part-time, a few shifts a week, but I'd have her here every day if I could – she's one of my best. You'll find her through in the public bar. There's two of the girls in there – she's the shorter one, dark hair. Not in trouble, is she?'

'No, we just want a word. Is there somewhere we can speak to her in private?'

'Yes. Tell her I said you could use the back room.'

The public bar was busier than the saloon, but not yet crowded. A few men were drinking, and a boisterous game of darts was underway at the far end. Two young women in their mid-twenties were behind the bar. The taller of them, with extravagant blonde hair, was serving drinks, but the shorter one, a robust-looking brunette with a firm jaw, appeared to be locked in a fierce altercation with a heavily built man a good foot taller than herself. Jago held Cradock back while he observed the proceedings. They weren't close enough to hear everything the barmaid said, but she was looking the man straight in the eye, and from the jut of her chin and the sharp working of her mouth he could tell she was having serious words with him. As they approached the bar they saw her fling her arm out towards the door and heard her say, 'Just get out.'

Jago watched the man skulk out of the door and waited at the bar while the barmaid adjusted a stray lock of hair that had fallen out of place during her argument.

'Was he giving you trouble?' he said.

'He probably thought he was,' she replied, 'but it was nothing. He's only been in here five minutes and he starts getting fresh. A bit forward, if you know what I mean, and when I told him to go and wash his mouth out he got a bit uppity. So I told him to sling his hook. I won't be spoken to like that. If a customer can't keep a civil tongue in his head he can go and buy his pint somewhere else.'

'What does your landlord think about that?'

'He says he wishes some of the other staff here would do the same. We've had girls working behind this bar who wouldn't say boo to a goose. They don't last long. Just kids, some of them. If you don't stand up to these types they'll be all over you. I tell them where to get off, and as far as I'm concerned they can take a running jump. Now, you two gentlemen look altogether more civilised specimens. What can I get you to drink?'

'Nothing, thank you – we're here on business. We're police officers and we understand you're Joan Lewis's sister-in-law. We'd just like to have a word with you in private – the landlord says we can use the back room, so perhaps you could show us the way.'

'Police? Right, well, yes, you'd better come with me.'

She beckoned to the other woman, who was pulling a drink at the far end of the bar.

'Cover for me for a tick, will you, Anne? Just got to have a word – shan't be long.'

She took Jago and Cradock into a room at the back of the pub and offered them each a chair.

'Mrs Marwell?' asked Jago. 'Is that correct?'

'Yes, that's my name. What do you want to know?'

'I understand you and your husband live with your mother in Carnarvon Road.'

'Yes, we did have our own place but we were bombed out, and she took us in. It's only one room – not ideal, but it's better than having to leave the area or get something temporary that's not fit for human habitation.'

'And your husband?'

'I know what you're thinking – what kind of man lets his wife work behind the bar in a place like this? I'll tell you what kind – a man who means well but doesn't bring enough money home of a Friday. He works at Addingtons, the varnish factory in Carpenters Road – they make something for putting on aeroplane wings now, for the RAF. Do you know the place?'

'Yes, I believe I've been past it, but never inside.'

'Well, it's not much to speak of, but at least he gets a bit of overtime – it's shifts, and he has to go in and do extra hours at all sorts of odd times, but it's still not enough. I want him to get into office work, accounts or something, but he'd have to study for exams to do that, and somehow he's never got time for it.'

'These air raids have made life busier for everyone.'

'I grant you that, but he manages to find time for his mates, and for his amateur dramatics. That's all been cut back, of course, what with the war and everything. They don't do proper performances like they used to, and I keep telling him he should use the time for studying, but he says they're doing play-readings instead, whatever that means. I suppose it means they sit around and read a play – strikes me as a complete waste of time, but it seems to keep him happy.'

'We have some bad news for you, I'm afraid. It's—'

'I know. It's about Joan, isn't it? You needn't worry – my mum's told me about it already. It's a terrible business, but at least she's at peace now – doesn't have to put up with all these bombs any more.'

'Were you close to Joan?'

'We got on all right, but I didn't see much of her, what with my working hours and hers both being a bit irregular.'

'Did you see her on Sunday?'

'Is that when it happened?'

'Yes, sometime after she finished work on Sunday evening.'

Elsie slowly shook her head. 'No. I was at work myself on Sunday evening. It's dreadful, isn't it? Just thinking of her being – you know. I always insist on Derek walking me home when these air raids are on. I'm not going out there on my own, I'll tell you that for nothing. You never know who might be prowling around in the blackout, do you?'

'Derek's your husband?'

'That's right. I was due to knock off at eight o'clock, but I stayed on a bit until it sounded like the bombing had stopped and it had all quietened down outside. Sunday night's Derek's fire-watching night, see, so I had to make sure he'd walked me home before it was time for him to go on duty. Mind you, it was more like me walking him home – the air raid had made him all jittery, and when he gets like that it's like walking home with a jellyfish. I don't know what he does on those fire-watching shifts – if an incendiary landed anywhere near him I think he'd run a mile. You should've seen him when he tripped over that sailor – nearly jumped out of his skin.'

'A sailor?'

'Yes. Some bloke lying in a shop doorway, legs sticking out all over the pavement. I knew he was a sailor, because of the uniform – nobody else wears those bell-bottomed trousers, do they? I wouldn't have noticed him in the blackout, only there was a torch lying on the ground beside him, still on, so I bent down and turned it off. Derek can't have been looking where he was going. You could smell the drink on him – the sailor, that is, not Derek. He looked like he'd had a few too many and passed out. Well, you know what sailors are like with the drink – we've had a few rough times with his sort in the pub over the years, I can tell you.'

'Do you happen to know who this sailor was?'

'No. A sailor's a sailor to me. But I'm pretty sure I'd seen him before. Judging by what I could see of his face, he was the one who'd been selling stockings in here earlier on.'

'What kind of stockings were they?'

'I don't know – I was too busy behind the bar to see them close up.'

'Would anyone else know his name?'

'I don't know. You could try the landlord, though – I can ask him if you like.'

'Thank you, but I think we'll ask him ourselves before we go. Tell me, though, when you came across the sailor in the doorway, where was it?'

'On the corner of Martin Street. You know – just down the High Street a bit, past Station Street.'

'And what time was it?'

'Well, Derek came for me just before half past eight, and we walked home, so it would've been a bit after that.'

'It's about ten minutes' walk home, I imagine?'

'Yes, we got home about twenty to nine.'

'And forgive me for asking a strange question, but when you saw the sailor lying there, was he wearing a cap?'

'A sailor's hat, you mean? I'm not sure, let me think. Yes, now I remember – he was sort of slumped in the doorway with his back against the wall, and his cap was pushed down towards his eyes a bit, still on his head but looking a bit precarious. Why do you ask?'

'It's just that we found a sailor's cap in Joan's flat, and we're wondering how it got there.'

'Sorry, can't help you with that – we just left him there and carried on home, back to my mum's house. I stayed in after that, and Derek went off back to Carpenters Road to do his fire watching.'

'Thank you, Mrs Marwell. I think that'll be all.'

'You're welcome, I'm sure. So what was Joan doing entertaining sailors in her flat?'

'I'm not suggesting she was. It's probably of no significance, but it's a little loose end that I'd like to tie up. Which reminds me – before we go there's another small matter you may be able to shed light on.'

He motioned to Cradock to pass the suitcase, then opened it and took out the tunic.

'Do you recognise this?'

She looked at it blankly. 'No,' she said. 'I haven't the faintest idea. Never seen it before.'

'Very well, in that case we'll let you return to your duties, and we'll see the landlord on our way out.'

They found the landlord serving drinks in the saloon bar, as before.

'Got what you wanted?' he asked.

'Yes, thank you,' said Jago. 'Mrs Marwell was most helpful. She happened to mention, among other things, that there was a sailor in here on Sunday selling stockings.'

'Look, I told you—'

'This is not to do with any informal commercial transactions that may or may not have been going on. I'm looking for a witness who may be able to help us, and I have reason to believe he may be a sailor who was in here on Sunday. If you can tell me his name I'd be most obliged.'

'Right, well, in that case it was young Ernie Sullivan. He's a local boy, used to be one of our regulars. I think he joined up a year or two ago, but he was always in here before that, and we still see him if he gets a bit of leave.'

'And is he usually in here selling things?'

'No, not usually.'

'Do you know where we can find him?'

'No, but his dad still lives up Windmill Lane. Don't know the number, but Ernie once said it's a flat over a greengrocer's, so if he hasn't moved or been bombed out, you should be able to find him round there.'

'Thank you. That's very helpful.'

'All right,' said the landlord. 'But remember – it wasn't me who told you.'

CHAPTER SEVENTEEN

'I was just wondering, guv'nor,' said Cradock as they came out of the Green Man and turned left up Stratford High Street. 'How much longer do I have to cart this old suitcase around? I'm beginning to feel like some sort of commercial traveller – I keep thinking people are expecting it to be full of brushes or cleaning products when I open it.'

'That's better than people looking at you and wondering what a young copper's doing with a suitcase,' said Jago. 'Good training for plainclothes work – learning how to blend in with your surroundings. But if we don't find anyone soon who can tell us whether it has any significance I'll give up. Elsie wasn't much help, was she?'

'No, sir, but that was a good tip about the sailor – selling stockings and all that. I don't suppose she'd have let him do it if the landlord didn't approve, though – he'd have been out on his ear. She could look after herself, I reckon. I wonder what would've happened at the Regal if she'd been the fire watcher instead of that Bert Wilson bloke.'

'You don't think much of him?'

'Well, he looked the part, didn't he? A real bruiser. But I wasn't so sure.'

'You weren't convinced?'

'No, I don't think I was. At first sight you'd think yes, he's a tough guy, the sort of bloke it'd be handy to have with you if you ran into a spot of bother down a dark alleyway. But if that was so, I'd have thought he'd put up more of a fight against whoever broke into the cinema that night. All sounded a bit convenient, didn't it? You know – he didn't see them, they grabbed him from behind, and they tied him up and gagged him before he could do anything.'

'So you think if it was an inside job he might've been part of it?'

'Not necessarily, but he did have keys.'

'Only for that night when he was on duty.'

'Yes, but he could've got a copy made some other time. Or he could've just let them in on the night. We've only got his word for it that he was on the roof when he heard the safe being blown. He could've let them in and then gone back up to where he was supposed to be.'

'Let's ask him a few questions, then,' said Jago. 'We'll drop in on our way back to the station – and if he's there we'll put your theory to the test.'

* * *

They walked up the High Street towards the cinema. On their right, Stratford Market railway station seemed to be untouched by the recent air raids, but a little farther on the Times Furnishings store had been obliterated by a direct hit. The breeze still carried the acrid tang of burnt timber.

At the Regal, they found Sidney Conway in his office. He confirmed that Bert Wilson was on duty and offered them the use of the room, then sent for the doorman. When Wilson arrived, the manager made a show of gathering up some papers and leaving.

'Mr Wilson,' said Jago. 'We'd just like to ask you a few more questions, if that's all right.'

'Fine by me,' said Wilson with a shrug.

Jago motioned to Cradock to take over the questioning.

'Right,' said Cradock. 'This break-in – the men who did it seem to have let you off lightly, don't they?'

'I suppose you could say that,' Wilson replied, 'although at the time there was no knowing what they might do.'

'I understand you had a set of keys to the cinema.'

'Yes, the fire watcher needs them to get around the building. What are you getting at?'

'Only that when someone like you is alone in a building at night with a set of keys and a safe full of money, and some other blokes get in and steal that money, someone's bound to ask whether you were in cahoots with them.'

'Cahoots? What are you talking about?'

'I'm talking about you having a finger in the pie, Mr Wilson.'

'What are you suggesting? That I let them in or something?'

'You wouldn't be the first.'

'Why would I do that?'

'For money, of course.'

'But that doesn't make sense. There'd only be a couple of nights' takings in that safe, say three or four hundred quid. There were two blokes who grabbed me, and they probably had someone keeping watch outside or downstairs, so there could've been three or four of them. If they split the money between them they'd get a hundred each, and for that they'd risk going to jail for blowing a safe, so what would they give someone like me for letting them in? Twenty, maybe? I earn two quid a week, so that means for ten weeks' money I'd risk getting eighteen months' hard labour, losing my job and possibly being out of work for the rest of my life. Why would I do that?'

'You take an interest in the courts' sentencing for cinema-breaking, do you?' Jago interjected.

'No, I don't – but I do take an interest in what goes on in cinemas. I read about a case in the paper, that's all,' said Wilson. He turned back to Cradock. 'Now look, I may be only a doorman, but I'm not stupid. I've got plans for my life. If Mr Conway can be a success, I reckon I can too. I'm as bright as he is, any day. Besides, I'm expecting to get my call-up papers soon, and if I come out of this war with a good record I'll be able to be something more than a doorman. I wouldn't chuck all that away for twenty quid.'

'Can anyone confirm you were on the roof when you said you were?' said Cradock.

'No, of course not. We only have one fire watcher on duty at night, so I was on my own. You have to believe me, though – I'm not a crook.'

Jago decided it was time for him to take over.

'All right, Mr Wilson,' he said. 'Thank you for that. There's something else I'd like to ask you. When we were with you and Mr Conway yesterday, I understood from what he was saying that you'd worked previously at the Broadway Super and he gave you a job when it was bombed, like he did for Joan Lewis.'

'That's right, yes.'

'So you knew Joan before she came to work here.'

'Yes.' Wilson was beginning to look irritated by this questioning. 'Look,' he continued, 'so I knew her. So what?'

'Just getting it clear in my own mind, Mr Wilson. I'd be interested to know what you thought of Joan – what kind of person was she?'

Wilson's expression softened. 'Well,' he said, 'she was just lovely. She was the kindest and gentlest person I've ever known.'

'Did you ever have reason to believe there might be another side to her character?'

'What are you trying to suggest?'

'I'm just wondering. Sometimes when we get to know someone we find they're not everything they seem.'

'Well, that's as may be with some people, but not with Joan. She was always really nice, the kind of girl any

154

bloke would be proud to have on his arm. When I heard she'd married Richard, I thought he must be the luckiest man in town.'

'Ah, so you knew Richard? Mr Lewis, that is?'

'I used to. I hadn't seen him for ages, but when Joan told me she was married and who her husband was, I realised that was the Richard I used to know.'

'When was that?'

'When we were boys. I got to know Richard when I joined the Boy Scouts – we were in the same patrol. I really liked it, but one day Richard said there was something new he'd found out about that was like Scouts but better. He said it had all the things I enjoyed, like the woodcraft and camping, but it wasn't all bugles and drums and parades like the Scouts. Richard said he was going to join that instead and asked me if I'd like to go with him, so I did.'

'What did you make of it?'

'Oh, I liked it. The man who started it was called John Hargrave – he'd been in the army in the Great War, a stretcher-bearer at Gallipoli, and he said the trouble with the Boy Scouts was that it was run by old generals who wanted to train boys so they'd be ready to go in the army and kill people. So he'd set up something that was all about world peace and international brotherhood, that sort of thing. Not that that worked out, did it? It all seems a very long time ago. In those days, though, he was very persuasive. I heard him speak once, and he was amazing – inspiring, really. He said the only country we should belong to is the world, and the only loyalty we should have is to mankind.'

Wilson paused and gave a short, cynical laugh, as if his own words had struck him as amusing.

'Anyway, this Hargrave, he was tall and handsome, very fit and athletic, and he had one of those strong faces – you know, perfect straight nose, square chin, the kind of face a leader should have.'

'The sort of man who attracts a following, then?'

'Oh, yes. I was only a lad when I joined, of course, so for me it was just a bit of fun, but some of the men had been through the war. Whenever there was any talk about the future, you could see they were sort of desperate to do something, anything they could, to make a better world, and White Fox – that's what Hargrave called himself – he always seemed to be sure that's what he was doing. I was in it because I liked the outdoor stuff, as I said, and the physical fitness, all that. But I thought making a new world was a good idea too – I didn't want to grow up and get killed in another war like the last one.'

'I don't suppose anyone did.'

'No. Of course, I don't think it's as simple as that now. Like I said, my call-up papers should be here any day and I'm ready to do my bit. When I went to register back in June I said I'd like to go into the RAF, but from what I've heard they don't necessarily take much notice of what you prefer, so I'll probably end up in the army. You never know your luck, though. I fancy flying – it's probably the only chance I'll ever get of going up in a plane.'

'So this organisation you and Richard joined – what was it called?'

'It was the Kibbo Kift. Funny name, isn't it? They used to say it means "proof of great strength" or something like that, in some old dialect from Cheshire.'

'Ah, yes, I remember hearing about it now. And it had a uniform?'

'Yes. We were supposed to make it ourselves, but my mum made mine, and I expect Richard's made his. It was green – a sort of Saxon tunic with a leather belt, and a hood, and shorts.'

Jago took the suitcase from Cradock and opened it.

'Like this?' he said, showing the contents to Wilson.

'Yes, that's it,' said Wilson. 'What are you doing carrying that around with you?'

Jago ignored the question, preferring to continue with his own.

'Could this have been Richard's uniform, Mr Lewis?'

'I couldn't say.'

'And you say you had a uniform like this too?'

'Yes, I did, but I haven't got it now. Looking back, I suppose it must all have seemed a bit ridiculous to outsiders. It wasn't just the clothes – we had special words for things, like a private language. People had animal names, too, like Batwing or Sea Otter, and there was lots of stuff about being like Red Indians. But when I was a kid I loved all that. So did Richard.'

'Did you keep up your friendship into adult life?'

'No. I stopped going to the meetings when I was

157

about fifteen – grew out of it, I suppose. Then Richard's family moved to a posh house in Windsor Road, and we lost touch – I've never seen him since. I only found out what he was doing when I met Joan at work and we discovered I used to know him. By that time he was in France, of course, so we had no chance to get together and catch up on old times.'

'And you say Richard was a keen member of the Kibbo Kift?'

'Yes, he was at the time, but I don't know whether he carried on. And later on I believe it packed up. Or rather, it turned into something else. About ten years ago, it was. That Hargrave bloke decided to make it some kind of political movement. He got them to wear green shirts and berets and grey trousers and changed the name to the Social Credit Party. Most people just called them the Greenshirts.'

'Was that after Richard had moved away?'

'Yes, that's right. So I don't know whether he was involved with them. From what I knew of him when we were younger, though, I wouldn't be surprised if he was.'

CHAPTER EIGHTEEN

Jago thanked Wilson and opened the door of the manager's office to show him out. Conway was just outside the door, with his back to it, and appeared to be adjusting a small display of leaflets on a table. He whirled round as the door clicked open.

'Ah, Inspector,' he said. 'Have you finished?'

'Yes, thank you,' said Jago. 'And thank you for letting us use your office. You can have it back now.'

Conway gave a brief nod of acknowledgement and stepped in through the doorway. Jago stood back to let him in.

'And perhaps we could have a word with you too before we go,' he added.

'Why, of course,' said Conway, settling into the seat behind his desk and motioning them to take a couple of chairs themselves. 'How are your investigations going?'

'It's early days yet, Mr Conway, but we're making

satisfactory progress. I trust you've had no more trouble in the meantime.'

'No, we haven't, I'm glad to say. Things seem to have settled back to normal, as much as anything is normal these days – and of course we're all still very shocked about poor Joan. Did you get anything useful out of Wilson?'

'That I can't tell you, I'm afraid. I'm sure you'll understand.'

'Of course, yes.'

'But I would like to ask you something about Mr Wilson. How would you describe his character?'

'Well, let's see. He seems a good enough fellow to me. I can't say I know him very well – he hasn't been working for me all that long.'

'Just your initial impressions would be helpful, though. Does he strike you as a reliable man, trustworthy?'

'I've no reason to think he isn't. In fact I took him on because I'd heard a good report of him, to do with what happened at the Broadway.'

'And what was that good report?'

'I was told he'd been on duty there the night it was hit. It was the same weekend the Stratford Empire caught a packet. I was sad to see that place go. I suppose it was lucky the theatre'd been closed for quite a few weeks, so nobody was killed, but it took a direct hit straight through the roof and was wrecked. Such a beautiful building.'

'Indeed. And Mr Wilson?'

'Yes, well, as you probably know, the Broadway Super was damaged when another bomb hit the cafe next door, early that same evening, and all those passengers in the buses going past were killed. Bert Wilson was on the front door at the Broadway, and it seems he was a bit of a hero. When I asked him about it he said it was nothing, he'd just got a few cuts, and his hat was blown off, but the manager at the Broadway told me Bert had gone straight over to the wreckage of the buses and helped pull the survivors out. With no thought to his own safety, he said. Cool as a cucumber. He reckoned Bert ought to be put up for one of those new George Medals. That's really why I gave him a job, and he hasn't done anything yet to suggest my judgement was wrong.'

'A reliable and honest man, then, in your opinion?'

'Yes. I wouldn't have taken him on if I thought he wasn't. But it's difficult to say. I mean, I think he's a brave man, but being brave doesn't always make you honest, does it? I remember there was a fellow a few years back who lost part of his hand in the Great War and won the Military Medal, then got jailed for forging cheques. He'd been brave, but he still ended up behind bars, didn't he?'

'Ah, yes. Three-fingered Jack they called him. I remember that case. Military Medal and bar, in fact. So do you have reason to think Mr Wilson isn't as honourable as he appears?'

'No, of course not. I'm just saying. You never know, do you?'

Conway stood up and paced round the office, his face suggesting he was reflecting on what he had just said. He stopped by a bookcase and distractedly brushed the top of a camera that was sitting on the shelf, as if removing some invisible dust.

'I told you I'm a photographer, didn't I?' he said, picking up the camera and passing it to Jago.

'I think you said you're a very good one,' Jago replied.

'Ah, yes, well I like to think I am. That's my Rolleiflex – it's a Standard, with a Heidoscop Anastigmat 75mm viewing lens. German, of course, but very good. I picked it up second-hand before the war.'

'It sounds like you have a passion for photography.'

'I do – I think it's the greatest invention of the last century. It's changed the world. I mean, who needs Rembrandt to spend months painting your portrait when a camera can capture a true likeness in one five-hundredth of a second? With photography, everyone can have beautiful pictures in their own home. If we all appreciated art and beauty more, I think the world would be a better place. It's not musicians and artists who start wars, is it?'

'Except Hitler, perhaps?'

'Yes, well, he's the exception that proves the rule, and I expect he was a very poor painter.'

Jago held the camera in front of his waist and looked down into the viewfinder.

'But you don't paint yourself?' he said.

'No, I just take pictures. I got the Rolleiflex because

162

it's what Cecil Beaton uses. I'm a great admirer of his work. I saw some of his fashion photos – beautiful women in beautiful clothes, just like in the movies, and they inspired me.'

'So is that the kind of photography you aspire to?'

'Yes. I realise I might've sounded a bit vague when I said that envelope of mine in the safe had some personal papers in it, but in fact they were photographs. The thing is, I was going to enter a national photographic competition, and I'd put some of my prints in the safe.'

'Why? Are they valuable?'

'They might be one day – it depends whether I manage to establish myself. I may not be Cecil Beaton, and I don't think I'd want to be a fashion photographer for the rest of my life, but I do have a talent.'

Jago was not surprised that Mr Conway thought he had a talent.

'So these are fashion photographs?' he asked.

'Yes, as far as that's possible in West Ham. Beautiful clothes are a problem, of course – women round here don't have the money for them, and neither do I – but there are still beautiful women to be found, and I try to capture the same sort of mood that Beaton had in those pictures of his that I saw. Languid sophistication – I think that's what I'd call it.'

'And the competition would help to establish you?'

'If I win it, yes. Any amateur photographer would be thrilled to win a competition. It's a recognition of your ability. I'd just like my work to be celebrated by other photographers with more experience than me.' His voice took on a more urgent tone. 'Look, Inspector, I think you understand me. I'd like to get those pictures back, so if you find whoever did this and you recover them, could you please return them to me? They were in a plain brown envelope, sealed with red sealing wax. I don't want them to fall into the wrong hands.'

'Why's that?'

'It would spoil my chances in the competition, of course – someone might recognise their quality and enter them as their own work.'

'I understand. We'll see what we can do, Mr Conway.'

CHAPTER NINETEEN

'Back to the station now, guv'nor?' said Cradock, putting the suitcase down as the cinema doors thudded shut behind them.

'Patience, Peter,' said Jago. 'Just one or two little calls to make before we do. There's one more person I want to show that uniform to.'

'Who's that?'

'Carol Hurst. We'll leave it at the station when we get there, but I want to call in at the bank first. Thanks to Bert Wilson we now know what it is, but I'd still like to know whether it was definitely Richard's. And what did you make of our Bert? When you suggested he might've been in on the job his answer was quite convincing, wasn't it?'

'I'm not sure, sir. He'd got it all off pat, hadn't he? As if he'd done all the sums before we came, and learnt it by heart.'

'He certainly seemed to have something of a gift for

arithmetic. And he thought a lot of Joan Lewis, didn't he?'

'Yes, but then maybe he didn't know her as well as he'd have liked to.'

'Possibly. Or perhaps he knew more about her than he wished to admit. Mr Conway speaks highly of her too, though, doesn't he?'

'Oh, yes, and he's a good judge of women, isn't he?' said Cradock with a stifled laugh. 'It's funny what you find out about people, isn't it?'

'You mean Sidney Conway as a would-be society photographer sensation?'

'Exactly.'

'He's entitled to his private life, though. And he does seem convinced that photography's changed the world.'

'Yes, and I get the impression he thinks he's going to change the world too. A bit too big for his boots, if you ask me.'

'Quite. Anyway, I'm not sure we can take what he said about Bert Wilson as a ringing endorsement of his doorman's integrity, can we?'

'No. I suppose the fact that a man rescues some people from a bus that's been bombed doesn't necessarily make him an angel, especially when temptation comes his way. If deep down he's dishonest, it'll come out in the end. You can't judge a leopard by its spots, can you?'

'You mean you can't judge a book by its cover.'

'Yes, same thing.'

'It's not the same thing at all,' said Jago, a note of exasperation creeping into his voice. 'If you can't judge a

166

book by its cover it means appearances can be deceptive. A leopard's appearance is never deceptive, precisely because it cannot change its spots.'

Cradock looked at Jago as if his boss had temporarily lost the balance of his mind.

'Are you all right, sir?'

'Yes,' said Jago with a sigh. 'I'm all right.'

A month or so earlier the banks had shortened their Saturday opening hours, blaming the change on the war, but on weekdays they were still open until two o'clock in the afternoon. It was five minutes to two when Jago and Cradock entered the National Provincial and were shown to the manager.

'I'm sorry to disturb you again, Mr Pemberton,' said Jago. 'I know your day is far from over when the doors close, but I need to see Miss Hurst again for a moment.'

'But you spoke to her only yesterday,' the manager replied. Neither his voice nor his expression reflected the lightness that Jago had noticed the previous day. 'Are you sure she's not in any trouble? This is a bank, Mr Jago, and we value our reputation for probity in all matters very highly.'

'There's no question of impropriety on Miss Hurst's part. It's just that she's a witness in a case we're investigating, and I need a little help from her.'

'Very well. There's a room upstairs that the staff use for their lunch break. It should be empty by now – you can talk to her there. But please don't take too much of her time. There's a lot of correspondence for her to type before she goes home, and the sun will be down before six. I don't like to have to keep the girls here after dark, not since the air raids started.'

The manager sent for Carol Hurst, and she took Jago and Cradock to the staff room upstairs. It was deserted. Closing the door behind them, she invited them to take a seat at a small round table while she made a pot of tea for them. Cradock put the suitcase down on the floor next to his chair and silently hoped for biscuits.

'Here you are,' she said, handing a cup of tea to each of them when it was brewed. 'Here's sugar too if you need it. I'm sorry I haven't got anything to offer you to eat.'

'That's quite all right,' Jago replied. 'A cup of tea is more than sufficient.'

Cradock smiled at the young woman sympathetically, hoping she might still remember a forgotten staff biscuit barrel, but she didn't seem to receive the message he thought he was sending.

'Now, Miss Hurst,' said Jago. 'I won't keep you long. I'd just like to ask you a little about Joan Lewis and Richard, her husband. My question might seem a little intrusive, so please forgive me, but it's been suggested to me that their marriage wasn't necessarily in what you might call a healthy state. Is that correct?'

'Who said that?' said Carol.

Jago did not reply.

'Oh, I see,' she continued. 'You're not going to tell me. That's your prerogative, I suppose. But if you want to know what I think, well, I hesitate to say, Inspector.'

'You can be frank with me.'

'All right, if you say so. I think Joan hoped for all the good things in marriage, but what you hope for in life and what you get can be very different, can't they? I suspect maybe she saw what she wanted to see in Richard and grabbed her chance in case it slipped away, but then she found out they weren't the perfect match after all. He wasn't quite the man she'd hoped for, and she couldn't be the woman he needed.'

'Do you have any evidence for that?'

'No, of course not. I mean, what can you tell about someone's marriage from the outside? You never really know what goes on behind closed doors, do you? I was very fond of Joan, and I know she chose to marry Richard – no one forced her into it. I think she married him because she loved him, but maybe it went just a little bit sour later on.'

'Why was that?'

'What can I say? It wasn't easy for her, you know. When they got married they had to go and live with Audrey, his mother. Well, everyone knows that's going to put the kybosh on it – I mean, a new wife living under her mother-in-law's roof? Two women in the same house like that, it's never going to work. I think it was just one of those cases where they didn't hit it off. Joan was a lovely girl, but I got the impression she felt she'd never quite matched up to the standards Audrey expected for her son. You've probably heard that sort of thing a thousand times.'

'I've been told Joan was lonely, that she didn't have many close friends.'

'She had me – we were close. She was like a sister to me – more than a sister, in fact. Ever since we first got to know each other doing all that prancing about exercise, like I said before.'

'Did you remain close?'

'You mean after she got married?'

'Yes.'

'Well, that always changes things a bit, doesn't it? I mean, she had a husband to look after. We were still more than just friends, though, I'm sure of that, even if we didn't see as much of each other as we used to. I think I was the only person she could really confide in. That's how I knew it wasn't all roses with her mother-in-law. Mind you, I don't say it was all Audrey's fault. She's had a basinful of trouble of her own to cope with. Her husband died, you know.'

'Yes, she told me. She said he was an investor.'

Carol gave a sudden laugh that almost caused her to spurt tea over her lap. She choked and wiped her mouth with a handkerchief.

'Oh, do forgive me, Inspector, I shouldn't be laughing at a time like this. It's just that the way I heard it from Joan it wasn't quite like that.'

'What do you mean?'

'Well, it's a kind of investment, I suppose, but judging by what Joan said he was more like a moneylender. You know, special loans for people who can't borrow money from the bank, and special interest rates to go with them. I believe they call it lending money on note of hand.'

'Yes.'

'And that was where the trouble started for Audrey, from what I can tell. You see, according to Joan, he made pots of money but he didn't like the thought of the taxman getting his greedy hands on it. He must've had some very clever ways of keeping it quiet, because when he died Audrey had no idea where he'd salted it away or how to find it. They lived in a big fancy house in Windsor Road – you know, those nice detached ones – but she had to sell it and move to the one in Carnarvon Road where she lives now. That's not exactly a hovel either – I certainly wouldn't turn my nose up at it – but it's not a patch on what she used to have. I feel sorry for her, really.'

'I see. Now, there's just one more thing I'd like to ask you about.'

Jago picked up the suitcase and opened it on the table, then took out the tunic.

'I wonder whether you can tell me what this is, Miss Hurst. Have you seen it before?'

'Yes, I have.'

'Can you tell me about it, please?'

'Yes. I went round to see Joan one day because I was going to a dance and didn't have anything to wear. I thought she might have a dress I could borrow. We were that alike in build we could pass for each other in the dark. She said to have a look in the wardrobe and help myself. So I had a look, and I noticed this hanging up right at one end. I didn't know what it was, so I pulled it out and said, "What's this?" She said it was Richard's. It was a kind of uniform for some group he belonged to. It had a funny name I'd never heard of. I can't remember what it was now. Something like the Kitty Kat Club, but more like made-up words, nonsense.'

'Was it Kibbo Kift?'

'That sounds like it. Meant nothing to me, but she said it was something Richard had been involved in when he was younger, a bit like the Boy Scouts. He liked it, but there was a spot of trouble when Charlie found out more about it.'

'Charlie?'

Carol laughed again. 'Ah, yes, I believe Audrey likes to call him Charles, but Joan said when he was doing his "investor" work he was just plain Charlie Lewis. Anyway, to start with, Charlie and Audrey thought it was just the same as the Boy Scouts, like I said – you know, camping, making fires in the woods and cooking on them, with a bit of tying knots and whittling thrown in – but when Charlie looked into it more he discovered it had some funny ideas he didn't agree with.'

'Funny ideas?'

'Yes, politics, and that sort of thing. To be honest, I haven't a clue what it was all about, but it was something to do with economics and money, and he clearly didn't approve of it. Maybe he thought it was going to poison

Richard's mind, but I don't know. It's the sort of thing Mr Pemberton would be able to explain – there's nothing he doesn't know about money. I may work in a bank, but that doesn't mean I know about things like economics. Social credit, that's what Joan said it was called. Charlie may have thought Richard would grow out of it, but it seems he didn't, and that's why they fell out.'

'And what did Joan think of these ideas?'

'I'm not sure she really understood them. A bit over her head, I reckon. I think she went along with what Richard wanted to do, at first anyway.'

'It's been suggested that Joan hid this uniform of Richard's because she didn't want Audrey to get her hands on it, but Audrey seems to think it's hers and Joan stole it from her. Do you know why that would be?'

'I'm not sure. I told you Audrey was a possessive mother, didn't I? Maybe she thinks Joan stole Richard from her. That old uniform's a part of Richard's childhood, when he belonged to her, so if she gets it back, she gets him back, out of Joan's hands. Like when soldiers capture the other side's flag in a battle, you know? And Joan might've wanted to stop Audrey getting her hands on it for the same reason – at least at the beginning, when Richard went off to France with the TA. Towards the end, though, I think it might've been just to spite Audrey.'

Carol's eyes darted across Jago's shoulder as the door opened behind him. He looked round to see Pemberton entering the room and rose from his chair.

'Am I interrupting you?' the manager asked. 'It's just that—'

'We were just finishing, thank you,' said Jago. 'Miss Hurst has been most helpful. And thank you, Mr Pemberton, for sparing her to talk to us.'

Carol got to her feet. Jago thought she looked a little flustered, as if worrying that she'd spoken to him for too long or said too much.

'I'll get back to work now, then,' she said hesitantly. 'If there's anything else you need to know, just ask.'

She made her way quickly to the door and slipped out past Pemberton without another word.

CHAPTER TWENTY

The bank manager stood by the door, regarding Jago with an inquisitive gaze as if to ask if he might similarly be dismissed and return to his duties, but Jago motioned to the chair that Carol Hurst had just vacated.

'Mr Pemberton,' he said, as the manager sat down, 'Miss Hurst was just talking to us about something called social credit, which she felt unable to explain, but she said you would know all about it. Do you think you could shed some light on it for us? Just the bare bones.'

'How touching,' said Pemberton. 'It's flattering to discover the staff think I know everything, but I can't claim that's really true. If it will help you, though, I'll happily try to explain as best I can. It's all to do with economics, and it's an idea put forward some years ago by a man called C. H. Douglas.'

His voice had become animated, which suggested to Jago that the bank manager relished opportunities to explain economic subjects.

'In layman's terms, please, if you can, Mr Pemberton,' said Jago, eager to forestall complicated musings. 'Simple enough for a policeman to understand.'

'Of course, yes,' Pemberton replied, his voice now slowing and taking on a schoolmasterly emphasis. 'You have to look at it in the context of the economic problems the world's had since the last war. Take the great depression we had in the early thirties, for example. Many people say that was caused by overproduction – too many goods being manufactured for the market to absorb. Douglas said the real problem was that in our kind of economy the costs of production are greater than the purchasing power that people have from their incomes. I confess even I don't understand the ins and outs of his economic argument, but to put it simply, I think he meant people just don't have enough money to buy all the things we produce.'

'And social credit is the answer?'

'Yes. He said the solution to all the economic problems we've seen in recent years is to introduce what he called a national dividend – an amount of money given to each person by the state to augment their purchasing power. Enough for them to choose whether to work or not, in fact. He claimed this would bring about an age of leisure, with prices stable or even falling, and an end to inflation. It would increase the freedom of the individual and make everyone more prosperous, regardless of whether they had a job or not. You might ask, of course, whether this wouldn't lead people to take advantage, and many would agree with you. The theory, though, assumed that all people are fundamentally good.'

'Not an easy conclusion to come to these days.'

'Indeed, but Douglas believed wars were inevitable as long as political leaders tried to achieve full employment, because the only way to do that was to increase exports by capturing foreign markets. I remember him giving a talk about it on the wireless five or six years ago – he said it's economic war that leads to military war. But who knows whether he was right? Either way, he said there's enough wealth in the country for everyone, but the problem is not everyone has access to it.'

'So we give everyone this national dividend and they have the money they need to buy things?'

'I think so, yes.'

'Is that the same as communism?'

'I don't think Douglas was a communist or even a socialist – he thought his ideas would give power to the individual, not to the state. I'm not really sure which category he fits into, I'm afraid, or whether he fits into any of them. I think he believed that in the future machines would do the work, and he may well be right. In banking we now have accounting machines instead of the old handwritten ledgers, and there's even talk of having robots instead of staff. Douglas believed automation would mean fewer jobs, but with social credit people wouldn't necessarily need a job to be economically secure and happy. Whether he thought we'd still need policemen I don't know. What do you think?'

Jago said nothing. As far as he was concerned, until such time as policemen were no longer required, his job was to ask questions, not to offer opinions on matters of public policy.

'Actually,' Pemberton continued, 'I don't think he was naive enough to think we'd ever have no need of police officers or armed forces. He argued that his social credit policy would remove the need for Britain to start wars, but that didn't mean other countries would never attack us, so I don't think he was calling for unilateral disarmament, for example, unlike some of our politicians in recent years. He said that that would be like saying a bank would never be robbed if it had paper walls – you'll understand why I remember that particular allusion.'

'So basically he was saying the government should give everyone a certain amount of money, regardless of whether they already have a job, and this money wouldn't have to be repaid?'

'I think that's it. Good news for people without a job, and bad news for loan sharks, you might say.'

'You might indeed. So that's what the Social Credit Party believes – the ones they call the Greenshirts?'

'Roughly, I think, but I'm not an expert, so I may be wrong. The main problem is that Douglas's system is so complicated, hardly anyone can understand it.'

'And what's your view of it as a banker, as far as you understand it?'

'My view is simple. I'd say it's not the kind of notion any serious banker would entertain for a moment.'

CHAPTER TWENTY-ONE

'That's interesting,' said Jago as they emerged from the bank onto the High Street. He strode off, heading in the direction of the town hall and West Ham Lane.

'What – all that stuff about economics? I didn't understand a word of it,' Cradock replied, hurrying to keep up and hoping they were returning to the police station, where at last he could say goodbye to the suitcase.

'I'm not sure I grasped every detail myself,' said Jago, 'but it's interesting because of what it tells us about the family. According to Audrey, Richard takes after his dad, but if we're to believe what Carol's just told us they're actually like chalk and cheese. You've got Charlie Lewis making a fortune out of back-street loans to people who are short of cash or can't make ends meet – probably charging interest rates that'd make your eyes water – and a son who believes the government should give everyone free money to spend. No wonder they didn't quite see eye to eye. I would've liked to be a fly on the wall if ever those two had got down to discussing economic policy. And I think I'd like to know a bit more about Charlie's business activities.'

'Shall I check up on him, sir?'

'Yes, find out whether he had proper premises to trade from, like those places in Stratford Broadway that advertise loans without security – you know, "five pounds to five hundred, with or without security", that sort of thing. And check whether he ever got a certificate for his business from the Petty Sessions Court. If he only died a couple of years ago it should all still be on record. If he didn't get one, see if you can find out whether he applied and was found not to be a fit and proper person, or whether he didn't apply at all. And find out whether there's any record of him taking out a moneylender's excise licence.'

'Yes, sir. And will that be it, then?'

'Will that be what?'

'You said we had one or two little calls to make. So was it just one – going to the bank? Are we going back to the station now? I'm starving.'

'It was two, Peter. Now that the landlord's told us the sailor selling stockings at the Green Man on Sunday was Ernie Sullivan and the name we found in the sailor's cap at Joan's flat is E. G. Sullivan, I don't think we need to wait for the navy to tell us where we can find him. We're going round to Windmill Lane to see if anyone's in. After that we'll go back to the station.'

Within a few minutes they had arrived in Windmill Lane and found the only greengrocer's shop in the street, just a few doors along from St Mark's Mission Church. They knocked on the door to one side of the shop. It was opened by a solidly built man of about fifty, of medium height and balding. His shapeless brown trousers looked as if they'd been worn for most of their life by a man a size or two bigger, with gathered handfuls of spare waistband overflowing a wide leather belt. With these he wore scuffed working boots and a black waistcoat over a grubby white shirt without a collar.

'Yeh? What do you want?' he said, leaning forward with one hand braced against the door frame.

'Mr Sullivan?'

'What if I am?'

'We're police officers, and we'd like a word with your son.'

'Which one?'

'Ernie. I believe he's a sailor.'

'He is, more fool him. At least his brother's got the wit not to volunteer for anything, especially the army or navy. He won't go till they make him.'

'Is Ernie in?'

'Why do you want to know?'

Jago was beginning to think Sullivan was asking more questions than he was, but he opted for calm patience.

'I'd like to speak to him, because I think we've found his cap.'

Sullivan's laugh was loud and sneering. 'Well, well, well – so we're in the middle of a war, but the police have time to return lost property in person. Three cheers for the modern policeman!'

'Your son is Mr E. G. Sullivan?'

'That's right. E for Ernest, G for George, after me. No one calls him Ernest, though – it's always Ernie.'

'I'd like to return his cap to him.'

'Leave it here, then, and I'll give it to him.'

'No, I want to return it myself, because I have one or two questions to ask him.'

'You're not telling me he's in trouble, are you? Leave the poor lad alone. You know what it's like when a sailor gets a bit of leave – you can't begrudge him a bit of fun.'

'He's not in trouble, but I think he may be able to help us. How long is he on leave for?'

'Just a few days.'

'And he'll be staying here?'

'Yes.'

'So I'll ask you again. Is he in?'

'If you must know, he went down the pub for a spot of lunch and a pint with a couple of his old mates. The Cart and Horses, at the end of the street. What's the time now?'

Jago checked his watch. 'Ten past three.'

'You won't catch him now, then. They'll have kicked him out at closing time, so if it's gone three and he's not back, he's probably gone off with his mates somewhere. Don't suppose he'll be long, though.'

183

'If he gets in within the next hour, can you ask him to pop down to West Ham police station? You know where that is, do you?'

'I know.'

'Tell him to ask for Detective Inspector Jago, and tell him I've got his cap.'

'All right. I'll send him down to see you. Can't guarantee what sort of state he'll be in, though. The poor lad's living it up while he can.'

CHAPTER TWENTY-TWO

Despite his unhelpful manner, it seemed George Sullivan had passed on the message as requested. The two detectives had barely got back to the station when a young man in Royal Navy rating's uniform arrived and asked to see Jago. On being brought to the CID office he looked around, taking in the scene with the same look of intrigued interest that he might have shown when going ashore in Alexandria or Singapore.

'Take a seat, Mr Sullivan,' said Jago as he closed the door behind the visitor.

'Thanks,' said the sailor. 'I'm not used to being called mister any more. It's A. B. Sullivan these days – Able Seaman Sullivan, that is.'

'Of course. Have you been in the navy for long?'

'I volunteered a couple of years ago. Usual reason back then, I suppose – thought I'd see the world.'

'And did you?'

'Some of it, yes. This time last week I was in the

middle of the Atlantic, on my way over from Canada. You've heard about the fifty American destroyers?'

'The ships Mr Roosevelt gave us in exchange for some bases?'

'That's the ones. Fair exchange is no robbery – that's what they say, isn't it?' He laughed, seeming to find this an amusing thought, but Jago's and Cradock's faces were both blank. 'Sorry,' he continued. 'You won't know what I'm talking about, will you? Pig in a poke's more like it. I'm serving in one of them at the moment – HMS *Stockbridge*, although I probably shouldn't tell you that, should I? A terrible old tub, she is – the sort of ship that'd roll on wet grass. The Americans sailed her up from Boston to Nova Scotia with her old name painted out, then we took her over in Halifax. I reckon they were glad to get rid of her. On the way out there to get her we thought it was going to be great – we'd been told the destroyers all had fridges and showers, not like ours, and they definitely weren't obsolete, whatever we'd heard. But when we tried to bring her back across the Atlantic, well . . . but that's another story, as they say. The main thing is we got here, and now she's in the Royal Albert Dock for a bit of refitting, and that means I've got a few days' leave. Couldn't be better for me – just a bus ride home.'

'Very good – I'm sure everyone's glad you got here in one piece. Now tell me, Mr Sullivan, when you crossed the Atlantic, did you bring anything of value back with you?'

'What do you mean? You're not the Customs and Excise.'

'No, but I've heard there was a sailor selling ladies' stockings in the Green Man on Sunday and I think that sailor may have been you.'

'So? What if I was? There's nothing illegal about it – I came by those stockings fair and square. They're not stolen, and anyway, I gave most of them away for nothing – as presents, like. There were just one or two ladies who insisted on paying for them.'

'What were these stockings made of?'

'Made of? I don't know. I'm a sailor, not a fashion designer.'

'Oh, come on. You went to all the bother of bringing them back across the ocean so you could sell them – you must've known what made them worth the trouble.'

'All right, then. If you must know, they're made of nylon. It's all the rage over there. I bought some from one of the Yanks. He said where he comes from the women are crazy about them. But what's any of this got to do with my cap? My dad said you wanted me to come down here because you'd found it.'

'Ah, yes, your cap.' Jago opened a drawer in his desk, took out the cap, and passed it to Sullivan. 'Is this yours?'

Sullivan looked inside. 'E. G. Sullivan. Yes, that's me. I'm glad you've found it – I'd be in trouble if I had to go back to the ship without it.'

'How did you come to lose it?'

'I've no idea. All I know is I definitely had it Sunday lunchtime at the pub, and I still had it when I went back there in the evening, I think, but I had a bit to drink, and when I got home that night I didn't have it.'

'Do you know whether you had it when you left the pub in the evening?'

'I think so, but by then I wasn't feeling too good. I must've ended up having a lie down and a little kip, because when I woke up I was in a shop doorway and I was cold.'

'What time did you leave the pub?'

'I think it was something like a quarter past, half past eight. I remember there was a bit of bombing going on somewhere, and I was quite impressed because most people stayed in the pub and carried on with their drinks. Not bad for civilians, I thought.'

'And when you woke up from your little sleep, did you still have your cap then?'

The sailor screwed up his face in concentration. 'Sorry, can't remember. I was a bit too far gone to care, I suppose.'

'What time did you wake up?'

'No idea. I can remember feeling cold and a bit stiff from lying there, but that's about it. One of your coppers stopped for a word, and I suppose I should've asked him the time – that's what they're for, isn't it?' He chuckled to himself. 'But I didn't.'

'All right. Do you know what time you got home?'

'Not sure – I vaguely recall putting the wireless on when I got home, the BBC programme for the forces. I thought there might be a bit of dance music on, but all I got was that religious thing, *The Epilogue*, so I turned it off. I think I went straight to bed then and fell asleep.'

Jago was not a devoted listener to *The Epilogue*, but he knew it was broadcast on the BBC's Forces Programme at ten o'clock on Sunday evenings, and he'd caught the end of it himself on the day in question.

'*The Epilogue* was on from ten o'clock to ten past ten,' he said. 'So you're saying you got home sometime between those two.'

'If you say so.'

'Can anyone vouch for the time you got home?'

Sullivan seemed to be trying to focus his thoughts before replying. 'Er, yes, my dad was in, I think.'

'You think?'

'I mean yes, he was in. But this cap of mine, where did you find it?'

'It was found at the scene of a crime.'

Sullivan's expression suddenly changed, his eyes widening in alarm.

'Crime? Now hold on a minute, what's this all about? All I've done is have a few drinks and lose my cap. I came down here in good faith to claim it, and now you're trying to mix me up in some crime.'

'Do you know a woman called Joan Lewis?'

'No.'

'And you weren't in her flat on Sunday evening?'

'I don't know what you're talking about. What flat? Where?'

'In Carpenters Road, Mr Sullivan. That's where we found your cap, and I want the truth, please.'

'Carpenters Road?'

'Are you denying that you were there? If you weren't there, what was your cap doing there?'

'Yes, I mean no. I mean – hold on, I don't understand. I . . .'

Jago fixed him with a cold, silent gaze. Sullivan looked round the office, as though hoping that help would appear. None did, and finally he spoke.

'All right, yes – yes, I was,' he said. 'I was in Carpenters Road, but I – no. No, that must be it – she must call herself something different now.'

'You're referring to Mrs Lewis?'

'Yes, exactly, that's it. I don't know any Joan Lewis, but if that's Joan Hayes's married name then yes, I do. She said she'd got married but didn't mention her new name, and I didn't think to ask.'

'She said this to you on Sunday?'

'Yes, but what's the problem? I bumped into her on the street near the Green Man in the afternoon. She's an old friend from when we were kids at school. I gave her a pair of those stockings, actually.'

'Did you go to her flat on Sunday evening?'

'Yes. I asked her if I could pop in some time, just for old times' sake, and she said yes. I said what about later that day, and she said she had to go to work – at the cinema. I asked her what time she knocked off, and she said she'd probably be home by half past nine. So I said I'd drop in then.'

'And she consented to this?'

'Of course. Why shouldn't she? We were old friends, like I said. It wasn't as though I was going to try anything on. She'd know that. She scribbled her address down and gave it to me.'

'What time did you visit her?'

'I don't know. I suppose it must've been about half past nine, but I didn't check the time when I got there.'

'You weren't there for long, then, if you were home in time for *The Epilogue*.'

'I suppose not. I certainly wasn't there for as long as I'd thought I might be. She said she wasn't feeling too well, but she still invited me in for a quick hello. We had a drink and a bit of a chat, but then I left. I could see she was going down with something – a touch of the flu, probably, I thought.'

'And you went straight home?'

'Yes. But look, what's going on? All I've done is have a drink with an old friend. So why are you giving me the third degree like this? What's the problem?'

'The problem, Mr Sullivan, is that Joan Lewis has been murdered.'

Sullivan seemed taken aback. He fumbled for his words. 'Murdered? But why would anyone want to do that?'

'That's what I intend to find out, Mr Sullivan.'

'Well, it wasn't me, right?' said Sullivan, his voice rising. 'And if you don't mind, I've got things to do today. I'm off.'

He strode out of the office, banging the door behind him, and Jago was left wondering whether the ferocity in the sailor's voice denoted anger, grief or something else.

Cradock went after Sullivan to ensure he had left the premises, then returned to the office and sat down.

'So,' he said, 'our Ernie was at Joan's flat after all, but not for long.'

'Yes,' said Jago. 'It must be about ten, fifteen minutes' walk from her flat to his end of Windmill Lane, less if he was in a fit state to run, so if he was home in time to hear a bit of *The Epilogue* he must've left the flat by about a quarter to ten, or five to ten at the latest. If he's telling the truth.'

'Do you think he was?'

'About what?'

'All that falling asleep in the street and not knowing what time it was. And everything else he said too, for that matter.'

'What do you think?'

'I'm just thinking we've found a sailor's cap in Joan's flat, and we've found a sailor with no cap, but he can't remember when he lost it – or where or how, for that matter. Very convenient, that.'

'Yes, but if he'd had too much to drink and genuinely can't remember when he lost it, all we know is that he was seen with it in Martin Street at some time after half past eight. Which reminds me, he said one of our men stopped for a word. Check with the duty roster to see who was on that beat on Sunday late turn and ask him if it was Ernie he spoke to.'

'Will do.'

'In any case, if he did kill her, it wouldn't be very smart to leave his cap there in her flat with his name stamped inside, would it? He might as well have left a calling card.'

'Yes, sir, but if he was drunk he probably wouldn't have thought of that, would he?'

'No. But nevertheless, the fact that we found his cap in Joan's flat doesn't necessarily mean he murdered her.'

'Right. So supposing he really did lose it – before he got to her flat, I mean. Someone else could've come across it, lying in the road or whatever. Do you think someone could've found it or stolen it and put it in the flat to incriminate him?'

'It seems unlikely, but it's a possibility. He was just lying in the street, dead to the world, after all. But if someone did take it, I doubt very much that young Ernie'll be able to say who it was, unless he's not telling us everything he knows.'

'So what next?'

'Next,' said Jago, 'I want you to phone up Addingtons in

Carpenters Road, that place where Derek Marwell works, and find out what shift he's on today. If he was with his wife when they saw Ernie in that doorway on Sunday, I'd like to know whether he can tell us anything else about it.'

CHAPTER TWENTY-THREE

The reply from Addingtons was that Derek Marwell's shift wouldn't end for another two hours, at six o'clock, so Jago decided now would be a good time to visit him. He made his way to the police station entrance, followed by Cradock, and stopped for a word with Frank Tompkins.

'We're just nipping up to Carpenters Road, Frank, if anyone wants us,' he said.

'Actually, sir,' Tompkins replied, 'I've got a man waiting to see you. He's just arrived. Young fellow, a bit down in the mouth – probably disappointed, I should think.'

'Disappointed?'

'Well, judging by the look of him, he's been in training for the Olympic Games – this year's ones, I mean, the ones that never happened. Athletic type, if you know what I mean.'

'Ah, yes,' said Jago. 'It was supposed to be Tokyo, wasn't it? Except they were too busy fighting the Chinese.

Then it was Helsinki, but they were too busy being invaded by Russia, and now everyone's too busy fighting everyone else. He'll have to wait for 1944 – that's when they're supposed to be held in London, isn't it?'

'I think you're right there, sir, but somehow I don't think we'll have finished the current spot of difficulty in time for that. Pity, though – your young man looks like he'll be too old if he has to wait till 1948, assuming even those games happen. He's in peak condition now, at any rate, as far as I can tell – perhaps we ought to see if he'd like to become a police constable. He's got the height for it, and bigger muscles than I ever had.'

'Ah, but you always had the cunning, didn't you, Frank?'

'Had? You should ask my missus about that. She reckons I've still got more than my fair share when it comes to dodging the chores.'

'So where is this fine specimen of British manhood?'

'I've put him in the interview room. You can't miss him.'

'Name?'

'He said it's Wilson – Bert Wilson.'

Jago and Cradock found Wilson sitting in the interview room, and from the sight of him they thought Frank's assessment of his mood wasn't too wide of the mark. He certainly looked preoccupied. As soon as they entered the room, he jumped to his feet.

'Hello, Inspector,' he said. 'I wasn't sure whether I should disturb you, but I've had something on my mind and I thought I should come and see you. It's about Joan.'

'Yes – what is it?'

'Well, it's more about Mr Conway actually. I don't mean to be disrespectful, but it's just that there was something about the way he was with Joan. He was always sort of, well, pestering her.'

'I see.'

Jago gestured towards the chair, and Wilson sat down again.

'How do you know he was pestering her?'

'She told me. I think it was because her husband was away – maybe he thought she'd be up for a bit of play, if you get my drift. But she wasn't like that. She was a lovely girl, like I told you before – sweet, gentle, tender-hearted. If it wasn't for Joan I don't know where I'd be now.'

'Why's that?'

'Why? I probably wouldn't have a job, that's why. When the Broadway got bombed I didn't know what I'd do – I couldn't go back to the job I'd had before that. But when Joan moved to the Regal, she said she'd put in a word for me with Mr Conway, and she must've done, because he took me on.'

'You told us you knew Joan before you both went to work at the Regal. What was the nature of your relationship?'

Wilson hesitated, a flicker of wariness in his eyes, but then looked straight at Jago.

'It wasn't a relationship,' he replied. 'We just got on well. She's been a good friend to me. People look at me, and because I'm big they think I'm confident. You know how it is – you're in the pub and someone's had too much to drink, they always think if you're a big bloke they'll look good if they can take you on, maybe land a punch or two. Conway's a bit like that. He likes to push me around at work because he knows I can't do anything about it if I want to keep my job. Joan seemed to understand that – it was as though she knew just what he was doing, and she'd be on my side. She was the kind of girl you could talk to.'

'You said just now that you couldn't go back to your old job. What did you mean?'

'Well, I'd been a doorman at the Broadway since the winter before last, and it was the first proper job I'd ever had – you know, the kind of job where you go to work every day and it's all above board and you pay your taxes – and I didn't get that till I was twenty-four. I left school at fourteen – couldn't wait to get out, like lots of kids. But all I could find was labouring jobs, just bits and pieces here and there, nothing solid.'

'And that's what you were doing before you started work at the Broadway?'

'No, for the last couple of years before that I had a different kind of job.'

'And that's what you couldn't go back to?'

'That's right – the bloke I worked for had died, you see, and that was the end of the job.'

'Which was?'

'Well, I was, er . . .'

He hesitated again, casting a glance towards the door as if looking for an escape route.

'You were what?' said Jago.

'I was, er, a debt collector. It's like the doorman job, really – you know, if you're big like me, people think you can do the strong-arm stuff and persuade the poor mugs to cough up the money they owe. Most of the time that's all it needs, though – if you look like you're capable of knocking them about, they'll pay up sooner than take a chance and find out the hard way.'

'But if the hard way was the only way?'

'Look, Inspector, I'm not saying I'm proud of what I did, but I needed the job and I had to do what I was told.'

'Was it a business you were collecting debts for?'

'Sort of. More a person, really.'

'And what was this person called?'

'He was, er, Charlie Lewis.'

'The father of your friend Richard Lewis?'

'Yes.'

'But you told us you'd had no contact with Richard since you were fifteen or so. Were you telling us the truth?'

'Yes, I swear. Straight up. I was desperate for work and I heard there was a bloke looking for a collector. It was only when I went to see him I found out it was Richard's dad. I remembered him from when we were kids, see, and he always seemed to have a bob or two in those days, so I thought he'd pay all right.'

'So you're saying you worked for Richard's father for

two years but never once saw his son, who'd been your childhood friend?'

'That's right. Charlie said it was private work. I didn't sit in an office all day where people like Richard might come in and see me. It was more like doing personal jobs for Charlie. Confidential, you know? Charlie paid to have a phone put in where I lived, and he'd call me and tell me where to go and who to see. It suited me fine – I only had to work when he needed me, and it turned out I was right, he did pay well.'

'But didn't you see this as an opportunity to get in touch with your friend?'

'No. Mr Lewis didn't want me to. He said I wasn't to talk to a living soul about my work, and that included his son. It sounded like they didn't get on. So I didn't – I couldn't afford to, could I? Then after two years Charlie died, and there was no more work for me. That's when I went to work at the Broadway and got to know Joan.'

'How close to her did you become? As a friend, you said.'

'Hold on a minute – I know what you're getting at. Was I sweet on her, you mean? Look, Inspector, I'm not the kind of bloke who sets their sights on other men's wives, especially when they're away serving their country.'

'Of course. But she was the kind of girl you'd have found attractive if she'd been unmarried?'

'If, yes – but that's a big if. She was a married woman, and I don't get involved with married women.'

'I see.'

'I hope you do. Now look, I came here to tell you about Conway, not to talk about my past, and I need to get down to the Regal now, so if you don't mind, I'll be on my way.'

He got to his feet and stood facing Jago, as if despite his flash of anger he was still waiting to be dismissed.

'Yes, by all means, Mr Wilson,' said Jago. 'Thank you very much for coming to see us.'

CHAPTER TWENTY-FOUR

Carpenters Road ran the length of a narrow strip of land bounded on its eastern side by the railway and to the west by the Waterworks River. Jago could remember when this, like the other channels that made up the Stratford back rivers, had been a filthy stream choked with rubbish, but after being dredged and widened just a few years before the war started, it was now surprisingly clean. The strip of land itself, however, remained an eyesore, every inch of it buried beneath seventy years of haphazard industrial construction. Now it was a warren of factories, works, chimneys and sheds, its air tainted by what seemed to Jago the smelliest industries imaginable. And as he drove down the road, he could see that the air raids had achieved what he would have thought impossible: added a new layer of disfigurement to its old ugliness.

The Addingtons varnish factory was one of the leading producers of noxious odours, and it was situated at the far end of Carpenters Road. By the time they got there, Jago and Cradock had been assailed by everything from the bitter fumes of paint factories to the sweet, cloying smells of perfume manufacturers. The particular output of Addingtons seemed to fall somewhere between the two.

The factory was a rambling, much-extended building of smoke-blackened brick, standing beside an untidy yard of unknown use. The detectives reported to the gatekeeper's hut and were asked to wait while Marwell was fetched.

The man who arrived a few minutes later looked in his mid to late twenties and seemed strikingly tall, although Jago wondered whether this was only because he was so thin, like a man stretched beyond his natural height. The legs of his stained overalls, not quite long enough, flapped round the top of his boots, but his arms were muscular. His hands were streaked with what looked like grease.

He glanced from Jago to Cradock and back again, as if uncertain whom he should be addressing. Jago spoke first.

'Mr Marwell?'

'Yes, that's right.'

'Detective Inspector Jago, and this is Detective Constable Cradock. We'd just like a quick word with you.'

'Of course,' said Marwell. He looked from one to the other again, and his hand went to the front of his overalls, as if he were worried that one of the buttons on his chest might be undone.

'Excuse me, Officers,' he said quickly. 'I must look a terrible mess, but it's dirty work here, and I'm just one of the plebs – it's only the men at the top who wear suits. Still, at least I'm doing my bit for the war effort, not just sitting around making money out of other people's misfortunes.'

'Are you thinking of anyone in particular?'

'No, I just reckon that in times like these there's plenty of characters who manage to do good business out of a war. If that were me, I'd feel ashamed – I'd rather do some filthy job in a factory for next to nothing but go home with a clear conscience. Like yourselves, I'm sure.'

Jago declined to follow this line of conversation.

'We won't take much of your time. I just want to ask you a few questions,' he said.

'Right. Yes, of course.' His voice was subdued. 'I suppose this is to do with Joan, is it?'

'That's right. You're aware of what's happened?'

'Yes, my wife told me yesterday – that's Elsie. You've met her, haven't you? She'd heard from her mother while I was here at work.'

Marwell took a packet of Capstan from his pocket and put a cigarette in his mouth. He struck a match to light it, but it went out. He struck another and managed to get the cigarette lighted. He tossed the spent matches away, his hand shaking slightly. He looked up at Jago.

'Forgive me, Inspector,' he said, extending the packet of cigarettes towards him. 'I wasn't thinking. Would you like one?'

'No, thank you,' said Jago.

Marwell offered one to Cradock, who shook his head.

'I'm sorry,' he continued. 'You must think I'm a nervous wreck. It's just the thought of poor Joan . . .' His voice tailed off for a moment. 'Really, it's the last thing I'd have imagined happening. I mean, people are getting killed in air raids every day – it seems like it's part of normal life now. But not something like this. My wife told me Joan had been strangled.' He gave a shudder. 'It's unthinkable.'

'How did you get on with Joan?'

'She was a nice girl. I can't say I knew her particularly well. I mean, your wife's brother's wife – it's one of those relationships we don't even have a word for.'

'What were your movements on Sunday evening?'

'Nothing special. It was my day off, so I was just generally catching up on odd jobs at home – mending my bike, things like that. I was due back on fire-watching duty Sunday night, so I was trying not to do anything too tiring in the daytime. Then in the evening I was at home, apart from going out to walk Elsie home from the pub. She gets a bit nervous with all these air raids, you see.'

'Your wife tells us that you passed a sailor lying on the street on your way home. Is that correct?'

'Yes, we did.'

'Do you remember what time it was?'

'Well, we left the pub at about half past eight, so it must have been just a few minutes after that.'

'And do you remember where this was?'

'Yes, it was on the corner of Martin Street. You know it? Down between Station Street and Angel Lane. He was lying in a shop doorway.'

'And later in the evening you came here for your fire-watching duty?'

'Yes.'

'Did that take you past Martin Street again?'

'Yes, it did.'

'Did you notice whether the sailor was still there?'

'No, he'd gone.'

'Can you remember what time that was?'

'Well, my shift started at ten o'clock and I was there on time, so I imagine it would have been about a quarter to ten, ten to ten, something like that.'

'When we spoke to your wife she told us the sailor was wearing his cap when you saw him on your way home. Is that correct?'

'Sorry, I don't recall. My wife's better at remembering details than I am – doesn't miss much, you know, our Elsie. She's very reliable in that respect. Very thorough.'

'Indeed. Well, thank you anyway, Mr Marwell. That's all we need to know at the moment.'

CHAPTER TWENTY-FIVE

At a quarter past seven on Wednesday morning Jago walked slowly down West Ham Lane towards Rita's cafe, lost in thought. He'd set off early to have time to think, but also to ensure that he'd arrive before Dorothy and be there to welcome her. He felt a strange warmth at the prospect of seeing her again. His brief visit with her to the Cenotaph on Monday evening had stirred memories of men long since lost to death, their faces, laughter and tears now decayed to dust, but she was different – so alive, so brightly present here and now in his life. He'd made up his mind not to live in the past, and she was the one who'd provoked him to break free of it. He wanted to be part of her world, not just to trudge through life in a bleak solitude and then slip away unnoticed.

In the midst of these thoughts he became aware of cheery whistling coming from behind him. He recognised the tune – it was 'Oh, Johnny, Oh', an American song from the end of the last war that had become popular all over again. The only person likely to be whistling on the street at this time of the morning was the milkman, and he turned round expecting to see a man – or these days possibly a woman – with a milk float and horse. What he saw, in fact, was the approaching figure of Cradock, walking briskly to catch up with him.

'Morning, guv'nor,' said the young detective constable, with a broad smile.

'You're looking very bright and breezy today,' said Jago. 'What's happened?'

'An early start, sir. You know – up with the lark, catch the best of the day.'

'Ah, I see. So you managed to get out of bed in time to catch Tom Gracewell.'

'That's right, sir. And I found out who was on the beat in Martin Street on Sunday evening. It was Ted Watson, and he was on early turn today, so I spoke to him too.'

'Good. What did he say?'

'Ted Watson, sir?'

'Yes. Did he confirm speaking to our sailor?'

'Yes. He said he found him lying in the shop doorway looking asleep and smelling of drink. He said it's not the first time he's come across men in uniform in that sort of state, but he reckons it's because now there's conscription they're getting all sorts of undesirables in the forces.'

'That doesn't surprise me. I've known Ted Watson for years – he's an old-timer.'

'Yes, a bit quaint, really, I thought. Very serious in the

way he talked. He had the *Police Code* off pat – you know, that bit where it says we should constantly endeavour to maintain the most friendly feeling with soldiers and sailors. He said it doesn't say anything about whether they're conscripts or not, so he endeavoured, and was very gentle with him. Said he doesn't take the same line with merchant seamen, because the *Police Code* doesn't say that about them.'

'Yes, but what does he say about Ernie Sullivan?'

'He said because the bloke was a sailor he didn't take his name, but judging by where Ted says he found him I reckon it must've been him. Ted said he just woke him up with a gentle prod of his truncheon and moved him on.'

'And what about the cap and the torch?'

'He said the torch was there, switched off, and the cap was there too, lying on the ground.'

'Did he make a note of what time he moved him on?'

'Yes, he doesn't miss a trick, does Ted – said the time was a quarter to nine.'

'And what did Tom Gracewell have to say?'

'Well, I asked him if he'd seen or heard anything on his beat that might suggest Joan was on the game, and he said no, nothing. In fact he didn't know anything about her, so either she was very good at keeping her affairs private or she was a decent, law-abiding resident. And the fingerprint boys said they had nothing on record for her.'

'Right. Thank you, Peter.'

'Oh, and yesterday evening I tracked down the regular ARP warden for Joan's road, but he said he hadn't seen anything significant. She'd only moved in about three weeks ago and she often seemed to be out in the evenings, so he'd barely seen her. Nothing suspicious to report, and no indication that there was anything immoral going on in the flat.'

'Very good. So I expect after all that you've worked up a good appetite.'

'Definitely, sir – especially if it's your treat.'

'Yes, well, just make sure you leave something for any other customers Rita may have today, won't you?'

They arrived at the cafe and were shown to a table by Rita. Jago was pleased to hear that they'd got there before Dorothy, and even more pleased to see her when she came through the door a few minutes later.

'Morning, dear,' said Rita, standing back slightly and looking her up and down, as was her habit. 'Very nice to see you.'

'Thanks, Rita,' said Dorothy. 'And how are you? Everything's going OK with the cafe?'

'All tickety-boo, thank you. It's a bit tricky getting the supplies in, what with the war, but mustn't grumble.'

'And how's your daughter? Emily, isn't it?'

'She's fine. She told me she'd had a lovely time at the pictures Sunday night with young Mr Cradock here. They went to the Regal, but I don't know what they saw. Anyway, is it eggs and bacon for everyone?'

'I think so, yes,' said Jago.

'Righto. Back in two shakes,' said Rita, and set off for the kitchen.

Jago turned to Cradock and raised an enquiring eyebrow.

'How strange. You didn't tell me that, Peter, did you? We spent all that time at the Regal on Monday morning talking about the money stolen from their safe, and you didn't even mention that you'd been there the previous evening.'

'Er, well, it was rather a private matter, wasn't it?' Cradock replied. 'Me being there with Emily, I mean. I, er, well, I didn't really want to bring it up. I suppose I was a bit embarrassed, really.'

'There's no need for you to feel embarrassed,' said Dorothy. 'You're among friends here, and I for one would like to know how you got on.'

'All right. But you won't tell Rita anything I say, will you?'

'Of course not. Now, was this the second time you've taken Emily to the movies?'

'Yes.'

'And did you take my advice? You didn't do anything to scare her?'

'Yes, I did – I mean no, I didn't. It was a bit scary for me, actually. She did that thing you talked about – you know, she looked me in the eye when I was talking to her, she smiled at me, nodded her head and leant towards me a bit, just like you said.'

As Jago heard Cradock's words, he had a disturbing

recollection of being in the churchyard at All Saints' Church, sitting side by side with Dorothy in the fading light of evening, and of the particular way in which she had spoken to him. He glanced up, hoping she hadn't noticed the look of surprise that he was sure must have crossed his face. Her expression betrayed nothing, but for some reason she was looking at him while she continued her conversation with Cradock.

'There,' she said. 'Just like I said – that means she likes you.'

'I'm not so sure,' said Cradock.

'So did you hold her hand this time?'

'No. I still wasn't sure whether I should. Especially if she does like me.'

Jago pitied the poor boy. He had the feeling that between them, Rita and Emily were weaving a web, and Cradock was the hapless fly. But he suspected too that this fly didn't mind being caught.

Cradock was spared further embarrassment by the arrival of Rita with their breakfasts. She set down a plate of bacon and eggs and a mug of tea in front of each one of them, wiped an imaginary spot of dust from the tablecloth, and went off to attend to her other customers.

Something in Jago compelled him to turn the conversation towards less personal matters.

'So, what news is there from the other side of the Atlantic?' he said as breezily as he could manage.

'Mostly it's about the election, as far as I can tell,' said Dorothy, 'although maybe that's because most of

212

the people I hear from over there are journalists.'

'That's the presidential election, is it?'

'That's right – on November fifth.'

Jago couldn't help laughing. 'What a great choice of date! The day Guy Fawkes tried to blow our parliament up with barrels of gunpowder in the cellar.'

'Yes, well I'm sure ours will be an exciting event, but hopefully not as exciting as that. I've heard your own elections here may be postponed, though. You're supposed to have a general election this year, aren't you?'

'Yes. The last one was in November 1935, and the law says a parliament can only last five years, so that means we ought to be having an election by next month. But now the government's talking about delaying it for a year because of the war, so who knows when it'll be? We'll just have to add it to all the fun we're going to have when this war's over.'

'Well, the result we get in the States next month could have a significant influence on how soon that day comes.'

'Is the war a big issue?'

'It certainly is, and especially what we can do to keep out of it. The Republicans have been saying Roosevelt's too keen on war and he's supporting you British too much when he should be building up our own defences instead, and the Democrats are accusing the Republicans of being sympathetic to the fascists.'

'Who do you think will win?'

'It's difficult to say. Back in June it looked like the Republicans would win and had a strong candidate in

Wendell Willkie, but now it's not so clear. Roosevelt's been ahead in the polls, but it could be a close-run thing.'

Cradock followed this conversation, looking from Jago to Dorothy and back again and realising that he didn't know the first thing about American politics.

'So what result would be best for us?' he interjected, hoping this remark would not sound too stupid. 'For Britain, I mean. Who do we want to win?'

'An interesting question, Peter,' Dorothy replied, to his ill-concealed pleasure. 'Although you have to remember it isn't always a clear-cut issue. I believe it was one of your English lords – Lord Morley – who once said an election offers the voters an opportunity to make a choice between two mistakes. You might think it's obvious that we should join the war on your side, but there are plenty of influential people in the States who want to keep the country out of it. Charles Lindbergh, for example. You know – the famous aviator.'

'The one whose baby boy was kidnapped?'

'That's the one. A few weeks back they set up a thing called the America First Committee – they're very opposed to Roosevelt, because they think he wants to drag America into the war.'

'And does he?'

'Well, I'm not sure I can tell you what he wants. He's talked a lot about keeping America out of the war too, but at the same time he's been helping you. We've been here before, of course. In the last war President Wilson did everything he could to keep America neutral. He'd

214

seen what the Civil War did to our country and he didn't want to put us through that kind of destruction and suffering again. When he campaigned for his second term in 1916 his slogan was "He's kept us out of war". And just like now, we weren't ready for it. It was only when German submarines started sinking our ships that he was finally persuaded, and Congress voted for war.'

'Roosevelt's the one who gave us those fifty destroyers, isn't he? Doesn't that mean he's on our side?'

'According to people I've spoken to in London, both candidates know that Germany's a huge threat to the USA, and that you're our last line of defence against it. My friends in Washington say President Roosevelt's biggest fear is that if Britain's defeated the Royal Navy will fall into German hands, and then Germany will be unstoppable – and America will be its next target. He can see you've got your backs to the wall and he doesn't want you to lose – that's why he pushed that destroyer deal through.'

'No wonder he's worried,' said Cradock, moved by a vague sense of obligation to be patriotic when talking to Dorothy. 'We've got the biggest fleet in the world.'

'It certainly worries me, dear, I don't mind telling you,' said another voice, joining the discussion. It was Rita, who had arrived noiselessly at Cradock's shoulder. Jago looked up and saw her staring down at him, notebook in hand, as if expecting him to say something.

'What's that?' he said. 'What worries you?'

'The war, of course. I'm a Gemini, see.'

'A Gemini?'

'Yes, my star sign. Geminis always worry, although you wouldn't know it because they hide their troubles behind their light-hearted exterior.'

'Really?'

'Yes. They're good-natured, kind and affectionate. And unselfish too. I thought you'd know about that sort of thing, Mr Jago, what with you being a detective. Understanding what makes people tick.'

'I see. For some reason the Metropolitan Police Service doesn't include star signs in its training for detectives.'

'They will one day, you mark my words. You can't just rely on fingerprints and alibis. You've got to understand the heart. Men don't see that kind of thing, though, do they? You want to get some women detectives, that's what you should do. Some Geminis. They're quick, you know – lots of insight into human nature. And Geminis make very good wives – that's what they say.'

'You don't believe in that nonsense, do you?' Jago replied, and immediately felt guilty when he saw Rita's crushed expression.

'It's not nonsense,' she said timidly. 'I find it very comforting, especially these days. There was an astrologist in the paper, an American lady.' She turned to Dorothy as if looking for sympathy and support. 'One of yours. Last year she predicted the war was going to start in the autumn, and it did. And she said Germany's going to lose, and Hitler's going to fall in 1943.'

'The papers are hardly likely to report an astrologist predicting that we'll lose the war, are they?' Jago retorted, unable to disguise the tone of impatience in his voice. 'Besides, what is the future? It doesn't exist, does it? So how can anyone predict something that doesn't exist? All we know is the present, and what we might remember of the past. That's all the truth there is, and all the rest is either made up or unknowable.'

'I don't know about that, Mr Jago,' said Rita. 'I don't think I'm clever enough to answer a question like that. All I know is we're at war again, and that means nothing but sadness and grief. I just want it to finish, and if someone says it's going to end, even if it's not till 1943, that gives me hope.'

Jago thought of his conversation two days earlier with Audrey Lewis, a mother clinging to the hope that her son missing in France had escaped or at worst had been captured – anything rather than killed. A hope that both sustained and consumed her.

'I'm sorry, Rita,' he said. 'I was wrong to speak like that. I do understand how you feel.'

'That's all right, Mr Jago,' she said. 'I know you mean well.'

There was an awkward silence, and Dorothy judged it was time to rescue both Rita and Jago from the difficult territory into which their conversation had strayed.

'You're right, Rita,' she said soothingly. 'We all need a little hope in our lives. They say hope's like a star – you can't see it when the sun's shining, only when everything around you is dark.' She paused, and gave Rita a warm smile. 'So what do you hope for, Rita?'

'That's easy,' said Rita, her face brightening a little. 'An end to this blasted war, and a good husband for Emily.' She looked at Jago and began to rub the table slowly with her cloth. 'Trouble is,' she continued, 'when you've got hope, the stronger it gets, the more it hurts when you don't get what you hope for. That's when you find out hope and grief come very close together. It's like it was with my Walter – I hoped and hoped he'd come back from the war, but he never did. "Hope deferred maketh the heart sick." That's what they say, isn't it? Well I can tell you, that's the truest thing I ever heard in my life.'

CHAPTER TWENTY-SIX

Jago and Cradock walked back from Rita's cafe with Dorothy until they reached the police station, where she said goodbye to them and continued on alone to catch the train back into the centre of London. Jago knew it might be embarrassing to wait and watch until she was out of sight rather than go straight into the station with Cradock, but there was a stronger fear in his mind too – a common one these days. The fear that at any moment, any day, a bomb could change a casual goodbye to a final and irreversible parting. So he stayed where he was, standing on the pavement and watching her back as she made her way up the street, despite the fact that Cradock waited beside him. He hoped she might turn round, and she did. They exchanged a brief wave, and Cradock sportingly waved too. Then she was gone.

'Right, Peter, let's get down to work,' said Jago briskly as they returned to the CID office. 'Any news on those fingerprints?'

'Yes, sir,' Cradock replied, mustering his most formal tone to reassure Jago that his waving to Dorothy would be treated as confidential. 'We've got a print confirmed for Evans, the fireman, on the back door handle, but nowhere else. We haven't found any for the ARP warden, Mrs Parks, but she said she was wearing gloves, so that's not surprising. By the time the two of them had been all over the back door handle there was nothing else identifiable left, and we're probably lucky that Evans's print survived.'

'So there's no other prints we can make use of?'

'That's right, sir. Oh, and by the way, sir, did you find out anything useful about those other cases – the Soho ones?'

'Yes, I spoke to Detective Superintendent Oates on C Division, where some of them happened. He said the first victim, Josephine Martin, who was known as French Fifi, was strangled with a silk stocking. The second one was strangled with a silk scarf, the third with a piece of wire, and the fourth with some blind cord. That's what made the detectives investigating think it was all the work of one man, but they haven't found a single clue to link them. What's more, they'd had a different suspect in each case, and one of them was actually in prison when another of the women was murdered, which obviously put him in the clear. They've come to the conclusion that even though most of the victims were prostitutes, it wasn't one man committing all the murders. In fact they think there was probably a different killer in each case, and the murders were actually crimes of imitation. The superintendent said it was possible, of course, that one of them had also been involved in our case, but he reckoned we might as well assume that our killer is a different person altogether.'

'So it could be anyone?'

'That's right. It could be anyone.'

'But still the kind of person who's likely to murder a prostitute?'

'As I said, it could be anyone.'

Cradock sat silent for a moment, lost in thought.

'I've been thinking, sir,' he said at last.

'Well done, Peter. About what?'

'About Bert Wilson, and about his jobs and all that. What he said yesterday about working for Charlie Lewis for two years without ever seeing Richard, who was his old mate. He wriggled out of it when you challenged him, with that business about not being in the office and Charlie not wanting him to talk to Richard, but I'm not convinced he was telling us the truth. And he must've known going round collecting debts for a man like Lewis was a pretty shady business. Supposing he's not the upright citizen he'd like us to think he is? If he's not, I could easily see him using his keys to help those safe-breakers get into the cinema.'

'That's possible, but you're not suggesting he could be involved in the murder, are you?'

'I don't know, sir. What if Joan found out he was going to let those thieves in and threatened to tell Conway or the police? He might've wanted to silence her. If Joan was having some kind of affair with

Conway, and Wilson knew it, he'd be scared that she'd tell Conway everything she knew.'

'But we don't have any evidence that she knew anything about the safe job.'

'That's true. But wait . . . supposing there was something going on between Joan and Wilson? He's pretty soft on her, isn't he? And he got quite prickly when you asked him how close he was to her. Maybe he was in love with her, but she refused to be unfaithful to her husband, so he killed her in a jealous rage.'

'That sounds a bit like a movie script. But in any case, did he have an opportunity to murder Joan? He was at the cinema all night, fire watching.'

'Yes, but you heard what that AFS bloke Evans said. He reckoned some of those fire watchers aren't above sloping off for a rest or a sleep, so why not slope off for a jealous murder?'

'It's possible, as long as he was back in time to be jumped on by a pair of safe-breakers. But his economic argument about risking eighteen months' hard labour for a twenty-pound cut was quite persuasive, wasn't it?'

'He wouldn't be the first crook to take on odds like that – especially if he thought he could get away with it. And Wilson was the only person with a lawful reason to be on the premises that night, wasn't he? Perfect cover.'

'Possibly. We'll see. Now, anything else to report before we go out?'

'Yes, sir. I checked up on those moneylending things, like you said – the certificate of good character and the excise licence. No record of either for Charlie Lewis, so I reckon his business was very private, like Bert Wilson said. He must've been an interesting character.'

'Yes, Audrey may claim he left her with no financial worries, but I doubt his clients would say the same. I've come across his sort before – they buy up bad debts for two-and-six in the pound, then use their powers of persuasion to get the debtors to pay them back the full pound on everything they owe.'

'And by powers of persuasion you mean Bert Wilson?'

'Yes. Not quite the gentle giant we might've taken him for after all.'

'A nasty business.'

'Indeed it is, and it sounds like Charlie Lewis was a nasty character. But he's somewhere we can't get hold of him now. We need to focus on the living.'

'What's next, then, guv'nor?'

'I think it's time we took a little stroll round to Cross Street to see whether we can catch young Beryl Hayes at home before she goes to work.'

CHAPTER TWENTY-SEVEN

At Beryl's lodgings Jago and Cradock navigated their way safely round the landlady and climbed the stairs to her door, where they were greeted by a bleary-eyed Beryl.

'I'm sorry, Inspector,' she said. 'I'm not long out of bed. It was a bit noisy last night, and I didn't sleep well.'

'The anti-aircraft guns?' said Jago.

'No,' she replied, lowering her voice almost to a whisper. 'It was Mrs Jenks, my landlady. She sleeps in the next room – I think it's her way of making sure I don't break her "no gentlemen visitors" rule. The thing is, she snores like a . . . Well, let's just say she snores very loudly. I'm starting late today, though, so I managed to have a bit of a lie-in.'

'I'm sorry if we've prevented you getting your sleep.'

'No, I was up and dressed before you arrived, as you can see.'

She was indeed dressed, and very well, in a smartly cut woollen suit. Surprisingly well, thought Jago, for a woman living in such humble surroundings. But then a lot of young women seemed to spend most of their income on clothes, in his limited experience.

'Can I get you a cup of tea?' said Beryl. 'I was just about to make one.'

'No, thank you,' Jago replied. 'We won't be here long.'

'All right. So how can I help you?'

'Well, I'm afraid I have to raise a delicate matter with you. I didn't like to mention it when we first spoke, as you'd only just heard what'd happened to Joan, but the fact is, the way your sister was killed bore some of the hallmarks of a number of other murders that've taken place over recent years. Please understand that this may have nothing to do with your sister's death, but in those cases most of the women were prostitutes, one of them from East Ham. So I have to ask you – do you have any reason to suspect that your sister might've been involved in that kind of activity?'

Beryl's eyes widened. 'You're saying my sister was a prostitute?'

'No, I'm not saying she was anything. I'm simply asking the question.'

'Of course she wasn't. Honestly, you policemen always think the worst of people. No, Joan would never do that. I don't think she'd ever have dreamt of it. Anyway, she had a job, didn't she?'

'Yes, of course, and I apologise for having to ask such an insensitive question. But it's not unknown for wives to be tempted in times like these – their husbands are away at war overseas, and they have to cope with all the pressures of life on their own. And you did say she was lonely.'

'Well, that's as may be, but it was natural for her to feel lonely if her husband was away overseas and missing. Look, I can assure you I have no reason to believe my sister had anything whatsoever to do with prostitution, and I hope that answer's clear enough for you.'

'Thank you, and again I'm sorry. I had no wish to upset you.'

'Yes, well never mind.'

'I must also ask you another rather delicate question.'

'Go on, then.'

'When I spoke to you before, I asked you if your sister had any male friends, and you said you weren't aware of her being close to any men in particular. But since then it's been suggested to us that your manager, Mr Conway, has what might be called an eye for the ladies, and may have had a particular interest in your sister. Do you know anything about that?'

'An eye for the ladies? I'd say that's a fair description. Have you heard about his inspections?'

'We've been told he's very particular about the staff's appearance.'

'Yes, he is, and he's especially keen to check the appearance of the female staff. Very thorough, if you ask me, getting all the usherettes lined up and checking their seams are straight. Quite the perfectionist.'

'Are you suggesting his attention to detail goes beyond the requirements of his duties as a manager?'

Beryl responded to his question with a knowing smile. 'That's a nice way of putting it, Inspector. The way he studies our details, you'd think he was going to paint us in oils. But then that's the thing – I think he fancies himself as some sort of artist, and you know what those artists are like for painting women.'

'An artist? I understood his interest was in photography.'

'Yes, well, I don't mean he actually does paintings. I mean I think he likes taking photos. Artistic photos. That's what they call them, isn't it? Like those postcards you hear about. He's keen on that kind of photography. The other usherettes warned me when I started there – said he likes the girls to model for him. Cheeky monkey, I thought. Let him try and get me to pose. I reckon that's what he had in that safe, you know – his private art collection, saucy snaps of any girl stupid enough to fall for his tricks.'

'Did Joan ever mention this?'

'I can't remember her saying. I think she must've been aware of it, but if you mean did he try it on with her, my guess would be no. I think he was a bit wary of asking the married women – you never know who might turn out to have a boxer for a husband. Mind you, he found a job for Joan fast enough when the Broadway Super was bombed, didn't he? Very attentive. Saucy Sid – that's what the girls call him.'

'But you're not aware of any close relationship between Joan and Mr Conway. Is that right?'

'To be honest, I don't know. She certainly never told me. If you want to ask that sort of question, you'd better talk to Cynthia Carlton. She seems to know everything about everyone else's business at the cinema.'

'Actually it was something Miss Carlton said that first suggested there might've been something between them, although I hasten to add she didn't make any specific allegation.'

'There you are, then. There's nothing that woman likes more than a bit of juicy gossip. The only time she doesn't like gossip is when it's about her, and there's plenty of that – about her and Mr Conway, too.'

'What do you mean?'

'If you don't mind, I'd rather not say. I don't like gossip, and I don't pass it on when I hear it.'

'Quite.'

'Not that there isn't things I could tell you if I had a mind to. Especially about that family Joan married into. For instance, did you know Audrey's husband was some kind of moneylender?'

'It has been said.'

'Oh, right. Shocking, isn't it? And her so respectable. And that Madame Zara?'

'Her name has been mentioned. Do you know her?'

'Not personally, no. But apparently Audrey's obsessed with finding her husband's money, only she can't, because he hid it. Since he dropped dead no one's been able to find it, so she thought if she got this Madame Zara to have a seance she could get in touch with the

228

other side – that's what they call it – and someone over there might tell her where to look. Funny idea if you ask me, asking dead people questions like that, but it takes all sorts, doesn't it?'

'And what about Richard, Joan's husband? Did he believe his father had hidden his money somewhere?'

'I don't think so. Joan never mentioned it, anyway. She did go to see Madame Zara herself once, though.'

'Why was that?'

'I think Audrey persuaded her to go along, to see if she could tell them anything about what'd happened to Richard – Joan hadn't heard a thing. Not that being in the dark was anything new for her – I'm not sure Richard even told her he was joining the TA in the first place.'

'Really? What makes you think that?'

'Oh, nothing really. It wasn't anything anyone said, just an impression I got. I may be wrong. But anyway, maybe Madame Zara thought the spirits would be more forthcoming if his wife and mother were both asking – I don't know.'

Jago moved to the room's one small window. The streaks of grime suggested it hadn't been cleaned for a long time. He looked down as a few spots of rain began to land on it, and saw only the backs of similar houses in the next road. He turned back to Beryl.

'Do you know where this Madame Zara lives?'

'Yes. Joan told me. It's 77 Eleanor Road. I remember that, because seven's my lucky number, and I thought an address like that might be double lucky, especially if your name's Eleanor. But mine isn't, of course. And by the way, I don't think Madame Zara's her real name. Joan said it was just made up – she's really called Vera. I've never met her, mind, so I just took Joan's word for it.'

'What happened when Joan went to see her?'

'She didn't say. I don't know whether she believed in that kind of thing. Audrey certainly did, though, as far as I can tell. As for Madame Zara, or Vera or whatever her name is, I reckon she's just been taking money off a foolish old woman. But if that gives Audrey some pleasure or comfort, let her do it, that's what I say. It's a free country.'

'Do you have any reason to think Madame Zara is deliberately trying to deceive her?'

'No. I just reckon Audrey can't get used to the idea of her husband dying and wants to go back to when they were together. Some people are like that, aren't they? Especially when they get older. They always seem to think the old days were better. But you can't live in the past, that's what I say. My boyfriend's always going on about the past, even though he's young, like me. Always talking about dead people I've never heard of. He calls it history, but I think it's just boring old stories. Politics, too.'

'He sounds like a serious young man.'

'Yes, well, he's a bit too serious for my liking. I'm beginning to think when they were handing out a sense of humour he was at the back of the queue – or maybe not even in it at all. Sunday night, for instance. There was a bit in the newsreel about some ship in Belfast, and I said to him, "Have you heard the one about the Englishman, the Irishman and the Scotsman?" and all of a sudden he snapped at me, said he hadn't, but he knew it was bound to end up that the Irishman was an idiot, and if we knew more about the awful things we'd done to Ireland we wouldn't be so cocky with our jokes. He said we don't belong there and we should get our troops out. It was quite an eye-opener. The way he flared up like that, you'd think I'd insulted his mother or something.'

'Perhaps his mother's Irish.'

'I don't think he's got a mother – not alive, anyway. But he's as English as you and me. He just seems to have this bee in his bonnet about politics and Ireland. But I thought that was all settled years ago – they're not part of our country any more, are they, except for that bit at the top? Men get so het up about politics, don't they? I don't know why. Me, I say leave all that to the politicians – that's what they're for. I'm young, and I think life's for living now. I don't want to go grubbing round in the past. Perhaps I will when I'm old, like Audrey, but for now I reckon if I've survived another night and haven't been bombed to pieces, I'll have a good time today and hope to be alive tomorrow. I'm very disappointed with that Martin. He seemed so promising at first, but I'm not sure I'm going to bother seeing him again – not since last time. He didn't even walk me home from the pictures – just nipped off with some flimsy excuse and didn't come back. What kind of gentleman is that?'

'I don't think I can comment on that.'

'Well, if ever I get married, I'm jolly well going to make sure I marry a gentleman. Someone like yourself – only younger, of course.'

Jago thought from her tone of voice that she was about to laugh, but she suddenly stopped and seemed plunged into some more sombre reflection.

'Is everything all right?' he said.

'Yes, I'm fine. It's just . . . Well, talking about getting married made me think. If I do, Joan won't be there, will she? That makes me feel sad, and it's reminded me of something else.'

'Yes?'

'When we were at the mortuary, with Joan, I didn't look at her hands. She was all covered up, and I thought I probably wasn't supposed to touch the sheet or anything. But I just wondered – did she have her rings on?'

'Why do you ask?'

'Well, I was down Manor Road yesterday, and I was passing by a pawn shop. I looked in the window and there was an engagement ring and a wedding ring in there that looked just like Joan's. I mean, wedding rings are all much of a muchness, aren't they, but the engagement ring was a bit unusual – it was a square emerald. It looked just like hers. I know she wasn't rolling in money, but I wouldn't have thought she'd have needed to pawn her rings.'

'Could you tell me which pawnbroker's it was?'

'Yes, it was at the top end of Manor Road, near where it meets Stephen's Road. I can't remember the name, but it's the only one in the street.'

'Thank you, Miss Hayes. That will be all for now. We'll leave you to get ready for work.'

'You're welcome. But let me know about those rings. If it turns out her Richard's dead after all, they might come to me, yes?'

Jago said nothing, but doffed his hat to her as they left.

CHAPTER TWENTY-EIGHT

'That was interesting,' said Cradock as the door shut behind them. 'What she said about Cynthia Carlton, I mean – the gossip about her and Conway.'

'You like a bit of gossip, do you, Peter?' said Jago.

'No, but it wasn't the impression I got when we were talking to Cynthia. I thought she was a bit sniffy about him. And when he started talking about how he looked after his girls and how sensitive he was to their needs, I thought she was going to laugh out loud. I can't quite see her being involved with him in that way.'

'Not now, I agree, but perhaps in the past? She did say there'd been a little history between them, and I got the impression it didn't have a happy ending.'

'So is it worth following up?'

'Oh, yes, definitely.'

Jago looked over his shoulder and saw a curtain twitch in the downstairs front window of the house they'd just left. He wondered whether it was Beryl, but he doubted whether she was allowed into the front room. Perhaps it was just Mrs Jenks the landlady keeping an eye on her gentlemen callers.

'Come along. The Regal's only round the corner, and if Cynthia's the manager's secretary I daresay she has to dance attendance upon him as soon as he gets to work.'

'If not before,' muttered Cradock.

'Now, now,' said Jago. 'Judge not. It's none of our business, unless someone's breaking the law. But if any of this has a bearing on Joan's death, I want to know.'

He set off at a brisk pace towards the end of Cross Street, with Cradock hurrying to keep up, then on to Stratford High Street and the Regal. A garish poster at the cinema's entrance proclaimed that it was showing something called *Dr Cyclops*, a film about which he knew nothing, while the B movie, equally unknown to him, was *Room for Two*, starring Frances Day and Vic Oliver. He smiled to himself. Every time he saw Oliver's name he wondered how Winston Churchill coped with having a comedian for a son-in-law. It was difficult to imagine the grandson of an English duke having anything in common with an Austrian-born music hall entertainer – except, of course, a young red-haired stage dancer called Sarah Churchill. Her father probably thought Vic Oliver was as common as muck, he reflected, but then Jago's own dad was only a music hall singer, so he'd probably think the same of him. Not that they were ever likely to—

Cradock's voice snapped him out of his musings.

'Shall we go in, guv'nor?'

'Yes, yes. Go and find out whether she's here.'

Cradock duly went off to find Cynthia, and a couple of minutes later she joined them in the foyer.

'Good morning, Miss Carlton,' said Jago. 'We were just passing. There was something I wanted to ask you, so I thought we'd drop in.'

'Do you want me to find somewhere we can talk?' she asked.

'No, that won't be necessary – it'll only take a moment. It's a rather private question, though, so perhaps we could step outside for a minute or two.'

Cynthia Carlton followed the two policemen out through the main entrance, and they found a quiet corner to one side of the building where there were no passers-by.

'So what is it you want to know?' she asked. 'Why all the secrecy?'

'It's not secret,' said Jago, 'but it is a little sensitive. When we spoke to you on Monday you said that Mr Conway had, as you put it, an eye for the ladies. Pardon me for asking a blunt question, but were you ever one of those ladies?'

Cynthia responded with a light-hearted laugh. 'Oh, what a sweet gentleman you are – so polite and proper. You don't have to mince your words, Inspector – we're not Victorians any more, are we? This is 1940, and I can live my life as I please. I've nothing to be ashamed of. Yes, I did have a relationship with Mr Conway, and it went a long way beyond typing his correspondence.'

'You speak in the past tense. Does that mean you no longer have that relationship?'

'It certainly does, and good riddance.'

'But you're still working here?'

'Of course, and why shouldn't I? Like I said, this is 1940, and I don't see why I should give up my job just because a man's behaved like a rat. If he doesn't like it, let *him* go and find somewhere else to work. And don't start treating me like some helpless young maiden who's been taken advantage of – I'm a grown woman and I can take care of myself. Why should I shed any tears over a man who seems to change his women like other men change their collar?'

'So he dropped you for another woman?'

'That's a blunt way of putting it, but yes, that's what he did. He couldn't resist her. "Such a sweet soul" – that's what he said when you came to the cinema, wasn't it? Honestly, it's enough to make a girl sick. I mean, now that she's gone, he's probably already eyeing up his next conquest.'

'You mean he dropped you for Joan?'

'Of course I do. You know he took her on at the Regal when the Broadway Super was bombed, don't you?'

'Yes.'

'Well, I think he'd seen her there and got her the job here so he could . . . how should I put it? Make his move? He wanted her a bit closer to the centre of his web, so he could pounce. And you know what I think? I reckon she was in the family way.'

Jago's face betrayed no trace of surprise. 'Why do you say that?' he asked.

'Oh, I don't know, just something I heard.'

'From whom?'

'I don't know, I can't remember. But I had this feeling, anyway – call it women's intuition if you like. Women notice these little things, in ways that men don't.'

'But did you ask her whether it was true?'

'No, of course not. I wouldn't do that, would I?'

CHAPTER TWENTY-NINE

A hint of mid-morning sun had broken through the clouds as Jago and Cradock made their way back from the Regal cinema to the police station. It brightened up the High Street and cast a warm, golden light on the stone colonnades and proud tower of Stratford Town Hall, which so far had survived the Luftwaffe's bombing raids. Cradock wanted to know what they were doing next, but he could see Jago was thinking, so he held his tongue. They turned right at the town hall and were just passing the magistrates' court when Jago stopped in his tracks.

'You know, Peter, I think we've got it wrong.'

'Got what wrong, sir?'

'The way Cynthia was talking about Joan just now . . . I've been waiting for someone to confirm our suspicions about Joan, about her being on the game, but no one has – not the bobby on the beat, not her best friend, not her sister, and not even Cynthia, who hears all the gossip. It would appear she's got nothing to thank Joan for, but the way she spoke, it sounded like she saw Conway as the villain of the piece, and Joan was just his innocent victim. She'd have good reason to blacken Joan's name, so don't you think if she knew anything about immoral goings-on in Joan's background she'd have told us?'

'She did say she reckoned Joan was in the family way.'

'Yes, but she didn't say it in a malicious way, and she didn't try to make anything of it. I shall certainly be asking Mr Conway whether it was anything to do with him next time we see him, but for now I'm thinking more about this business of prostitution. As I said, I think we've got it wrong – or rather, I've got it wrong. Judging by what Superintendent Oates said, it seems clear that Joan can't have been murdered by the Soho Strangler, because there was no such person – it was just an idea the press latched on to and made a meal of it.'

'But you said he thought it could be a crime of imitation, sir. So it could be someone who didn't do those other murders but who still wanted to kill a prostitute.'

'Yes, but that's the point. I've been considering the possibility that she was murdered because she was involved in prostitution, but I think I was barking up the wrong tree.'

'Does it make any difference?'

'You mean whether she was on the game or not? In one sense no, I don't think it does. She's a murder victim, and we'd investigate it the same whether she was a prostitute or not. It just means I don't think we need to spend too much time and energy trying to see a link that isn't there. I don't think that's the reason why she was murdered.'

'But that puts us back to square one, doesn't it? I mean, she could've been murdered by anyone, for any reason under the sun.'

'Yes, that's about the measure of it, I think. We need to keep an open mind and broaden our horizons.'

They arrived at the police station and went round to the yard at the back, where Jago had left his car. The Riley Lynx was gleaming attractively in the sunlight.

'Hop in,' he said to Cradock. 'We're going to see a man about some rings.'

'You mean the pawnbroker?'

'Exactly.'

Jago slid into the driver's seat and started the engine, and they moved off in the direction of Manor Road.

'So what is it we're looking for?' Cradock asked as Jago steered the car deftly into the middle of the road. Cradock glanced to the side and saw that they were avoiding a bomb crater in West Ham Lane that had been temporarily, and unevenly, filled in with rubble – which itself had no doubt been conveniently provided at the scene by the same high-explosive bomb.

'What Audrey said – a narrow gold wedding ring and an engagement ring set with a small square emerald.'

'Sorry, sir, I realise I should know this, but what colour's an emerald?'

'Ask any Irishman.'

'Sir?'

'The Emerald Isle – it's green, the colour of Ireland.'

'Oh, yes, I see. I don't know much about engagement rings.'

'One day, Peter.'

They drove on in silence to Manor Road, Cradock hoping they'd find the pawnbroker's soon so he could avoid having to delve deeper into the question of engagement rings with his boss. To his relief he spotted the traditional sign of three golden balls hanging above a shop ahead of them on the street, and Jago slowed the car to a halt outside the small and rather dingy premises.

The sign over the door indicated that the shop belonged to one William Horncastle, or perhaps had once done so in the past, and the word 'pawnbroker' was painted alongside it. A notice in the window promised 'liberal advances'. As they pushed the door open it set a bell ringing, and a man emerged immediately from a doorway behind the counter.

'Good morning, gentlemen,' he said, with a deference that seemed too oily to be sincere. 'How can I be of assistance?'

'Mr Horncastle?'

'That's me.'

'I'm Detective Inspector Jago and this is Detective Constable Cradock, from West Ham CID.'

'I see. Come to check my licence, have you? I've got it right here if you want to see it. Everything's strictly above board here, you know – no shady business.'

'No, I don't need to see your licence. I want to know what you can tell me about a couple of rings you've got in your window.'

'Certainly. Which ones?'

'A plain gold wedding ring and an engagement ring with a small square green stone.'

The pawnbroker came out from behind his counter and reached into the window to remove a tray holding the rings.

'These ones?' he asked.

'Yes,' said Jago. 'A green stone's an emerald, isn't it?' he added, pointing to the glittering square set into the engagement ring.

The pawnbroker picked up the ring and turned it round in the light.

'In a manner of speaking, yes, but not quite. An emerald is a green stone, but not all green stones are emeralds, as you might say. What we've got here is a green stone all right, but if that's an emerald, I'm a Dutchman.' He placed the ring back on the tray. 'It's glass.'

'How can you tell?'

'It's got facets. A real emerald's quite hard, so the facets don't wear. If you get one like this, with worn facets, it's likely to be glass. I haven't bothered to get it checked, but I reckon I'm right, so I only gave him fifteen bob for it, plus a quid for the wedding ring. He seemed happy with that, and off he went.'

'When was this?'

'Just yesterday.'

'Did you satisfy yourself that they weren't stolen?'

Horncastle laughed. 'Pawnbrokers Act 1872? Yes, Inspector, I know my responsibilities, and I've studied that very carefully. I can assure you that if I'd suspected they were stolen I'd have handed him over to one of your constables. I've done that a good few times before now. You get to know the types. You can read their faces. But in this case it was a local – lives just round the corner. He's been in before.'

'What's his name?'

The pawnbroker thought, then shook his head. 'Sorry, I can't quite recall at the moment. It'll be in the pledge book, though.'

He reached under the counter and produced a large leather-bound journal, then leafed through the pages and turned the book round for Jago to read. The page was laid out in nine columns, all completed in a neat copperplate hand. He pointed to the bottom of the page, where Jago saw an entry recording that two rings had been pawned for a total of one pound fifteen shillings. It was dated the previous day.

'Is that the one?' he said.

'Yes, that's it,' said Horncastle.

Jago slid his finger across to the columns showing the name and address of the pawner. He turned the book slightly so that Cradock could read what it said: Mr Hosea Evans, 46 Stephen's Road, West Ham, E15.

'Thank you,' said Jago. 'That's most helpful. Is there anything else you can add to what you've told us?'

The pawnbroker pursed his lips thoughtfully, then shook his head again. 'No, I don't think so.'

'Did he say how he'd come by the rings?'

'Yes. I don't like to be too nosy – people can get a bit embarrassed. But like I said, I know my responsibilities, and if a bloke comes in to pawn an engagement ring it's a bit unusual, so I asked him.'

'And what did he say?'

'He said they were his grandmother's, and she'd left them to him when she died.'

'Well,' said Jago, 'that was very thoughtful of her, wasn't it?'

When they got back to the car Jago didn't start the engine straight away. Instead he sat holding the steering wheel in silence, deep in thought. Cradock began to fidget in the front passenger seat.

'Do you think that Horncastle fellow was telling the truth about the engagement ring, sir?' he said. 'About it being a fake, I mean. Supposing it's real?'

'It doesn't matter for the next twelve months, because Evans can bring the ticket in and redeem it any time he likes for his fifteen shillings plus a few bob interest. The real question is whether it actually belongs to Evans or not.'

'So that business about his grandmother – do you reckon he just made that up?'

'Well, it would certainly be a convenient coincidence for her to have the same taste in rings as Joan.'

'Does that mean we need to go back and see Evans again?'

'Indeed it does.'

'Any chance of a bite to eat on the way, sir?'

Jago sighed. 'We'll see,' he said.

Jago had never had children, but in this moment he felt like the father of a four-year-old. It was the way young Cradock sometimes came out with these streams of questions, fired randomly at him in the assumption that he'd know all the answers. Still, he supposed, better that than a detective constable who asked no questions. Not for the first time, he resolved inwardly to rein in his natural reactions and do his best to develop the boy. He abandoned his attempt to think.

'Now, I have a question for you, Peter,' he said, with what he hoped was not too theatrical a note of patience in his voice. 'Apart from this little business of the rings, there's the mystery of Charlie Lewis's missing money, Joan's missing husband and the unknown father of Joan's child. In all these cases, the person most likely to know the answer is dead – or in Richard's case, possibly dead but certainly out of contact. Now, who's the only person we haven't spoken to yet out of those we know had dealings with Joan before her death?'

Cradock thought for a while, his face showing the intense concentration he was applying to the task. Suddenly his frown eased.

'I've got it,' he said. 'That medium lady, Madame Zara. You mean you think she can get in touch with some of those dead people and turn up some evidence for us?'

Jago already regretted his attempt to cultivate Cradock's mind.

'I most certainly do not. What do you take me for? That sort of stuff's for gullible fools – but those mediums are experts in reading people.'

'Reading people?'

'Yes, it's one of their techniques. They ask you questions that could apply to anyone, then they use whatever you say to convince you that they know something about you. I'm just wondering whether she worked that trick on Joan when they had the seance that Beryl told us about – the one that Audrey took her to. I don't like these people, but I'll take evidence from anyone if it'll help us find out who murdered Joan Lewis.'

CHAPTER THIRTY

'Can you see number 77 yet?' Jago asked over the noise of the engine.

'Not yet, sir,' Cradock replied. 'Must be down the far end, I reckon.'

Jago drove to the end of Eleanor Road and parked the Riley at the kerbside, facing the green expanse of West Ham Park.

'Nice place to live,' he said, turning the engine off. 'All those trees, grass, fresh air. Pity about the anti-aircraft gun, but I don't suppose the estate agents mention that. Let's see if Madame Zara's at home. If she's that gifted, she should be expecting us.'

They walked the short distance back towards number 77, a neat little terraced house with a green front door. A smart maroon-and-black saloon car was parked outside it. Jago's knock at the door was answered by a man in his sixties with extravagant whiskers and an equally extravagant waistcoat under his grey jacket. As Jago took in the man's appearance the word 'flamboyant' came to mind.

'Good afternoon, sir,' said Jago, showing his warrant card. 'I'm Detective Inspector Jago of West Ham CID, and this is Detective Constable Cradock. We're looking for a lady called Madame Zara.'

'Well, you've come to the right place. Come in, gentlemen.' He ushered them into the living room.

'And you are?' asked Jago.

'Ballantyne's the name, Greville Ballantyne. What's it about?'

'We're investigating the death of a young lady called Joan Lewis. We've been told she attended a seance conducted by Madame Zara with her mother-in-law, Mrs Audrey Lewis, in connection with the whereabouts of the deceased's husband, Richard.'

'I see. If you'd like to take a seat, I'll fetch her.'

He left the room, and Jago took in the surroundings. What he saw reminded him of a museum, or perhaps a film set. It was tastefully decorated, but in a particularly turn-of-the-century style. A couple of framed music hall posters on the wall in an alcove caught his eye, and he was about to take a closer look when his host returned. Ballantyne stood aside to make way for a woman, who crossed the room towards Jago with her right hand outstretched.

'How do you do, Inspector,' she said, taking his hand and shaking it limply. 'Madame Zara, astrologist and medium.'

249

Her voice struck Jago as an intriguing mix of Yorkshire and the 'correct' English affected by BBC wireless announcers, as if perhaps she'd once had elocution lessons but they hadn't been entirely successful.

'And in case you were wondering,' she added, 'this is my husband, so if this is an official visit I suppose you should call me Mrs Ballantyne.'

'Thank you. I'd been given to understand that Madame Zara was a stage name.'

'Yes, that's correct. My friends know me as Vera – that's my real name. It means "faith". I'm a Pisces, you see, born on the nineteenth of March, and my mother knew that that would make me a faithful and caring person, so she gave me an appropriate name.'

Here we go again, thought Jago. *There must be more horoscope-lovers around than I'd thought.*

'What's your zodiac sign, Inspector?' the woman continued.

'I'm afraid I don't know,' he replied.

'You should, you know. Some people ignore what's written in the stars for their life, and they're the poorer for it. What's your birth date? I may be able to give you some helpful insights.'

'Well, supposing I were to tell you my birthday was the twelfth of November.'

'Then you are a Scorpio.'

'I see, and what would the stars say for me?'

'They would tell you this is a week in which you should do what you feel is right. It's up to you. Your

250

planets are favourable for action, so if you're thinking you should take the plunge on some matter, this could be the time to do it. But is that your real birth date?'

'Surely the stars should be able to tell you that.'

'I see you are sceptical, Inspector. That's a pity. It's difficult to help those who have no trust. I expect you would say a policeman cannot trust anyone or anything, but surely even policemen have to trust sometimes. I'd be happy to give you a personal reading – my fees are very modest – then you'd know your ruling planet, your lucky number, and the birthdate of your most suitable marriage partner, for example.'

'I don't think that'll be necessary, thank you.'

'Or for your colleague?'

Cradock glanced at Jago and shook his head. 'No thanks, madam.'

There was a brief silence, broken when Ballantyne stepped forward, rubbing his hands together.

'Shall I make some tea?' he asked.

'Yes, please, dear,' said Vera. 'A cup of tea for you, gentlemen?'

'That would be very nice,' said Jago.

'And as it's getting on for lunchtime,' Ballantyne continued, 'perhaps I could make you a sandwich. Would cheese and pickle be all right?'

From the corner of his eye Jago saw Cradock's eyes light up.

'That would be most kind,' he said. 'But are you sure you can spare the butter?'

'Actually, we don't have any. You know what it's like now the ration's down to two ounces. Would you mind margarine instead? I can't abide the stuff myself – goodness only knows what it's made of.'

'Margarine will be fine.'

Ballantyne left the room, promising to be back soon.

'So how can I help you?' said Vera when the door closed behind him.

'Well, as I said to your husband, we're investigating the death of a young lady called Joan Lewis. We've been told she attended a seance conducted by you, with her mother-in-law, Mrs Audrey Lewis. Is that correct?'

'Yes, that's right.'

'And you've known Audrey for some time?'

'Oh, yes. Actually we're sort of related. Not really, that is, but our husbands are cousins, or were, until poor Charles passed away. That's why she originally came to me for help when she wanted to get in touch with him, you see.'

'And the time Joan came with her, what happened?'

'Audrey wanted to contact Charles, but it proved not to be possible. Then she asked me if I could get any news of her son, Richard.'

'Joan's husband.'

'Yes. He's been reported missing in France, and Audrey's very concerned. But we weren't able to find out anything.'

'Why was that?'

'Joan wasn't a believer, so we couldn't get through to anyone. She was a sceptic, like you. She had this little smirk – like she was laughing at me.'

'I expect you're quite perceptive about people. Did you pick up anything in Joan that might help us understand what happened to her?'

'She seemed very ordinary. Not much colour to her, a grey sort of person. She was flat, emotionless, but then she didn't know what'd happened to her husband, so naturally she was preoccupied. All I can say is she was what you might call a closed book – one that I couldn't open.'

'I see. Have you had any other contact with her, before or since that seance?'

'No. I probably wouldn't have met her at all if she hadn't been Audrey's daughter-in-law.'

'And you didn't learn anything that might shed light on why someone would want to kill her?'

'No, nothing at all, really. Audrey did most of the talking – well, she tends to do that when younger people are present. She just asked if I could make contact with the spirit world and find out what'd happened to Richard.'

'But it didn't work.'

'On that occasion I wasn't able to make contact, but in a way that's a good thing. It could indicate that Richard's still alive – he'd only be contactable if he'd passed away.'

'Hmm. And what did Joan have to say about that?'

'Joan didn't really say anything, as far as I can recall. If anything, she seemed rather indifferent, as if she didn't care, but whether that was about the seance or what'd happened to her husband I really couldn't say. I'm sorry I can't be more helpful, but that's the only time I've met her.'

The door opened and Ballantyne entered with cups of tea which he distributed to his wife and the two detectives. He disappeared again, to return moments later with a plate of sandwiches for each of his guests, one of which Cradock seized appreciatively.

'Thank you,' said Jago, setting his plate down on the delicate Edwardian occasional table beside his chair. 'It's a very nice house you have here, Mr Ballantyne. So close to the park.'

'Yes. We've only been here since last year. After a lifetime of touring and living in theatrical digs it was strange to have a home of our own, but since we bought this place it's been wonderful.'

'You have a theatrical background? I thought perhaps you had when I saw the posters on the wall over there.'

'Oh, yes, I was a professional vocalist. Mainly in the music halls, you know. In fact, I was going to ask you something – about your name. It's rather unusual.'

'It's Cornish.'

'I see. Pardon me for asking a personal question, but are you by any chance related to Harry Jago?'

'That was my father's name.'

254

'And was he a singer?'

'Yes, he was, actually.'

'Then I knew him.'

'Really?'

'Yes, we both worked the music halls back in the old days, and our paths crossed more than once. In fact I remember him saying one night – it was at the Leeds Empire, I think, although I may be mistaken there – that he'd become a father. He was so excited. He'd had a son, and I suppose that was you, unless you have a brother.'

'No, I was his only son. Did you know him well?'

'Well enough to share a drink with him to celebrate your birth. I seem to remember our celebrations were quite extensive. I envied him his good fortune – sadly my dear wife and I have never been blessed with children. He was very proud of you then, and I'm sure he'd be just as proud of you now. He was a fine fellow, your father, and I was sorry when I heard he'd passed away. But that was years ago, wasn't it? You must have been just a child.'

'That's right. He died when I was fourteen.'

'Well, he was a splendid chap, always lots of fun. Like me, though, he never made it to the top. I think he struggled at times.'

'In what way?'

'Financially, of course, but then we all did. You didn't make a lot of money if you were in the bottom half of the bill. But he had trouble with his health, too, although I don't know what it was.'

'I never knew that, although I do know he and my mother went through some hard times. You must've had a more successful career than him, judging by this lovely home.'

'I wouldn't say that. We've only got this place because we came into a little money – a legacy, you know.'

'I see. I noticed a very nice car outside too. Is that yours?'

'Yes, there was enough left to buy that.'

'A Singer, isn't it?'

'Yes,' Ballantyne laughed. 'My little joke, I suppose. If I'm going to own a car, it really ought to be a singer, like me. It's not new, of course, but the man I bought it from said it'd only had one careful lady owner, a clergyman's widow. He said it's got independent front-wheel springing, which is apparently the latest thing and very good, and you can top up the battery without taking out the floorboards, although I must confess I'm not entirely sure what topping up the battery means. There's a little garage round the corner where a man does that sort of thing for us.'

'It sounds excellent. I know my father never made enough money to own a car.'

'Well, perhaps if he'd lived longer . . . He had a wonderful voice, and I'm not just saying that.'

'I'm sure he's right, Inspector,' said Vera. 'My husband was a very fine singer himself in his day, so he should know. He's a professional coach now – teaching young girls who want to be singers, who fancy themselves as the next Deanna Durbin. They won't be, of course, but it helps to pay the bills.'

'And who am I to dull their fantasies, deny their dreams?' said Ballantyne. 'I see it as my duty – in days like these, people need a little romance in their lives.'

'You must excuse my husband,' said Vera. 'He used to sing romantic songs, and he still thinks girls swoon at the sound of his voice. Mind you, they did when we first met. I was on the stage too, in those days. I was an acrobatic dancer, thrown about all over the stage twice nightly by a couple of handsome young men. It's a miracle they never dropped me – I probably wouldn't be here today if they had. I was young then, of course.'

'And very beautiful,' said Ballantyne.

'Then, yes, perhaps,' replied Vera. 'It's funny, isn't it? When you're twenty you never think you might be fifty one day. You see a woman of that age and you laugh at her, because you've still got everything she's lost. You don't think you'll ever be her yourself. Men pay you attention when you're twenty, but when you're fifty they don't even see you. It doesn't seem to work like that with men. My husband's sixty-two, but he dyes his hair and cuts a grand manner, and the youngsters think he's a suave and intriguing man of the world. Strange how a young woman can fall for a man old enough to be her father, yet no young man gives a second glance to a woman of my age. I don't need to consult the stars to tell you that, Inspector.'

Ballantyne looked a little disconsolate at her description of him, but he said nothing. Jago wondered whether she'd noticed this, because she changed the subject.

'I'm sorry to hear you lost your father at such a young age, Inspector,' she began. 'Have you ever contacted him since he passed over to the other side?'

'No, and I've no plans to do that.'

'But you should. There's a lot more interest these days in spiritualism – it's been growing ever since the last war. So many people have lost loved ones, and the chance to get in touch with them is very precious to them. Sir Arthur Conan Doyle said spiritualism is the greatest revelation mankind has ever had and will draw all religions together.'

'Well, I'm afraid you're talking to the wrong person. I'm too much of a sceptic.'

'As you are about horoscopes. And yet I sense you're facing a difficult decision, and it concerns another person, someone who's important in your life. Astrology can help. Millions of people believe in it, including some very important figures.'

'Yes, I've heard Hitler and some of his pals are very keen on it.'

'Well, he's not one of the people I was thinking of, but if our leaders paid more attention to his horoscope they might be better able to thwart him. It's the key to understanding the man. He's a Taurus, and his horoscope has Saturn in the tenth house. If they studied that they'd know it's the sign of immense ambition, authority and success, but also that if he lets that ambition control him it will all end in defeat. A man with that kind of ambition will think the world's there for the taking.'

'So Hitler's ambitious? You don't need a horoscope to know that.'

'But don't you see? For all we know, Hitler may have decided to invade Poland or France on the basis of advice from his astrologists. If our leaders consulted our own experts on the stars we might be able to anticipate his moves and save lives. Churchill's no fool. I've written to him about it and I'm expecting a positive reply.'

'Right, but I'm more concerned about events a little closer to home.'

'And I share that concern, Inspector. It may surprise you to know that my work has already saved people's lives right here on our own doorstep.'

'Really?'

'Yes, a girl who works at a local cinema came for a reading a while back and I told her the stars said it wasn't a good week for undertaking anything underhand or secret. She came back the following week and said her manager had told her to go to a rival cinema to spy on the competition, find out what they charged for their ice creams or something, but because of what the stars had told her she didn't go. And do you know, that very night that cinema was bombed. If I hadn't told her what was in the stars she might well've been one of the people killed there.'

'Was that Joan Lewis?'

'No. Why? Did she work in a cinema?'

'Yes.'

'I didn't know that. No, it wasn't her. It was a young woman called Cynthia. A bright girl, I thought, and she had the intelligence to respect the stars.'

Jago and Cradock said goodbye to the Ballantynes and made their way back to the car. Jago noticed a cheeky expression on the younger man's face that he'd seen before.

'What are you grinning at, lad?' he said.

'I was just thinking what an odd pair they were, sir. How about that Madame Zara, or should I say Madame Vera? All that stuff she was coming out with about you having to make a difficult decision and take the plunge . . . Was she right?'

'That's none of your business. And even if it were, you should pay no attention to it. Everyone has to make difficult decisions, and these people say things like that because they sound personal, but they could apply to anyone. Ten years ago there were none of these horoscopes in the papers, but now you see them everywhere. It's just a fad.'

'My mum reads hers every day.'

'Good luck to her, then. We didn't have them when I was a young man. Can you imagine what your horoscope would've said in 1916? "A good day for going over the top – look out for opportunities to be cut down by enfilading machine-gun fire"? No, it's all about making people feel happy and confident when life's just the opposite.'

'People do say these psychic types can see into your heart, though, don't they?'

'Well, I can assure you she wasn't looking into mine. And even if there were someone important in my life, it wouldn't be you, so it's none of your business. These people just use tricks. At its most innocent it's all pure poppycock, but at its worst it's creating a public mischief.'

Jago looked through the car's side window back towards the Ballantynes' house. He was about to start the Riley's engine, but put the key back in his pocket.

'Wait here a moment,' he said to Cradock. 'I need to pop back and check something.'

Before Cradock could answer, Jago was out of the car and striding towards the Ballantynes' front door. He knocked, and Ballantyne opened it.

'Just one more thing,' said Jago apologetically. 'I wonder whether you might do me a favour. Could I come back sometime and talk to you about my father? When this investigation's over, of course. I was so young when he died, I thought I'd have him for ever. It hadn't occurred to me to ask him about his life, the things he'd done before I came along. Now I've no family left, so there's no one to ask. You're the first person I've met who knew him when he was a young man, on the stage, and, well, I'd like to hear some more of your stories about him.'

'Why, of course,' said Ballantyne. 'I should be delighted. You could perhaps come and join us for tea and a gentle trip down memory lane, as they say. I would enjoy thinking back to those good old days myself. Just get in touch when you'd like to do it.'

'Thank you,' said Jago. 'I will.'

CHAPTER THIRTY-ONE

Jago drove in silence. He felt irritated – how dare that woman put ideas in his head about a 'difficult decision' and 'taking the plunge'? If he'd only been considering whether or not to buy a new hat he would have taken it lightly, but as soon as she'd said it his thoughts had flown to Dorothy. It was annoying. He knew it was standard fare with that kind of person – as he'd told Cradock, they just came out with some general statement like that knowing it would produce an echo in most people's minds. But in his case the echo had been Dorothy – and for that he was more annoyed with himself than with Madame so-called Zara. He tried to push the thought away: he wasn't going to have his actions dictated by some self-appointed mind-reader.

'So those seances,' said Cradock. 'That's all a bit weird, isn't it?'

Jago felt his body twitch. Surely the boy wasn't starting to read his thoughts too? He turned to Cradock to check his expression, but found nothing disturbing in it.

'All that stuff with mediums and fortune-telling, I mean,' Cradock continued. 'Strictly speaking, it's not legal, is it? We could nick her under the Vagrancy Act 1824, couldn't we?'

'Strictly speaking, you're right, although I must say I don't recall hearing of anyone being convicted in my time, so I'm not proposing to take any action unless we uncover some kind of racket. It's just a shame that people get exploited. It was the same after the last war. All those people grieving, and someone says there's an afterlife like a paradise where all the lads who've been shot or blown to pieces will live on, physically whole. I suppose people who'd lost loved ones didn't want to accept that death was the end, so they turned to people like her to try to contact them. She as good as said it herself.'

Jago turned the car into the eastern end of Windmill Lane and stopped.

'But right now I'm more interested in our sailor friend Ernie,' he said. 'I want to know whether his memory about Sunday night's improved. Let's just pop into the Cart and Horses, in case Ernie's in there having a lunchtime pint. His dad said he was living it up.'

The pub was busy when they went in, the air heavy with the smell of beer and cigarette smoke, but there was no sign of the sailor. They came out again and Jago looked down towards the other end of the street, where the Railway Tavern stood on the corner of Angel Lane.

'He must think he's in clover living here, with a pub at each end of the street,' said Cradock, following Jago's gaze.

'Yes, we'll take a look down there if there's no one at home,' said Jago. 'But we'll see if there's anyone in first.'

They walked down Windmill Lane, where the lingering smell of beer in their nostrils gave way to the more pungent odours from the London and North Eastern Railway's cattle depot. A little farther on they came to the flat they had visited the previous day. Jago knocked on the door.

They heard the sound of feet clattering down stairs, and the door opened. The man before them, however, was neither Ernie nor his father.

'Is Mr Sullivan in?' Jago enquired.

'Depends which one you want.'

'We're looking for Ernie.'

'Well, I'm sorry, you've missed him. He's gone up west. He said he was going to the theatre, so I reckon he must've gone to the Windmill – it's probably the only theatre still open in London. Cheeky lad. I bet it's where all the sailors go when they've got a bit of leave – so they can remember what girls look like, eh? Maybe if he tells them he lives in Windmill Lane they'll give him a discount. Either way he'll come home with empty pockets. He likes to have a good time, does my brother.'

'Ah, I see.'

'And who are you?'

'We're police officers. Perhaps you could tell me who you are.'

'Don't see why not. I'm Martin Sullivan.'

'And you're Ernie's brother.'

'Like I said, yes.' The young man stood on the doorstep, affecting a cocky expression as if challenging him to ask another question.

'Do you know when he'll be back?' asked Jago.

'No, I don't, but I'll be sure to tell him you called. He'll be so sorry he missed you. Now, as it happens, I'm just on my way out myself, so if that's all, I'll bid you good day – I'm a busy man.'

'That will be all, Mr Sullivan. We may see you again.'

'Bye, then,' said Sullivan. He edged past them on the doorstep and closed the door behind him, then hurried away down the street.

'Charming fellow,' said Jago to Cradock as they turned away.

'Yes, a bit full of himself,' said Cradock. 'He'll come a cropper one day with that sort of attitude – and it might not be long, if I'm right.'

'Right about what?'

'Well, I've just remembered – I've seen him before. It was at the Regal, when I was there with Emily on Sunday night. The film ended, and we all stood up for the national anthem, and then they played "Spread a Little Happiness"'. Just right for a war, eh?'

'Get to the point, please.'

'Sorry. Emily needed to powder her nose, so she went

off to the Ladies, and I went to the Gents. It was very busy, of course, and as I was going through the door, he barged in ahead of me, then had the cheek to turn round and say something very rude to me. Quite foul, it was. Anyway, he went straight off into one of the cubicles, so I was out before him. When I got out, there was this long line of women queuing for the Ladies, including Emily, so I signalled to her that I'd wait for her there. I thought I'd keep an eye out for him too, and have a word with him about his language.'

'Very commendable. And what did he say?'

'Well, that's the funny thing. In all the time I was waiting for Emily, I never saw him come out of the Gents.'

'Perhaps you were too busy thinking about Emily and didn't notice.'

Cradock looked suddenly bashful.

'No, sir, really – he just never came out.'

CHAPTER THIRTY-TWO

Back at the car, Jago checked his watch. DDI Soper had instructed him to report at six o'clock sharp to brief him on the progress of the case. Probably just so Soper could keep the area superintendent off his back, he imagined, but he needed to keep an eye on his time this afternoon. Cradock's mention of what he thought he'd observed on Sunday evening had put him in mind of the break-in at the Regal again. Blowing a safe open with gelignite was undoubtedly a serious offence, but even so, it was only money they'd taken, not a life: he needed to keep his main focus on Joan's murder. And something was niggling him.

'Peter,' he said.

'Yes, guv'nor,' said Cradock, keen to please.

'That green outfit – the tunic and what have you. We carted that suitcase halfway round the borough before Joan's friend Carol finally confirmed that it was Richard's – or at least that Joan had said it was.'

Cradock briefly considered correcting his boss on the matter of who had done the carting, but instead simply said, 'Yes.'

'And Beryl said Joan asked her to look after it because she didn't want Audrey to find it.'

'Yes.'

'Now, when we showed it to Bert Wilson, he said it was what he and Richard both used to wear when they were boys in that Kibbo Kift thing. And yet when we asked Richard's own sister, she said she'd never seen it.'

'I see what you mean, sir. Elsie's only a couple of years younger than Richard, so she must've seen him dressed up for his meetings or whatever when they were kids.'

'Exactly. I think she knows more than she's told us, and I want to know what it is. We need to pay her a visit.'

'You haven't forgotten what the pawnbroker said, have you, sir? You said we need to talk to Evans about those rings.'

'Oh, yes, the blasted rings. No, I hadn't forgotten. I suppose we'd better see the man.'

They found Evans at home, in his shirtsleeves and wearing a pair of worn-out slippers. He appeared not to have shaved. When he opened the door to Jago and Cradock he welcomed them in, but he sounded preoccupied.

He showed them through to the kitchen, where he edged past Jago to remove a newspaper from one of the chairs.

'Have a seat, gentlemen,' he said. 'Can I get you a cup of tea? My wife's not here, but I think I still know how to work a kettle.'

It sounded like an attempt at a joke, but he delivered it in a voice that was somehow morose, not like his breezy manner the last time they'd seen him. 'Forlorn' was the word that crossed Jago's mind.

'Yes, please,' said Jago. 'Is your wife well?'

'Oh, yes, fit as a fiddle,' said Evans. He found the tea caddy and dropped a couple of spoonfuls into the pot sitting on top of the range, then poured in boiling water and left it to brew. 'But like I said before, she goes out to her sister Cissie in Epping for the night, on account of the bombing. She went off a bit early today – the trains are playing up again. But it's terrible, isn't it? There's no such thing as a front line any more – it's all happening right here. To think a woman can't spend the night in her own home because of this war. It's not like it was in the old days, when the men did the fighting and the women stayed safe at home.'

'Yes,' said Jago. 'I remember what Mr Chamberlain said last year, when he was still prime minister. He said if we do end up in a war, even if we're not all in the firing line we may all well be in the line of fire. He might not've been right about everything, but he certainly got that right, didn't he? It makes no difference whether you're a soldier or a shop girl when the sirens go.'

'It's wicked, that's what it is,' said Evans. 'I miss my Amy when she goes out there, and I wish she didn't have to, but it puts my mind at rest to know she's away from the bombing at night. I can be thankful for that, at least.'

He poured three mugs of tea and handed one to each of his visitors. He failed to offer them sugar, but Jago didn't ask.

'You'll have to forgive me, Inspector,' he continued. 'I'm a bit down in the dumps. Sometimes when Amy's not here and I'm on my own, things get on top of me. It's not just her I miss, it's everything. We have a word for it in Welsh. We call it *hiraeth* – there's no English word for it. It's a bit like homesickness, but it's more than that. It's what I feel when I get to thinking about Wales, and the past, and the way things used to be. That's when I start wanting to be back there.'

'I'm told Wales is very beautiful.'

'Oh, yes,' said Evans. 'But not all of it, mind. When I left school I worked in the quarry, and you couldn't call that beautiful.'

'Are you still in touch with people from those days?'

'With some, yes. Why do you ask?'

'It was just what you said about wanting to be back there. And when you went to work in the munitions factory – that was in Wales too?'

'Yes, it was – during the Great War.' His lips began to twitch into a faint smile, but in a moment it was gone. 'You'd have thought all those years in the quarry digging holes in the ground while the earth exploded behind me would've suited me to being a soldier, but they didn't seem to need me. It was hard work, I can tell you, but at least I wasn't underground. Most people seem to think if you're Welsh you spend all your time either coal mining or singing in male voice choirs, but I never had to go down the pit. Very glad of that I was, too. If I had, it would've been at Gresford, and you know what happened there.'

'The underground explosion.'

'Yes. Two hundred and sixty-six men killed, including two of my school pals. Six years ago, and I still have dreams that I was in it too.' For a moment Evans seemed lost in his own thoughts. He sipped his tea, cradling the mug in his hands.

'And the rest of them aren't much better off, are they?' he went on. 'How is it we're more than a year into another war, with everyone telling us the country's got to live off what we can produce, yet half a million of them are out of work? And instead of putting them back into work to dig the coal we need to make the steel for ships and tanks, some bright sparks, English no doubt, are saying they should be dragged out of their villages in the valleys and put to work clearing up the bomb sites in London. It doesn't make sense.'

Jago felt sorry for Evans, but had to do his job.

'There's something I need to ask you, Mr Evans,' he said, drinking the last of his tea. 'Could you please show me your pawn ticket?'

Evans looked puzzled. 'Pawn ticket?' he asked, as though he'd never heard of such a thing.

'It's no good, Mr Evans, we've seen the entry in the

272

pawnbroker's ledger. I'm talking about the pawn ticket he gave you yesterday for two rings.'

'Ah, that pawn ticket,' said Evans.

He moved to the mantelpiece over the range, where he reached behind the clock and pulled out a mix of papers. He singled out one small ticket and passed it to Jago.

'Here it is.'

Jago read out what was written on the ticket: 'Pawned with W. J. Horncastle, pawnbroker, of 37 Manor Road, West Ham, for the sum of one pound and fifteen shillings, one lady's wedding ring and one engagement ring.'

He looked Evans in the eye. 'Now, Mr Evans, tell me how you came by these rings.'

'They were my grandmother's,' Evans replied. 'I've had them since she died, but things have been tight recently – you know how it is. I'd kept them for sentimental reasons, but my wife and I don't have any children, let alone daughters, so we'll never have a use for them. I just decided it was time to turn them into some useful cash to help pay for my wife's train fares out to Epping.'

'You're sure they didn't belong to Joan Lewis, the woman you found dead in her flat in the early hours of Monday morning – the day before this ticket was issued?'

A sudden anger flashed in Evans's eyes.

'What are you accusing me of? Stealing them? Why is it people like you can't leave honest, hard-working men alone? You should be out there catching the real criminals. Why aren't you doing something about those bloodsuckers on the black market who make money out of other people's misfortune? Or those blighters in the docks stealing food from under our noses? Why aren't you cleaning up the streets, getting rid of those immoral women who prowl about luring men into shameful behaviour and wrecking marriages for the sake of money? I've tried to live honestly, but all I've seen is crooks who flourish, including at my expense. It's not right.'

Jago listened carefully to what Evans was saying, waited for him to calm down, then continued.

'When we spoke to you on Monday you were careful to let us know she wasn't wearing any rings when you found her, weren't you? You didn't have time to notice anything else, but you made sure we went away thinking she didn't have any rings on.'

'But it's true, she didn't. Loads of women have rings like that, but those ones I pawned were my grandmother's. Ask my wife – she'll tell you.'

'But your wife's not here, is she? Perhaps we'd better continue this conversation down at the station.'

'I'm happy to carry on whenever and wherever you like, Inspector,' Evans responded. 'But look, can't we talk about this tomorrow? I'm meant to be on duty in half an hour, and if I'm stuck at the police station people might die. It's my night off tomorrow, so come and see me tomorrow morning when my wife's back from her sister's.'

'How do I know you'll be here?'

'Don't you worry about that. I'm always here when

Amy gets back from Epping. She's more precious to me than anything in the world, and I don't feel easy until I know she's safely home.'

Jago studied Evans's face. He couldn't help liking the man, but there was something about his easy charm that made it difficult to tell whether he was lying.

'All right,' he said at last. 'I'll give you the benefit of the doubt. What time does your wife get back from Epping?'

'She's always back by half past ten, sometimes sooner if she can get an earlier train. I'm usually home before her, and she doesn't like to think of me being here cold and tired on my own waiting for her.'

'Right then, Mr Evans, we'll be back to see both of you at half past ten tomorrow morning.'

'Don't you worry, we'll be here.'

Evans sounded confident and reassuring, but Jago wondered whether he detected a hint of relief behind the bravado.

CHAPTER THIRTY-THREE

'This shouldn't take long,' said Jago as they pulled up outside Audrey Lewis's house. 'That's assuming Elsie's in.'

His assumption was proved correct. Elsie Marwell greeted them at the door with a neutral expression that revealed nothing about her feelings on seeing the police return. She invited them in and closed the door behind them.

'It's just a quick question I need to ask you, Mrs Marwell,' said Jago. 'It won't take a moment.'

'Of course. What do you want to know?'

'You remember we showed you that green tunic yesterday?'

'Yes,' she said cautiously.

'You said you'd never seen it before. But since then it's been suggested to us that it was the uniform of an organisation that your brother belonged to – something that he and your father fell out over. So I'd like to ask you again. Do you recognise it?'

Elsie let out a sigh, but whether of resignation or frustration Jago couldn't tell.

'OK,' she said. 'Yes, I do. It must've slipped my mind yesterday. I was a bit shocked to hear what'd happened to Joan, so I wasn't quite myself. Yes, it was something Richard belonged to when he was younger.'

'And there was a disagreement between him and your father?'

'Yes. That wasn't long before my father died. Richard had some rather foolish ideas about politics when he was younger, and he didn't like it when Dad challenged him. But someone had to, otherwise he'd have gone on believing those stupid notions for ever. Dad was right – it was all a lot of romantic nonsense and could never work in the real world. My father was a realist, you see, and that's why he was successful in business. He never had any time for idealistic claptrap. He used to say that in the end it's all about pounds, shillings and pence, and the more of that you have, the better your life will be. Other people can talk about inner peace, he said, but that doesn't put bread on the table. Only hard graft does that, and he always worked for his family – he wasn't going to wait around doing nothing and expecting other people to pay his bills.'

'So clearly you agreed with your father.'

'Yes, of course I did. I thought Richard was naive and indecisive, and lacking in ambition, but I hoped he'd see sense eventually.'

'Do you think he did?'

'Yes, I think he did, to some extent at least. I think when things started getting so bad politically in Europe he realised fancy ideas like giving people free money weren't realistic. The only thing that made sense in the world as it is was to fight, and I think that's why he joined the TA.'

'Your mother wasn't pleased to discover I had that uniform, but she didn't say why. She didn't want to talk about it. Why do you think that was?'

'She probably just thinks like me. That that part of Richard's life is in the past, and it's not who he is any more. He'll come home from this war a hero, and that'll open doors for him. I think our mother's probably worried that it'll be bad for his career prospects if people find out he used to be mixed up with the Kibbo Kift, so she'd rather all that was buried in the past, where it belongs.'

'And you think she's right.'

'Yes, I do. He was an embarrassment to our father, and I don't see why he should be an embarrassment to our mother as well. He means everything to her. That's why she didn't want him to join the TA.'

'She hasn't mentioned that to us.'

'Well, I don't suppose there was any need to. She was just worried as a mother.'

'Did he tell you before he joined up?'

'Yes.'

'But not Joan?'

'I don't know.'

'Someone told us they thought he hadn't.'

'Well, I wouldn't know what passed between him and his wife, would I? He might've thought she'd get tearful, try to stop him. I could imagine her doing that.'

'What was Joan's attitude to Richard's past?'

'I think she went along with whatever he wanted to do. To be frank with you, I think all that stuff about politics and economics that he was interested in was above her head. I don't think she understood it. I think the romantic side of it appealed to her, the idea of making everyone happy in three easy steps – she was a pretty soft sort of girl, a bit of a dreamer – but I don't think she was bright enough to see through it for the nonsense it was. If our father had lived longer he'd have been against them marrying, I'm sure.'

'I've been thinking, sir,' said Cradock as he got back into the car outside Audrey Lewis's house. The obvious retort sprang immediately into Jago's mind, but he didn't like to discourage the boy.

'Well done,' he said. 'Are your thoughts in a fit state to share?'

'Yes, I think so. I've been thinking about that brother of Ernie's we met, Martin Sullivan, the one I recognised from the Regal on Sunday night, who disappeared into the toilets and never came out.'

'I remember. What about him?'

'Well, the first time we met Beryl, she mentioned she'd been at the Regal Sunday night with her boyfriend. I thought that was a bit peculiar myself, her going to the pictures where she worked, but anyway, the thing is, when we talked to her this morning, she said he didn't walk her home at the end. He just nipped off and didn't come back. And she said his name was Martin. Now, I know there might've been a dozen blokes at the Regal called Martin, but if he disappeared like that at the end it makes me wonder whether his other name's Sullivan.'

Cradock sat back in the passenger seat, as if bracing himself to hear his reasoning demolished, but Jago simply nodded his head.

'Good thinking, Peter,' he said. 'So what do you suggest we do next?'

'Go and ask Beryl what her boyfriend's surname is and where he lives?'

'I think that would be very sensible.' Jago checked his watch again. 'If she's working tonight, she'll be at the Regal already. If she's not, she could be at home, but I'd rather not provoke her landlady to wrath, so let's try the cinema.'

They drove to the Regal and told the page boy in the foyer they needed to speak to Beryl. There was no sign of Conway, but the boy was happy to take his instructions from Jago and soon reappeared with Beryl. She was wearing her usherette's uniform and carrying her torch.

'I'm sorry to drag you away from your work, Miss Hayes,' said Jago. 'I really will only keep you for a moment. It's just that when we spoke to you last time you mentioned your boyfriend's name was Martin.'

Beryl gave him an apprehensive look.

'Don't worry,' said Jago. 'I'm not here because anything's happened to him. I just need to know his surname, and his address.'

'It's Sullivan,' she replied. 'Martin Sullivan, and he lives in Windmill Lane. It's number 41, a flat over a greengrocer's shop – you can't miss it.'

'Thank you. And you said he didn't walk you home from the cinema. I believe you said he just nipped off with some flimsy excuse and didn't come back.'

'Yes, that's right.'

'What was the flimsy excuse?'

'Well, it was a bit personal, really. He said he wasn't feeling too good, said he had a touch of gippy tummy and would have to go to the Gents. He said he might be a long time and I wasn't to wait, I'd have to see myself home. Then off he went. Not so much as a sorry or a goodnight, or see you again, or even hang on a bit and I'll walk you home.'

'Annoying for you, I imagine.'

'Yes, of course. But I hadn't known him for very long, and to tell the truth I wasn't all that bothered about him, so I thought fine, I'll be off home by myself and you can forget about another date, even if you want one.'

'So how did you happen to meet in the first place?'

'He just started talking to me one night at the Regal.

Came out with the usual sort of chat, said he'd like to get to know me better, so we went out for a drink a couple of times. It turned out he was very interested in cinemas and quite fancied working in one himself. Said he'd like to be a cinema manager. I told him he'd have to start at the bottom and work his way up. He said something a bit cheeky then, but it made me laugh, so he said maybe he could start out by taking me to the pictures. I thought he meant go somewhere else, but he said no, the Regal, so I could sit back and enjoy the film for once while the other girls did the running about. I suppose that was his sense of humour or something, but anyway, I said yes, so that's how we came to be there on Sunday evening. Not a big romance, as you can see – he turned out to be a bit of a disappointment.'

Jago thanked her for the information, and he and Cradock took their leave. They returned to the car.

'You were right, Peter,' said Jago. 'About his name. Well done.'

'Thanks, guv'nor. Shall we go and ask him what he was up to?'

'That'll have to be tomorrow. Right now I have to go and see Mr Soper at the station.'

'Right, sir. The thing is, I'm thinking if Martin Sullivan was in the Gents all that time and I didn't see him come out, could that be because he was hiding and came out later when everyone had gone home and let the thieves in?'

'Clearly, Peter. That's a reasonable conclusion to draw. It also prompts another question – did he get any help from Beryl? And for that matter, was Joan involved in some way? After all, it turns out she knew another Sullivan from the past, didn't she? Ernie, I mean.'

'There's something else too, sir. I've just thought. We've got a man who behaves oddly at a cinema that has its safe blown open the same night, and he seems to have a bee in his bonnet about British troops in Northern Ireland. I mean, blowing things up and Northern Ireland – do you think there could be some kind of link with the IRA?'

'It's an interesting idea, Peter. The Irish Republicans have certainly been very active over the last year or two, especially with that big bomb in Coventry just a week before the war started.'

'Do you think our safe-breakers could've got their explosives from the IRA?'

'I don't know. I've heard some reports of them using gelignite, but I'm not too well up on how they make their bombs. Most of the accounts I've read talk about things like aluminium powder and rubber balloons.'

'Rubber balloons? You mean like balloons for children's parties?'

'Yes, I believe they use acid that has to burn through the balloon before it detonates the explosives, so it gives them time to get away. Something like that, at any rate. I'm not an expert.'

'Sounds a bit barmy to me. I thought they used clocks.'

'Yes, well, as I said, I'm no expert. And whether the IRA's in the habit of supplying gelignite to people who want to steal money from cinemas I certainly don't know.'

'Could we find out?'

'Oh, yes, Peter. We'll find out.'

CHAPTER THIRTY-FOUR

Divisional Detective Inspector Soper was standing in his office, looking out of the window when Jago entered.

'You wanted to see me, sir. About the case.'

'Ah, yes, the case,' said Soper. 'Got your man, eh?'

'What man, sir?'

'I don't know his name. Tompkins told me you've brought a Welshman in to do with that young woman's murder. The usherette. Good work. Case closed, eh?'

'No, sir.'

'What do you mean?'

'I mean there is a Welshman, but we haven't brought him in. We've been to see him to ask about some rings he's pawned, and I very much suspect those rings belonged to Joan Lewis, the woman who was murdered, but we haven't charged him with anything yet.'

'I see. Well, what about that safe-breaking business at the Odeon?'

'The Regal, sir.'

'Yes, the Regal. Where have you got to with that?'

'We don't know who did it yet, but we've got our eyes on a young man called Martin Sullivan, who we think may've hidden in the cinema when it closed that night and helped whoever blew the safe to get in. But we're not sure yet. It appears the young man also has an interest in Irish politics. DC Cradock has raised the question of whether there might be a link to the IRA.'

'I knew it – Irishmen. I told you, didn't I?'

'Well, sir, actually I don't think you—'

'Yes, explosives, cash – it's as plain as the nose on your face. It's the work of Irish Republicans.'

'Except they're not Irishmen, sir, as far as we can tell.'

'Scratch at the surface, John, and you'll find an Irishman underneath. You just have to scratch hard enough.'

'Yes, sir.'

'Now, if there's any trace of Irish Republican activity in this business, you must talk to Special Branch. You know what they're like – that sort of thing's definitely their parish, and they won't want us tramping all over it. Who's that high-up in Special Branch that you got pally with when you were seconded to them?'

'I think you must mean Mr Ford, sir, but I don't think I can claim to be pally with him – he is a detective superintendent, after all.'

'Well, acquainted with, then. But he must be quite pally with you if he wants you to go and work for him.'

Soper's words came as a surprise to Jago, but his face didn't show it.

'Excuse me, sir, but how did you know that? I've never mentioned anything of the sort to anyone here.'

'In my job I hear things, John, and that's one of the things I've heard.'

'Well, I can assure you I have no plans to transfer to Special Branch. The experience was useful, and so's the connection with Detective Superintendent Ford, but I like my job here.'

'I'm glad to hear it, John – I wouldn't want to lose you. Filling vacancies is the very devil of a job these days, with the force so stretched.'

Jago was still wondering whether he was being commended as a valued officer or identified as a potential source of unwanted paperwork when Soper continued.

'So anyway, if there's the slightest whiff of the IRA in your investigation, I advise you to go and report it to your friend Mr Ford at the earliest opportunity. I don't want them coming down on me like a ton of bricks for encroaching on their responsibilities.'

'Yes, sir. I'll call him immediately, and see whether he can give me a few minutes tomorrow.'

'That's the ticket. And get those chaps behind bars, or we'll all be in trouble.'

'Yes, sir,' said Jago, suddenly feeling the need for an early night. 'We'll do our best.'

CHAPTER THIRTY-FIVE

The only time Detective Superintendent Ford could give him was first thing in the morning: at a quarter past seven, in fact. As Jago made his way to the railway station he hoped the track had survived the night's bombing, and was relieved to find that the service was running at something close to normal. By ten past seven he was sitting in Ford's office at New Scotland Yard.

'So, you think you might have an IRA connection to your case,' said Ford. 'Tell me about it.'

'Well,' Jago began, 'as I said on the phone last night, it's just a possibility. But with explosives involved, and a suspect with an unusual interest in Irish politics, I thought we should check with you. We heard a lot about the IRA bombing campaign last year, but it seems to have quietened down now.'

'Yes, but it hasn't stopped. I'm just thankful no more lives have been lost. We had those bomb attacks on phone boxes and cinemas in November and December, but by then the Prevention of Violence Act had come in, so we could deport suspects and stop others entering the country. And then De Valera cracked down hard in the South – he banned the IRA and interned a lot of suspects. The only incidents we've had since then are two shops bombed in Birmingham in February, and then a bomb in Oxford Street. No attacks in Scotland or Wales yet, because the IRA don't want to upset the Scottish or Welsh Nationalists. The last incident we know of – because the bomb worked – was in Westminster in March.'

'So are there still IRA cells active in England?'

'There may be. We're keeping an eye on known sympathisers in the London area, including on K Division, where you are – and that's where we had our first breakthrough, the summer before last.'

'When that car was stopped in Ilford? A random check, wasn't it?'

'Yes, and if your chaps hadn't taken a look in the boot and seen all that potassium chlorate, that would've been the end of it. I know they let them go when the men in the car produced a receipt to show the chemical wasn't stolen, but they had the gumption to take their names and addresses. And then, thank goodness, one of your men was suspicious enough to tell his station officer, who called us.'

'And it turned out they weren't what they seemed?'

'Too true. We raided one of the addresses, in Dagenham.'

'Also on K Division.'

'Yes, and we found a notebook full of names and addresses, and when we checked them against our files we found quite a few were IRA suspects. That was really helpful – it's amazing how often the IRA have left incriminating documents and papers lying around for us to find. We raided the addresses in the notebook and found all sorts of things – sticks of gelignite, detonators, fuses, the lot. We made a lot of arrests too. All thanks to your men.'

'The people you arrested – were they all Irish? The reason why I ask is that our suspects aren't, as far as we know. They're as English as you and me.'

'Well, that's an interesting point. We've traditionally looked out for Irishmen, but we think they've tried to use people born here with English accents instead, because they don't attract the same attention. When we got the ringleader of the Liverpool bomb attacks last year it turned out he wasn't an Irishman at all – he was a seaman from Manchester. He got twenty years' penal servitude for conspiracy, possessing explosives, and causing an explosion.'

'The Home Secretary said something last year about foreign involvement too. Was he talking about Germany?'

'I think it's generally assumed that he was. We think there's been contact between the IRA and German military intelligence, and I suspect MI5 may know more about that than they've told us. Some people are worried that if the Germans took it into their heads to invade Ireland, the IRA suspects we've deported might act as some kind of fifth column there.'

'That all sounds very big. Is it really possible that our three in West Ham could be mixed up in it?'

'Anything's possible, I suppose. Only last year we raided an address in Manor Park and found all sorts of stuff for making bombs – detonators, fuses, alarm clocks and suchlike. And that's in East Ham, right next door to you. But on the other hand I've checked the names you gave me last night and they're not on our files as sympathisers.'

'I see. I was wondering how they'd come by their gelignite, too. Could that be through the IRA?'

'It's possible. We know the IRA stole gelignite from quarries in the Midlands, and when we raided a house in Birmingham we discovered a store of two-ounce sticks. They'd hidden it there and passed some on to their contacts in London. So if your chummies had links with the IRA in London they might've got their hands on some of that.'

'That doesn't necessarily make them bomb-makers, though, does it?'

'No. And if all you have at the moment is a gelignite wrapper from a safe-breaking and a young man who's interested in Irish politics and might've stayed in the Gents too long at the cinema, I don't think you need to go in with guns blazing. I suggest you just treat it as an ordinary case of larceny but let us know if you turn up anything more telling.'

'Thank you. There's something else I'd like to ask you about before I go. Nothing to do with Ireland or gelignite, as far as I know.'

'By all means.'

'I just wondered whether you can tell me anything about an organisation called Kibbo Kift.'

'That woodcraft lot? Oh, yes. An odd bunch, definitely. We've kept an eye on them since they began – the Home Office has been a bit concerned from time to time about what they might get up to.'

'And have they got up to anything they shouldn't have?'

'Not really. They got going just after the war – about 1920, I believe – when people were shouting about radical change and there were all kinds of odd new movements. Quite a few prominent people supported it. They wanted to get away from industrialised society and raise up healthy leaders committed to peace and internationalism. As far as I'm aware, their activities seemed to consist mainly of rambling, hiking, arts and crafts, fancy costumes and mumbo-jumbo ritual. Dramatics, too – acting in little plays. A bit of a cult, if you ask me. In the early days I think people were worried they might be communists and linked to Moscow, but we came to the conclusion they were just a bunch of pacifist cranks. You know – enthusiastic but not dangerous, and not of any serious political significance. They saw themselves as an elite group leading society into a new future, but they were never very big – they numbered in the hundreds rather than the thousands.'

'And they turned into the Greenshirts?'

'Yes, that's right – in 1931, I think. Their leader got them all wearing green shirts and berets, and marching on the streets with drums and banners. They got a bit bigger then – several thousand at one point. They blamed all our economic problems on the international bankers and reckoned they'd be able to abolish poverty, hunger and unemployment by reorganising the economy. Of course, there was concern about any political group that started parading about in uniforms, so we had men in their meetings too, keeping tabs on what they were up to. The Greenshirts reckoned they were standing up to the Bolsheviks and fascists alike, and got into fights with both. They started to attract more public attention then, because they were out on the streets instead of camping in the woods, but they only started wearing their uniform in public in about 1932, and then of course four years later the Public Order Act came along and they had to stop wearing it.'

'I don't suppose they were very pleased about that.'

'No, I think it hit them pretty hard, and they've rather faded away since then, although they still get up to occasional stunts. In February one of them dressed up in a green jacket, shirt and tie, strolled into Downing Street and shot an arrow through a window at Number 10, with a message on it saying "Social credit the only remedy".'

'Ah, yes, I've heard a lot about social credit.'

'You probably know more about it than I do, then. Anyway, the incident wasn't the biggest threat to the state, although I suppose if Chamberlain had been looking out of the window at the time it could've been more serious.'

'Was the archer put away?'

'No, it turned out he'd been called up and was due to join the forces that same day. He was just charged with insulting behaviour and bound over for a year.'

'All pretty harmless, then.'

'So it seems, yes. But we're still watching them and preparing regular reports. We don't regard them as a threat in the way that the Blackshirts were – or are – but they're still an unusual bunch, with some pretty odd ideas.'

'Odd ideas sincerely held,' said Jago. 'What a lot of trouble that can mean.'

CHAPTER THIRTY-SIX

Jago took Superintendent Ford's advice regarding the Sullivans and decided to keep his powder dry. He'd press Martin Sullivan a little about his movements on Sunday evening first, before getting too carried away with the possibility of suspicious political leanings. He would track him down as soon as he'd kept his appointment with Hosea Evans.

At a quarter past ten on Thursday morning, therefore, after he'd briefed Cradock on some of what he'd been told at Special Branch, the two men set off from the police station for the ten-minute walk to where Evans lived. Jago had given the fireman the benefit of the doubt the previous day, and found himself hoping Mrs Evans's testimony would bear out her husband's claim concerning the rings. Not that he was being swayed by any sense of sympathy for Evans, he assured himself. If the man had committed a crime, he must be held to account for it, and there was something about stealing rings from a dead body that was particularly distasteful. It was dishonourable. But there was also the reputation of the fire service to consider. People had been quick to spread rumours after a number of firemen were convicted of looting from fire scenes, and he had no desire to embarrass the local Auxiliary Fire Service by prematurely arresting one of its members.

They reached the junction with Church Street, and Jago was reassured to see that the parish church of All Saints had come through another night's bombing unscathed. For the second time in as many days a memory of sitting in its churchyard came unbidden into the forefront of his mind, this time of talking quietly with Dorothy about the stars, and war, and life. It had felt as though she were peeling away layers of the armour he'd built up to protect himself, but in a way that was only for his good. He remembered too with a pang of guilt how in that same conversation he had spoken harshly, paining her in a way that he would never have wanted.

He pushed these thoughts away as they crossed into Marcus Street. Here the scene was less tranquil: halfway down it, a bomb had left a large crater in the middle of the road, on either side of which two houses – or possibly three, it wasn't easy to tell – had been reduced to an uneven pile of matchwood and rubble. The rescue workers were still there, but it looked as though they were packing up their trucks to go. Jago guessed that if anyone had survived the explosion they'd have been removed to a rest centre or hospital by now. He stopped to ask whether he and Cradock could lend a hand, but the answer was a polite no, with thanks.

At the end of Marcus Street they turned right into Stephen's Road, looking for number 46, where Hosea and Amy Evans had their home. Jago had begun to count down the terraced houses from the one nearest to them, but he could soon tell that 46 was going to be in a section that was showing signs of serious damage. As they got closer to the house they could see that the glass had been blown out of all its windows, the slates had been blasted off the roof, the chimney stack had disappeared, and the front door was swinging open. Jago peered in at the door and saw wrecked furniture in the small front room that opened directly off the street. He knocked on the door and called, but there was no answer.

He turned away. The only activity he could see in the street was the relatively new sight of a small squad of Pioneer Corps soldiers shovelling the last of the debris onto the back of an army truck, in which they would presumably soon be transporting it to barges and dumping it on the Essex marshes. Any other civil defence workers who might have been there earlier had gone.

He was about to set off with Cradock in search of an ARP warden when a woman hailed them from across the street. She was middle-aged and wearing a floral-patterned cotton overall with an almost-matching turban.

'Excuse me,' she called as she approached them. 'Are you looking for Mr Evans?'

'Yes, we are,' said Jago. 'We're police officers.'

'Come with me, then. He's in my front room. I'm a few doors further up and missed the worst of it.'

She took them into her house, which indeed seemed to have got off lightly in comparison with number 46 and its immediate neighbours. They found Evans sitting in an armchair with his head in his hands. Beneath the overcoat he was wearing, which like his hair was covered in grey plaster dust, his legs appeared to be clad in pyjamas. He looked up as they entered.

'Mr Evans?' said Jago.

Evans responded with a blank gaze that seemed to go straight through him and out to the street beyond.

'Mr Evans,' Jago repeated, his voice subdued. 'Your house has been hit?'

'Not my house,' said Evans in a flat monotone. 'My Amy.'

He closed his eyes, and the tears began to course down his cheeks and drop onto his coat.

'I'm sorry,' said Jago, squatting down on the floor beside the chair.

'She came home yesterday afternoon after you'd gone,' Evans whispered. 'Said she'd decided I was right, she should try it again for a night, sleeping at home. Said if it was my night off she'd have me there to look after her, and it wouldn't be as bad as when I was out on duty.'

'But—' Cradock began, but Jago hushed him.

'We went to bed in the Anderson shelter in the back yard, and she wasn't too bad at first, but then when the anti-aircraft guns started up she got very jittery – held on to me and wouldn't let go. I said I'd go and get her some cotton wool so she could stick it in her ears and keep some of the noise out, and I'd fetch her a nice tot of whisky to help her sleep. So I went into the house. I was only gone a few minutes.'

His voice broke. Jago put an arm round Evans's shoulders as the fireman struggled to regain his self-control.

'I'd just gone upstairs into the front bedroom to find some cotton wool when there was this almighty bang behind the house, half the ceiling fell in on me, and I could see stars where the roof should've been. I knew what must've happened. I got down the stairs as quick as I could and out the back door, and then I saw it. The bomb had landed right on our Anderson shelter. There was nothing left. Nothing. She's not there any more. We hadn't even said goodbye.' His voice trailed away into a quiet sob.

'I'm sorry, Mr Evans,' said Jago.

Evans nodded his thanks.

'Have you got somewhere to go?' Jago asked. 'You can't stay in your house if it's got no roof.'

'The station officer's been round already,' Evans replied, his voice flat. 'Our fire station's only just down the road and it's got a dormitory, so he said I can stay there until I get myself sorted out.'

He looked up, as if he'd just remembered who his visitors were.

'But that's not why you came here, is it?' he said

sadly. 'You were going to ask my Amy about those rings, weren't you?'

'I was,' Jago replied.

'Well, I don't care any more. I don't care about anything. You know I wasn't telling the truth, don't you, about being on duty last night. How come my Amy said she was going to stay at home with me because I could look after her all night if I was on duty? That's what you're thinking, isn't it?'

Jago nodded.

'Well, I was lying, wasn't I? I said I was going to be on duty just to get you off my back long enough for me to tell Amy what to say. She's always been a better person than me. I didn't deserve her, and I was going to make her lie for me.'

Evans stood up, wrapping his coat round himself. He looked Jago in the eye.

'Yes, you're right,' he said. 'Those rings belonged to that woman who was murdered in her flat. She didn't need them any more, and I did. Life doesn't get any cheaper just because one day you get a job as a fireman – a rasher of bacon costs the same, and you still have to find the rent. I know what I did was wrong, but we were in a bit of a sticky patch moneywise, and when I saw those rings it was just a temptation I couldn't resist. I thought no one would know, and we'd get a bit of cash to tide us over. I reckoned if I didn't sell them but just pawned them, I'd be able to get them back, and then perhaps I could've returned them to that poor woman's family, if she had one. But now I suppose I'll never know. Does this mean I'll go to prison, Inspector? I've never been in trouble before.'

'That's out of my hands, Mr Evans. If you've been a man of good character up to now, you must hope the court will take that into consideration. The only thing you need to know right now is you're under arrest.'

Jago heard his own words as though they were spoken by someone else, but in his stomach he felt something like a shard of ice biting into him. It was a deep, cold anger at the death of this woman Amy Evans. Whether it was directed at the man who'd dropped the bomb from the sky, the dictator who'd commanded the action, the God who'd allowed it to happen, or the universe for being a place where such things occurred, he couldn't tell. All he knew was the intense disgust that gripped him, the sense of futility that he'd known as a young man in the trenches. He wanted to scream his rage, but he remained outwardly silent, emotionless. He was certain of only one thing. The law must take its course in respect of Hosea Evans, but the real crime was not a weak man's theft of a dead woman's rings. It was the pointless killing of a frightened woman who wanted to stay by her husband.

CHAPTER THIRTY-SEVEN

With Evans locked in a cell at West Ham police station, it was time to pursue Martin Sullivan. Jago didn't know what kind of job the young man did, if indeed he had one, nor why he seemed not yet to have been caught up in the net of conscription to the armed forces, so he and Cradock set off for the flat in Windmill Lane, hoping to find him at home. This time they took the car: Jago had a feeling that this was going to be a busy day.

They arrived at the flat, and Jago's sharp rap of the door knocker brought an immediate response. It was George Sullivan who opened the door, dressed in what appeared to be the same clothes as he'd been wearing the last time they'd seen him.

'Oh, it's you lot again,' he said, looking them up and down. His voice was sullen. 'What do you want this time?'

'I'd like to have a word with your son Martin, Mr Sullivan. Is he in?'

Sullivan jerked one thumb over his shoulder. 'Up there.'

He stood aside so that Jago and Cradock could come in. They climbed the stairs, followed by the rhythmic stamp of Sullivan's boots on the wooden treads. At the top they went into a small living room where Martin Sullivan sat reading a newspaper. He glanced at them and went back to his reading.

'What do you want to know?' said Sullivan senior.

'What makes you think there's something I want to know?' said Jago.

'Don't make me laugh. Your sort never comes round just to pass the time of day.'

Jago turned his attention to the son. 'Mr Sullivan, can you tell me where you were on Sunday evening?'

Martin Sullivan put his paper down, but had barely opened his mouth before his father spoke.

'He was here, with me.'

'The whole evening?'

George Sullivan looked at his son, who gave an almost imperceptible shake of his head.

'No, not all the time. Martin and Ernie were both out for a bit. Martin got in before Ernie did. What time was it, now?'

'It was about a quarter past nine, I think,' said Martin.

'Ah, yes, that's right,' said George. 'I remember – a quarter past nine.'

'And what about your other son?' Jago asked.

'Ernie? He, er . . . He got in a bit after ten, about a quarter past, maybe, and we bedded down in the Anderson shelter for the night.'

'All three of you?'

'Oh, yes, we were all there together.'

Jago kept his eyes on Martin Sullivan. 'I understand you were at the Regal cinema on Sunday,' he said.

If the young man was surprised to be told his whereabouts by a police officer his face did not betray it. Instead he looked affronted.

'What? What's going on here? You been spying on me? What kind of police state are we living in?'

'No,' said Jago, 'we haven't been spying on you. It just came up in a conversation we had with someone.'

'Who?'

'I can't tell you that at the moment. All I want to know is whether you were at the cinema. That's quite a normal activity. So were you?'

'Well, yes, I was, as it happens. Not that it's any of your business. Just an evening out with my girlfriend. So what?'

'And would you mind telling me what time you left?'

'About ten past nine, just after the film finished. I told you, I was home by about a quarter past.'

'Did you walk your girlfriend home?'

'No, I didn't, if you must know.'

'You leave her to fend for herself in the blackout, do you?'

'No, of course I don't. Normally I would've walked her home, but as it happened I was feeling a bit ill, so I went to the toilets. When I came out I couldn't see her, so I reckoned she must've given up waiting for me and gone.'

'Did you explain to your girlfriend that you were feeling unwell?'

'I'm not sure. I told her I had to go to the Gents, but I didn't go into the details. Well, you don't, do you? Then when I was looking for her I started feeling ill again, so I went straight home.'

'Have you seen her since?'

'No. It's not like we're engaged or anything. We've just had an evening out once or twice. Besides, between you and me, I'm not so sure I'm the marrying kind.'

'Really? Why's that?'

'Because of what happened to my dad.'

George Sullivan cut into the conversation. 'Now then, Martin, there's no need to go into that.'

'Why not, Dad? It's not as if you did anything wrong. It was her fault.' He spoke now to Jago. 'It was my mum, see – she just walked out when I was twelve, left him to it. And don't ask me where she is now. I don't know.'

'I'm sorry to hear that, Mr Sullivan.'

'That's all right. We managed.'

'By the way, that reminds me. Is there any Irish blood in your family? Your mother, perhaps?'

'What? What's that got to do with anything?'

'I was just wondering. Is there?'

'No, of course there isn't. I'm as English as you are, and my dad too. Ask him.'

'That won't be necessary. It's just that I understand you're interested in Irish politics, and I wondered why.'

'Who told you that?'

'Never you mind. Is it true?'

'What if I am? I'm interested in Irish politics the same as I'm interested in American politics or French politics or Italian politics. I'm just interested in what's going on in the world. Nothing illegal about that, is there? Or is it a crime to think now?'

'There are no laws against what you think, Mr Sullivan. Only against what you do.'

'So,' said Cradock as they drove back from Windmill Lane in the direction of the police station, 'he reckons he was ill. Not very convincing, was he?'

'He didn't inspire me with confidence,' said Jago, 'but if his father's telling the truth he's got an alibi. Martin can't have been home by a quarter past nine and hiding in the cinema at the same time to let someone in when everyone had gone home.'

'I reckon they're all in it together, sir – that Martin, and his dad, and his brother Ernie too. Very convenient that they were all in the shelter together all night, isn't it? A bit too convenient, if you ask me. Especially if they're tied up with the IRA. Did you ask that Superintendent Ford at Special Branch about the gelignite?'

'Yes. He confirmed that the IRA have stolen gelignite and supplied it to some of their people in London. But whether that means that's how our safe-breakers got it is another matter.'

'I expect they could find out, though.'

'Special Branch don't necessarily know everything, Peter.'

'Yes, of course, but they know more than we do.' Cradock's eyes widened with a kind of boyish enthusiasm. 'It must've been exciting for you when you worked for them, sir.'

'Well,' said Jago, 'I was only with the Branch for a six-month secondment, so it was hardly a career.'

'Interesting, though, I bet.'

'Yes, it was. Mind you, all that business I was involved in with the civil war in Spain is history now. The fascists won, Franco's got total power, and now the only reason we're interested in Spain is because we're worried he might join up with Hitler and Mussolini and grab Gibraltar.'

'Gibraltar will never fall,' said Cradock confidently.

'I believe that's what they said about the Maginot Line,' Jago replied. 'Even Special Branch couldn't prevent that little disaster. Anyway, Superintendent Ford's advice was to treat our cinema job as an ordinary case of larceny, so if there's any heroics required, we'll leave it to them.'

'Yes, sir. Still, I wouldn't mind doing a bit of that myself some day. Special Branch, I mean.'

'I dare say,' said Jago. 'And if they need your services, I'm sure they'll let us know.'

CHAPTER THIRTY-EIGHT

When they reached Stratford Broadway Jago slowed the car and pulled over to the kerb, where he stopped. He was thinking.

'Before we go back to the station we need to see if Mr Conway's in,' he said. 'He's probably expecting us to give him an update on the break-in, and we might profitably put one or two questions to him too. Interesting fellow, isn't he?'

'Yes, and very ambitious,' said Cradock. 'So's that Elsie, I think. I wonder if they've ever met – they'd probably get on well together if she wasn't already married.'

'From what we've heard about him so far, I'd say he might not regard that as too great an obstacle.'

'True. He's certainly what they call a go-getter. That reminds me – when we were talking to Vera Ballantyne about horoscopes and all that, she said Hitler was ambitious, didn't she? She said a man with that kind of ambition's going to think the world's there for the taking.'

'And?'

'Well, that sounded just like what Conway said the first time we spoke to him at the cinema, didn't it? He said he had big plans, and the world was out there for the taking.'

'Are you suggesting Mr Conway's another Hitler? Is he going to march into the Forest Gate Odeon and annex it?'

'No, it's just that it struck me. I suppose it made me think about whether ambition's always a good thing. It can be a bit unpleasant, can't it?'

'Well, it certainly is in Mr Hitler's case. I think it depends on the person – some people handle it better than others. I suspect there's something of the dreamer in Conway.'

'Same as in Joan? That's what Elsie said, isn't it?'

'Yes,' said Jago, pulling out into the traffic again. 'I think Joan had her dreams. Or maybe "hopes" would be a better word. But I don't get the impression she was the sort to scheme and plot to get what she wanted. That's the difference between someone like her and the Conways of this world. There's nothing wrong with a bit of ambition, but the trouble is it can make you selfish – you end up seeing other people just as stepping stones to what you want, so you tread on them on your way.'

'You reckon that's Conway's problem?'

'I do. But what I'm wondering is whether it was hope that cost Joan her life.'

Cradock was still pondering this new thought when they arrived at the Regal cinema.

* * *

Conway met them in the foyer. Striding across the richly carpeted floor, he threw open the door to his office with what Jago thought was a rather grand gesture and swept in behind them.

'Good morning, gentlemen. I trust you've come with good news. Have you found my envelope yet?'

'The envelope from your safe?' said Jago.

'That's right, the sealed one.'

'Not yet, I'm afraid, but we'll let you know as soon as we recover it, if we manage to. And the money?'

'What?'

'You haven't asked whether we've found the cinema takings that were stolen from the safe in your office.'

'Oh, yes, of course. The money. Is there any news?'

'Not yet. Forgive me for asking, but I get the impression you're possibly more anxious about your missing envelope than you are about your employers' money. Is that correct?'

'Of course not – what a ridiculous idea. I've told you, there's nothing in that envelope except a few silly old photos. It's just that the deadline for submissions to the competition is coming up, and I'm very keen to have them back before that.'

'Silly old photos, you say. That's a very modest way for a man to speak about his own art. We've been discussing your pastime with someone who claims to know something about your photographic work. That person described them as "saucy snaps". What do you say to that?'

310

'What? Who said that? I'll, I'll ... Who told you that?'

'I can't tell you at the moment, Mr Conway.'

'Well, whoever it was, he's a fool and a Philistine who knows nothing about art. Saucy snaps? I'll give him saucy snaps. My work is art, and my photographs are artistic images, quite possibly soon to be judged as works of outstanding artistic merit. If, that is, you manage to get them back in time from whoever stole them – something you don't seem to be having much success at, as far as I can see.'

'We're doing our best, Mr Conway.'

Conway did not reply immediately, as if he had heard the sudden burst of petulance in his own voice and was regretting it.

'Thank you, Inspector,' he said, composing himself. 'I'm sorry for speaking sharply. It's just that I'm anxious about the competition. Please excuse me.'

'That's all right, Mr Conway. But I must ask you another personal question.'

'Yes?' said Conway warily. 'What's that?'

'It's been suggested to me that you were involved in a relationship with one of your staff. A personal relationship, if you know what I mean. Is that correct?'

'I'm not sure I do know what you mean. Which member of staff am I supposed to have had this relationship with?'

'With your secretary, Miss Carlton.'

'Who told you that?'

'It was Miss Carlton herself, actually.'

This answer seemed to knock the stuffing out of

Conway. He moved to his desk and sat down behind it. There was an unfamiliar look of uncertainty in his eyes.

'I see,' he replied slowly. 'Well, in that case yes, it's true. But I don't see what business that is of yours. It's got nothing to do with your investigation.'

'Perhaps so. But what interests me is that she claims you ended that relationship. Is that true?'

'Yes, it is.'

'Why did you end it?'

Conway thought for a moment, then pursed his lips and looked up at Jago. 'If you must know, it's because I grew tired of her. She has a superficial charm, but it became clear to me that behind that she is shallow. No depth. No mystery. I assume you won't need to tell her this, Inspector, but between you and me I look for something more in a woman. I want a woman with character, who's been through the fire, as it were, who's been tested and has overcome. A woman who deserves to stand beside me in the future. That's not too much to ask, is it?'

Jago thumbed silently back through his notebook, then stopped and ran his finger down a page.

'You perhaps won't be surprised to learn that that's not the reason Miss Carlton gave for the end of your relationship. She says you dropped her in favour of Joan Lewis, and I think you'll agree that does have something to do with my investigation.'

Conway looked shocked. 'Joan? No, it's not true! She was a married woman.'

'Such things are not unheard of, Mr Conway.'

'Yes, of course, but no, you've got it wrong. The only relationship I had with Joan was the normal contact between employer and employee. There was nothing improper about it at all.'

'So you're saying Miss Carlton is mistaken?'

'No, I'm not. I'm saying Miss Carlton is lying. Can't you see? She's just bitter because I didn't want to carry on with her. She's jealous and immature, and quite frankly she's jeopardising her future employment in this cinema. It's outrageous, and I won't have it.'

'So you were not in an intimate relationship with Joan Lewis.'

'Intimate relationship? What do you mean by that?'

'I mean the kind of relationship that's intimate enough for a woman to get pregnant.'

Conway's face took on an expression of outraged astonishment. 'What? Are you saying Joan was—'

'Just answer the question, Mr Conway.'

'I most certainly did not have such a relationship with her, and I've nothing more to say on the subject.'

'Very well. That will do for now. But there's just one more thing I'd like to ask you, and that's to do with the theft from your safe.'

'By all means,' said Conway, visibly calming himself. 'What do you want to know?'

'Simply this – do you have any reason to suspect that someone working at the cinema could've been involved in the theft?'

'What they call an inside job, you mean? No, I don't. I know you said there was no sign of forced entry, but I've told you before, the only people with keys are myself, my secretary and whoever's on fire-watching duty overnight, which on this occasion was Wilson. I regard him as a trustworthy fellow, and whatever Miss Carlton's personal shortcomings might be, I've no reason to believe she'd do something like that.'

'Providing the thieves with a key isn't the only way a member of staff might be involved. If there's no sign of forced entry, it could be because someone let them in from the inside.'

'Well, in that case it could be anyone, couldn't it?'

'Perhaps, but it also seems they were sure enough of where the safe was to go straight to your own office and break into it. Your man Wilson said they didn't ask him anything when they attacked him and tied him up. They knew exactly where to go. Could someone who works for you have given them that information?'

'Yes, but the safe was in my office. That would be a fairly obvious place to look for it, wouldn't it?'

'There's no sign on the door saying "manager's office". It's just a blank door.'

'Yes, but it's right next to the pay box. It wouldn't take much to work out that's where the safe might be.'

'Right. So you've no reason to suspect that any member of your staff might've told these thieves where to look?'

'No, I haven't. Are you asking this because poor Joan

was murdered on the same night as the break-in? Are you saying there's a connection?'

'What do you think?'

'No, it's not possible. Joan would never do anything like that.'

'And her sister?'

'What? Beryl? That sweet little thing? No, it's impossible. My staff are all very loyal – not just to the company, but to me personally. Good leadership creates trust, and trust creates loyalty, Inspector.'

'An interesting thought, Mr Conway. I'm sure you're right – a man can't get far without loyal staff. Is Miss Hayes on duty at the moment?'

'Yes, she is.'

'In that case, if you don't mind, I'd like a brief word with her.'

CHAPTER THIRTY-NINE

As soon as Conway had left the office to fetch Beryl, Jago ran an eye quickly over the papers on the desk, but he saw nothing of interest. He imagined the manager would send a page boy to find her rather than trouble himself, so he refrained from moving anything in case Conway returned too soon.

'So do you think Beryl really could've been in on the job?' said Cradock in a hushed, conspiratorial voice. Jago thought this unnecessary, since Conway had closed the door behind him, perhaps not wanting passing members of staff to see the two police officers back to interview him again.

'I don't know,' he replied. 'But I'm certainly going to ask her.'

Their conversation was terminated by Conway's return, followed by Beryl Hayes.

'Thank you, Mr Conway,' said Jago. 'Would you mind leaving us for a few minutes? We won't be long.'

Conway opened his mouth as if to object, but appeared to change his mind. He marched out of the office without a word and closed the door behind him with a little more force than before.

'What is it, Inspector?' said Beryl, standing before the detectives in her usherette's uniform.

'As you may know, we're investigating not only the death of your sister but also a theft that occurred here at the cinema on the same night.'

'I had heard about a break-in – someone blew the safe, didn't they?'

'That's right. Now, I'd like to ask something, and please think carefully. Do you know anything at all that might shed some light on that incident?'

'No, I don't. I mean, I was here that evening – I told you that, didn't I? With my boyfriend, not on duty. But I thought they said the break-in was later, during the night. I'd gone home by then.'

'Yes, but are you aware of anything that happened before or after that time that might help us?'

'No, I'm sorry. Why would you think I did?'

'Did anyone ask you about the layout of the cinema – where the offices were located, for example?'

'No. Who'd be interested in that? I mean, people sometimes ask where the toilets are, or the cloakroom, but those are pretty obvious – there are signs up.'

'What about the manager's office?'

'That's different – there's no sign on his door, but then I suppose he likes his privacy. So would I, I think, if I had to deal with all the customers' gripes. Martin took a dislike to something and wanted to complain to the manager, so I told him where to go, although I don't know whether he went or what it was exactly he wanted to complain about. But I can't think of anyone else wanting to know.'

'This would be your boyfriend, Martin Sullivan.'

'That's right.'

'I see. Has anyone ever asked you to supply them with a key to the cinema?'

'Certainly not, and I wouldn't have one to give them anyway.'

'Has anyone asked you to do anything that might've helped them to break into the cinema?'

'No, of course not.'

'And do you know whether anyone approached your sister Joan with the same intention in mind?'

'No. What are you trying to suggest?'

'We're just examining possibilities, Miss Hayes. There's a chance that the thieves might've tried to gain information from someone who worked here, so we're just checking.'

'Well, no one's asked me, and I wouldn't have told them if they had. And the same goes for my poor sister, I'm sure. She needed that job. She'd moved out of Audrey's house and had to pay her rent, and find money for her lessons. They weren't cheap, from what I gathered.'

'Lessons?'

'Singing lessons. She had a good voice, always used to sing around the house when I was a kid. When she got married she didn't seem to sing so much, but lately she got interested in it again, even joined the local dramatic society so she could be in one of those romantic Ivor Novello musicals. *Careless Rapture*, I think it was. Silly, maybe, but I think she'd seen that girl from East Ham singing everywhere, making records and on the wireless. What's her name?'

'Vera Lynn?'

'That's the one. I think Joan reckoned if a girl from East Ham could do that, a girl with the right voice from West Ham could too. I think she felt trapped, you see, and she was desperate to do something about it. She felt like a prisoner in Audrey's house, and when Richard was reported missing she grabbed her chance to move out.'

'And did she feel trapped in her marriage too?'

'That's not for me to say, but I got the feeling she was beginning to think that way. Whether she'd had enough of Richard or not, I think she wanted to escape, and becoming rich and famous was about the only chance she'd have of doing that. Like I said, it was probably a silly idea, but she'd started having singing lessons, and they didn't come cheap.'

'Do you know who was teaching her?'

'No, she didn't say.'

'Do you think she might've been tempted to disclose information about the cinema if someone had offered her money?'

'Never. She might've been silly and romantic, but she was an honest girl.'

'Thank you, Miss Hayes. You've been most helpful.'

'You don't think Joan had anything to do with those safe robbers, do you?' said Beryl, looking anxious.

Jago gave her a brief smile. 'That will be all, thank you. You can get back to your duties now.'

Beryl waited for a moment, as if expecting Jago to go on, but when he didn't she turned on her heel and left the room.

As soon as she'd gone, Conway scurried back into the office and closed the door.

'So did she have anything to do with it?' he asked, his eyes probing Jago's face for signs of a reaction.

'It's too early to say,' Jago replied. 'But thank you for your cooperation. It's much appreciated.'

Jago led Cradock out of the office, leaving Conway staring silently at their backs.

CHAPTER FORTY

The sun had come out while they were in Conway's windowless office, and when the cinema's front doors swung shut behind them it was for a moment dazzling. Jago stood still, shading his eyes with his right hand. When they had adjusted to the light he glanced to one side, then nudged Cradock's arm.

'Hello,' he said. 'Look who we've got here.'

Cradock followed the direction in which Jago was looking and saw a man in the uniform of a Royal Navy seaman studying a poster displayed outside the cinema. From his side view of the man's face he recognised him immediately, as had his boss.

'Hello, Ernie,' said Jago, walking up to the man.

Ernie Sullivan turned round to see who had greeted him.

'Oh, hello, Inspector. I didn't expect to see you here.'

'Nor I you. Checking the programme, are you?'

'That's right. I've got to get back to my ship the day after tomorrow, and I fancied seeing a movie before I go, so I thought I'd see if there was anything good on here tonight or tomorrow. Looks like there isn't, though.'

'Shame. But since you're here, I wonder if I might ask you a quick question.'

'Be my guest.'

'It's about last Sunday. Could you possibly clarify a couple of small points for me about when you got home that night?'

'Sure. Fire away.'

'You said you went to bed soon after you got home, yes?'

'That's right.'

'You didn't mention whether that was in the house or in the shelter. Can you tell me which it was?'

'Yes. It was, er . . . It was the shelter.'

'And you said your father was at home when you got in, but you didn't mention your brother. Was Martin at home too?'

'Er, I'm not sure.'

'Not sure? Those Anderson shelters aren't exactly spacious, are they? Surely you'd remember whether there were three of you tucked up in there together or only two?'

'Yes, but I, er . . . Look, that was Sunday and now it's Thursday, and to be honest, I've been doing quite a lot of meeting up with old pals and having a few drinks, if you know what I mean, making the most of my leave, so I might've got a bit muddled up. But yes, now I remember – I know Martin was at home. Yes, definitely – he was.'

'You'll have to do better than that, Mr Sullivan.'

'What do you mean?'

'I mean I don't believe you. I don't think you're telling me the truth, and there's something you need to understand. I don't like lying, and I don't like perjury, especially when the person who I think is lying to me is wearing the king's uniform. I expect the navy would take a dim view of that too.'

'Perjury? This isn't about me, is it? Is this something to do with Joan getting murdered? Are you saying my dad and Martin are mixed up in that?'

Jago ignored his questions. 'This is about you, Mr Sullivan – it's about you giving me the truth. So I'll ask you again – are you really sure Martin was at home? Sure enough to give evidence to that effect in a court of law? Or is this just a story you've cooked up with your father and brother? You see, I think it is, and I think you just didn't cook it up in enough detail to make it plausible. Now, what's the truth?'

Ernie seemed uncertain how to respond. He chewed his lip nervously before blurting out his reply. 'Look, Inspector, this is difficult for me. Believe me, I didn't want to . . . It's just that I didn't know how to . . .' His voice trailed off uncertainly.

'You didn't want to what?'

'I didn't want to get involved. Look, I've grown up in a family that hasn't always stuck to the straight and narrow. You understand me? In that kind of family you learn to cover for each other. But I'm not a crook, I swear it, and I don't want to be one. And anyway, if you think I was up to something illegal with those nylons you've got it wrong – I bought them and sold them, and I gave away more than I sold.'

'So perhaps you can reconsider what you've said and tell me exactly what did happen when you got home on Sunday evening. First of all, was your father in?'

'Yes, it was like I said – Dad was at home.'

'And your brother?'

'No, Martin wasn't in. But I don't know where he was or what he was doing.'

'And you went to bed soon after you got home, in the Anderson shelter, as you said.'

'That's right.'

'What time was that?'

'About half past ten, I should think.'

'And your father went to bed in the shelter too?'

'No. He said he was going to stay up a bit longer. I didn't hear him come into the shelter, but then I usually go off to sleep pretty quickly – when you're in the navy you learn to sleep anywhere and any time. I did wake up once, though, when the bombs were landing a bit close, and I checked the time – it was getting on for midnight. There was still no one else in the shelter then, but when I stirred again a bit later they were both there, in their beds.'

'Your father and your brother?'

'That's right. They must've come in sometime after midnight.'

'Thank you, Mr Sullivan. Are you expecting to see them today? I'd like a word with them.'

'You're not going to tell them what I've just said, are you?'

'Only if I have to. The fact that they weren't in when they told me they were doesn't necessarily mean they were involved in criminal activity. But if I find they've been up to no good somewhere else, what you've said could become relevant to my enquiries.'

'I just don't want them to think I've shopped them. But seriously, Inspector, believe me, they're not murderers.'

'I haven't said they are, Mr Sullivan. I just want to speak to them.'

'All right. Dad didn't mention where he was going, but he said he'd only be out for a couple of hours. I don't know when Martin's planning to get back.'

'Very well, that will be all for now. I'll see them later. In the meantime, perhaps you'll find something more to your taste at a different cinema.'

Cradock glanced back over his shoulder as they returned to the car, noting that Ernie Sullivan had set off in the opposite direction to their own.

'Do you think he'll tip his dad off, sir? Or his brother? If he does, it'll give them a chance to make up a new alibi before we see them.'

'Maybe, but I'd be surprised if those three managed to concoct anything half convincing, judging by their performance to date. What did you make of Ernie's version of events?'

'He was struggling, wasn't he? Couldn't get his story straight. He didn't know what his dad and Martin had told us, so he couldn't work out whether he was getting it right or not.'

'So what does that tell us?'

'Well, I still think all three of them were mixed up in that safe-breaking. I told you I reckoned that story of them all being in the shelter together all night was a bit too convenient, didn't I?'

'Yes, and now that alibi looks decidedly feeble. If Ernie's saying he was alone in the shelter until after midnight, his dad and his brother have no one to testify that they couldn't have been in the cinema at the time Wilson says he heard the blast.'

'Exactly.'

'Mind you, of course, if George and Martin weren't in that shelter from half past ten or so until after midnight, it means Ernie doesn't have an alibi for that time himself, does he?'

CHAPTER FORTY-ONE

Jago noticed Cradock rubbing his stomach with one hand, a pained expression on his face, just as a lorry lumbering past down Windmill Lane made a particularly grinding gear change.

'Is that you making that noise, Peter?' he said. 'What's the matter?'

'Nothing, sir. Just feeling a bit peckish. I wondered whether we might be going back to the nick soon for a bite to eat.'

'Not yet,' said Jago, climbing into the car. 'I'm interested in those singing lessons of Joan's that Beryl mentioned. I'm just wondering who her teacher was, and I think it might be worthwhile making a slight detour via the park, so jump in.'

Ignoring Cradock's sigh of disappointment, he drove east down Stratford Broadway and on into Romford Road, then took a turning on the right towards West Ham Park. He pulled up a little short of the park itself.

'Here we are,' he said. 'Out you get.'

With Cradock in his wake he strode up to a green door and knocked on it. After a short wait the door creaked open, and a man greeted them with a smile.

'Hello, Inspector. How nice to see you.'

'Good afternoon, Mr Ballantyne. I'd like a quick word, if that's all right.'

'Of course. Come in.'

They followed him into the living room.

'Have you come about your father?' said Ballantyne. 'I've been thinking about him a lot since you called yesterday, and about the good times we had.'

'No, I haven't.'

'I'm afraid my wife's just slipped out to the shops somewhere, and I'm not sure where she's gone or when she'll be back, but I can make you a cup of tea if you'd like one.'

'No, thank you. We shan't be here for long.'

'Very well, but take a seat at least. How can I help you?'

'It's about Joan Lewis,' said Jago, easing himself onto the comfortable sofa. 'When we were here yesterday in connection with her murder your wife told us she'd met Joan, but you didn't mention whether you knew her yourself.'

'Yes, that's right. But if I recall correctly, I don't believe you asked me, Inspector. You seemed to be more interested in my wife's seances.'

'Your wife mentioned that you coach young girls who want to be singers.'

'That's correct.'

'It's come to my attention since then that Joan Lewis was having singing lessons. I'd just like to know whether she was getting those lessons from you.'

'Ah,' said Ballantyne. 'Yes, well, I was rather afraid you might ask that question at the time, but you didn't, so I, er . . . well, I suppose I thought I would let that particular sleeping dog lie.'

'Why?'

'It was the judgement of an instant, Inspector, the spur of the moment. Had I reflected for a second longer, I might have ventured the information, but I didn't, and alas, there it is.'

'So you were giving Joan singing lessons?'

'Yes, I was.'

'But why did you prefer to conceal it?'

'I was afraid there might be a misunderstanding. I suppose I was just nervous about what questions you might ask.'

'You mean you had something to hide?'

'Not from you, Inspector, not from you. But you will recall that my wife was present.'

'So?'

'Vera means the world to me. I've come to depend on her for everything – the truth is, I'd be lost without her. I've always loved her, since first I saw her, but in the theatre there are many temptations, and when I was a younger man I, er—'

'You succumbed?'

'Let's just say that I didn't always make the wisest of choices. But I assure you, all that was a very long time ago, and she forgave me, and I've been faithful to her ever since.'

'So what did you have to worry about?'

'When you were with us she made some comment to the effect that it's strange how a young woman can fall for a man old enough to be her father, and I remember wondering why she'd said that. I thought perhaps she suspected me of improper behaviour, that she didn't trust me, and I was afraid there might be other things you knew about Joan that would make my innocent lessons seem compromising in some way.'

'You mean you were aware of something potentially compromising about Joan?'

'No, of course not. I didn't know anything about Joan's private life. I was just worried what you might come out with, and I thought the simplest thing would be to keep out of it.'

'Were you emotionally involved with her?'

'Absolutely not. Look, Inspector, this is what happened. Joan heard that I gave singing lessons and she asked me to coach her. I said I would, and we started – I would visit her flat once a week. There's no denying it, she was a pretty girl, and neither can I deny that I could have fallen for her – in my mind I was still the young man I was forty years ago, full of strength and energy. But then I caught myself in the mirror and realised that in fact I'm just a silly old fool. The very idea of it was ridiculous. Besides, she'd shown no interest in me and had neither said nor done anything to lead me on. So I concentrated on helping her to improve her singing, and that was all there was to it. The poor child had a dream of becoming a singer, and I was just doing what I could to help her.'

'When was the last lesson you gave her?'

'It was last Wednesday – the Wednesday before she died.'

'Did you see her after that?'

'No.'

Jago heard a key turn in the front door, then the sound of it shutting. A woman's voice cried 'I'm back', and the door to the living room opened to reveal Vera Ballantyne.

'Oh, sorry to disturb you,' she said.

'Not at all,' said Jago. 'Do come in.'

She smiled and entered the room, depositing a shopping bag on the floor and then sinking into an armchair with a sigh of relief.

'Don't let me interrupt you,' she said. 'I'll get you a cup of tea when I've recovered.'

'No thank you, Mrs Ballantyne. That's very kind, but your husband's already offered, and I've declined.' He turned back to Ballantyne. 'Just one last question, if you don't mind, Mr Ballantyne. Can you tell me where you were on Sunday evening?'

Ballantyne shifted his gaze to the ceiling and looked thoughtful. 'Sunday? Ah, yes, I was in Birmingham, visiting an old actor friend from my performing days. I went up on the train Sunday morning and got back Monday afternoon.'

'And your friend will be able to confirm that for us?'

'Oh, yes. He's a wonderful man – the sort of chap who'd do anything for a pal.'

'So you were here on your own, Mrs Ballantyne?'

'Most of the time, yes, but I don't mind. If you work in the theatrical world you get used to being apart.'

'Including Sunday evening?'

'No. I'm not so good on my own after dark nowadays, what with all the air raids, but Audrey came over to stay the night. She's very good like that.'

'Thank you. You've both been most helpful.'

'Before you go, Inspector,' said Ballantyne, struggling to his feet.

'Yes?'

'I've got something for you.'

Ballantyne crossed the room and opened the door of a Victorian mahogany chiffonier that was a little too large for the room but nevertheless to Jago's eye a magnificent piece of furniture. He pulled out a cardboard box and began rummaging through it.

'Ah!' he said at last. 'Here it is. After we spoke last time – about your father – I had a look through some of my old mementos and I found this.' He handed Jago a theatre handbill. 'I told you I'd appeared with your father in the old days, when we were both touring the halls. I dug this out because I thought you might like to see it – we were both on the programme together at the Hackney Empire all those years ago.'

The sheet was dated 1902, and Jago had already

seen Ballantyne's name listed as the twelfth act on the programme, followed by the name of another man identified as a 'character comedian'. His eyes skimmed down a few more acts and then he read the words 'Harry Jago, popular vocalist'.

He heard his own voice soften as he spoke. 'Thank you, Mr Ballantyne, that's very kind of you.'

He handed the programme back, but Ballantyne waved it away.

'No, you keep it,' he said. 'It'll be something for you to remember your dear father by. I've got my own memories of him – he was a good chap.'

'In that case, I should like to very much. Thank you.'

Jago took the handbill and carefully folded it in half. He noticed that Cradock seemed to be studying his face.

'Come along, Peter,' he said. 'It's time for us to go.'

He slipped the handbill into his pocket, and they left.

CHAPTER FORTY-TWO

'And before you ask,' said Jago, 'yes, I know it's past your lunchtime, and yes, I know you're starving, so yes, we will stop at the first coffee stall we come to and I'll buy you a sandwich. Cheese and pickle? You seemed to be keen on that yesterday.'

'Oh, yes, guv'nor, that'd be perfect.'

Eleanor Road was not a likely location for a coffee stall, but they found one as soon as they turned onto Romford Road, and Jago parked the car behind a lorry. To Cradock's delight, he bought not only cheese and pickle sandwiches but also a currant bun and a coffee for each of them. A man in overalls who might have been the driver of the truck and a couple of young women in the khaki uniform of the Auxiliary Territorial Service were standing in front of the stall, so Jago ushered Cradock away a little to where they could talk without being overheard.

'Well, what did you make of that?' he said.

'Of what, sir?'

'Of Ballantyne's story – him and Joan.'

'Oh, right,' said Cradock through a mouthful of sandwich. 'He seems a likeable old buffer, but those singing lessons sounded a bit dodgy. Old man like that alone with a woman like her? I mean, he was the one who reckoned it was all about helping to make young women's dreams come true. Maybe he wasn't just teaching her how to practise her scales.'

'He seemed quite honest when he was talking about his past indiscretions, though, don't you think?' said Jago. 'He gave the impression that he'd learnt his lesson and put that sort of behaviour behind him.'

'Well, he would say that, I suppose, given that she's been murdered. He was certainly quick to write himself out of the picture as far as getting up to anything with Joan was concerned – even though he'd as good as admitted his wife thought that's exactly what he'd been doing. He also made sure to tell us he was just a silly old fool, and maybe that's right – there's enough years between him and Joan. But maybe he was really more of a sugar daddy. I mean, from what he was saying about his legacy it doesn't sound like he's short of a bit of money to splash around.'

'And his alibi?'

'Spent the night with an actor who'd do anything to help a pal? If you ask me, I think we ought to have a word with Mrs Ballantyne on her own as soon as we get the chance.'

'You're right. But if you've got your strength up now, we need to see those Sullivans again.' Jago checked his watch. 'If Ernie's prediction was right, George at least might be back in half an hour or so.'

'Yes, sir. Can I make a suggestion, sir?'

'Of course.'

'Why don't we stop off and see if Audrey's in on the way? She only lives just over the road there, doesn't she?'

'Yes. But what's your thinking?'

'Well, Beryl said Joan started having her singing lessons because she felt like a prisoner in that house, and possibly in her marriage. We know Joan and Audrey didn't get on, so maybe we should hear Audrey's side of it.'

'True. Good thinking, Peter. We need to find out whether she can confirm what Mrs Ballantyne said about them being together on Sunday evening too – we'll drop by and see if anyone's at home.'

The turning to Carnarvon Road was only yards from where they were standing, so they left the car where it was and walked to Audrey's house. Their knock at the door brought no response, but just as they were about to turn away the door opened to reveal Derek Marwell.

'Ah, good afternoon, Officers,' he said. 'I wasn't expecting you.'

'We were just passing, sir,' Jago replied. 'But actually it's your mother-in-law we were hoping to see.'

'Ah, she's out, I'm afraid. There's only me in the house – I've just got in from an early shift. It's non-stop, you know. I'll be back there at midnight on fire-watching duty, and then I've got another early shift tomorrow. No time to sleep, even – sometimes it feels like I live in that place. Anyway, I shouldn't keep you on the doorstep. Would you like to come in? She might be back soon, for all I know.'

'We will come in for a moment, thank you. We can't stay long, but you may be able to help us yourself.'

Marwell took them into the same room in which Audrey had previously entertained them.

'Do sit down, gentlemen,' he said. 'I always find it a little awkward having visitors, what with it being Audrey's house. She's kindly taken us in, but it's not the same as having your own place, is it? I still feel somehow as if I'm trespassing. Elsie doesn't, of course – this was her home before we were married. We did have our own little house until quite recently, but we were bombed out when the air raids started, and Audrey's let us have a room here.'

'Yes, your wife told us.'

'Of course. It's not ideal, but we've just got to put up with it. No houses are being built now, and they say it could be years before anything's available. On the night we were bombed the ARP people took us to one of those rest centres, but it turns out they were only designed to shelter people for a few hours – just some chairs and blankets, a cup of cocoa and a sandwich, not a place to live. We'd lost everything – all we had was the clothes we stood up in – but the council seemed to have no idea what to do with us. Elsie was very angry about it. She feels these things, you know.'

'I can understand that.'

'Audrey's been good to us. She's not exactly flush with money, but she's letting us have the room free, so we can save up for a deposit on another place. I thought we should move out and rent a flat, but Elsie said no. She wasn't brought up renting and she wants us to have a house of our own.'

'We were told that Elsie's father had put a considerable amount of money away somewhere but that your mother-in-law hadn't found it yet. Is that correct?'

'Yes. I hope they find it, although I suspect there may be some mystery about how he came by it, if you know what I mean, so that might explain why it's not been easy to trace. Elsie's certainly very keen to find it, because then we could get our own home. Mind you, if she did find it I'm not sure she'd tell her mum – I think she'd want to take the lot and get out. Anyway, one way or another we could do with coming into some money out of the blue, like Vera and Greville did.'

'You know Mr and Mrs Ballantyne well?'

'Not terribly – I've met them when they've been here visiting Audrey. Ridiculous name, isn't it? I can't believe anyone could really be called Greville Ballantyne – he must've made it up for the stage. Talk about grand – I call him Burlington Bertie when he's not around to hear. They were as poor as church mice when I first met them, but now they seem to be living in clover.'

'Yes, they told me they'd come into some money a couple of years ago.'

'That's right – it was just after Elsie's dad passed away. I sometimes wonder whether he'd lent them the money privately, and they just kept quiet when he died, hoping no one knew about it. He made his living out of lending at exorbitant rates, from what I've heard, but maybe he made some loans at more reasonable rates to friends and then conveniently popped his clogs. I don't suppose there'd have been any paperwork to complicate things.'

'I understood from Mr Ballantyne that it was a legacy.'

'Really? Well, that shows how much I know, then. As I said, I don't know them well. I'd just like to have some of their luck. Elsie's convinced her dad salted his money away. She says he once told her he'd got a little nest egg hidden somewhere, and the bird sitting on it wouldn't sing to the taxman, whatever that means. But please don't tell her I said that, will you?'

'While we're talking about Mr Ballantyne, there's something I'd like to ask you.'

'Of course. What is it?'

'It's to do with Joan. We understand that she was taking singing lessons.'

'Really? I didn't know.'

'And the person who was coaching her was Mr Ballantyne.'

'Well, that makes sense, I suppose. I mean, he used to be a professional singer, so what better person to teach her?'

'I'd like to know more about Joan's relationship with him, and that's what I came here to ask your mother-in-law, but I wonder whether you can shed any light on it for us yourself.'

'Relationship? No, I'm afraid I can't. I know he's a friend of the family and a singer, but I don't know any more than that.'

'I understand you're involved in amateur dramatics.'

'Yes, I am.'

'And that's related to the world of singing, isn't it?'

'Not really. We do plays, but there's no singing in them, except perhaps the occasional song in a Shakespeare comedy. But you don't have to be a good singer to do them.'

'I just wondered whether you might've come across any information in the course of your dramatic activities that might be relevant to our enquiries.'

'No, sorry.'

'Are you sure?'

Marwell paused for a moment, his eyes closed in concentration, then abruptly opened them. 'Well,' he said, 'there is just one small thing.'

'Yes?'

'It may be just gossip, but I've heard he used to be a bit of a ladies' man, and I've also heard it suggested that perhaps he still chances his arm in that respect from time to time. Nothing that I could prove, though.'

'You didn't ever hear Joan say anything about it?'

'No, but I'm not sure that's the kind of thing she'd

have confided in me. I mean, it's more the sort of thing women talk to each other about, isn't it? Unless they want a male friend to go and punch him on the nose, in which case I don't think I'm the man she would've chosen for the job.'

'Your wife hasn't ever mentioned anything?'

'No, but I'll ask her when I see her, if you like.'

'Thank you. Tell her to contact us, please, if she does know anything.'

'Is there anything else I can help you with?'

'No, Mr Marwell. We'll leave you in peace now.'

CHAPTER FORTY-THREE

'Well,' said Jago as he and Cradock returned to the car. 'We didn't learn much about Joan and Ballantyne, but what Marwell said about the money was interesting. First thing tomorrow morning I want you to check with all the local estate agents and find out who handled the Ballantynes' house purchase – someone should remember if it was only a couple of years ago. Whoever did it should be able to tell you who the Ballantynes bank with, or were banking with at the time. Then get on to the bank manager and find out where the money came from.'

'Yes, sir.'

'And now let's pop down to Windmill Lane.'

It was only a few hours since they had last visited the Sullivans' home. This time George Sullivan met them with a look of weary exasperation.

'For goodness' sake,' he said. 'Don't you people ever give up? Haven't you got anything better to do than come round pestering the local residents?'

'Good afternoon, Mr Sullivan,' said Jago. 'We'll come in, if you don't mind.'

With a resigned shake of his head Sullivan let them in. He took them up the stairs and through to the kitchen at the back of the flat, where Jago was surprised to find both Martin and Ernie.

'Well, well,' he mused. 'A full house.'

Cradock slipped round behind the three men and stood near the door to the outside stairs that led down from the flat into the back yard.

Jago acknowledged the two sons with a brief glance but addressed his first comments to the father.

'Right, Mr Sullivan, I want to ask you again about your movements on Sunday. Earlier today you said all three of you spent the night together in your Anderson shelter, but I now have evidence that makes me doubt that.'

'What are you talking about?' said Sullivan. 'What kind of evidence?'

'A witness claims you were not all here when you said you were.'

'It's a lie. Who told you that?'

'I'm not at liberty to say, I'm afraid.'

Sullivan responded with a menacing glare at Jago, and looked as though he was about to add some threatening words, but he was interrupted by his elder son.

'Shut up, Dad,' said Ernie. 'They're not idiots.' He turned to Jago. 'You don't have to worry about me, Inspector. I'm big enough to take care of myself. I know what I said about not telling them, but I've changed my mind. If they're mixed up in any way with what happened to poor Joan, I'm not going to lie for them – they deserve whatever they get. You can tell them what I said. I don't care any more.'

'What?' shouted his father. 'It was you? You ungrateful, two-faced little—'

George Sullivan launched himself at Ernie and began pounding him with his fists. The sailor, considerably lighter on his feet, parried most of the blows and then drove a punch into his father's stomach, sending him reeling, breathless, into the corner of the room. Martin stepped forward and tried to help him up, but George, fighting for his breath, pushed him away. He attempted to get to his feet, but the effort was too much for him. He fell back, crashing into a heavy oak sideboard. Ernie stood over him, rubbing his knuckles.

'As I was saying, Mr Sullivan,' said Jago, addressing the defeated man on the floor, 'I don't believe your story about Sunday night, and I'm inclined to believe you were actually at the Regal cinema helping yourself to the contents of the safe.'

'It's not true,' Sullivan hissed.

'I also believe that your son Martin was there with you.'

'You're mad,' said Martin.

Ernie took a step towards Jago. The confident air had suddenly faded from his face: he looked baffled.

'What?' he said. 'I don't get it. Are you saying my dad and my brother were out robbing a cinema?'

'Yes, that's exactly what I'm saying.'

'And you think I had something to do with it?'

'No, Mr Sullivan, I don't think you did.'

Ernie Sullivan was still puzzled. 'So you mean this is nothing to do with Joan?'

Before Jago could answer, he saw from the corner of his eye Martin Sullivan hurling himself towards the back door. He shouted a warning, but Cradock had already seen. He stuck out a foot and sent Martin flying to the floor. The young man jumped back to his feet and seized the door handle, but the door wouldn't budge. He rattled it noisily, but to no avail.

'This what you're looking for?' said Cradock, holding a key aloft. 'Someone's locked it, I'm afraid.' He slipped the key into his pocket.

'Thank you, Peter,' said Jago, as Cradock pushed Martin and his father onto chairs at the table while Ernie stood to one side, a silent spectator. 'And now perhaps you'd better attend to the other door, in case anyone else should have a sudden desire to leave.'

There was no key in the other door, so Cradock took up position in front of it, blocking this remaining way out.

Jago surveyed the room, and something tucked behind the clock on the mantelpiece caught his eye. He crossed to the fireplace to take a closer look.

'What do we have here?'

'I don't know,' said George. 'You tell me.'

'It appears to be a brown envelope. A somewhat bulging one, sealed with wax – or rather, formerly sealed with wax.'

'Really? So is it a crime now to have a brown envelope in your house?'

'That depends on what's in the envelope, doesn't it? It looks as though there's more than just a letter.'

'So?'

'Are you a betting man, Mr Sullivan?'

'What's it to you if I am?'

'I don't mind an occasional wager myself. What would you say to a little bet that I can tell you what's inside that envelope without looking?'

'I don't know what you're talking about.'

'I suspect you know that if I open it I'll find some photographs inside.'

'I told you – I don't know what you're talking about.'

'Let's see if I'm right, then.'

Jago covered his hand with a clean handkerchief and removed the envelope from behind the clock. It was clear that the wax seal was broken and the flap had been opened. He rejoined George and Martin Sullivan at the table, then gently shook the envelope over it. Half a dozen photographs and some negatives spilt out. He scrutinised the photos and recognised the face of a woman.

'Bit saucy, aren't they?' said Martin with a smirk.

'Shut up, you fool,' said his father, glaring at him.

'It's too late for that,' said Jago. 'Now, tell me, what do you know about these photos?'

'Nothing,' said George. 'Never seen them before.'

'It's too late for that too. Right, you're under arrest,

both of you. You are not obliged to say anything, but anything you say may be given in evidence. Now, sit still where you are and don't try any funny business. I'd like to take a look at something else that caught my eye over there before we take you down to the station.'

'Please yourself,' said Sullivan senior, his voice as surly as his face.

Jago stepped back across the room to the fireplace, next to which was a cupboard. The door was open, revealing a pile of newspapers neatly stacked on a shelf. He reached in and took the copy lying on top of the pile, then held it up.

'Well, well,' he said. 'This looks interesting.'

The masthead of the paper bore the words *An Phoblacht*, and underneath in English *The Republic*. It was dated July 1937.

'A bit behind in your reading, are you, George?'

'It's a keepsake,' Sullivan muttered. 'I kept it for historical interest, if you must know – that's the last one published before it was shut down.'

'Shut down by whom?'

'By the Irish government.'

Jago opened the paper and studied the inside pages briefly.

'There's an article here about the Republican Army Council,' he said, as lightly as if he'd just found a report on a football match. 'Seems to be all in favour of it. That'll be the Irish Republican Army, I suppose. Friends of yours?'

'I'm interested in politics, that's all,' said George.

'And Irish politics in particular?'

'Any politics. There's nothing illegal about being interested in politics.'

'No, but as you may be aware, there are some aspects of involvement with the IRA that are.'

'I haven't done anything wrong.'

Jago put the newspaper down on the table and took another look into the cupboard.

'I suppose this is of interest to students of politics too.' He pulled out a sheet of paper and held it up for Cradock to see. 'It's a proclamation,' he said. 'Let's see.' He read from the sheet: '"We call upon England to withdraw her armed forces, her civilian officials, and institutions and representatives of all kinds from every part of Ireland . . . and we call upon the people of all Ireland at home and in exile to assist us in the effort we are about to make in God's name to compel that evacuation and to enthrone the republic of Ireland."'

Jago placed the sheet on the table, next to the newspaper, and turned to Martin.

'I've heard it suggested that you might share some of these views. Is that correct?'

Martin said nothing but looked at his father, his eyes pleading for help.

'Leave the boy alone,' said George. 'It's nothing to do with him.'

'Does your interest in Ireland extend to doing a little fundraising for the IRA? Perhaps emptying the safe at

348

the Regal cinema and donating the proceeds to them?'

'You're talking nonsense. I'm not a criminal. Look, as far as I'm concerned the Irish Republican Army has a good cause. So what? I'm entitled to my belief, and there's nothing you can do about it. You can shoot me if you like, but it won't make any difference – I believe they're right.'

Once the two suspects were safely locked in the cells, the detectives returned to the CID office.

'Those photos, sir,' said Cradock. 'I couldn't see them from where I was standing. What did Sullivan mean when he said they were a bit saucy?'

Jago handed him the envelope.

'Have a look for yourself,' he said. 'And take care of them. We'll need to show them to Mr Conway so he can confirm they're his and that they were in the safe.'

'Which will prove that the Sullivans were the safe-breakers, right?'

'Not necessarily proof in itself, but certainly strong evidence. Get them checked for fingerprints. If we find George Sullivan's on any of those photos he'll have a hard time maintaining he's never seen them.'

'Yes, sir, will do.'

Cradock let some of the photos slide out of the envelope onto the desk and examined them.

'I see, sir. They're a bit, er—'

'Glamorous? Yes. If those Sullivans'd had more sense they'd have thrown the whole lot away. They might've been in the clear then. But you can see why I suspect they may've taken a liking to them and decided to keep them. He makes the women look like Hollywood stars, doesn't he? Very languid. I'm surprised they didn't catch their death of cold.'

'Oh, and look – that one there.'

'Yes. You know who that is, don't you?'

'I do. It's Cynthia Carlton. What a lark.'

'Now, now, Peter. The poor woman may be quite embarrassed when she finds out what we've got, so we'll have to treat her very carefully. Make sure nobody else sees those – I don't want to hear you've been passing them round the station.'

'I should think Conway might be a bit embarrassed too.'

'Really? I'm not so sure. For him this is art, and he's the artist, and I'm sure it was all done in the best possible taste. We may just have to remind him of the provisions of the Obscene Publications Act, even though it doesn't actually define what obscene means.'

'He'll probably have a pretty good idea, though.'

'Precisely. I'm not sure there's anything in that envelope that a magistrate would be likely to judge obscene, but it'd be wise for Conway not to cross the line in future. For now, all we need to know is that they're his. We'll have to tell him we're keeping them as evidence, and if he wants them for his competition he'll have to get some more prints made. I think I'll advise him to get the permission of the ladies concerned before he submits them, too, if he hasn't already done that, otherwise he might discover he's acquired a black eye or two.'

'Shall I get a search warrant from the magistrate to search the Sullivans' house too?'

'No, that'll take too long. Get in touch with the superintendent and ask him for a written order to search. If we suspect they might have explosives hidden on the premises, he can do that – just say we're asking for it under section 73 of the Explosives Act 1875. Tell him we've got reasonable ground for believing an offence has been committed with respect to an explosive and it's an emergency. We don't want the house blowing up while they're locked in the cells. That should do the trick.'

'So young Ernie's dropped them right in it, hasn't he? Without his alibi they're sunk. But what I don't understand is what's in it for him?'

'Perhaps it's simply the satisfaction of knowing that he's done his civic duty.'

Cradock looked at Jago cautiously. Sometimes he just couldn't tell whether his boss was being serious.

CHAPTER FORTY-FOUR

Cradock looked at the clock on the wall of the CID office. It was coming up to five o'clock, the time when people with normal jobs might start thinking about going home. Sometimes he envied them: in the CID you had to put in whatever hours the job required. He wondered how Jago had put up with it all these years, and whether that was why he'd never married. Too busy to find the time? It was a question he was certainly never going to ask: the detective inspector wasn't the sort of man you could expect to get to know, especially if you were a detective constable. He never dropped his guard.

He was lost in these thoughts when Jago came in through the door.

'Right, Peter,' he said. 'It's about going-home time now, isn't it?'

Cradock's face brightened. 'Time for us to knock off, you mean, guv'nor?'

'Knock off? At this time? Don't be ridiculous. No,

I meant for the bank. That fellow Pemberton down at the National Provincial said he didn't like to keep the girls at work after dark, and it's nearly sunset now, so Carol Hurst should be just about finishing work. There's something I want to ask her.'

'Really, sir? What about?'

'I'm curious to know whether there's anything more she knows about this idea of some kind of affair between Joan and Conway. It was Carol who first told us she thought Joan was a bit of a flirt, and she also said she thought her marriage had gone a bit sour, but she didn't say anything about an affair. Yet when we spoke to Cynthia Carlton yesterday, she claimed Joan had been having an affair with Conway, and she even suspected Joan was in the family way. You'd have thought Joan might've said something to her closest friend about all that, wouldn't you?'

'I suppose I would, yes,' Cradock replied. 'And there was something about those photos we found.'

'Yes?'

'Well, it's just that there weren't any of Joan in that envelope.'

'Well done, Peter – very observant of you.'

'Thank you, sir. Mind you, I'm not sure it means anything. The fact that Conway persuaded those girls to let him take their picture doesn't mean he was in that kind of relationship with any of them.'

'There was one of Cynthia, and it appears she was one of his old flames.'

'Yes, but maybe he included that one because he'd finished with her. He might've thought it'd be bad taste to put a picture of his current girlfriend into a competition, especially if he knew Joan was . . . well, you know.'

'In the family way?'

'Yes,' said Cradock, embarrassed to feel his face flushing.

'You may have a point, but in any case we'll have to speak to Conway about those photos, and before we do I'd like to know whether Carol can tell us anything more about this relationship he had with Joan, if it really happened. There's something else, too. The last time we spoke to Carol, she was starting to tell us about Richard Lewis and his funny ideas about economics, and the big falling out he had with his dad, but then the bank manager came in and interrupted us. There's bad feeling in that family, isn't there? And it seems to be all about money – Charlie Lewis's money. I want to know if she can tell us more about that.'

'And there's no time like the present, eh, sir?' said Cradock, making little effort to conceal the glumness in his voice.

'Exactly,' said Jago, picking up the phone. 'I'm going to call the bank now.'

Ten minutes later Jago parked the car outside the bank in time to meet Carol Hurst as she emerged onto the street.

'There's a rather nice ABC tea room just down here,' he said after they had exchanged greetings. 'I expect you know it. They do some very good toasted tea cakes, and I thought you might like to join us for one.'

He felt a tinge of disloyalty to Rita and her cafe on hearing himself recommend a rival establishment, but was reassured to notice that his suggestion seemed to have brought a new spark of life into Cradock.

They found a table in a quiet corner of the tea room, and Jago ordered tea and toasted tea cakes for all three of them.

'I don't want to keep you long, Miss Hurst,' he said. 'I expect you've had a tiring day and you'll be wanting to get home before the sirens start, but there's just a couple of things I'd like to ask you. First I must thank you for introducing us to your manager, Mr Pemberton, the other day. He was most helpful in explaining social credit to us.'

'Did you understand it, then?' said Carol with a barely suppressed giggle. 'It sounds like just giving everyone money for nothing, and I can't see that ever happening. But as long as you got what you wanted, that's fine.'

'We got enough for our purposes, I think. When we spoke to you before, you said Joan agreed with Richard's convictions about social credit, but his father didn't. Did Joan ever give any indication of what their disagreement was about?'

'She mentioned it, but I'm not sure I followed it all. From what I remember, she said the idea with social credit was that the government would give ordinary people money for nothing, so they could spend it and keep the economy going, and Richard reckoned that'd be good for everyone.'

'But his father didn't?'

'No. Charlie reckoned it was like fairy tales – something only children and fools would believe in. He said he'd worked hard for his money – although as I told you before, he didn't believe in sharing it, especially not with the taxman, and possibly not even with his wife. Joan used to say Charlie reckoned it sounded like the communists in Russia or the fascists in Germany – both lots said they could abolish unemployment and create jobs for everyone, but they could only do that by ruining their economies. He said private enterprise and capitalism were the only things that could create prosperity. That's about all I can remember. Joan told me Richard would get quite cross about it. He said it's all very well to say capitalism works when you're the one with the money, but there can't be prosperity if you don't share it. Apparently he had a big row with his dad about dodging his taxes, and they ended up not speaking to each other.'

'And Joan supported Richard in all this, you say.'

'Well, yes, but I can't say Joan ever struck me as an expert on economics. I mean, she was an usherette, not a bank manager. That's how they first met, actually, her and Richard. He saw her at the pictures, when she was working, and chatted her up. That was two years ago, I think. They wanted to get married, but apparently Richard's dad disapproved. Wanted something better for his son, I suppose. But then he died sometime later that year and couldn't disapprove any more, so they got married at the beginning of last year. I was there – at the wedding, I mean. It was a freezing cold day. Nothing fancy – just a quick, simple affair at the register office.'

A waitress in a blue dress brought their drinks and tea cakes and deposited them on the table with a smile, then left.

'How did the rest of the family take to that?' Jago continued.

'Him marrying her, you mean? There wasn't any fuss that I noticed. They seemed pretty indifferent – but then Charlie'd just died, and Audrey was very cut up about losing him, so I suppose she was more preoccupied with that.'

'But you implied before that Joan's relationship with Audrey was somewhat strained – "It wasn't all roses," I think you said.'

'Yes. Mind you, I was only looking in from the outside, wasn't I? It didn't seem very good to me, but then again their circumstances weren't ideal. I mean, they were living in his mother's house. Are you married, Inspector?'

'No.'

'Well, neither am I, and never have been, but like I said, it's well known, isn't it? If you marry a man and have to live under your mother-in-law's roof there's always going to be trouble. You can't have two women ruling the roost in a household, or in a marriage, and if your mother-in-law won't let her little boy go, how can he ever be a proper husband?'

She seemed to wait for agreement, but Jago treated her question as rhetorical. Confronted by his silence, she continued.

'I told you before that I thought Audrey was possessive, and she was – the sort of mother who thinks the apron strings are a fixture for life. Joan used to say Audrey would insist on baking his favourite cakes for him and giving them to him in front of her as if to make out she was incapable of pleasing him. I think things got a bit tense sometimes, and the reason why Joan moved out was because she wanted to be herself.'

'But that was after Richard had been posted to France. Why didn't they set up their own home before?'

'Money, I suppose – lack of. He didn't earn a packet, you know. And of course that was the other reason why they had to wait to get married. You know what the banks are like.'

'What do you mean?'

'Well, they don't let their clerks marry until they're earning two hundred pounds a year.'

Jago had heard of this before, but it seemed to be news to Cradock, who opened his mouth as if to ask a question. Carol answered before he could get the words to his lips.

'Don't laugh, Constable. It's because a clerk starts on a hundred and twenty a year – less if it's a woman, of course – and the banks think that's not enough for him to support a wife, so they won't let him get married until it's crept up to two hundred, which takes about five years. They're worried that if he gets married when his salary's below that, he might put his fingers in the till. It makes me laugh, but I think Joan found it frustrating, having to wait.'

'So Richard was a bank clerk,' said Jago.

'Yes, that's right.'

'Which bank?'

'The National Provincial, same as me.'

'In the same branch?'

'Yes. Why?'

'You haven't mentioned that before.'

'Well, you never asked me before, did you?' Carol tilted her head to one side, like a schoolmistress waiting for a slow pupil to answer, but Jago was lost in his own thoughts.

'No,' he replied eventually. 'No, I didn't.' He took a slow sip of his tea and continued. 'Now, I want to ask you about another member of the family. You've made it clear that Joan didn't get on terribly well with Audrey, but what about Elsie, her sister-in-law? What was her response to the marriage?'

'Elsie? I'm not so sure what she felt about it. Surprising, really, because she was just like her dad – spoke her mind, you know. She definitely agreed with his views, too – she didn't approve of free handouts to anyone. But Joan never said whether she'd had any trouble with Elsie.'

'I see. And what about Joan's relationship with Richard? You said you thought they married for love, but it went sour later.'

'Yes, well, she married Richard, not his family, didn't she? I think she fell for him hook, line and sinker when they met, and it was all wonderful to start with. Love at first sight, that sort of thing.'

'Soulmates?'

'That's what she thought. At first, anyway.'

'But not later?'

'Yes, that's the thing, you see. Richard might not've agreed with his dad about politics or the way he made his money, but Charlie was a strong man, and Richard took after him in that respect. He had a strength of character that Joan didn't have.'

'Strength of character? But his sister told us he was naive and indecisive, lacking in ambition.'

'Elsie said that? Well, like I said, she speaks her mind, but that sounds to me like her dad speaking. Charlie had no time for his son, and she'd think Richard disagreeing with their dad was a weakness, a character fault. She's never had a good word to say about him.'

'So what do you mean by Richard's strength of character?'

'Well, put it like this – he had ideas about life, knew where he was going. Joan seemed happy just to tag along behind him, and that appeals to some men, of course, but I had the feeling Richard needed someone with a bit more spark of their own. He was what people call self-obsessed, I think, bound up in himself. He always did what he wanted to do and expected her to fall in line behind. I never saw him show any interest in her life. They were all lovey-dovey at the beginning, but after a while it seemed to me he lost interest in her. Joan said that as time went by he stopped showing her any affection, just got on with his own life. She told me once how she really wanted children, but he wasn't interested. That happens sometimes, though, doesn't it? A man falls for a good-looking girl and they get married, but then he finds she hasn't got much depth behind the looks, not much to hold his attention, and the next thing you know he gets the roving eye.'

'Do you mean he was unfaithful to her?'

'Oh, no, I don't think so. But I do think perhaps he could've been, if the right woman had come along. I just mean there were things he wanted to do in life, whether or not Joan fitted in with his plans. Some men are like that, aren't they? Only care about themselves, don't seem capable of loving anyone else. It was like that when he joined the Territorials, she said. He just decided to do it, and never even discussed it with her.'

'I see.'

'Do you really? I sometimes wonder whether any men understand women. I think the thing about Joan was she wanted to be loved. She wanted to have one person in the world that she really knew, deep down, and even more someone who knew her as she really was and loved her all the same. She thought she'd found that in Richard.'

'But she was disappointed?'

'Exactly. But don't get me wrong – I'm not saying it was all Richard's fault. He was a good man. I'm sorry, I shouldn't say "was" – it's just that with him being missing for so long I'm beginning to think the worst. He *is* a good man. He can't help the way he is, and I don't think Joan really gave him a chance. If she wanted to marry him she should've accepted him as he was and loved him. She might've thought she deserved better, but so did he.'

Jago thought he glimpsed a tear brimming in Carol's eye, but before he could be sure she flicked a finger across it and it was gone.

'One last question, Miss Hurst,' he said. 'You told us before that you didn't know whether Joan had any men friends, but I got the impression that perhaps you thought she might have. The question I have to ask you is rather delicate, so forgive me, but the fact is that one of the people we've talked to about Joan has suggested she might have been having an affair. Was that true?'

Carol looked shocked.

'No, she wasn't that kind of girl.'

'So no men at all?'

She hesitated before answering.

'Well, in all honesty I can't say that, but I don't want you or anyone else to think badly of poor Joan. The truth is there was one man – but only one man. She wasn't the kind of woman you seemed to think she was when we first spoke.'

'Who was this one man?'

Carol's expression suggested she was struggling with how to answer.

'I don't know as I should say. I don't want to betray a confidence. I know she's dead, but even so, it was her private business.'

'I'm afraid nothing is private in a murder case, Miss Hurst.'

'But I'm sure it had nothing to do with her being killed.'

Jago looked her in the eye and spoke firmly. 'I'd be grateful if you would assist me by telling me who Joan was having an affair with, if that was the case. Was it?'

Carol looked down into her lap and nodded her head. 'Yes, it was,' she said quietly. 'If you must know, it was Derek. But please don't tell him I told you.'

'Her brother-in-law?'

'Yes, Elsie's husband. I told you what'd happened in her marriage. I think it was simple, really. She needed to be loved, she wasn't getting love from Richard any more, and then he wasn't even here. Derek was different. She told me he made her feel like she was loved. She felt there was someone who valued her. He's not flash, he's not brave, he'd make a terrible soldier, but he needed her. I think it was as simple as that – he needed her, and she needed to be needed. I know he was a married man, but him and Elsie . . .' Her voice dropped to a whisper. 'You know, I think she hates him. But I've said more than I should. I'd like to go now, please.'

Jago sat back in his chair, taking in what she had said. 'Thank you, Miss Hurst,' he said. 'That's very interesting, and you've been most helpful. I won't take any more of your time – we'll say goodbye for now, and thank you again for your help.'

He got out of his chair and stood by the table as Carol Hurst picked up her handbag. She clutched it defensively to her chest as she made for the door.

'Right, Peter,' he said, once she had left the tea shop. 'We need to find Derek Marwell and hear what he's got to say about this. If it's true and his wife's found out, there'll be hell to pay – and for all we know, maybe it's already been paid.'

CHAPTER FORTY-FIVE

As soon as they were out of the ABC tea room's door Jago strode briskly to the car, Cradock half a step behind him. He slipped into the driver's seat and started the engine.

'Quarter past six,' he said, checking his watch. 'Let's see if Marwell's still at home.'

He glanced over his shoulder to check the traffic, but it was almost blackout time, and anyone who could be at home would be there by now. At least there'd been no sirens yet, he thought, so if they were lucky they'd get this done before the Luftwaffe paid their nightly call. He set off for Carnarvon Road. When they reached the house he knocked on the door, and after a short wait it was opened by Audrey Lewis. Before he could ask for Marwell she welcomed them in.

'What a pleasant surprise,' she said. 'You're just in time to join us. Do come through to the dining room. We're about to start.'

Curious to know what was about to start and who 'we' were, Jago turned to Cradock with a shrug and followed her down the hallway. Audrey led them into a room and shut the door behind them. Inside, the blackout curtains were drawn, but the electric light was off: the near-total darkness was relieved only by a paraffin lantern with a red glass set on a table. In this dim light Jago was struck by how sparsely the room was furnished – just the table, a few wooden chairs and a small cabinet. It reminded him of the room in which Joan's body had been found.

'Take a seat, gentlemen,' said Audrey softly. 'I think Madame Zara's about to make contact with the other side.'

Jago noticed Cradock's uncertain look and motioned him to sit down at the table. He recognised the other people sitting round it: Audrey to his left, then her daughter, Elsie, then Madame Zara, and finally Derek Marwell and Greville Ballantyne. All had their eyes closed, none of them acknowledging the two policemen's arrival. Jago kept his open.

Madame Zara gave a low moan, then expressed greetings to someone unseen.

Audrey leant towards Jago and whispered: 'That's Black Hawk, her spirit guide.'

Jago said nothing. He thought he glimpsed Madame Zara's eyes opening slightly, then quickly closing as she uttered a long sigh.

'He says he has a message about Richard,' she said.

Audrey let out an almost inaudible gasp. 'Tell me – please tell me – where is Richard?'

'He's safe and well, in France.'

'Oh, thank you,' said Audrey, louder, her voice now breaking. 'What else can he tell me?'

'Nothing. That is all. But he says he has a message for the policeman. Something you need to know about Joan – he says he knows who killed her.'

There was a gasp from Jago's left as he scraped his chair noisily back from the table and stood up.

'All right,' he said sternly. 'That's enough. If he knows so much, ask him to tell us about the baby.'

'Baby?' said Audrey, her voice rising to match his as her eyes opened wide. 'What baby? What are you talking about?'

Jago noticed that all eyes were now open, including those of Madame Zara.

'I'm sorry, everyone,' said the medium. 'We have to stop now. I think we've upset the spirit guide – he's fading away.'

'What's all this about a baby?' demanded Audrey, ignoring her friend.

Jago strode to the door and switched on the electric light.

'I'm talking about the baby Joan was expecting,' he said. 'If your spirit guide can't tell me, perhaps one of you can. Who knew about it?'

No one spoke.

'I'm waiting.'

Another silence followed. Jago could see that everyone was avoiding his gaze. Only Cradock was looking at him eagerly, waiting for something to happen.

'All right, if none of you's willing to tell me, I'll tell you.' He turned to the medium. 'Mrs Ballantyne, you knew, didn't you?'

His use of her real name seemed to deflate her other-worldly air. She looked around the table, as if seeking help.

'No, of course I didn't. How could I?'

'Because you're a medium.'

'But no one in the spirit world told me anything about a baby.'

'That's not what I mean. It's because you're a medium that people tell you things – things that other people don't know.'

'Joan didn't tell me anything.'

'I'm not talking about Joan. I'm talking about someone else who came to see you – a young lady from the cinema, called Cynthia Carlton. You told me yourself, didn't you, when you were boasting about saving her life? She's the only person who's admitted to suspecting Joan's condition, and you're the only person in this room who's mentioned knowing her. She'd found out, hadn't she? And she told you. It's true, isn't it?'

Vera Ballantyne's head dropped. She gazed down into her lap and nodded. 'Yes.'

'Right. And who else knew?' He stared at Audrey expectantly.

'All right,' she said, 'I knew too. Vera mentioned it to me.'

'Why didn't you tell me earlier, Mrs Lewis?'

'Surely it's obvious. Put yourself in my shoes, Inspector. Why would I want to do that? She'd brought shame on her husband and his family, and when I heard she'd died I hoped no one would ever know. I thought it was something we could keep within the family.'

Jago glanced at Elsie, but her face remained impassive.

'And you, Mrs Marwell? Did you know?'

Elsie returned his gaze, her eyes widening in astonishment. 'No, I certainly did not. I had no idea.'

'Your mother didn't tell you?'

The question seemed to anger her, and she replied through gritted teeth, looking Jago in the eye. 'No, she didn't.'

Jago turned to the men.

'Mr Ballantyne. Did you know?'

Ballantyne looked shocked. 'No, certainly not. How would I know about something like that? It's women's business, surely.'

'And finally you, Mr Marwell.'

Derek Marwell gulped. He opened his mouth, but no words came, and as his eyes flitted from one person to another round the table it looked as though he couldn't think of what to say. Finally he turned towards his wife, looking at once guilty, frightened and beseeching.

Elsie Marwell said nothing at first, but her face flashed with anger, as if a dam within her had been breached. She sprang from her seat and leant forward towards her husband where he sat, her finger stabbing at his face.

'You pathetic liar,' she hissed venomously. 'You

thought I didn't know, didn't you? What did you take me for? I knew what you two were up to – amateur dramatics my eye. She didn't love you, you know. She did it to spite me and my mother. What are you? Useless, that's what. You're so incompetent, you couldn't even have an affair with my sister-in-law without getting her pregnant. You killed her, didn't you?'

Marwell sat in shocked silence as Elsie turned to Jago.

'I know what he did, Inspector. That cap you told me about – the sailor's cap you found at the flat. He must've known what he was going to do that night. He was going to murder the woman who was about to reveal what a useless swine he is. Then when we found that sailor stretched out on the street he could see the man was so drunk he'd passed out, so he went back to that shop doorway – he'd have to walk right past him on his way to his fire-watching duty. And when he saw the man was still there, with his cap on, he stole it and left it in her flat where he knew you'd find it. You'd draw the right conclusions, and he'd be in the clear.'

'What are you talking about?' cried Marwell, his eyes widening as at last he found his voice. 'This is all madness, Inspector. Don't listen to her.'

'You're the one who's mad,' said Elsie. 'You were so scared when you found out she was pregnant you panicked, you decided to kill her, and when you saw that sailor you thought it'd be an easy way to cover your tracks. You couldn't bear the thought of having to be a man and take responsibility for your actions, so you decided to get rid of Joan and let someone else swing for it. You're just a coward. I despise you.'

Marwell crashed his chair back and stood up, glaring at her.

'Shut up, you stupid woman,' he sneered. 'You're not so bad at amateur dramatics yourself, are you? But you're not fooling anyone. I know what you're doing – you're trying to pin the blame on me when you're the one who did it. You couldn't accept a rival, could you? Joan was everything you're not – she had imagination, a sensitive spirit, a gentle and caring heart. It was only knowing her that made me see you as you really are – as hard as nails and as cold as ice.'

Cradock got out of his chair and moved discreetly to guard the door.

'Mrs Marwell,' said Jago quietly to Elsie. 'He betrayed you, didn't he? Humiliated you. And you wanted revenge.'

Elsie's expression turned from rage to panic as his words sank in.

'Help me, Mum,' she pleaded. 'Tell him I didn't do it!'

Audrey took a packet of cigarettes from her handbag and lit one, then rose from the table and took up a position standing beside a bookcase. She drew slowly on the cigarette before speaking.

'She can't have done it, Inspector,' she said at last. 'Elsie got home last Sunday night at twenty to nine, and an hour later Derek went off to do his fire watching – or whatever else it was he had in mind to do that night. As soon as he'd gone, Elsie said she needed a word with me. She told me what her husband had been up to, and we talked about it. We were together for the rest of the evening, and we didn't get to bed until after midnight.'

'So,' said Jago to Marwell, 'you set off to your fire watching at twenty to ten?'

'Yes.'

Jago now addressed Elsie. 'And can you confirm that was the time your husband left?'

'Yes.'

'And Mrs Lewis, you say you and your daughter were together, just the two of you, from then on until after midnight, when you retired to bed for the night?'

'That's right.'

'But Mrs Ballantyne has told me you stayed with her that night, at her house.'

He turned back to Vera, who was looking very worried.

'Mrs Ballantyne,' he said, 'that's correct, isn't it? You told me Audrey was with you that night. But she can't have been here with Elsie and with you at your house at the same time, can she? I'd like the truth now, please.'

The medium seemed to have lost the power of speech. Her eyes flitted around like those of a cornered animal.

'I, er . . . I-I . . .' she stuttered, then fell silent again.

Audrey Lewis stubbed out her cigarette in an ashtray on the mantelpiece and drew herself up with a straight back.

'All right, Inspector,' she said, 'I'll give you the truth. I'm a mother, and I can't abandon my daughter. Can you blame me for wanting to protect her? But she asked me to tell you she hadn't killed Joan. I said what I said to protect her, but it was a lie. Yes, a lie, and I don't care. I admit I wasn't with Elsie.'

Marwell spun round to glare at his wife.

'So it was you,' he said. 'You killed her, you evil witch.'

He flung himself towards Elsie and grabbed her by the throat.

'You murdered my poor Joanie,' he said, choking on his tears as he shook her back and forth.

Cradock leapt forward and prised the man off her, pinning his arms behind his back. Marwell collapsed like a rag doll, weeping uncontrollably. Elsie staggered back, rubbing her hands against her throat.

'It's not true, Inspector,' she gasped. 'I never laid a finger on her.'

Jago was silent. Elsie looked at her mother uncomprehendingly.

'But Mum,' she cried, 'what are you saying? Don't do this to me!'

'Don't worry, my love,' said Audrey. Then turning to Jago she said calmly: 'It's true, Inspector. I was not with Elsie that night. But I can assure you with all my heart that I know Elsie did not kill her. Because I did.'

'Mum?' said Elsie again. She scanned the room, her eyes wide with pain and confusion.

'Inspector Jago,' said Audrey, her voice steady and measured, 'I have only one true friend in this world, and that's Vera. I'd always had my doubts about my son's wife and the quality of her commitment to him, but it was only when dear Vera told me what one of her clients had said that my worst fears were confirmed. As you so astutely suspected, Vera was visited in her professional capacity by a young woman who works at the cinema, and during their consultation this young lady let slip that a colleague of hers was expecting a baby. That would normally be of no interest to me, but then Vera said the girl had revealed that the colleague in question was my daughter-in-law, Joan. She'd said the pregnancy wasn't showing yet. I imagine that to her this was just another salacious detail, but to me it was clear as day that if Joan was indeed pregnant the child could not be my son Richard's. I discussed with Vera what we should do about this, and we decided we should confront Joan with what we'd learnt and ask her if it was true.'

'So you went to Joan's flat on Sunday evening,' said Jago.

'Yes, we went there together. As we got near the flat we saw a man leaving, in the moonlight. We weren't close enough to see who he was, but he seemed unsteady on his feet, and when he said something Joan giggled like a schoolgirl. She was behaving no better than a common prostitute. When he'd gone she closed the door, but we went over and rang the bell, and she opened it. We went in and confronted her – I told her I knew she was pregnant, and demanded to know who the father was.'

'And what did she say?'

'She said it was my daughter's husband, Derek. I couldn't believe it – that she could stand there as bold as brass and say such a wicked thing. I told her she'd betrayed both my son and my daughter. She had the nerve to stand there, looking down her nose at me, and laugh in my face. She called me something I cannot repeat, and said Vera was a witch. Then she flew at me like a cat, her fingers like claws. It took both of us to fight her off. She ran into the bedroom and tried to shut the door, but we pushed our way in. We struggled together and I tripped her so she fell to the floor. Vera sat on her and slapped her face. There was a chair knocked over beside me, with a pair of stockings draped over it. They looked expensive, and all I could think of was stories I'd read in the newspapers about prostitutes who'd been murdered by an unknown man using a stocking. Then Vera said, "Get one of those harlot stockings and let's teach this bitch a lesson.'"

'No!' gasped Vera. 'Audrey!'

Audrey ignored her. 'I grabbed it,' she went on, speaking faster, 'and wrapped it round her neck to frighten her, but all she did was spit in my face. I don't know what happened next – all I remember is feeling a terrible anger raging inside me. I remember screaming at her, and the next thing I knew the stocking was tight round her neck – and she wasn't moving any more. I looked at Vera. I said, "She's dead. What are we going to do?" She said, "We'll do nothing – just leave her here and go. No one'll see us in the blackout, and we'll go back to my place. I'll say you were with me there all evening and all night." So that's what we did.'

A look of horror crossed Vera's face.

'No, no, it wasn't like that,' she said, backing away towards the wall. 'You've got to believe me, Inspector. It wasn't me. I wasn't there. She's lying.' She looked around helplessly. 'It wasn't me, I tell you. It was her – she made me do it.'

Her words became unintelligible through her tears. Jago beckoned to Cradock, and they crossed the room together. Jago took hold of Audrey's arm, and Cradock Vera's.

'You're both under arrest,' said Jago.

Vera's voice turned to a subdued and pitiful moaning, but Audrey stood motionless, her face fixed in an icy glare.

CHAPTER FORTY-SIX

When Jago arrived at work the next morning, Station Sergeant Tompkins drew him to one side.

'Someone's come to see you, sir,' he said. 'He was here first thing – Mr Ballantyne, husband of one of those women you brought in last night. Young Cradock's got him in the CID office, waiting for you.'

'Thanks, Frank,' said Jago.

He went straight to the office. As soon as he entered the room, Ballantyne jumped to his feet, clutching his hat with both hands before him in a beseeching manner.

'Good morning, Mr Ballantyne,' said Jago. 'How can we help you?'

'Help me?' said Ballantyne, his voice drained of its former confidence. 'There's only one thing you can do to help me. Let me see my wife – I beg you. I must see her.'

'I'm sorry, Mr Ballantyne. That won't be possible at the moment.'

Ballantyne's already distressed face crumpled. He seemed to be fighting back tears.

'That's what I feared you'd say. But I can't just stay at home waiting. She's my wife, Inspector, my wife – can you understand? She's all I have. I can't imagine living without her.'

'She's been arrested in connection with a very serious crime, Mr Ballantyne.'

'I know, I know. I'd give anything just to turn the clock back and prevent this terrible thing happening. Our home's like a grave without her – my grave.'

'Actually,' said Jago, 'there's something I need to ask you about your home.'

Cradock slipped a piece of paper across the desk to Jago, who picked it up. He scanned what was written on it, then looked up, noticing a hint of wariness in Ballantyne's eyes.

'When we spoke to you on Wednesday,' he continued, 'you said you bought the house last year with a legacy you'd received.'

'Yes.'

'A legacy of two thousand, one hundred and sixty pounds?'

'Er, yes. But how did you—'

'How did we know? We checked with your bank, and that's the only large sum that's been paid into your account in the last five years. The curious thing is that you deposited the money in cash. But I assume the solicitor didn't pay you the legacy in cash. Am I right?'

'Yes, well . . . It was actually a loan of sorts.'

'Of sorts?'

'It was a loan from my cousin Charles.'

'Mr Lewis?'

'Yes, that's right, but it was what you might call an informal loan, unofficial.'

'What do you mean?'

'How can I explain? You have to understand – we'd lived in theatrical digs all our lives, moving from one cheap lodging house to another, barely getting by, with no security for the future. We'd saved a little, but nothing like enough to have a comfortable retirement in a home of our own. Then my cousin asked me to look after a bag of his. Well, I say asked, but in fact he told me, and he wasn't a man to say no to. Just for a few weeks, he said, so I agreed, although I suspected there was something fishy about it. He was a somewhat unorthodox businessman, if you know what I mean. The bag was locked, too. He insisted that we tell no one he'd given it to us, and if anyone asked, we were to say we knew nothing about it. The next thing we knew, he'd had a heart attack and died.'

'And I suppose your curiosity got the better of you?'

'Well, yes, naturally I opened the bag – he wasn't to know, so I forced the lock, and found it packed full of five-pound notes. A small fortune. Knowing Charles, I thought it was highly unlikely that anyone would know he'd left it with me, probably not even his family, but still I waited for a month, just in case.

When nothing happened, I paid the money into the bank. I reasoned to myself that he was a moneylender, and he'd given me this money temporarily, so in a way he'd loaned it to me, and since no one was likely to know about it, now that he was dead I wouldn't have to pay it back – it'd effectively become a gift. That was just over a year and a half ago.'

'During which time I believe Audrey has enlisted the help of your wife to hold seances in order to try to find her late husband's missing money.'

'Er, yes. But I think Audrey imagined it was a far greater sum. Vera was unable to establish through her gifts where such an amount might be, and she agreed with me there was no point in complicating matters by mentioning this comparatively small sum that he'd, er, loaned us.'

'So she deceived Audrey?'

'Well, er, I cannot vouch for my wife's gifts, Inspector. I'm sure she, er, acted in good faith.'

'Oh, yes, I'm sure she did – good faith that made sure his little nest egg remained safely in your little nest.'

Ballantyne looked crestfallen. 'I'm sorry, Inspector, there's nothing I can say. I feel as though I've let you down – and let your father down, too. I was foolish. Having that money in my hands and thinking that with my cousin dead probably no one knew I had it was just too great a temptation. I know I should've resisted it, but I failed, and there it is. But whatever may happen to me now is nothing compared with what poor Vera's facing. I just can't believe it, Inspector.'

Watching the miserable scene playing out before him, Jago felt sorry for Ballantyne: just a weak man overcome by temptation. He felt a bitter regret too that this man had been a link with his own father which would now be broken.

'I understand,' he said. 'I wish it hadn't worked out like this, but both you and your wife will have to give an account of yourselves before the law.'

By mid morning, Divisional Detective Inspector Soper had returned from one of his occasional meetings at Scotland Yard with his fellow DDIs from the other twenty-two Metropolitan Police divisions, the four area superintendents, and the chief constable of the CID. When Jago reported to his boss's office with Cradock it seemed to him that an hour spent in this elevated company had left Soper feeling rather more elevated than usual himself.

'Come in, John,' he said grandly, as if inviting him into the Throne Room in Buckingham Palace rather than this gloomy office that stank of cigarette smoke and hadn't seen a paintbrush since the Wall Street Crash.

'Thank you, sir,' said Jago, as he and Cradock entered the room.

'Now, John, I understand you've got a couple of women in the cells for that murder, so I just want to know the main points before I see your full report. Just the headlines, though – I'm a busy man.'

'Yes, sir. The women are Audrey Lewis and Vera Ballantyne, also known as Madame Zara, and they've both been charged with murder.'

'Madame Zara? Sounds a bit foreign to me.'

'No, she's not a foreigner, sir. She's a medium, and a friend of Audrey Lewis. It turned out the murder was nothing to do with prostitution, and nothing to do with the Welshman Evans, except that he stole her rings. He'll be up before the bench on Monday morning for that.'

'Good. We need to make an example of looters. I don't understand why the courts seem to be letting them off with just a few months in prison – the Defence Regulations say they're supposed to be shot.'

'Yes, sir. In Evans's case, however, we've recovered the rings, and he's just lost his wife in an air raid, so I'm hoping the magistrate won't be too hard on him.'

'I see, right. You mentioned something about finding a sailor's cap at the scene of the murder. Was that anything to do with it?'

'The sailor had visited Joan Lewis at her flat and left it there by mistake, but he didn't kill her. Joan's sister-in-law, Elsie Marwell, tried to make something of it because she thought her husband, Derek, was the murderer. She accused him of stealing the cap from the sailor while he was lying drunk on the street so he could leave it in the flat to incriminate him, but she didn't know Ted Watson had already moved the man on before that, so he couldn't have.'

Soper appeared to be struggling to digest this information. Jago wondered whether it was his own fault – perhaps in trying to be concise he'd created some uncertainty in his boss's mind as to whether Derek Marwell himself was lying drunk on the street while allegedly stealing the cap – but the DDI had asked for the main points only, so that's what he was doing his best to give him.

'We've also interviewed Vera Ballantyne's husband, Greville, in connection with some missing money that Audrey Lewis was trying to find,' he continued. 'It was salted away somewhere by her late husband. She doesn't know where, and neither do we, but what we do know is that Charlie Lewis entrusted a bag stuffed full of cash to Greville, who was his cousin. Vera Ballantyne knew Audrey was looking for it, because Audrey'd asked her to enlist the help of the spirit world in finding it, but Vera wasn't going to tell her about the money Charlie had left with them, because she and Greville intended to keep it for themselves. We haven't charged Ballantyne yet, because he maintains it was a loan, but I think he fraudulently converted the money to his own use, so we're probably going to be charging him with larceny.'

Soper nodded his head in a sign of understanding as Jago finished this account, but his eyes looked tired.

'And what about that safe-blowing job at the cinema?' he asked. 'Just briefly.'

'We've got two men in custody, sir. Martin Sullivan, who I mentioned before, and his father, George.'

'Jolly good.'

'They're both going to be charged under the Explosive Substances Act, 1883. The son hid in the cinema and let his father in. They stole the weekend's takings from the safe, and also a packet of photographs that belonged to Mr Conway, the manager, and which we later found at the Sullivans' house. The photos were a bit saucy, so we've got to break it gently to one of the ladies concerned that we've got what she probably thought was a private photograph. She's Conway's secretary, so it's a delicate business, but I'm sure we'll manage.'

'And the stolen money?'

'We haven't found it yet but we're expecting to receive an order to search from the superintendent later today so we can go through the house. If we find some explosives too it might be enough to put them away for ten years. We also found some Irish Republican documents. It turns out that although the two Sullivans are English, they're IRA sympathisers.'

'What did Superintendent Ford make of it?'

'He's pleased. He thinks they might've stolen the money because the IRA's short of funds at the moment, but they're probably not bomb-makers, although I expect Special Branch'll join us when we do the search.'

'So I was right, then, wasn't I?' said Soper, his voice brightening.

'About what, sir?'

'About it all being the work of Irish Republicans.'

'Yes, sir – and I did mention to Mr Ford that you

were the second person in West Ham CID to suspect an IRA connection.'

'Second? What do you mean? I said that from the very beginning.'

'Not quite, sir. In my report to Mr Ford I noted that it was Detective Constable Cradock who first drew my attention to that possibility. Isn't that right, Peter?'

'Yes, sir,' said Cradock, a broad grin creasing his face as he drew himself up to his full height.

A hint of an amused smile tugged at Jago's lips, but he regained his impassive expression as he turned back to Soper.

'So as you can see, sir, DC Cradock has done very well.'

'Well, yes,' said Soper. His voice was hesitant and, thought Jago, a little suspicious. 'I suppose he has.'

'And deserving of congratulation.'

'Of course, yes. Well done, Cradock,' he said. 'Well done. Keep up the good work.'

'Yes, sir,' said Cradock. He smiled keenly at Soper, pleased by this approval and not least by the fact that as far as he could recall, this was the first time the DDI had got his name right.

'Right, carry on, then,' said Soper. 'I'm sure you both have duties to attend to.'

'Yes, sir,' said Jago. 'We do indeed.'

CHAPTER FORTY-SEVEN

By a quarter to twelve Jago had completed his duties. The order to search had not yet appeared, but he'd briefed Cradock and would phone in later to check whether it had turned up. Now something else was in his thoughts, a far more pleasurable prospect: he was going to see Dorothy. It was only two days since he'd last been with her, but it felt like a week. This time he wouldn't be sharing her with a crowd of other people, either. It would be just the two of them.

The first thing he'd done the previous evening when he got home from a long day's work confident that he'd got Joan Lewis's killers behind bars was to phone Dorothy. As always, his call to her at the Savoy reminded him that they lived in different worlds. Yes, she was only there because her newspaper had put her in the same luxury hotel as the rest of the American press corps, but that was only part of the difference. Their backgrounds were separated by more than the

Atlantic Ocean, and he sometimes wondered whether the gap between them was any less bridgeable.

He'd wanted to know whether she'd be free for lunch today, and he'd been excited when she said yes. He was about to suggest he introduce her to some more traditional British cuisine when she cut in with a proposal of her own. It would be her surprise, she said: 'Just meet me outside the Ministry of Information in Malet Street when I've finished my meeting there, and I'll take you somewhere that I think you'll enjoy. I should be out by twelve-fifteen.'

At ten past twelve Jago got off the Central Line Tube train at Tottenham Court Road station and took the short walk to Malet Street, in the heart of Bloomsbury. The ministry was housed in what had been for just the couple of years between its construction and the onset of war London University's new Senate House, an imposing art deco fortress in white stone that soared nineteen storeys above the street in a demonstration of strength and solidity. To Jago it seemed like a piece of America transplanted into London, the capital's first New York-style skyscraper: a home from home for Dorothy, perhaps.

He couldn't help feeling some amusement at the transformation it had now undergone, in purpose if not in appearance: from the academics' lofty pursuit of truth to something more banal. Taken over by the government when war came, it was now, he imagined, stuffed full of civil servants immersed in censorship, propaganda and no doubt all manner of nefarious tasks. He looked up at the rows of windows towering over the neighbouring streets and wondered which one of them masked the office of Mr A. J. Mitchell, the official who'd originally brought Dorothy into his life. He smiled at how he'd resented the idea of being forced to nursemaid an American war reporter. Now here he was pursuing her across London for the pleasure of sharing lunch with her.

She emerged punctually from the building and waved as she strode towards him.

'Come along,' she said, grabbing his arm and marching him back the way he'd come. 'We'll take the Tube.'

'Where are we going?' he asked.

'I'm not telling you – it's a surprise. All I'll say is we're taking the Northern Line to Strand station, but then we have to get off because the line's closed from there to Kennington.'

'Why's that?'

She lowered her voice. 'Apparently there's an unexploded bomb lying close to the tunnels under the Thames, so the trains can't run.'

'You're very well informed.'

'I am. I'm a journalist, and I know a lot of people with interesting jobs. But there's no need to worry – I don't repeat everything I hear. Except maybe to a policeman.'

She flashed him a smile, which he returned, and at Strand station he discovered she was right: this was as far as the train went, and all the passengers got off. As they negotiated the final steps up to street level Dorothy grabbed his arm again.

'This way,' she said, heading away down the Strand. Within moments they were at the south-east corner of Trafalgar Square. To their left was the ugly cocoon of corrugated iron thrown up round the equestrian statue of King Charles I to protect it from bomb damage, which Jago had last seen when he'd met Dorothy here a few weeks ago. But now something had changed: right beside it there was an area of rubble forty or fifty feet across where a crater had been filled in.

'I expect you heard about the bomb,' said Dorothy.

'Yes, I heard there'd been something, but not the details,' said Jago. 'I see the king survived, though,' he added, nodding towards the corrugated iron, which appeared unscathed.

'Yes, but that's only because the bomb went ten feet or more down into the ground above Trafalgar Square station before it exploded. I spoke to a man who told me they reckon it was a 250-kilo bomb, and he said ten people sheltering at the bottom of the escalator were killed. I can't write about it, of course, because of the censors, but keeping these things out of the papers doesn't stop people finding out – anyone who tries to use Trafalgar Square station will know, because it's still closed until they've fixed the bomb damage. But at least it hasn't stopped us getting here, has it?'

She led him off round the crater site towards Nelson's Column, but he still didn't know their destination. The last time they'd met here Jago had been the one in charge, taking her for a bus ride all the way to Tower Hill, but now as they entered the square again he could only ask where she was taking him.

'To lunch, of course,' she replied. 'But we're going to have a cultural experience too, to repay you for the ones you've organised for me – only this time it won't be the best fish and chips in West Ham. It'll be the finest music in the world. In there.'

She pointed to the National Gallery, ranged along the northern side of the square, and at once he understood. The gallery was no longer the place to go to see art: all the treasures had been evacuated, like the children, to places of refuge around the country where they'd be safe from bombing. The cultural experience she must have had in mind was the lunchtime music concerts.

'I see,' he said. 'You mean Myra Hess, the pianist – those concerts she's been organising.'

'That's right. Have you been to any?'

'No – it's not the kind of thing I do, and I don't know enough about music to appreciate it.' He felt wary of admitting that he'd never been to a classical music concert. 'I've heard about them, though,' he added. 'I should think everyone has. It's certainly a great idea for brightening people's lives up. But chamber music's probably more your cup of tea than mine, isn't it?'

'If you mean I like it, then yes, I do. But this'll be the

first of these lunchtime concerts I've been to. I'm writing a piece about them, because people've heard about them even in America. I interviewed Sir Kenneth Clark the other day – you know, the director of the National Gallery – and he told me all about it.'

'You move in more exalted circles than I do. So he gave you a couple of free tickets, I suppose.'

'Certainly not. We'll be paying our shilling to get in, just like everyone else, only I'll be treating you. That's one of the interesting things about the whole idea – they only cost a shilling because they're for ordinary people, and the money goes to help the musicians who lost their jobs when the government closed down all the concert halls. But we'll need to be quick – it starts at one o'clock.'

Dorothy steered him towards the classical portico which marked the entrance to the gallery, scattering pigeons in all directions. They hurried past the square's elegant fountains, now turned off for the war and surmounted by brutally functional loudspeakers, and up the steps to the road between the square and the National Gallery, where the traffic was light enough for them to weave through the cars and buses to the other side. Jago pulled a handful of change from his trouser pocket and picked out a florin.

'Put that away,' said Dorothy. 'I told you this is my treat.'

Jago obeyed. 'Very well,' he said. 'But what about lunch?'

'Lunch is on me too. You may have heard they do food here now – a bunch of women volunteers run a sandwich bar for people who go to the concerts, and I've heard it said that the sandwiches are the best in London. They say the honey and raisin ones are the most popular.'

'Sounds good to me,' said Jago, although he still felt a little uneasy at not paying.

They joined the queue at the entrance and were soon inside. They made their way towards the eastern end of the building, through rooms which had once been adorned with some of the world's finest paintings but were now empty, their precious contents scattered to secret hiding places far from London.

'They've had to move the concerts too,' said Dorothy. 'The room where they used to be held has a glass dome over it, so when the big air raids began the gallery moved them to a safer room in the basement.'

The room was already crowded when they reached it, and uncomfortably airless. Every seat was taken, but people were standing round the edges or sitting on the floor. It seemed to Jago there must be three or four hundred of them, of all ages, and their appearance suggested that they came from all walks of life.

'Obviously very popular events,' he said as they found a place where they could lean against the wall.

'Yes,' said Dorothy. 'When I interviewed Sir Kenneth, he said there's too much music around that's supposed to be cheering us up but actually drives any intelligent person into an even worse despair. What he called "patriotic imbecilities".'

'Very well put, I'd say.'

'He said he thought people were crying out for something to take them away from all the muddle and uncertainty of war, and that's what he and Myra Hess wanted to give them.'

'I see. So is Myra Hess playing for us today?'

'Yes. That's why I suggested we come today. She doesn't play every week, because I think she wants to provide work for other musicians, but today she's playing a couple of Brahms sonatas.'

'German, then. We didn't hear much German music in the last war.'

'I guess that's not surprising, but apparently these concerts include lots of German classics, and the audiences like it.'

'Perhaps we've become more civilised,' said Jago. 'Though I doubt it.'

A man and a woman appeared on the makeshift platform and were greeted with a burst of applause from the audience. The woman cut a diminutive, stout figure in a black ankle-length dress, with a single string of pearls at her neck. She looked about fifty, with a strong, confident face, and her dark, centre-parted hair was swept back over her ears. Jago recognised her immediately from newspaper photos as Miss Hess. The man, with moustache, glasses and thinning hair, looked a good dozen years or so older. He was wearing a dark grey lounge suit with a waistcoat and a plain tie. Jago didn't recognise him, but the programme named him as Lionel Tertis and confirmed that the instrument he was carrying in his left hand, with a bow in his right, was a viola.

A hush descended as they began to play. Jago considered himself an ignoramus in matters of classical music and assumed it would go straight over his head, but from the start he was intrigued by the way the two instruments seemed to speak to each other. There was something stirring about it, but also a feeling of melancholy and a hesitancy that reflected his own mood exactly. He closed his eyes. Soon he was immersed in the music, borne along by it and unaware of his surroundings. Only the tumultuous applause at the end of the second sonata broke the spell.

It was Dorothy who spoke first.

'So, did you like it?'

'The music? Yes, I did – very much.'

'I hoped you would. What did you like about it?'

'I don't know, really. I'm no judge of music, but it definitely affected me, as though it was taking me somewhere else, away from here, and I was looking at everything from higher up – looking at myself from the outside. Do you ever feel like that – suddenly seeing yourself and wondering what on earth you're doing?'

'I do, yes.'

'Well, it made me think about how a man like Brahms could give his whole life to writing that kind of music, and how someone else could give their whole life to playing it, and then I was wondering what I give my own life to. Locking up villains, I suppose.'

He'd answered his own question and was about to continue, but realised his train of thought was leading straight to the question he didn't want to discuss with anyone, not even Dorothy – the question of what he really wanted to fill his life.

'So,' he said, as lightly as he could, 'where do we go for those sandwiches?'

CHAPTER FORTY-EIGHT

'Did you know a bomb went off here yesterday?' said Dorothy, changing the subject as they made their way to the sandwich bar. She sensed that Jago had something on his mind and didn't want anyone intruding. 'Apparently it landed on the other end of the gallery last week without exploding, so the Royal Engineers were here for days trying to defuse it, but it went off during yesterday's concert just as everyone was in here listening to Beethoven's Razumovsky String Quartet.'

'I didn't know that,' said Jago, grateful to her for sparing him further probing.

'From what I heard, they were in the middle of the third movement, the minuet, when there was a huge explosion,' she continued. 'And the amazing thing was, the quartet just played on as if nothing had happened – didn't miss a note. I hope one day I'll be allowed to write about it.'

'Were there casualties?'

'Apparently not – but a lot of damage to the west end of the building.'

They reached the sandwich bar. Jago declined the recommended honey and raisin sandwiches which Dorothy chose for herself, and opted for ham and chutney instead, with a generous slab of fruit cake and a cup of coffee. They took their lunch away to the quietest corner they could find.

'You're right about the sandwiches,' said Jago appreciatively as they began to eat. 'They're very good.'

'I told you so. Sir Kenneth said the profits from the food and coffee all go to the Musicians' Benevolent Fund, same as the takings at the door. The problem is, they can't fit so many people in down in the basement, so now the concerts are in serious financial trouble.'

'Does that mean they'll have to stop?'

'Fortunately not. It seems my own home town's stepped in to help. He told me the Boston Symphony Orchestra held a special festival of British music just recently to raise money for your lunchtime concerts here and sent over enough to keep them going right through the winter.'

'That should cheer the place up. Especially if they keep selling this fruit cake.'

'I'm glad you like it. I wanted to give you a treat to celebrate the end of your case. You've got it all wrapped up now?'

'Yes, but it was a peculiar business. We ended up arresting the victim's mother-in-law and another woman last night at a seance.'

'A seance?'

'Yes. Who'd believe it? In 1940. You must think we're still living in the Middle Ages here. Mind you, I suppose you have that kind of thing in America too.'

'Oh, yes. I don't know about now, but when I was in my first newspaper job in Boston I found out there were dozens of spiritualist churches in the city. And before that, when I was a kid, my parents took me to a talk by your Sherlock Holmes man, Sir Arthur Conan Doyle. It was at Symphony Hall, in 1922, and I thought it would all be about his stories, but actually he was talking about spiritualism, which I'm sure they didn't agree with. He was passionate about it. The place was packed, too. He talked a lot about the afterlife – he said people would have bodies just like we do, and clothes and houses, even furniture.'

'And what would they do for all eternity? Apart from polishing the furniture.'

'He said they'd work, but there'd be abundant leisure too.'

'That sounds just like the Greenshirts.'

'The what?'

'Just some group I came across during the investigation. They started out calling themselves the Kibbo Kift and said they'd make a better world, then they turned into the Social Credit Party and reckoned we should save the economy by giving free money to everyone. Then we'd have a wonderful future of leisure without poverty. Two sides of the same coin, though, in a way, I suppose.'

'What do you mean?'

'Well, the spiritualists and the social credit lot both got a following because of what happened in the Great War, and I think it was all about what people wanted to hear. They'd listen to anyone who promised them a better world to come, whether it was in this life or not.'

'You can't blame them for that.'

'I don't. It's just that I'm a bit sceptical about politicians who make big promises, and when it comes to all that psychic stuff I find it even harder to swallow. I've seen too many con tricks in my time – from hustlers playing Find the Lady on the streets to business fraud and embezzlement, you name it. Did you ever hear about the photographs of fairies that some girls in Yorkshire took during the last war? They said they were real, and even the great Conan Doyle believed them.'

'Oh, yes, I think that story went around the world. We certainly heard about it in the States.'

'Psychic photography, that's what they called it – quite a craze. Someone even took a picture of the Cenotaph on Armistice Day that got in the papers. That was in 1922 as well, I think – and it showed extra faces that were supposed to be spirits of the dead or something. People got very excited, but it was obviously a fake.'

'So I'm guessing when you went to that seance yesterday you weren't expecting to be impressed?'

'What do you think? Look, my dad died when I was a boy. I loved him and I still think about him every day, but I don't believe he can speak to me through some woman in a sitting room with the lights off in Stratford. As far as I'm concerned, life is life and death is death, and never the twain shall meet.'

Dorothy thought for a moment. 'I don't buy it either,' she said. 'But you know, Conan Doyle said something in that talk that really shocked me. He said ten members of his family went off to the Great War, and not one survived it. His own son died. I'm sure he must've desperately wanted to speak to his boy again, to be in contact with him, and if someone came along and said they were speaking on his behalf from beyond the grave, he'd want to believe it was true.'

'People who've suffered want a better future,' said Jago, 'and some of them will believe anyone who promises it. That's probably how even Hitler got elected.' He paused. 'Sobering thought, eh? Still, it's the here and now that matters. And all things considered, I must admit it's a whole lot more enjoyable to be here at a concert with you, eating nice moist fruit cake, than it is chasing cranks and criminals round West Ham.'

'Well, congratulations on finishing the case. You must be very pleased.'

'I am. But to tell you the truth, I feel a bit bad about it too. I think we did her a disservice – Joan, that is, the woman who was killed. There were things about the case that made it look as though she might've been involved in immoral goings-on, as they say.'

'What my mother would've called a lady of negotiable virtue?'

'Exactly. And we were quick to assume that the circumstances of her death meant she was. But she wasn't – she was just a lonely young woman earning an honest living as a cinema usherette. Her life had got complicated, but I think that was just because she'd been disappointed in love and was trying to find the real thing.'

'Like we all do.'

Jago hesitated. The way Dorothy spoke so freely about her emotions was both enviable and disturbing.

'Well, er, yes, I suppose. Her best friend said all she wanted was to have one person in the world who knew her deep down as she really was and loved her all the same. But in the end what she got was the opposite – murdered by someone who wouldn't accept her for who she was. As far as her mother-in-law was concerned, Joan was a big disappointment – she wanted the perfect wife for her son, so she tried to control Joan and make her into something she wasn't.'

'But it's over now. You've got justice for Joan.'

'Maybe, but I still don't feel like celebrating. Pretty much a whole family's been wiped out. Joan's dead, her husband Richard's missing in action and very likely killed, her mother-in-law may hang for murder, and her sister-in-law's marriage looks finished. It's the war that's done it, isn't it? I mean, supposing Richard hadn't joined the Territorials and gone off to fight in France. Would his marriage have survived? Because if it had, none of this would've happened. It seems unjust.'

'You're right – there's precious little justice in war. But we have to believe we can make something better after it, otherwise we'd have nothing to hope for. It's like Rita said, isn't it? "Hope deferred maketh the heart sick."'

CHAPTER FORTY-NINE

A tall young man in army officer's uniform strolled into the sandwich bar with a woman of similar age who was bemoaning how stuffy the gallery's basement was. Jago himself was feeling too warm and had a sudden desire for fresh air. He also wanted to be somewhere he could talk without being overheard.

'Shall we go outside?' he said. 'We could go and sit on the steps at St Martin-in-the-Fields.'

They left the gallery and crossed Charing Cross Road to the neoclassical church building which had stood there since the early eighteenth century. Now a sign outside advertised a canteen it was running day and night in the crypt for members of the armed forces.

'I remember they always gave a welcome here to soldiers in the last war too,' said Jago. 'The vicar called it "the church of the ever open door". There's plenty of space for us to sit out here and have a quiet chat without being bothered by anyone.'

He took off his overcoat and spread it on the stone steps so that Dorothy could sit on it.

'Thank you,' she said. 'That's kind of you. Now where was I?'

'You were saying something about hope deferred making the heart sick.'

'Oh, yes. And having something to hope for. I just think that even when we can't see justice anywhere, we still have to hope – perhaps that's when we need it most of all.'

'It's easy to say that, but I saw plenty of men in the war who were full of hope – hope that they'd survive and go home. But they didn't. You know, when we were at the Cenotaph on Monday I said those men it reminded me of were my family, but that wasn't true. Maybe when I was first in the army it was – I did get to know the men I was serving with. But then time passed, and one by one they got killed off. Towards the end, I think I chose not to know them – to know their names, yes, but not to know them as people, in the way their real families would've known them, because I knew the chances were they'd soon die. And I didn't let them know me either – because I'd probably soon be dead too. The truth is I think I didn't want to matter to them.'

'Is that still how you are now?'

'I don't know.'

'Don't you think we all want to be known? To be accepted by someone, even loved by them? Is it just women who feel like that, or is it possible for a man too?'

'But that's the problem. I'm not just a man. I'm a policeman, and that means if you have feelings you don't show them. I'm expected to submit to every regulation, obey every order and never question it. When I'm on duty I'm not supposed to think about anything except that duty. One of the first things they taught us when I joined the police was that lounging about was the worst sin you could commit. They called it "gossiping", and any officer they caught doing that was for it. And I always had to be civil and polite to the public, never get angry, listen respectfully to whatever they said.'

'But you're off duty now.'

'Am I? I'm not sure I ever am.'

Jago twisted round and looked back down Charing Cross Road to where a police constable was on point duty, directing the traffic.

'You see that man down there? And that blue-and-white striped armlet on his left sleeve?'

'Yes.'

'Well, that means he's on duty. It goes back to the old days, when policemen had to wear their uniform all the time, so they put the armlet on to show they were on duty. At training school they drummed it into us right from the start that whether we were officially on duty or off, our responsibility to the public was the same – to prevent and detect crime by all possible means. In other words, I was to be a policeman twenty-four hours a day, seven days a week. It's been like that for twenty years now, and I don't feel as though I'm me any more.

I'm just this detective that you see before you.'

'But I don't just see a policeman. I see John Jago, a boy who grew up and found the world was a cruel place full of bad people, but who's done his best to be good and true. I see a man, a human being. You need people you can talk to from the heart – people who can understand you as a person, not just as a policeman.'

Jago didn't know how to answer her. Who did he have that kind of relationship with? The only person who came anywhere close to it within the Metropolitan Police Service was his old friend and colleague Frank Tompkins. And outside the force? Well, there was Rita. She seemed to understand him, but it wasn't what you'd call a deep or intimate relationship. Apart from her, over all these two decades he hadn't let anyone into his life – there was just too much risk of being hurt.

He looked up and caught Dorothy's eyes. They were warm and peaceful, and yet they seemed to see straight into him. He looked away quickly. When Carol had described Joan she might just as easily have been speaking of him. He recognised the ache he'd felt inside – it was a longing for intimacy, to know just one other person and to be known truly, deeply and totally by them. The realisation sent an unexpected surge of pain through him, and he bit his lip to stop it.

'I don't know if I'll ever change,' he said.

'While there's life there's hope – that's what people say, isn't it?' said Dorothy quietly.

'They do these days,' he replied.

'And I suppose you could say while there's hope there's life, too. That's why it's important to know what people's hopes are – you need to know what they long for to understand them.'

Jago nodded. He felt as he had when he was nine years old, standing on the edge of the swimming pool at the West Ham Municipal Baths and being told to dive in. Now, here, he realised he was staring into the distance and saying nothing.

'What are you thinking?' said Dorothy.

'Oh, I'm sorry,' he replied, looking at her. 'I was miles away. I was thinking about when we were having breakfast at Rita's on Wednesday. You asked Rita what she hoped for.'

'That's right. She said she hoped for an end to the war and a good husband for her Emily.'

'Yes. But I noticed you didn't ask me. You didn't ask what I hoped for.'

'No, I didn't. I sensed it was maybe what Rita wanted me to ask her – or maybe what she was hoping you might ask her. But I wasn't so sure it was a question you wanted to answer yourself. So you're right, I didn't ask you. But then you didn't ask me what I hoped for either.'

'I see. Yes, of course, you're right. I'm not used to talking about things like that.'

'So shall I ask you now?'

'Yes, please.'

'OK. What is it you hope for in your life, John Jago?'

He immediately wished he hadn't invited her to do

this. He struggled to find the words to reply. For all these years in the police he'd been the one who asked the questions and had the right to expect answers. Intrusive probing by journalists was to be batted away. But this was not just a journalist. This was Dorothy, and the door she was knocking on was one that he knew he wanted to open. It just felt as though the hinges were rusted fast.

Her eyes were locked on his. Again he looked away, like a guilty suspect. He wanted to escape, but even more he wanted not to. He willed himself to meet her gaze.

'I'm sorry,' he said. 'I don't find this easy – talking about what I feel inside. I think I got out of the habit many years ago.'

'I understand that,' she replied, her voice gentle and reassuring.

He forced himself to keep speaking. 'It's just that hope can be very painful, and when hopes don't come true, sometimes all you can do is let them die – or make them die.'

'I'm sorry. I shouldn't have asked.'

'No, I want you to ask. I don't think there's anyone else in the world who'd ask me a question like that, and I need it.'

'So, John, what do you hope for?'

He thought carefully. 'I'm not sure I could answer a big question like that in one sentence,' he replied. 'It just feels so complicated. But if I have to, I think I'd say this is what I hope – that by the time I die I'll have mattered enough to someone for them to remember me.'

*　*　*

408

When Jago got home that evening the light was fading. He knew that Dorothy had said goodbye on the steps of St Martin-in-the-Fields and returned to her hotel to write about the National Gallery concerts for her readers in America, while he had returned to his own world at West Ham police station. He also knew he'd spent the afternoon in the CID office waiting for an order to search that was now promised for the morning, but by the time he got home that evening the rest was a blur.

He let himself into the house, more conscious than usual of its emptiness, and switched on the wireless to break the cold silence, but the talk in progress was earnest and depressingly dull. He snapped the broadcast off with a flick of his wrist. Soon the sirens would go, he thought. He should put the kettle on and make a flask of tea to keep him warm in the shelter that night. But he felt listless and turned instead to the cupboard where he kept his Scotch. He took out the bottle and a glass, poured himself a tot and sat down in his favourite armchair. Not for the first time, he thought of the night to come and whether he would see the day that followed.

He reached into his jacket pocket and felt a piece of paper. Pulling it out, he recognised the old handbill that Greville Ballantyne had given him. It was crumpled. He rested it on his thigh and tried to smooth it with his hand.

The image of Ballantyne's face as he'd last seen it rose like a ghost in his mind. *How will that poor man remember me*, he thought. *I'm the one who took his wife away, who stole all that was precious in his life to destroy it. I'm the law, I'm the bringer of vengeance and death. If he remembers me now, it'll only be to hate me.*

He looked down at the handbill and ran his finger gently along his father's name. His father's memorial. *Will there be someone who sits down one day and remembers me like this,* he thought, *or will I just be forgotten?* The words were captive in his mind, and the silence of the room remained unbroken. He felt his eyes moisten as he raised his glass to the handbill and took a sip.

He thought of the question Dorothy had asked him, and wondered what she'd made of his answer. To be remembered. Was that a strange thing to hope for? He didn't know, but he had a feeling she would understand. There was only one person in the world that he wanted to be remembered by, and her name was on his lips as the darkness slowly fell.

ACKNOWLEDGEMENTS

As in all the Blitz Detective novels, some of the events in this story really happened. A bomb did explode in the middle of Beethoven's Razumovsky String Quartet during a lunchtime concert at the National Gallery, London, in October 1940, although I have taken the liberty of moving its date by a day or two. I'd like to thank Zara Moran and her colleagues in the National Gallery Research Centre for letting me consult their archived materials on this explosion and also the Myra Hess lunchtime concerts, and for their efforts to find answers to my questions. Thanks are due also to my old friends Tim and Janet Griffiths for their expert counsel on Beethoven and Brahms.

A Tube station named Trafalgar Square may sound fictional to the modern reader, but in 1940 it was fact (nowadays it's part of Charing Cross station), and a bomb really did hit it in October of that year, causing extensive damage and taking the lives of ten people who were sheltering at the bottom of the escalator. I'm thankful to Nick Cooper, author of *London Underground at War*, for his help in providing me with details of this incident. Sadly, it was just one of many instances during the Blitz when people seeking a refuge from the bombing, whether in a Tube station or an Anderson shelter, were killed when bombs landed not on their home but on their supposed place of safety.

The bombing of St Thomas's Hospital in 1940 also took place as described in the book – and lest anyone be troubled by my version of the name, I plead that I have relied on E. M. McInnes's 1963 history of the hospital, which says that the name St Thomas' Hospital was officially adopted in 1948 but traditionally the more usual form before that was St Thomas's.

Other real-life events inspired elements of the story, all of them occurring on K Division of the Metropolitan Police, where Detective Inspector Jago is based. Three men were arrested and tried for explosives offences after police raided a house in Manor Park (part of the County Borough of East Ham) in 1939 and found various items of bomb-making equipment, while significant breakthroughs in the prevention of terrorist bomb attacks were made in Ilford and Dagenham.

It's worth noting too, for any readers wondering, that the Kibbo Kift, the Social Credit Party and the Greenshirts were all real organisations.

I'm indebted to Frank Chester, who served in the Royal Navy as a lieutenant on the Arctic convoys and was awarded the Distinguished Service Cross. Frank's pin-sharp memories of life in London before the war and at sea during it were of great help, and to me all the more remarkable given that when he shared them with me he had already celebrated his hundredth birthday.

As always I'm grateful to Roy Ingleton for his help on police matters, and as always too I could not have got to the end of another book without the constant support and encouragement of my wife, Margaret, and my children, Catherine and David.

MIKE HOLLOW was born in West Ham, on the eastern edge of London, and grew up in Romford, Essex. He studied Russian and French at the University of Cambridge and then worked for the BBC and later Tearfund. In 2002 he went freelance as a copywriter, journalist, editor and translator, but now gives all his time to writing the Blitz Detective books.

blitzdetective.com   *@MikeHollowBlitz*